STUNG!

Mighty John Marshall

"MIGHTY"

John Marshall

www.mightyjohnmarshall.com

Spring Point Press
207-767-4225
SpringPointPress@aol.com

STUNG edited by:

Mary Foley
John Plunkett
Dee Dee Richardson

Cover design by John Gaudet

Photo of ball players by Albertine Feury

ISBN. 0-9754285-051295

To the 1950s and 1960s...and the memories they gave me.

PREFACE

If life is a baseball game then I guess I'm in the 7th inning stretch, but back then it was the top of the first. It began when Elvis was in Graceland, Kennedy in Camelot, and Yaz still ruled left field at Fenway. Most of my baseball games took place with best friend, Jimmy Peters, in the old Western Cemetery in our home town of Portland, Maine.

In the middle of the cemetery there was a big vacant space where we could chase a long fly ball without stumbling over the dead. There were no stones, just well-worn summer grass that had an odor all its own. Maybe it came from the waste of wandering creatures of the day and the night. Maybe it came from the soles of sneakers that had stomped all over it from years of playing *flies and grounders,* a baseball game that just two can play with one hitting, one fielding, and both laughing, hollering, and insulting each other. Maybe it was a mixture of all that plus age, dirt, salty air, and finally *death* that lingered in that special place. Whatever it was, for Jimmy and me, it was part of our growing up. We were happy there...for a while.

STUNG

1

Although I had been teaching in Southern California for over twenty years, my heart and mind were still back in the old neighborhood, back in my childhood where it seemed that no violence existed. You could go away and leave your doors unlocked, and everything would be there when you got back. Kids could play outside without worrying about Chester The Molester waiting in the shadows. Your next door neighbors actually knew you as well as their own. They made you feel safe if your mom or dad were away, and there was always a mom *and* a dad. It was life according to the gospel of Ozzie and Harriet. Kids never gave a second thought to drinking out of the same soda bottle as their friends, and nobody was the worse for it. For 50 cents you got two full length features, a Three Stooges short, and a couple of cartoons. The milkman and the postman were just part of your extended family, and if no one was home they would let themselves in and drop off their deliveries. They might even turn off a light that had been left on accidentally. There were no computers, cell phones, or video games. What there was, was family, and it didn't get any better than that. When something or someone messes up your world, innocence can soon be a victim.

Today, my world was being invaded by something *evil*. The fact that I could read the Portland Press Herald on line made it even more difficult to let go of the "good old days". This morning when I saw the headlines about the body count and the mystery that started to fester with this latest discovery, I felt that it couldn't be happening in the neighborhood that was suspended in time in my mind.

At first, according to the small article in last Tuesday's paper, there were two bodies. Two old winos that nobody cared about, not the cops, not the neighbors, and apparently no concerned relatives. There was no mention of how they died. It did say where they died, in the Western Cemetery. That's just up the street from where I was born. The paper didn't say whether foul play was involved or not. There was speculation that drugs might have been the cause. There had been a lot of drug deaths in Portland during the previous six months.

MIGHTY JOHN MARSHALL

Drugs? How did drugs sneak into my world of things sweet and good? Who wasn't looking when that boogieman came to town? The two men, listed simply as Mr. Holt and Mr. Nelson, would be buried without fanfare or ceremony. There was no mention of where they were from or anything they might have accomplished in their unnoticed lives. The opening of the latest Wal-Mart was given more press.

Things changed early Saturday night when 12 year-old Paul Feeney was discovered lying face down just inside the cemetery gates. It was a dog-walker who stumbled over the small lifeless boy, almost hidden by the tall grass and brush. It was just after sundown. At first, according to the paper, the dog-walker thought the boy was just sleeping. There were no visible signs of injuries, but on further examination it was evident that the boy was dead. Paul Feeney was from one of Portland's most prominent families. Both John and Sandra Feeney were attorneys who knew the sins and secrets of most of their wealthy clients. Their firm was the largest in Portland, and it has long been hinted that John Feeney was in line to be the next Democratic nominee for Governor. There was no way the death of *his* son would be treated with the same cavalier attitude as the first two victims, Mr. Holt and Mr. Nelson. That's what they surely were, *victims*. That's what Paul Feeney was too. No accidents here.

The Sunday paper went on to say that young Paul had gone to shoot his new BB gun in the old cemetery with Steve Winchell, his best friend since the first grade. The gun was a birthday present from his father. It was an original RED RYDER, the same kind Paul's father had been given on his twelfth birthday. It also said that Steve had not come home. His parents were urging friends, neighbors, and anyone who could help, to go up to the cannon on the Western Prom. They would receive flyers with Steve's picture and instructions whenever they got there. There was a photo of Steve's mother in the paper holding an 8 x 10 of her son, and a plea to those who might have taken him that Steve was diabetic and needed insulin.

I finished the article that also listed relatives, friends, and accomplishments for which the Feeney boy was most proud. At the end there was a mention that a reward fund was being set up by the Feeney family for any information leading to the arrest and convic-

3

tion of the killer or killers. I picked up the phone to call my brother Joe who still lived in the old neighborhood. Like me, Joe was a history teacher. He had Paul Feeney in his class the previous year. Joe and I both knew his dad from our student days at Cheverus High.

"Lo," said the lazy voice on the other end.

"Wake up, Dickhead. Its past ten there!" I said with great affection for the older brother who was my childhood hero. He meant more to me than anyone else...well, almost. We talked or e-mailed daily, and were still as close as if we still shared that same upstairs bedroom at 89 Pine. I hadn't been home in a long time, not since Mom passed away. Joe knew why. My obsession with my first love and that old cemetery just wouldn't fade away. It took me ten years to make the break to the West Coast. Joe would never come out here where he said all those liberal weirdoes lived, but we didn't need to breathe the same air to remain the closest of brothers.

"Hey, Dipshit, go away. I'm on vacation," he said with the same affection I afforded him.

"What's happening out there?" I asked. "You got some kind of serial killer or what? What's the paper leaving out? No one knows more about what's going on in that town than you. They don't call you the freakin' *Mayor of Portland* for nothing."

"Yeah, and don't you forget you'll never be more than the Mayor's little brother...ha ha ha," he snickered with that king-shit attitude that was just another part of his nature.

Everyone in Portland who knew us both knew him as Joe and me as Joe's brother, Charlie. It was if I didn't exist at all without being connected to Joe. It's just the way it was. I really didn't mind at all.

"Have they found the Winchell kid yet?" I inquired.

He paused, as if not to ruin my day. "Yup. Unfortunately you're not the first to wake me. Lisa Ibrahim from the paper called about an hour ago to see if I could say a few words about Steve. He had been another one of my students...Damn good kid...always polite...never gave me any problems. They found his body up by the crypts at the far end of your old stomping grounds. Paul Feeney was found near the front gates, but Steve was about two hundred yards the other way. They must have run in different directions. I'm thinking there was more than one attacker. Those kids were good little athletes...They could run. The killer or killers had to be athletic themselves. That's what I'm thinking. You have to rule out any of the ordinary drunks that might be hanging out in there."

"Who would want to kill two innocent young kids...and then just leave their bodies to be found so easily?"

"Lots of whack-jobs in the world, Charlie. Look at those snipers who killed all those innocent people down in D.C. And what about that Dahmer asshole who kept his victims' heads in the fridge for a late night snack? What made that Speck character in Chicago kill all those nurses and then go in for a sex change in prison. Whack-jobs, Charlie, whack-jobs!" Joe always had an answer for everything...just not the answer you necessarily wanted to hear.

"Do they know the cause of death on either of the boys, Joe?"

"If they do they're not saying yet. You remember Frank Blanchette from King Junior?"

"Yeah, nerdy little kid. Why, what's up with him?"

"He's a pathologist now, heads up the Forensics Department for the Portland Police Department."

"Do you think you can get some inside information from him?"

"Dunno. He comes into O'Toole's on occasion. He goes to the bar, throws back a few brewskies and leaves. I never see him talking with anyone."

"Well, loosen up the purse strings, you cheap bastard, and buy him a couple."

"Yeah, yeah, yeah...I'll send you the bill!"

"Don't ever change, Joe. My heart couldn't take it."

"Don't worry, I won't." Joe was proud of the fact that he was as stingy as Jack Benny.

"Damn!!!" I shouted as I looked at the time. "I've got to get going. Please give me a call with any fresh news. I have to head up to the park and help set up a party for the incoming freshman. Even in slow Sunday morning traffic that can be a chore. Besides, there's a pretty little English teacher who's new, and if I'm not there those kids will walk all over her...Ya know what I mean, Jose?"

"Call me, Joe, you California beach bum...So you got a new babe?"

he teased.

"I got more babes than you'll ever have. You haven't had a date since the Johnson Administration...ANDREW JOHNSON!"

We both chuckled and hung up at the same time. It was good therapy. No matter how bad the news we found time for a laugh.

John Lennon wrote, "Whatever gets you through the night is all right." For some that means drugs, alcohol, or a warm body. It could be a combination. Making wise cracks is how I get through the night. It's instant. It's my fix. Sometimes I keep it to myself and have a private laugh. No matter the tragedy or the horror it just seems to make the boogieman go away, if only for a while.

As I put the receiver back in its cradle, my heart felt a chill for two boys I had never known and for two homeless men nobody seemed to know. I still couldn't believe this was happening in my hometown, and in *my cemetery playground.* I had spent so many happy summer days on the open field in the center of the cemetery grounds, playing ball and listening to my transistor radio as WJAB- THE BIG JAB blasted the hits. For me, and I think for best friend Jimmy Peters, there was a sense of security among the silent population. There was a certain acceptance, almost a welcoming, that I have never forgotten. It was also there that the love bug first bit me in the ass. Jimmy and I had a number of puppy love infatuations, but nothing like the one that came into my life during the summer we were both seventeen.

You should know that Jimmy and I were inseparable through junior high and high school. Joe was my brother and my protector, but Jimmy was my best friend. We reveled in our childishness from the days in the seventh grade when we would sit in the back of Mrs. McDonough's class and check out which girls were then wearing bras, and which still had tee-shirts showing underneath their blouses. Our immaturity continued through our senior year in high school when Fr. Morrison said to the graduating class, "You came to us as boys and you are leaving today as men... except for *two* I won't mention." He looked our way. He didn't need to. Everyone knew. He held back a smile as we waved to a round of applause.

Our personalities, tastes, and senses of humor were perfectly matched. Making wise cracks and goofing off were our trademarks. I remember the time in junior high when our baseball coach benched us for not taking a game seriously. Ricky Romano had hit a game-winning home run; and a local reporter came over to Jimmy asking, "Hey, what's the name of the kid who hit that home run?"

"Him?...oh...ah...That's Jimmy Peters."

"Yeah, that's Jimmy with a Y," I confirmed.

Sure enough, next day in the sports section of the paper was the headline: JIMMY PETERS' HOME RUN WINS GAME FOR KING JUNIOR HIGH. Coach Jackson never did find out how that happened, but he did have his suspicions.

We never fought over girls until that magical summer, although we had made a lot of them mad with our immaturity. We would play basketball games in the school yard, not for money but for girlfriends. If I lost, I would tell my girl I had just lost her to Jimmy. He would do the same, and give away the girl he was seeing. They would swear at us; and we would act so shocked, and then fall to the ground laughing.

Jimmy and I always had a good time whether in school or at each other's house. Anywhere we were together was fun; and, when we made that old cemetery our home away from home, we found our own private sanctuary. We also found the girl who would almost come between us. Her name was Cindy.

2

From the time Jimmy and I were twelve until that *special* summer day when we first saw Cindy, our Saturday morning ritual was pretty much the same. The only exception was when the cemetery was knee-deep in snow.

After Jimmy and I had finished playing ball we would sit under the big old elm tree near home plate and have lunch. We would always bring Italian sandwiches, mine from DiPietro's and Jimmy's from Amato's. Each of us swore that his sandwich was better, but they both pretty much tasted the same. "It's all in the oil," they say. We washed them down with Pespi. There was no argument about that. Then we would finish them all off with a couple of good belches and taste them all over again. Thems eats!!!

Jimmy and I would always pick up the papers, bags, and empty soda bottles. We would drop any leftovers in the grass behind home plate for any hungry critters to find. I think we felt it was the neighborly thing to do for our quiet spectators. We respected the home they let us play in.

As I think back on it now, Jimmy and I were the only two that cemetery let have a "free ride". It was as if it was *their* way of saying thanks for leaving their home in the same condition we had found it. To those who were careless and sloppy, there could be consequences.

I remember Tommy Caine got frightened by a grass snake while he was taking a whiz on a Civil War general who had breathed his last in 1889. Tommy jumped and peed all over his sneakers. Jimmy and I were holding on to our sides, laughing our asses off. Tommy swore it was a rattler, and then he swore at us. Tommy never came back.

Bill O'Neal came running by Jimmy and me one summer day, sweating more than usual and stammering that there was "something" or "someone" leering at him after he had tossed a soda bottle near one of the mausoleums.

"I think I woke it up. Run you guys. Let's get the hell out of here!!!"

Bill screamed as he ran home.

"What a nimrod!" Jimmy said, ala Bugs Bunny. No one could do Bugs Bunny like Jimmy Peters. That would always crack me up.

Bill never came back, but his mother did call our mothers saying that "William" will not be allowed to go to that awful cemetery again.

"Well la di da!" That was Jimmy's response.

Through those carefree years most of our other friends had similar experiences, and all had reasons why they couldn't or wouldn't come up to the cemetery to play.

"Too many bugs up there! I get bites all over my back," bitched Lyman Meserve. "I go up there for one day and I itch for a week."

"My mother says I have to watch my little brother and sister," Dickey White complained. "Plus, I'm getting paid for it. There's no money to be made up in that old bone yard."

Even Claudia Barlett, the bravest girl in the neighborhood, stayed away. "My parents said to keep away from you two. They said one of the teachers at school told them you guys were pervs."

"McDonough!!!" Jimmy and I said at the same time and in the same tone that Jerry Seinfeld complains about "Neuman" today.

As so the summers came and went. Jimmy and I rarely missed our Saturday morning routine up in the old cemetery. Events that change routines seem to come on quickly and without notice. It was in late June of our seventeenth year when it happened to us, when our lives took a new direction. It was the day a new family moved in across the street from Jimmy and his family.

"I went over and said hello to the Chamberlains today," Sara Peters said to Jimmy and me as we were watching American Bandstand.

"That's nice," he replied back as if it had absolutely no importance to us, and it didn't.

"They just moved down from Bangor. They have a boy, George, your age. I think it would be nice if you and Charlie invited him to play ball with you." Mrs. Peters suggested in her natural friendly manner.

"Think again!" Jimmy said in his natural *don't-bother-me-while-I'm-watching-TV* manner.

That little remark caused Sara Peters to turn off the TV. She stood in front of it, saying, "James Aron Peters, you and Charlie go over there and act like good neighbors, and say hello to George. He would probably like to have new friends to chum around with."

"Chum around? Who are you, Mary Poppins?...I saw the fat little bugger when they moved in. The only think he wants to chum around with is a couple of cheeseburgers," Jimmy argued.

I didn't say anything. I could tell Jimmy was just prolonging the inevitable. The only way to get life back to normal was to go over there and say hello; then come back and say George would let us know when he would have some time to "chum around."

As we made our way across the street, we noticed one thing different from the way the front lawn used to look. Before it was just a normal *I-don't-care-if-you-notice-me* type of lawn. Now there was a bunch of big pink-plaster flamingos in various forms of stance and a sign that read: FORGET THE DOG. BEWARE OF THE OWNER.

"Well, there goes the neighborhood," I said.

"What a bunch of maroons!" Jimmy replied in his Bugs Bunny voice.

We rang the bell. The door opened and George's father stood there, blocking the doorway like a bouncer at a bar. He had on a dirty white tee-shirt with big yellow stains around his arms pits. He looked like he would tip the scales at about 350 pounds. His thick hair was chopped in a crew cut, which no self-respecting Elvis fan would ever do. Pushed back on the top of his big head was an undersized Yankees baseball cap. We hated him immediately. He popped a big wet cigar out of his yellow-brown stained teeth; and, with tobacco juice running down his chin, growled, "Ya, what do ya want?"

"You're not an Elvis fan, are you?" Jimmy asked, as if he couldn't resist doing so.

"NO! Hate him! Why?"

"Just taking a survey." Jimmy forced a smile. "Sir, my name is Jimmy Peters and this is my friend, Charlie Sullivan. We were wondering if your son was home."

"George? Ya, why? Has that shithead killed another cat?"

"Ah...no...not that we know of," I managed to say as I looked at

Jimmy for some reason to carry on with this conversation.

"Killed a cat?...I'm sure that was an accident," Jimmy said diplomatically.

"ONE'S an accident!...SIX is goddamn cruel!!!" barked back Mr. Chamberlain. "GEORGE!!!" He yelled up the stairs while trying to relight his soggy cigar.

"I'M ON THE SHITTER!" came the reply from the second floor.

"You boys want to go up? He should be done in a minute," George's father beckoned us in.

"Well, actually, we're late for choir practice," I stammered as Jimmy nodded affirmatively. "But if George would like to play ball with us next Saturday, tell him to meet us at the cemetery just up the street. There's a big field in the middle where we play."

"Ya?" Mr. Chamberlain acted surprised. "You wanna play ball with George? Huh, he might like it up there. Good place to bury cats!" Then he laughed and started to cough. Tobacco flavored spittle jumped everywhere, showering Jimmy and me.

"I'm gonna strangle my mother," Jimmy whispered as we left down the front steps and passed the pink flamingoes, all the while trying to rub off any wet goo left on our faces.

The next Saturday morning George waddled through the gates chomping on bubble gum like it was going out of style. He dropped the wrappers as if he would follow the trail in case he got lost in his new surroundings. It wouldn't be long before he would forget about the wrappers and the mound of bubble gum that swelled his cheeks.

Jimmy explained the rules. "Listen up, Georgie-Porgy-puddin-n-pie. Miss a meal and I bet you cry."

The fat kid was not amused at Jimmy's little ditty. I looked at my friend with eyes that said, *Cut the shit. He could kill us and forget about the cats.*

George and I took the field while Jimmy prepared to bat.

Things went well for a while, and George looked like he might be enjoying the game more than other things he might have done when he was alone. Other than ridding the neighborhood of cats, we could only guess what those other things might have been. But the fun of this day was about to end for the new kid in town.

STUNG

As he chased a long fly ball, George, huffing and puffing, ran face first into a hornets' nest which hung low in a maple tree. The nest was disguised by big leafs that only a tree that had seen a lot of years could produce. The bees were home and they were pissed! As chubby George ran in circles, screaming and crying and jumping up and down, he looked like the Tasmanian Devil in a whirling dervish. Jimmy and I began yelling for him to run two blocks away. Bees are territorial and two blocks are about as far as their boundaries stretch. For some reason, it's one of those lessons your mom teaches you after you've been stung and not before. I guess, even though you know that little factoid, you don't think about it when the pain is more than you can bear. George, in his stupor and to our amazement, found his way to the front gates without even looking at the gum wrappers he had dropped on the ground. A passing fire truck spotted him and hosed him down, drowning the little torturers who fought like kamikazes till the end. George never played with us again and was rarely seen outside his house.

I heard later that the Chamberlain family had moved back to Bangor where George soon gained reputation as a *loner*. I also read ten years later that he had raped and killed a waitress from Mooney's Country Bar. The prosecutor said the waitress was found naked in an abandoned warehouse over near the Airport. She had hundreds of tiny needles, like so many bee stingers, stuck in her body. According to the trial transcript George tied her up, poured honey all over her body, and then dropped a bag full of hungry rats next to her. The Coroner testified that she may have died in one of several ways or a combination of several, but most likely her heart finally seized in terror as the crazed rats began to feed. At the trial Chamberlain said the voices, buzzing in his head, made him do it. The jury didn't buy it, and they made George do life without parole at Thomaston State Prison.

I remember all those happenings just like it was yesterday, but the reason that old burial ground still has a hold on me is because of a girl. A pretty girl takes precedence over baseball, Italian sandwiches, rock-n-roll, and even best friends like Jimmy Peters.

She was just outside the fence as Jimmy and I were leaving. It was the same day George Chamberlain was attacked by those bees. I can still see those long legs walking down the hill on Vaughn Street.

She was wearing short shorts, Clorox-white against her caramel-colored body. Her long blond hair was swept back in a ponytail, and it bounced up and down against a tiny black tank top that reached down to her belly button. I was paralyzed immediately and ready to be her teenage love-slave. So was Jimmy.

Jimmy spoke first as he pushed me over a stone. I stubbed my toe and fell against the fence. Jimmy said something lame like, "And where have you been all my life?"

Not to be outdone I said something lamer, "Hellooooo Baaaaby!" just like the Big Bopper in that old rock-n- roll classic, <u>Chantilly Lace</u>.

She smiled at Jimmy and gave me one of those, "*Gawd!!!-Get-a-life*" looks.

Then Jimmy said I wasn't The Big Bopper, just The Big Loser, and that didn't click with her. She turned her smile on me and said, "You're kind of silly, but you're cute. What's your name?"

Excitedly I blurted out, "Ahh...my name is Charlie and you can call me that, or Charles, or Chuck, or doofus, or just snap your fingers and I'll come running."

I was hooked like a trout on a blood worm. I remember thinking Fr. Duffy was going to get an earful the next time I went to confession. This girl was worth any penance, at least that's what I thought at the time.

She said her name was Cindy; and I just had to make myself look like a bigger idiot by saying, "Is that spelled, SIN-DY?"

Jimmy gave me that *how-stupid-are-you* look, but she smiled coyly and whispered like Bridgette Bardot, "But of course."

I was seventeen and I was a goner. Cindy never did say how old she was. She reminded me of Barbara Eden on <u>I Dream of Jeannie</u> except Cindy showed her belly button. The TV censors wouldn't let Jeannie do that.

"Are you from around here?" I asked in hopes that she had just moved into one of the row houses in my neighborhood.

"Yes, my home is around here, but I don't know you well enough to tell you exactly where. Guess you'll just have to get it out of me some way. Got any ideas how?" she teased.

"Well, let me tell ya, Missy. I'm gonna die tryin," I said, mimicking

John Wayne and making Jimmy ill at the same time.

"I'm gonna barf right here, I swear," Jimmy said as he threw our baseball high up into the air and waited to catch it.

Suddenly, there were two or three tiny bees sitting on her left shoulder. I went to brush them off, but she grabbed my hand and said, "Uh uh, no touching." She waved her finger back and forth as if scolding me.

"But, there are bees on your shoulder and I was just going to shoo them away."

"They are my friends. They won't sting me." She put out her left hand. The little bees jumped onto it, and then she tossed them gently into the air.

"They are so small. They must be baby bees," I suggested.

Cindy watched them as they buzzed off. Then she strangely remarked, "Those *babies* are older than you, Charlie." Then, as if not meaning to be so mysterious, she said, "But I think you're cuter." She smiled and gave me a small kiss on the cheek.

"Oh man, if there were three bees sitting on Charlie's shoulder he'd be running for his mommy," Jimmy said, trying not to be left out and still hoping to win her favor.

"Well, I'm not afraid as long as Cindy's here," I boasted.

"Awe, Charlie, you are so sweet!" the girl said as she gave me a gentle hug.

"That's it. Here come the big chunks first." Jimmy pretended to stick his fingers down his throat.

"James is so childish," I remarked in a mocking tone.

"Oh, and you're Mr. Grownup I suppose." Cindy teased.

"I could be Mr. Anything or Mr. Anyone for you," I bragged.

She laughed softly as she twirled her ponytail and set her eyes on mine.

Jimmy was sensing that I had won her over and said sarcastically, "Well I hope you two will be very happy. Just don't send me any wedding invitations." Then he threw his baseball glove across the street. Jimmy didn't get mad often, but when he did he would always throw something. Usually it was a stick or a rock, but never his glove. That mitt meant more to him than his sister. I guess I knew how he felt. I would have been the one throwing my glove if she had picked him over me.

When afternoon thunder-clouds began covering the West End, Cindy said she had to go. All of a sudden there was urgency in her eyes, as if she had lost a little confidence in her ability to mesmerize. As she hurried off she told me to meet her the next Saturday if it were a sunny day, under the big elm near home plate.

"Sun, rain, hail, snow, floods, tornadoes, even a chance to meet Elvis won't keep me away," I shouted after her.

"Just be here if it's sunny," Cindy hollered back, and then she disappeared down the hill.

"Hey, if she's new around here, how did she know where home plate was?" Jimmy asked.

"Guess she's just smart. After all she picked me." I gloated.

"That means she's stupid!" he fired back.

As Jimmy retrieved his glove we headed for his house on Danforth Street. He kept throwing his glove in front of him, and then he picked it up and threw it again. Jimmy was quiet until we approached his back stairs. It was then he turned to me and said, "Just remember, beauty is only skin deep." He threw his glove one last time.

"C'mon, Jimmy, don't let this ruin our friendship."

Then he repeated one more time, with a more sinister delivery, "Beauty is only skin deep, *my friend*."

"And just what do you mean by *that*, my friend?"

Jimmy drew closer to my face, "Well, if beauty is skin deep, then we should SKIN her. HEH HEH HEH...HEH!!!

Jimmy was my best friend, but he did have his dark side. But I laughed too. So I guess I have a dark side as well. Maybe all God's children got a dark side.

3

The seven days leading up to my next meeting with Cindy made up the longest week of my life. "Slower than molasses running up hill," is what Joe would say. He would usually be referring to my running from home plate to first base, but, in this case, I use the phrase in the context of time. All that week it seemed like I called the weather phone every thirty minutes to get the forecast. When Saturday *finally* came around, the sun was out. My moment had arrived. The anxiety made me realize my world would never to be the same again. As much as I wanted to say hello to the next chapter of my life with Cindy; I didn't want to say goodbye to those happy days I shared with Jimmy, waiting for the page to turn.

Jimmy and I had talked frequently during the past week, and he had stopped throwing his glove or anything else. I can never remember a time when we weren't the best of friends for very long. He had only one request, other than to tell him *everything* we did. And that was to ask her if she had a friend.

I arrived through the front gates with my head down and my hopes up. Would she be there when I raised by eyes? Would she be as pretty as she had appeared last week? Had my mind made her even more alluring and captivating during the previous seven days when I thought of nothing else but her beauty and her way of almost hypnotizing me? The mind can play tricks on you when you are blinded by desire, or when you are in the throws of fear. It could be twice as tricky when you are falling in love *and* afraid at the same time.

When I got to the edge of the field, where the tombstones ended and the grass began, I looked up slowly and she was there. She was radiant with the sun shining off her golden hair, even more beautiful than my mind had imagined. I approached almost in embarrassment. Without Jimmy around I was half as confident in my ability to be "cute". As I got nearer my knees grew weaker. I wasn't even close to being a grown man. I was Jell-O. No, I was freakin' Barney Fife trying to get up the nerve to ask Thelma Lou out on a first date.

"Nice to see you again, Charlie." Cindy smiled with her sensuous lips and glowing eyes.

"Hello."

"Is that all you have to say, 'hello'?" she asked.

"Hello, Cindy."

"What happen to, 'Hello Baaaaaby'. Are you only silly when your friend is around?"

This wasn't how I imagined it would be. I thought I would walk right up to her and confidently shake her hand or maybe give her a small kiss on the cheek. Then we would sit down under that old elm, talk, listen to my radio, and get to know each other. Jimmy's prodding of, "Make sure you get some elbow-tit," wasn't something I was concerned with. I wanted to be Dobie Gillis not Hugh Hefner.

"Come, give me a kiss on the cheek and sit down with me, if that's what you want. We can talk and listen to your radio if you like. And don't worry about what Jimmy would do. Do what you want to do ... Dobie." My mouth dropped opened. My heart began racing, not because I couldn't help being in love with her, but because *she knew what I was thinking*. I started to back away, but she stepped forward and said so softly and sweetly, "I mean...Charlie" Her green eyes looked into mine, and I began to feel better, safer.

When she took my hand the fear and anxiety seemed to leave; and, almost in seconds, I felt comfortable. Quickly it seemed like we had known each other for a long time, and I was at ease. We leaned back against that tree, holding hands and quietly becoming the friends I had hoped we would. The fact she seemed to know what I was thinking became somewhat comforting as well. If she still wanted to be my girl, after knowing everything about me, I figured I had nothing to be worried about.

"Cindy, how do you know what I'm thinking?" I asked, as if it had a simple answer.

"It's just a trick. You know, like a parlor game. My mother taught me. It's like a family trait." She then held my hand tighter and whispered, "In time, I may teach you, but for now you'll just have to guess what I'm thinking. Although, I just might have to give you a few clues."

Then I began to get a small idea of what was on her mind as she turned and gave me that first kiss ɔn the lips. I could hear Jimmy again. *If she kisses with her mouth open she'll do the deed, my friend. You better tell me everything you two do. You owe me that. I'd tell you.*

It was there, behind home plate near the big old elm tree, that Cindy changed my world forever. On my transistor The BIG JAB was playing <u>Sugar Shack</u> by Jimmy Gilmer. Cindy mentioned how much she liked sugar and that it was sweet kissing me. *Oh, man. She's smooth.* Little did I know. That first kiss was innocent and gentle, and I thought Jimmy might have to wait another time to hear the kind of lurid encounter he was hoping for... or would he? Cindy smiled seductively as she clicked off the radio, saying she wanted all my attention. Never taking her eyes off mine, she took out the antique-looking clasp that was holding her ponytail together. She shook her hair till it settled softly over her shoulders. Knowledgeable beyond her years, she gently pushed me down on the shady grass and stretched her long body over mine.

Her strawberry fragrance was intoxicating. She was the spider and I was the helpless fly. Her green eyes seemed to grow bigger, but maybe that was because they were about an inch away from mine. Again she pressed her lips on my lips, gently at first, but quickly her advances grew more aggressive. With more strength than I could muster she rolled us through the grass; and, with the last tumble, I found myself now on top and breathing heavy.

My mind was trying to catch up with what was going on, but there wasn't time to comprehend everything. My head was spinning. The cemetery grounds seemed to be moving up and down like a sea of tombstones.

Cindy locked her hands together behind my head and pulled me forward till we kissed again. But this time her mouth *was* open, and I felt her tongue searching for mine. As she pried my mouth wider it seemed like her tongue darted down my throat. I swear she could touch my tonsils.

Before our meeting, as I was walking down Vaughn Street, I was making up stories in my mind that I would tell Jimmy to make him more jealous. What was happening now was more than I had imagined and more than Jimmy would have ever believed.

Cindy withdrew her tongue only to get some air, air that I desperately needed as well. With her lungs full she proceeded to plunge her tongue deeper and deeper, and I didn't have the strength or the desire to resist her. She was now in complete control for whatever would happen next.

With the crickets singing their love song in the tall grass behind us; and with the eerie feeling that someone was watching, she was ending my childhood.

Now, sitting upright over me, she lifted her tank top to expose small but perfect breasts. It was like looking at one of those Playboy magazines that Jimmy kept under his bed.

She then removed her top, pulling it up over her head and tossing it to the side. She stretched her arms back, placing her hands on the ground behind her and pushing her young breasts up, closer to me.

For a moment I thought I was having the kind of dream teenage boys with raging hormones hope to have when they close their eyes. But this was more real than any juvenile fantasy.

Cindy smiled, plying her talents. "You like my fried eggs?" she whispered in her sex kitten way.

WOW! How did she know that's what Jimmy and I called them? She is amazing!

I realized I didn't even know her last name, but I was sure it wasn't Modesty.

"I can't wait for breakfast," I barely managed to say. My mouth had gone dry.

With that she cupped her breasts in her hands and brought them to me. "Charlie, this is what you want. And I want it too."

Adam could have resisted Eve and that apple in the Garden of Eden easier than I could have turned away from Cindy at that moment. As I gave in to temptation she seemed to lose control as well. She moaned, "Oh, John, it's been so long."

Oh yes, I wanted to ask, "Who the hell is John?", but I didn't want to *lose the moment* as they say. I felt I couldn't stop to ask about old boyfriends. I just wanted her. She said she wanted me.

Cindy's fingers were long and thin, and as they crawled up my legs it felt like they were working independently of each other. She continually kissed me deep into my mouth as if she was devouring me. She was doing everything to me I had hoped she would. To her, my mind was an open book, and she was reading every page.

Guilt took a vacation with buttons popping and belts unbuckling. We melted into one mass of naked flesh. If someone had been looking on they couldn't have told my hands from her hands, or distinguished my moans from her moans. She took all I had to give, and then lay silently beside me for about thirty minutes.

As I started to regain some sense of control she kissed me on the forehead and asked if I would come back to see her the next Saturday. I could barely get the yes-words out when she kissed me again, hard and fast. It was if she wanted to repeat what had just happened, but I could hardly walk by then.

As we were hunting for all our clothes, scattered over a pretty good distance, she said, "Don't ask, Charlie."

"Don't ask what?" I said, fastening the belt that my dad had given me for my birthday.

"Don't ask about John," Cindy replied while fastening that old looking hair clasp and forming a new ponytail.

"How did you know I wanted to ask that?" I tried to button my shirt but I failed to match the right button with the correct buttonhole. I was so nervous I was lucky I didn't have the damn thing on inside-out.

"Let's just say it's woman's intuition," she smiled as she lowered her tank top down over her breasts.

"Cindy, I felt like there was someone watching us," I warned as I tucked my shirt into my pants.

"If someone was, it wasn't him, Charlie. He's somewhere in Massachusetts."

"But, he is an old boyfriend, right? You're still not seeing him?" I asked in apprehension, hoping she would say she hated him and he was a big mistake.

"I haven't seen him for years," she said matter-of-factly as she put her arms around me.

"Years? How many years? You're like… only seventeen, right?"

Cindy didn't answer that. She just said, "Let's just say I will never see him again, and he never meant as much to me as you do. How's that?"

"That sounds pretty good," I conceded as I gave in to her answer.

She gave me a gentle hug, the way she had done last Saturday when Jimmy and I had first met this mysterious girl. "Thanks for loving me, Charlie. Please don't stop feeling that way about me, no matter what."

"No matter what? What do you mean by that? You're not married, are you!?!" I exclaimed like that would be the worst thing ever.

She pushed her fingers slowly through my hair and soothingly said, "You do have an inquisitive mind don't you? Don't worry. I'm your girl now." She then kissed me, deep again into my throat. I remember thinking that her kisses tasted like honey, and that her tongue really *could* reach my tonsils.

"Just trust me, Charlie. And don't ask so many questions. All you need to know is that I really love you, and only you. Okay?"

Cindy was the most exciting girl I had ever met, but I had to admit she was a little strange. I guess I was just intimidated by her mysterious ways, but I really did love her. I didn't know love could come on that fast, but it did.

As I reached to hug her one more time I noticed those little bees that I had first seen last week, gathering again on her shoulder. By instinct I went to brush them off.

"No, Charlie, they mean no harm," she said as she pulled out of my reach. She waved her arm and those on her shoulder, about ten by now, buzzed off to be with the others swarming on the tree behind us.

"You act like you know them, and they act like they know you. That's really weird. It's almost like they are pets," I remarked. "You know what's weirder. I have been coming to this cemetery to play ball for five years, and I have never seen bees that small. Come to think of it, I've never seen tiny bees like that anywhere."

She smiled and said I probably just hadn't noticed them before, that I had been to busy playing ball.

"Oh yeah? Do they have little bees like that in Massachusetts?"

"As a matter of fact I've seen bees just like them in Massachusetts," she stated, like she had an answer for any question I might ask.

I soon felt the kid coming out in me again and said, "I told my mom I would be back by five."

I can just see it now, *Hi Charlie. Did you have fun with Jimmy today?* she would ask as I came up the stairs. I'll say, *Oh yes, Mom. We played ball, and then we worked on our Eagle Scout merit badges.* She would then say, *That's nice, Dear. Now wash up for supper.*

As I walked toward the cemetery gates after kissing Cindy goodbye and assuring her I would be back the next Saturday, I realized there was no going back to the world of Ozzie and Harriet. I was growing up. I felt happy and sad at the same time. I had crossed the threshold to adulthood. Maybe too soon, I wasn't sure. There was a warning sign that flashed across my mind: DANGER. But it flashed off as quickly as it flashed on, and I ignored it.

Cindy stood there under that big elm until I got to the front gates. As I turned and waved I noticed the swarm of bees behind her was growing larger. I wanted to yell for her to be careful, but I sensed she was aware of her surroundings. When I got across the street I turned again to see if she was still there. But she was gone and so were the bees.

She never gave me a phone number or an address. She didn't mention anything about her parents or whether she had any brothers or sisters. She never really said for sure that she was seventeen. And she never did say whether she had a friend for Jimmy. He would soon be throwing things again.

I headed for home with my head still swimming. I had a lot to learn about women. I once made out with Joanie St. John at a party and got some *elbow-tit*, the way Jimmy had taught me. He said girls wouldn't notice if you were careful, and, if you were successful, you would have something to brag about to your friends.

I said to myself, *They notice all right. It's guys who are stupid and unaware.*

I flipped on The BIG JAB just in time to hear Elvis sing, <u>I Got Stung</u> (By A Sweet Honey Bee...YEAH!)

4

Soon, Saturday was almost every day of the week, and I saw Cindy almost constantly. Only rain would keep Cindy away. She never would say why. There were exceptions for me too, such as driver's ed. classes and, by now, a part-time job at a small hardware store down the street. Joe and Jimmy knew where I was and what I was doing in my free time.

Jimmy was working at the I.G.A down on St. John Street that summer. We saw less and less of each other. But I knew he would always be there if I needed a friend, and the time was fast approaching when I would need him

Life was good, and it stayed good most of the summer as Cindy and I found all the pleasures of young love. Then one day, out of the blue, she dropped a bomb on me. Cindy said that after Labor Day she was going away, and that she needed my help to make it possible. Her big green eyes were flooded with tears. The tears even seemed to cause her physical pain as well. She grabbed my hand and held it so tightly that for a moment I thought I would lose circulation. I had never seen her so vulnerable. She looked like a little girl who had lost her mommy at the mall, and not the woman who was always in control.

"My help? What can I do? Besides, I don't want you to go away." I held her to me, as close as I could. I was almost panicking. I had never been stung like this before, and I knew it was going to hurt for a long time. Maybe for the rest of my life.

"Charlie, there is something I want to tell you...a secret," she softly whispered in my ear.

"What is it?" I asked, trying to guess it before she could answer. *Maybe she's going to tell me that trick of reading minds. I saw a gypsy lady do that at Old Orchard Beach and always wondered how she did it. Maybe she's going to tell me her real age. Or worst of all, maybe she's going to tell me she's going back to that John guy from Massachusetts.*

"I'm not sure you will understand or if your will believe me," she said nervously as she walked me over to sit down by the old elm tree.

"I'll believe anything you say. I love you!" *Maybe she's going to tell me why she doesn't like to come out in the rain...Or maybe she's dying from an incurable disease.*

She hugged me that gentle hug, the way she had the first day we met. I can't explain it, but in some ways her little hugs meant more to me than the passionate kisses we had shared all summer long.

"I've waited for someone like you, Charlie, for a long time... someone...who would truly love me."

"What's a long time, Cindy? You're only seventeen, right?" I demanded to know.

"Do I look seventeen? Then I am seventeen." She smiled through her tears. "And, no, I'm not going back to anyone anywhere. I will always love you, Charlie." Then she almost laughed through her tears when she said, "And I'm not going to teach you how to read minds. Ask the old gypsy you once saw."

"Cindy, just what is it you have to tell me?" I stopped trying to guess in my mind. What was the point? She seemed to know everything I was thinking, including how much I would like to be able to read *her* mind.

She paused for a moment, "This may not be the right time. There are still a couple of weeks before I have to leave. Let's spend as much time together as we can."

This is good. This will give me time to try and convince her to stay.

She smiled at my thought, all the while knowing what I didn't know. There would be no tomorrow. Our last kiss would be today.

For the next hour or so there was little conversation. There was no need for it. We had come to the point where we didn't need to talk. We just needed to hold on to each other. I no longer had any concern for those tiny bees that always seemed to be so close to her. I figured they were attracted by her strawberry scent. I know I was. Sometimes my mom would ask if I had been out picking strawberries. The scent was all over my clothes. I once wiped Cindy's face with a handkerchief, and hid it in a drawer with my baseball cards. The sweet smell lingered. I still have it to this day. It's my most cherished possession.

As I sat quietly holding her I let my mind wander and think.

Her invisible family that I had never met, that to my knowledge had no last name or permanent residence, was taking away the very reason I had for getting up in the morning.

In the beginning I thought Cindy belonged to a family of gypsies who were always on the move, and sometimes lived out of their cars or trailers. You know the type. They pull up to your house and tell you your chimney's about to topple, or your driveway needs to be re-sealed. Before you know it you're forking over a few hundred bucks for repairs to a chimney that soon topples anyway and a driveway that starts showing cracks a few days after these wanderers are long gone. Could Cindy be a part of that crowd? The idea seemed as logical as any other. And then there was Jimmy Peters' idea about her secret life.

One Sunday, a few weeks after I had met Cindy, Jimmy's family invited me to go along on a trip to the lake. At first I didn't want to go. I wanted to be with her, but I also wanted to see Jimmy and get his thoughts about my mysterious girlfriend.

Of course, Cindy's name came up before Jimmy and I could be alone. After the obligatory teasing from his sisters, Polly and Priscilla, that "Charlie's got a girl friend" and "Charlie and Cindy sittin' in a tree...blah blah blah," Jimmy and I went out on his boat.

It was there, in the middle of Sebago Lake that he offered up his theory. Sitting on the edge, with his feet dangling in the water, Jimmy said, "I think she's on the run. She's got the cops on her tail...where I'd like to be...heh heh heh." Jimmy looked up at me with his eyes squinting in the sun.

"Peters, you're such a perv," I said, now wishing I had gone to see Cindy instead of going to the lake to hear Jimmy's crap.

"Maybe she goes from town to town searching for a one armed man like Dr. Richard Kimble on that new TV show, The Fugitive," Jimmy continued sarcastically.

"Well, if she's searching for a guy with a small dick, I'll give her your name," I fired back.

"Hey Man, my *being-on-the-run* theory isn't that crazy. If not the cops, maybe she's a runaway. Yeah that's it. Her old man is probably trying to get in her pants, or her mom is a drunk who's farming her out to do tricks for a bottle of hooch. You never know, my friend. It's getting to be a big bad world out there."

All of a sudden I was hoping my gypsy theory was the real one, but Jimmy's runaway theory seemed more likely. Hopefully not for the reasons he stated.

We spent the rest of the day water skiing and goofing off, like the best friends we always were.

As I sat there next to Cindy with my legs trembling and by heart hurting she knew I wanted the answers to all my questions; but she just kissed me in her very "special" way, and said to meet her there tomorrow. She made me promise to wait for the answers and purred in my ear the gentle words, "I will love you forever, Charlie."

"Forever? Hell, I should have my driver's license by then!" I teased.

"I like the way you can still joke, Charlie. It's gift. Use it well."

A light rain began to fall and she said it was time for me to leave. She hurried off down the hill and out of sight. The bees followed.

Who was this mystery girl? Who were her parents? Where was she from? Where was she going? How can anyone have bees for pets? Why did the rain bother her so and, most of all, why couldn't I see her again after Labor Day?

Frankie Valle & The Four Seasons sang on my radio, <u>Big Girls Don't Cry.</u> They never told you that, sometimes, big boys do.

While walking down Carroll Street to Thomas Street to home and the security of my room, I went over in my mind all the conversations that I had with Cindy. When we talked, which was rare as other things occupied our time, we talked mostly about music, movies, and baseball. Well, to be honest, it was me who talked about movies, music, and baseball. Cindy just listened, I guess now, out of courtesy. I don't think she really cared about the rumors circulating that Paul was dead and now there were only three Beatles. She really didn't give a rat's ass that the Red Sox had no chance of winning the pennant, or that there was a new James Bond movie playing at The

Strand. No sir. It seemed her world revolved around that cemetery and our romantic encounters there. Come to think of it, that *was* better than seeing the Sox win a World Series. There's always *next year* in baseball, but there would be no *next year* with Cindy.

I got up early the next morning. What the hay, I couldn't sleep anyway. The sun was out, but it was unusually cool for the end of August. The wind was coming in off the ocean with an extra strong gale. There had been a long drought most of the summer with just a few showers now and then, but not enough to make the farmers care. It was predicted to last through the fall, but they didn't have the sophisticated satellite pictures they have today. A storm was brewing, but nobody knew except for Dad. "My knees are aching. There's going to be a storm." Who needs the Weatherman?

I went downstairs and my dad, an early riser, was cooking breakfast. He was a tall man at six feet two who always dressed as if he were going someplace special, like to church or out to dinner. He always had a fresh flower in his label, and his shoes were always shined. His face was freshly shaved, and his wavy white hair was always combed. The aroma of Old Spice followed him around everywhere he went. I first learned to make wisecracks from him.

"Good morning, Charlie. You're up early, aren't you?" Always the jokester he went on, "Would you eat a fried egg if I boiled it?"

If he knew the fried eggs I was thinking about, he would have boiled me. "Thanks, Dad, but I'm not hungry." I plopped down in a flowered vinyl kitchen chair.

"No breakfast. Are you feeling okay?"

I lied and said, "Yeah Dad, I feel fine." Then I flipped on the radio, a sure sign to him that I was telling the truth. I just didn't want to talk.

I really didn't crave a shot of rock-n-roll at the time either, but I got one just the same as BIG JAB GOOD GUY, J. J. Jeffries, announced, "Here's Del Shannon from a few years back, and I wonder where she'll stay...my little run, run <u>Runaway"</u>. With each repeat of those words, I began to think more and more that Jimmy was right.

It's strange how you can hear a song a hundred times and never think about the words until their meaning hits home in your own life. Next up the Beatles. (She Was Just Seventeen When) <u>I Saw Her Standing There</u>. When J. J. played Roy Orbison and <u>It's Over</u> (Your

Baby Won't Be Near You Anymore) I shut him down.

I left the house at 11:30. It took about twenty minutes to make the journey; but I wanted to give myself extra time, extra time to practice my, *It-was-nice-knowing-you-and-I-really-want-to-wish-you-the-best* line. The truth was I really did hope that, wherever she was going and whatever she would be doing. As I walked though the alley that runs in back of the row houses where Joe and I lived and knew all the neighbors, I wondered if they had any idea that the boy they had known for seventeen years had lost his innocence in the old cemetery. If they saw me today would they think I was on my way to play baseball?

Would Mrs. Flaherty yell, "Hey Charlie, how's your mother? Tell her to bring you and Joe over for some ice cream real soon." She still saw us as little kids. I think they all saw us that same way back when neighbors were part of our extended family.

Would Mr. Devlin shout, "How ya doin', Charlie? Tell your dad I got extra tickets to the Red Sox. Me and the family would like you and Joe to come with us to Boston if you can."

As I passed by Mrs. Conley's open window I could smell fresh bread. It even made me pause and inhale some of the air. Cindy's scent was my favorite today, but before Cindy, bread was number one. Mrs. Conley waved out the window and said, "Stop in on your way home from playing ball, Charlie, and I'll give you some bread to take home to supper."

I waved back "Thank you, Mrs. Conley. You're very kind, I'll do that."

I could hear her say to her husband, "He's such a good boy." *Ya, right!*

I knew none of them would say, "Hey, Charlie, I hear you been bangin' some broad up in the bone yard." Growing up wasn't as fun as I had once thought. When you do, ice cream never seems to taste as good. You get your *fresh* bread at a giant supermarket that had just defrosted it. You still love the Red Sox, but you learn they are just men with weaknesses and dark sides. They are not the gods you once placed on a pedestals.

I looked up and saw the sun was falling behind dark clouds and drops of rain were starting to make patter sounds on the ground. Cindy hated the rain. I guessed it was a hair thing. I didn't know for sure, but I knew it wouldn't keep her away on this day. I'll just add it to my list of questions along with, "Who *was* this John guy from her past?" I hadn't let go of that. The only name I wanted on her lips was Charlie.

Early last evening I bought her a gift, a gold chain with a heart that opened up and revealed a small picture of me. On the back, I had the man at Day's Jewelry Store etch in tiny letters: LEST WE FORGET.

When John Wayne retired from the army in the movie, <u>She Wore A Yellow Ribbon,</u> his cavalry troop presented him with a watch with those words on it. At the time, I thought that was cool. If it could make John Wayne cry, it should make Cindy remember me.

The rain was falling harder as I approached the front gates to my old haunt. My heart felt like it would leap out of my chest. I wanted to run back home and pretend the clock was turned back to the beginning of summer when my biggest concern was getting my driver's license, and I was still a boy. But a man's gotta do what a man's gotta do.

Cindy was always there before me, but not today. At least I couldn't see her. Maybe she was seeking shelter from the storm that was really intensifying with each passing moment.

When I reached the very spot where she had always stood under that old elm, lightning flashed and thunder crashed. A big branch at the top exploded and fell to the ground. A hornets nest came down with it. And I had visions of being the next George Chamberlain, running and screaming, and praying that the pain would stop.

The bees scurried out of their demolished home, but, instead of attacking me, they just swarmed under another branch. It felt like they were looking at me and saying, "Hey, not your fault, act of God. But that fat kid, he bashed our friends' nest with his big fat head, so he got what was coming to him."

I stood there for an hour letting the cold rain have its way with me, the way I wanted her to. I couldn't believe Cindy would let the storm keep her away, not on the day she promised to answer all my questions and maybe kiss me a final goodbye.

When the unexpected happens your mind starts to play Sherlock

Holmes. You think of all the possible reasons why things go wrong. Maybe she was sick or hurt somewhere. Maybe she didn't have warm clothing for a cold rainy day. Maybe vanity did play a role, and she didn't want me to see her unless she felt she was perfect. Maybe she had a chance to jump a train like the bums down at The Hobo Grounds, which was just farther down the hill.

Then, the worse thought of all, maybe Jimmy was right. Beauty is only skin deep, and she didn't really care at all. *Elementary, my dear Watson, elementary.*

After another 30 minutes had passed I took my gift and placed it, with love, under that old broken tree. The bees still swarming there seemed to make room for me as if they understood.

I went to Jimmy's to wait out the rest of the storm, and to renew our friendship. He and I hadn't spent that much time together since Cindy came into my life, and I needed his wisdom and understanding. I even needed his, *I told you so. I told you, beauty is only skin deep.* Going through a rite of passage is best shared with your best friend, especially when the passage hurts so badly.

I told Jimmy about the entire relationship, the good and now the bad. He listened intently and hung on to each word like he was in total disbelief. After I was through with my story he gave me some Hallmark crap about pain fading with each new day, and that when God closes one door He opens another. Then he said with a straight face, "My friend, I've gone all the way with a dozen girls as pretty as Cindy, and they all came back begging for more." We looked at each other for about ten seconds without saying a word, and then broke out into uncontrollable laughter. I needed that. We hugged each other and punched each other in the arm. Lest we forget.

I know what you're wondering. Yes, I did go back the next Saturday and many more Saturdays after that, but the only ones there had been there for over a hundred years. My Cindy was gone. The gold chain with locket was gone too. Probably some old bum, looking for cans and bottles, found it and hocked it. Jimmy and I never played ball there again. That was for kids.

5

"Who wants ice cream? Who wants ice cream?" shouted Andrea Rios.

"I do. I do. I do," answered an endless chorus of young voices as they pushed and shoved their way to the head of the line. I remember when it was my turn to host the freshman reception many years ago. When they rushed for the free food, I just screamed at them, "BACK OFF, you little mutants!!!"

She didn't say anything. She just looked at them with caring eyes. They lined up quietly behind each other, with a please-and-thank-you coming out of each one of them. *She's magic*, like Samantha Stevens on <u>Bewitched</u>, but Andrea Rios didn't even have to twitch her nose. All the other teachers looked on with awe and wonder as well.

A month ago these kids were 8th graders, but now they were on their way to becoming the next freshman class at John Marshall High School in Oceanside, California.

The annual picnic at Capistrano Park was put on by the faculty. Andrea Rios was our newest member and according to our unwritten rules: the newest teacher has to be the main hostess, sort of a baptism under fire. But it was the kids who were baptized by this young charismatic teacher.

Her ease, and the way she conducted herself around the kids, was genuine. She spoke Spanish as well as she did English She didn't talk down to them and was always respectful, referring to them as, Mister or Miss, and not by their first names. She got respect in return.

The way she held on to my arm as she laughed and talked with each student made me feel special ...actually... honored.

Bob Piccone, the math teacher, gave me one of his *hubba-hubba* looks. Piccone was very active in the local Republican Party and was running for the state house in Sacramento. He came over to ask for Andrea's vote, and also to mention that he was single and ten years younger than me. Then he pointed and said, "By the way that's my Vette over there...if you want to go for a ride sometime."

When Andrea asked, "Is that why I should vote for you?" as she held my arm tighter, Piccone got flustered, mumbled something under his breath and walked away.

She made all the kids feel special, and no one has made me feel that special in a very long time.

I met her for the first time about a month ago when I heard my name over the school intercom. "Charles Sullivan to the Principal's office" and then repeated again. The voice was that of the Principal, Bernard Allen.

On my way down the hall to his office my mind was wondering what he wanted on this last day of the school year. My guess, he wanted me to take a over a summer class because some teacher had just canceled out. It could be he was going try to convince me, one more time, to head up the debating team next year. Most likely, it would be to answer some irate parent's complaint that I didn't understand how hard History was for junior; all those names and meaningless dates.

As I entered his office, I spotted the big picture that now hung on the wall behind him.

"Barn, is that what you want me to see, a new portrait of yourself?"

"For God's sake, Charles! That's John Marshall, the first Chief Justice of the U.S. Supreme Court, for whom this school is named. You do talk about him in class, don't you?" the old Principal exclaimed as his blood pressure started to rise.

"Huh! Sure looks a lot like you, Barn...same beady eyes, same sour puss."

Frustrated, he shook his head and mumbled, "Mrs. Allen said I should retire. I could have years ago. I must be the oldest living principal in California. Why don't I listen to her?"

"When you do, take that picture with you. That guy is ugly!"

"I thought you said it looked like me!...Oh, never mind." The Principal sat down behind his cluttered desk, piled high with manila folders that contained everything from job applications to requisition forms for new text books. On the corner was a picture of a young Bernard Allen with his platoon buddies in Korea. He was sixteen when he left his daddy's farm to join the marines. He told the recruiter he was eighteen. His wife, Georgia, told me that was the only time he ever lied in his life. Each year they hold a reunion. Out of the original sixteen in the picture, there are only five still alive.

"I only get drunk once a year," he told me the first time I asked about the black and white photo. "We have one drink for each one of our buddies who has gone on to his last reveille. They were a great bunch of guys."

I was careful not to disturb the sacred picture as I placed the final grades for my students on top of the massive pile. It was then a vision of loveliness caught the corner of my eye. She was sitting on the small couch near the bookcase where Barn kept his collection of Zane Grey novels.

"Charles, I want you to meet Miss Andrea Rios. She'll be teaching freshman English starting in the fall. I thought you might show her around. Her class will be across the hall from yours. "Miss Rios, this is Charles Sullivan"...the head of our History Department."

"Yabba Dabba Do!!! Things are looking up in Bedrock, hey Barn?" I happily said, irritating the old Principal at the same time.

Principal Allen, wiping sweat from his forehead with a few coffee filters, lamented, "Miss Rios, you'll have to excuse Charles. He's Irish. I'm told some of them drink...a lot! He means well but he's like an untrained puppy. You have to whack him on the head with a rolled up newspaper every now and then. Hopefully it's the heavy Sunday edition of the L.A. Times."

"Nice to meet you, Mr.Sullivan," said Andrea Rios "My mother's family came from Ireland," she said with a slight Chicano accent. It just added to her charm. "Principal Allen speaks very highly of you."

I gave Barn a look as if to say, *That'll be the day!*

She smiled broadly as she reached out to shake my hand, as if amused at my immaturity. The fact that she wasn't offended was a relief to Barn, whose lectures on sexual harassment were a source of pride for him. I felt like telling him that I might need a refresher course, but I held my tongue. I'm sure the thought had already crossed his mind.

Miss Rios looked to be in her early 30's. It was hard to tell. I'm not good with ages. I gave up guessing a long time ago when I was seventeen. Her perfect white teeth that revealed that winning smile, were surrounded by full lips. Her skin was flawless. Her blue eyes, with no need for makeup, were oversized like Tweety's in the Looney Tunes cartoons. All of a sudden I was feeling sorry for Sylvester. "Thuffering thuckertash!" That cat must have really wanted that bird.

The strangest thing was that she acted as if she had no idea of her immense beauty. The little cross that hung gently around her neck was fitting. She seemed like such an innocent. It was then I could hear Jimmy saying in my mind, *Looks can be deceiving.* I pushed him aside, but he came back with another one of his cliches, *Remember, my friend, the Devil has a pretty face.* One more shove and he was gone, for the time being. Almost as strange to me was why she was still *Miss* Rios. Surely she must have had hundreds of proposals. Could it be that she had one special love that she could never forget. Maybe we had something in common other than being on the faculty together at Marshall High.

After a little more small talk with Barn, Miss Rios and I set off for the *El Grande* tour.

"And Charles, don't call me Barn unless we're outside school property," the Principal shouted as we left his office. He always called me Charles.

His better half, Georgia, told me that he really didn't mind me calling him Barn. In fact, he actually liked it. Barn and Georgia Allen were like second parents to me. They had no children of their own. They were always there for me, and I was always there for dinner on Wednesdays and Sundays. In the last ten years I never spent a major holiday without them. Christmas doesn't seem like Christmas in Southern California when you have spent so many in the snow. Barn and Georgia had a way of making it feel good just the same. Did I tell you, I love them? Well, I do.

As we walked through the school, Miss Rios said, "Please call me, Andrea."

"Ditto," I said. "I mean don't call me Andrea. Please call me Charlie. Everyone calls me Charlie, except Barn. He calls me Charles."

We both laughed.

Suddenly Jimmy was taking up room and board in my head again. *What a maroon you are!*

"Why does Mr. Allen call you, Charles? Why doesn't he call you, Charlie?"

"Well, I don't mind telling you. I guess it will show you what kind of a man he is," I said as I invited her to sit down on a bench in the cafeteria.

"Would you like a soda?"

"Pepsi, your favorite, would be nice. Thank you. I've always had a sweet tooth. I don't think I could live without sugar." Her smile was mesmerizing.

"How did you know Pepsi was my favorite?" I asked somewhat perplexed.

"Oh, just a guess. You look like a Pepsi man," she said as she sipped her drink.

"I suppose if I ask you what a Pepsi man looks like, you'll just give me a description of myself."

"You're so smart, Charlie. Now, tell me why the Principal calls you Charles."

"Did you notice the picture on his desk?"

"The black and white one, the one with the soldiers?"

"That's the one. His wife first told me the story many years ago. One of the marines in that picture was his older brother, Charlie Allen. Barn joined the marines a year after Charlie, and within a year they ended up together in the same outfit in Korea. Barn's father had fought in that same division in World War I, and reluctantly went along with his youngest son joining up at such a tender age. He was proud of both of them, but often told Charlie to make sure he looked after his brother."

I found the emotion of the story getting to me as I was telling it, knowing what I was going to say next. I hardly knew this young woman, but somehow I wasn't embarrassed to continue. She reached for my hand and I went on, "Well, they were together in the center of a heavy fire fight as the marines were assaulting the harbor at Inchon. Suddenly, a hand grenade was tossed into their midst. Charlie Allen jumped on it, smothering the blast with his body...and saving his little brother. He died within minutes in Barn's arms. His last words were, 'Tell Dad I did my best'."

I had to stop for a minute. I finished off my Pepsi, giving myself more time to tell the story. Andrea's big blue eyes were welled with tears, making it more difficult for me to continue. I just looked at the empty bottle, peeled off the label and went on, "The guys in the outfit always called him, Charlie, as did Barn and all his friends. However, Barn's dad always called his oldest son, Charles. It was out of respect for a boy who never had much of a childhood. It seemed Charlie Allen was always a man, looking after Barn and working hard on the farm with his dad so that Barn could go to school. You see, Andrea, I find it very easy to tell Barn and Georgia that I love them because I do. But, Barn is one of those people who finds it difficult to say those words so freely, except to Georgia. She told me that by calling me Charles, as his father called Barn's brother, is Barn's way of telling me he loves me too."

Andrea wiped her eyes on a napkin from the dispenser on the cafeteria table. "I should go back to his office and give Principal Allen a great big hug."

"Hey, I told the story. I should get the hug!" I teased as my composure returned. She looked at me now as if we were *old* friends Her soothing smile made me feel like I had known her forever, or that I had seen her somewhere before. I wouldn't forget a beauty like Andrea Rios.

I soon learned that she wasn't just another pretty face. With a 4.0 from Pepperdine, Marshall High was lucky to have her on the staff. We talked and walked all over the school. I introduced her to all the teachers still left on the premises.

As we came to her room she said her family was from Ventura and that she had a sister, Denise, who was a dispatcher for CHP. I thought that could come in handy next time I got a ticket. Her dad had retired from Cal-Tran, and her mother ran a small child care while Andrea was growing up.

She said she liked baseball, and even though she was a California girl the Red Sox were her favorite team. She even liked the same kind of music that Jimmy and I grew up with.

Wow!!! Is this the perfect woman or what?

MIGHTY JOHN MARSHALL

After the tour I walked her to her car and we exchanged phone numbers. I told her to call me anytime, for anything. She said I could do the same. She smiled that enticing smile and gave me a gentle hug. It was then I could smell the strawberry fragrance that danced from her wine-colored hair. More than a song or an old movie, it's the smell or fragrance from long ago that can trigger the sharpest memories.

I breathed it in and thought of Cindy, and the way things used to be. Once in a while when I'm feeling down I'll take out the handkerchief that I still have, the one with Cindy's fragrance. A breath of her scent still remains. It's all I have left of her, not a picture or a love letter, just a faint hint of the intoxicating fragrance she used to wear. Now it was back and present in this new teacher at Marshall High, Miss Andrea Rios.

We said our goodbyes, and I watched Andrea drive away as Jimmy Peters tapped me on the brain, *Beauty is only skin deep.*

You're wrong, Jimmy. This time you are wrong!

Andrea had taken me up on my offer, to call on me for anything. The day after Barn introduced us she phoned to ask if I would help with the festivities that were now coming to a close on this classic California day, swept by warm Santa Ana winds.

She was a big hit with the incoming class. They all felt a part of the John Marshall High School Family after spending just a few hours with their new English teacher, Miss Rios.

I also called her several times, just to talk. I was enchanted by her voice. We went out for pizza on a few Saturday nights. We took in a movie or two and spent time with my family, the Allens.

My good friends, Rick Snyder and Mitch Mitchell, were not seeing as much of me this summer. When you have a chance to spend time with an angel you take it. I hadn't put my friends on the back burner since Cindy, when Jimmy was moved to the side.

Andrea took off for Ventura after the picnic in the park to spend a week with her family. She promised to be back by the 4th of July to watch the fireworks with me. I really didn't care about the fireworks. I really did care about Andrea. There was just *something* about her.

I was uneasy and comfortable at the same time when she was around. Why would this bright and beautiful young woman want to spend so much time with me? *When God closes one door, He opens another*. Shut up, Jimmy! I just never realized He took so long between door openings.

6

Monday was a normal summer day off, laundry, grocery shopping, cleaning up some to make sure my little bungalow on Mission Avenue wouldn't be condemned by the board of health. Friends, Rick and Mitch, would be over in the evening for our monthly poker-party. With Andrea out of town, it gave me a chance for a little male-bonding. Monday went according to schedule, no problems, good friends, lots of laughs. I won twenty bucks and even better, made the guys burn with envy. They met Andrea when I brought her by the radio station where they both worked. They now play the old-time rock n' roll records that were *hit-bounds* back when the BIG JAB was THE PUNCH OF GREATER PORTLAND.

Before we finished the first game, before the pizza arrived, the teasing began.

"What in all that is holy makes her see anything in you, Charlie boy?" Mitch asked as he popped the top on a can of Budweiser.

"What in all that is *unholy*?" chided Rick as he threw down a Jack-high hand.

"She's a little young isn't she, Charlie?" asked Mitch. He shot a glance at Rick as if to encourage more teasing.

Rick obliged. "Is she a teacher or a student?"

I didn't say anything. Frankly, I didn't know what to say. They were riding me pretty good, but there was still a lot of truth in their words. What is it she sees in me?

"You must be like a father-figure to her," Rick suggested.

"More like a grandfather-figure." Mitch howled in laughter.

"You lucky shit. Yeah, you lucky shit," they both murmured.

I have to admit I was feeling pretty lucky. There's been no one since Cindy who's made me care so much. Still, there was something in me that warned me to take it slow this time. *Don't go off the deep end, Charlie boy. There's no way back after that. Nothing left but the splat!!!*

The game broke up early, around 9:30. Mitch and Rick "The Slick"

Snyder had the early morning shift on KIMA—GOOD TIMES AND GREAT OLDIES.

After they left I decided to phone Andrea to say a quick hello, but the number she had left for her parents' house had been disconnected. I must have written it down wrong. Guess I am getting old. *Just as well.* Her parents probably go to bed early. Tonight, so did I.

Tuesday morning was routine, until those CNN headlines revealed that the normally quiet seaport town of Portland, Maine was shocked with the discovery of four bodies found inside an old cemetery.

As I put my razor down I listened closely, and hoped the anchor was talking about the two homeless men and the Feeney and Winchell boys. I turned off the faucet and wiped the foam off my half-shaven face. I walked slowly toward the TV as if that would make a difference in what he would say next. It didn't.

"All four girls were freshman at the University of Southern Maine," he said with little emotion in his well trained voice.

"FOUR GIRLS! FOUR GIRLS! FOUR GIRLS!" I kept repeating out loud. I couldn't believe what I was hearing. This can't be true. This kind of thing can't be happening, not in the very place where Jimmy and I had found such comfort, and where I had found such love.

My mind held on to a picture of serenity and joy, and I found it difficult to create an image of death and young life snuffed out way before it's time. I felt dizzy and the room began to spin. It could have been the result of too much greasy chips and pizza from the night before, but there was more than that making my stomach churn.

The newsman, with chiseled good looks just moments ago, began taking on the appearance of some zombie or fiend that you might have seen in one of those Night Of The Living Dead movies. His snow-white capped teeth dripped blood as he slowly repeated, "Fffooourrr Giirrrlllsss." He then smiled, like the Grinch stealing Christmas presents in Whoville. His formerly tanned skin was now ashen gray, and his perfectly hair-sprayed head was crawling with maggots. His eyes were red dots, like in those Polaroid photos I took of Andrea over at the Allen's. Those damn red dots! Only his eye-dots were pulsating like small hearts that began to beat louder and louder. BA-BOOM! BA-BOOM!! BA-BOOM!!! And then

DOUBLE EXPLOSIONS!!!!!! that splashed green slime all over his jacket and tie. His tongue which was now a scaly snake was swishing back and forth, and licking his goo-covered suit. The demented beast growled on; but all his words ran together, making the anguish more painful by keeping the rest of the facts unknown.

If not for the ringing of the phone, the newsman might have grown even more grotesque. With each successive ring he morphed back into the pretty-boy he was hired to be. The spinning room started to slow down. Reality was taking control again.

The mind can play evil tricks when the system is shocked, and mine had just been given a quadrupled jolt. The total of dead, found in my old playground, was now eight. It's been less than a week since the first two were discovered.

I could see by the caller ID it was Joe. At least he wouldn't catch me by surprise with the latest terror from back home.

"Hey there, Ugly. I'm not going to ask what's new. I just found out," I said with a low and serious voice.

"You found out what?" snapped the voice on the other end.

"I just saw on CNN that four USM girls were found dead in the old cemetery."

"Screw CNN! They never get anything right. Turn on FOX!!!"

"Never mind CNN, FOX, or PMS-NBC. What's going on!?!" I asked in frustration.

"Don't fudge your undies, Little Brother," Joe said with his know-it-all attitude.

"All right, Big Brother, play like Joe Friday and give me the facts."

"Well, from what I've been able to find out from John Plunkett over at the college, the girls were pledging to be in a sorority. Part of the deal was to spend the night in the cemetery. They were all from out of town, and were supposed to enter college in the fall. They had made a special trip to fulfill the requirements early so they could move right into the sorority house. They hadn't been told about the recent murders. Now, what CNN failed to tell you, Bro, is that only three girls were killed. One is still alive, but the cops want to keep it quiet until they have a chance to talk to her... that is if she comes around. She's in a state of shock and under heavy guard at Maine

Med."

Before I could respond, Joe added, "I also talked to Ben Matthews at the Sheriff's Office. None of the bodies, not one of the seven had any major wounds, cuts, bites, or bruises. I don't know about the girl in the hospital. Looks like they ought to call Mrs. Fletcher over at Cabot Cove to help solve this one. Not even that old TV wench would have a clue."

I didn't say anything for a moment. I was just like a sponge, absorbing everything Joe said.

"Maine Medical Center is just a stones throw from that cemetery." I finally replied.

"No shit, Sherlock. That's why there's a ton of security up there."

"Where were the girls from?"

"Plunkett said they were from Massachusetts. Two were on full sports scholarships. They called in the State Medical Examiner to perform the autopsies. I understand that Frank Blanchette in the Portland office was pissed because John Feeney wasn't happy with Blanchette's work on his son Paul or the Winchell boy. That's all I have for now."

"All right, Joe. I'll be in touch...But if you get anymore info, no matter how trivial, call me...immediately."

He belched in agreement. It was just another way he said goodbye. Nothing fazed Joe, except the Red Sox. Nothing could get him more upset than a fly ball hit over the Green Monsta' by an opposing player. "Take that shit-head out now! He couldn't strike out his grandmother!"

As for me, I needed some secure surroundings. I finished dressing in my jeans, and I picked a tee-shirt that read "MAINE, THE WAY LIFE SHOULD BE".

Next I drove over to see Barn and Georgia. Maybe what I really needed was a shoulder to lean on, or a pat on the head from someone who would say, "There, there, everything is going to be all right. I'm sure it's not as bad as it seems. They'll catch the killers. Soon everything will be peaceful again."

As I pulled into the driveway I could see Barn up on a ladder with a giant bottle of Windex. He insisted that he have the cleanest windows on the block. Barn took pride in everything he did. That's why he did everything well. I suppose it was from the marine training he received over at Camp Pendleton when he was a much younger man.

"Hey, Old Man, don't fall. Not at least until I've had a good meal," I teased.

"Charles, has anyone ever told you that you're a wise-ass?" he shouted down from his perch with a chuckle.

"Just you, Barn, just you," I hollered back.

Barn climbed down and as he walked to meet me on the porch I could see he was sweating hard and breathing heavy; but he still had muscles in his arms that could make the Hulk jealous. His white hair hung down over his forehead. When he tried to push it back it refused. His eyes were chestnut brown and honest. Simply put, he was a hard working, loving man.

"What are you doing over here on a Tuesday? You know Wednesday is the day Mrs. Allen makes your favorite beef stew." He tried to make light conversation. He really knew what was on my mind as he put the Windex and paper towels down on the front porch swing. "Mrs. Allen and I heard the news about the strange happenings going on back in your home town," he said sympathetically as he put his hand on my shoulder.

"I just talked to my brother. I guess there were three girls who died. There's one still alive, but she's unconscious."

"Well, that's good...I bet she'll pull through. C'mon inside, out of this hot weather and we'll talk."

Georgia met us at the screen door. She had a big jug of lemonade in one hand, while balancing three glasses in the other. She frosted the glasses before she poured the drink.

"That's what makes my lemonade tastes so good," she liked to brag.

Georgia was a tall thin woman where Barn was rugged and short. Her hair was silver and pulled up in a bun like Aunt Bee on The Andy Griffith Show, only Georgia was about a half foot taller and 150lbs lighter.

It seemed, besides their obvious love for one another, the only

43

thing they had in common were chestnut brown eyes.

Barn loved the Dodgers. "I'm always true to Dodger blue," he liked to remind fair-weather fans. If the Dodgers ever play the Red Sox in a World Series, Barn and I would have to watch in different rooms. The tension would be too great.

Georgia loved the ballet and the symphony, while Barn had his Dodgers and the <u>Westerns Channel</u>. He could cuss with the best of them, but no such words would come from Georgia.

For as long as I've known her, going on ten years; she always wore an apron in the house, just like my own mom had done. I teased her in similar ways.

"This apple pie is great, Georgia. Did you *buy* it yourself?"

Then she would come over and pretend to take it away from me, and I would take it and run. It's a ritual we both enjoyed.

I remember saying to her once, "What do you see in Barn? You could have any guy in town."

"Mr. Allen would starve to death and never find a clean shirt if I weren't around," she laughed.

"Mrs. Allen would have the most run down house in the neighborhood if I weren't here," Barn chimed in.

They always referred to each other as Mr. Allen and Mrs. Allen. It reminded me of the way Andrea always referred to her young students as Mr. or Miss.

"Its respect that holds a marriage together," they both said in harmony. They were a perfect match, and just what I needed in troubled times.

We sat down around the kitchen table, where all problems are solved.

For the next four hours I brought them up to date on my whole life including my happy days in that old cemetery with Jimmy and Cindy; and how Jimmy and I had found it so peaceful. I told them we had felt as safe there as we did in our own rooms. Now the memories of my growing up were being interfered with by the horror and reality of today. Good memories are very special. They are something you own, like a car or a home. You don't want anyone breaking in.

After I finished my story Georgia brought me a piece of pie, and said with a smile, "Here, Charlie. Have some of my freshly *purchased* apple pie."

We all laughed and talked for a while about upcoming school projects and other simple but happy things. We were creating future memories.

Then Barn took me by surprise when he said, "Charles, there's something else we have to talk about." He looked at his wife as if to give her a queue.

Georgia responded as requested, "I suppose you boys want to talk baseball. I've got some work to do in here so take your business out on the porch. There should be a nice breeze now that the sun is going down. Take some lemonade with you...shoo shoo!!!" She pushed us gently out the door and disappeared into the kitchen.

Barn and I took up residence on the old weather-beaten couch-swing on the front porch. As we sat down his demeanor took on that father-to-son look. He didn't say anything for a minute as if he were thinking how best to express his thoughts.

He then took a deep breath and said, "Charles, I want to talk to you about Andrea."

"Now that's a subject I wouldn't flunk in school," I responded with pride.

"Charles, please just listen for a while," he instructed. He got up and began pacing back and forth. He ran his fingers through his unruly white hair.

I began to get a bad feeling. I could see he was serious. "Is there anything wrong? I tried to call her last night in Ventura, but couldn't reach her. Is she all right? Has there been an accident?" I now asked nervously.

"Charles, I'm sure she's just fine. Now *please* be quiet and listen." He stopped his pacing and stood in front of me.

I rested my back against that old porch-swing and waited for the next shoe to drop.

The old man began, "It was last winter. I was trying to decide among the forty applications for the freshman English position when I got a call from an old and dear friend who asked me to consider one more candidate. That candidate was Andrea Rios."

"You made a great choice, Barn!"

"Please, Charles!!!" He was becoming more irritable. "I can only tell you as much as I can without stepping on the toes of confidentiality. I realize this is not a doctor/patient or priest/penitent situation, but what is in an employee's *god damn* private file is just that, private!"

"Barn, just what is it you're trying to tell me in your own awkward way?" My curiosity factor was in full gear.

"More than something I want to tell you, it's something I want to ask you."

"Ask me what?"

"I'm asking you not to get romantic notions when it comes to Andrea," he blurted out.

"ENHHHH!!!...Wrong...next! Barn, I'm already crazy about her. You and Georgia seem to like her too. Is it because she's that much younger than I am?"

"Hell, no! Don't get me wrong, Charles. We think she's a wonderful girl too from what we know, being around her these last few weeks. But what do you really know about her? There's always more to people than first impressions. All you see is a pretty woman, alone in the city with very few close friends. You don't really know her past. Yes, you know she's from Ventura. You know her parents' names. You know she's as smart as they come, and she turns heads everywhere she goes."

"And that's bad?" I asked.

He paused and looked down with his hands cradled behind his back, reminding me of Spencer Tracy in <u>Look Who's Coming To Dinner</u>. Tracy, talking to his daughter and her fiance, was trying to explain all the difficulties a black man and a white woman would have in this world. His speech and manner were now manifested in my friend, Bernard Allen.

Barn looked up and said," Charles, you know how Mrs. Allen and I feel about you. We just don't want to see you get hurt."

"I appreciate that, Barn, but you're still not getting through to me."

He took another breath, sighed, and went on, "When I called you to the office that day to meet her, I wanted you to be the one to show

46

her around. Of all the hound dogs on that staff...you were the one I trusted to be a gentleman. I wasn't trying to *fix you up*! I just wasn't thinking at the time. I didn't realize you might get serious about her."

"Too late for that now!" I stood up and started pacing the porch myself. As he paced left, I paced right. The conversation continued.

"Well, I blame myself. I should have made it clear from the start. I realize I'm creating a mystery here. I'm sorry about that, I really am. When she gets back in town I'll talk to her and see if I can get her to release some information...so you can understand why I'm asking you to back off."

"Barn, a little hug here and there, or an innocent small kiss on the cheek is all that has happened, but if she wants no more than that she should tell me herself." I pleaded my case.

"To tell you the truth, I don't know why she hasn't told you herself. Maybe it's just not easy for her. Hell, I don't know. I was asked not to say anything, and I promised I wouldn't. Listen, Charles, this has been a long day, first the troubles in Portland and now I'm burdening you with more grief. Go home and try to get a good night's sleep, and hopefully everything will work out here and in Maine."

I continued pacing, not really listening closely. My mind was going into overdrive, "Barn, are you saying...she's *married*?"

The old man looked surprised; like we were playing *Hot and Cold*, and I was getting warm. "Damn it, Charles!!! I'm not saying anything! Don't ask me anymore questions." The Principal's blood pressure was rising.

"I know!!! She's working under cover. Don't tell me she's a *narc*!...a *married* narc!"

"Charles, please go home and do as I ask. Wait till I have a chance to speak to her. Meanwhile, I'm going in and find out where Mrs. Allen hid my bottle of Jack Daniels." As he turned toward the screen door the old man hugged me and whispered, "Trust me, Charles, just trust me."

7

It was about ten o'clock that same night when I arrived back at my place. I did trust Barn, and I respected his position as Principal. I understood that he had to separate friendship from his job, but that didn't mean I wouldn't try to find other ways to learn the secrets Andrea was hiding. Just because I had the summer off didn't mean my curiosity was on vacation.

I hadn't turned off the TV in my rush to get over to the Allen's this morning, and CNN greeted me when I opened the door. I wanted to turn it off before any more bad news could keep me up all night, but that damn curiosity thing got in the way. I sat there in the dark with just the light from the screen, and watched as they recapped the events of the day. That Ken Doll model who first broke the bad news was gone, and Barbie was in his place.

She narrated the details as new footage was shown. "With the deaths of the four coeds, that brings the total to eight dead since two homeless men were found last Tuesday in the Western Cemetery. Portland Police are giving very little details as to the cause of the deaths, and are not saying if there are any suspects at this time. Police have set up a barricade around the perimeter of the cemetery to make sure no more people enter. There has been some speculation that the blockade was also constructed to prevent the attacker or attackers from escaping. Chief Ray Richardson did say there was a possibility the culprits were still in the cemetery, hiding. Richardson said his men had made an initial sweep after the two young boys were found dead, but nothing suspicious was discovered. Police are waiting for a special canine unit to arrive and hope to take the dogs in sometime tomorrow. CNN does have a crew on the way, and we hope to have more details with a live on the scene report when they arrive."

The film from the area, provided by a local TV station, was an aerial view of the cemetery and other parts of the surrounding neighborhood. I could see the baseball field where Jimmy and I had spent so many happy days, and where Cindy had won and broken my heart.

I saw the big mansions along the Western Prom where the rich sea captains of a century ago had built their massive homes. The camera swept down Cassidy Hill along the back gates of the cemetery and down to Danforth Street where Jimmy used to live. Seeing it all again, after all this time, just made the tragedy more unbelievable and sadder.

I didn't understand why the cops thought someone could be hiding in there. I remember most all of that area. It's not all that big. In the daylight there were very few places to hide. Those tombstones weren't that huge, except for a small row of crypts up back and one big mausoleum. Of course, back then Jimmy and I just ignored them. We were only interested in the big field in the center of the grounds. And Cindy and I didn't wander far from that big elm tree near home plate. I was hoping Joe was right, about one of the girls still being alive. Apparently CNN didn't have the sources he had. I tuned off the news babe and sat there in total darkness, contemplating the events of the day. Then the questions started popping up in my mind, like so much spam in my e-mail.

Was Andrea married? If so, why would she keep it a secret?

Was her husband a famous person? Maybe a movie star...and she didn't want her students to be distracted?

Was her real name, Andrea Rios? Might I, or someone else, recognize her real name?

And what about Barn? Why would he agree to keep her secret? It wasn't like him to be so evasive. He did say an important friend asked him to give her the job. He discarded the other thirty nine applicants without a second thought...hmmm...That is strange.

Could she really be working for the law...undercover? Sure, we've had problems with drugs at Marshall High, but no more than any other school.

I couldn't believe another beautiful girl I cared about could be almost as mysterious as Cindy. I didn't know anything about Cindy's past...And Barn was right...I don't know all that much about Andrea, except her parents have a disconnected phone number. I'm positive I wrote that number down correctly. Two beautiful girls...both very mysterious...with that same strawberry scent...*weird*. Of course, it could all be just one big coincidence.

Finally, I asked myself the question that you probably ask yourself from time to time. *Am I crazy, or is it just the rest of the world that's nuts?* Don't answer that. You are probably right. Either way, it's pretty freakin' scary.

I hopped up and headed for bed, anxious to get this day behind me. Hopefully tomorrow would be one of those ordinary boring days I used to complain about...but no more.

When your phone rings at 3 a.m., you know it's not good. It's either a wrong number and you won't be able to get back to sleep, or news that couldn't wait till daylight. When it's not the phone; but a banging on your door, that can *only* be bad news. No chance it's Publisher's Clearing House with a bunch of balloons and a check.

THUMP! THUMP!! THUMP!!! The pounding continued.

"Hold your horses," I yelled as I jumped into my pants and stumbled across the floor.

I opened the front door a crack, keeping the safety chain taut. A bright light blinded me and then an unknown voice asked, "Are you Charles Henry Sullivan?"

"Yes. What the hell do you want?"

"Please open the door, Mr. Sullivan."

"Not until you answer my question."

"My name is Robert Russell. I'm a detective with the Los Angeles County Sheriff's Office," he said as he lowered his flashlight.

I immediately thought there had been an accident...Rick, or Mitch, or one of my students...or God forbid... Andrea! As Detective Russell presented his credentials I loosened the safety chain and bolt. I could see he was not alone. A uniformed cop stood on each side of him.

As the law stepped in I turned on the living room light. "Now, what's this all about? Has there been an accident?"

"Mr. Sullivan, do you have any weapons on you or in the house?" Russell asked in a routine manner, but it wasn't routine to me.

"WHAT! NO!!!...I don't have any weapons!"

"Well, do you have any beer?...Just kidding!...Lighten up, Mr. Sullivan, and you'll get back to bed, and we'll get back to the donut shop as soon as possible." The cop lit up a huge cigar without asking if it was all right with me. He took a couple of big puffs and then said, "You like that one? It always cracks me up."

I was hoping this was a bad dream brought on by the excitement of the previous day; but it was real, and so was this slovenly dressed cop who made Columbo look like he was on Mr. Blackwell's best-dressed list.

"Do you mind if my men look around? I do have a search warrant, but it would be better if you...just cooperate." He smiled like a big Cheshire cat, and then picked cigar remnants from his lips.

"Look around, Cipowicz. Let me know if you find the TV remote. I've been hunting for it for two days." I was reaching that *I-don't-give-a-shit* point we all come to when we are overwhelmed by events.

"Oh, good one! Can I use that, Mr. Sullivan?" He pulled out a small notebook from his back pocket. "Please, sit down." As I did he asked, "Do you know a Kathy Kostenello?"

I watched his two men go into other parts of the house. I didn't really mind as I realized this wasn't about Andrea, and I couldn't think of any student by the name of Kostenello.

"Name doesn't ring a *bell*, and I'm not saying that as a teacher trying to be a smart-ass. Who is she? Does she go to Marshall?"

"She's a student all right, but not here. Miss Kostenello is a freshman at the University of Southern Maine. The Portland Police Department thinks you might know something about an assault that took place in their town, and that's why I'm here."

I immediately thought she might be one of those sorority girls mentioned on the news. But how the hell was she connected to me? I was speechless and this seasoned detective, crude as he might have been, picked up on my facial expressions as the thought of the recent killings crossed my mind.

"Mr.Sullivan, you do know something, don't you?" the Detective pressed.

Finally I spoke, "Well, I know there have been some attacks back there. That's where I'm from, but there is *no* way I had anything to do with them. I haven't been back there in years!"

"Cool your jets! I know. I checked. You've been here, but the people in power back there want to question you just the same. As a matter a fact they have a gift for you." Russell threw a plane ticket down on the coffee table. "Your flight leaves Thursday and I am personally going to drive you to the airport, and I do accept tips." He chuckled to himself.

"The place is clean, Detective," the uniform cops reported as they left through the front door.

"But if they know I was here all the time, why the hell do they want to talk to me?"

"Beats me, Pal. I just do what I'm told, and you'd better do the same. By the way, don't try to disappear. My men will be watching. I'll pick you up Thursday at seven. Don't bother having breakfast waiting for me...I'll pick up something on the way...ta ta! Enjoy the rest of your day," Russell said as he followed the other two outside.

"Yes, thanks, I think I'll have a party!" I yelled after him. "We're going to have lots of fresh coffee and donuts. Too bad you're not invited."

I just sat there on the couch for about a half hour, staring at a blank TV screen. I didn't need it on. The pictures playing in my head were all I could see. I thought about the name, Kathy Kostenello, but I just couldn't make a connection. *Oh great! Another mystery girl. Well, if everything comes in threes it should be smooth sailing from here on.* Maybe Joe would know.

I went to the bathroom to get an aspirin and found my TV remote in the medicine cabinet. That didn't surprise me as I once found the toothpaste in the refrigerator. I decided to go back into the living room for the rest of the night. There was no way I was going to be able to sleep. I clicked on the tube for a change of scenery. There was Judge Judy yelling at a some poor slob, "Sir, not on your *best* day will you be as smart as me on my *worst* day. Are we clear on that?"

I answered right along with the dumbfounded defendant, "Yes, Your Honor." At the moment I didn't feel I had any smarts at all. I was just one dumb-ass fool in love and now in some kind of trouble.

8

Another trip to see Barn and Georgia and phone calls to Rick and Mitch to let them know the latest installment in *Let's Play With Charlie's Head*, and I was just about ready to fly 3000 miles back to where I was born. They all had my cell phone number and I had theirs. I wish I had been able to get in touch with Andrea, but that was not to be. Barn, still holding tight to her secret, said he would let her know I had gone to Portland.

I had talked to Joe too. He didn't know the Kostenello girl who Detective Russell had mentioned; but he said he would check with John Plunkett, one of his informants over at the University. I could tell Joe was *really* concerned about my new predicament. I asked him to pick me up at the Portland Jetport. His reply, "Take a cab. The Red Sox are playing the Yankees, and I don't want to miss it." I like to think it was his way of putting me at ease, by acting like me being hauled back to Portland was no big deal. Of course it could be he was just being an asshole. You can never tell with Joe. He was like the Tony Soprano of our little corner of the world when we were growing up. All the other kids looked up to him as the leader. A little Irish godfather, that was Joe; minus the guns, money laundering, and killings, but with the same attitude. The neighborhood kids knew, if there were sides to be chosen for anything, it was best to be on Joe's side.

I said to him, "Thanks for nothing. If I get the chair I hope the jolt will knock your TV off the air."

"If you get the chair, I'll sell tickets...ha...ha...ha"

From now on I *am* going to call him in the middle of the night.

Detective Russell was punctual. I was waiting on the steps when he pulled up, exactly at 7, in an unmarked vehicle. Well, let me clarify that. It was a baby blue Camero convertible, about 30 years old, with a tattered top. The motor coughed like it was in bad need of a tune up. Smoke and exhaust fumes poured out from the broken tail pipe. There were mismatching golf clubs thrown about in the back seat along with several open and empty Dunkin Donuts' boxes. On the bumper were several stickers, one of which read: I BRAKE FOR BLONDS, and another that read: MEET ME AT HOOTERS.

At first I was worried that if my neighbors saw me getting into a cop car their response to reporters would be, "Mr. Sullivan was a very quiet man. He pretty much kept to himself. He seemed very nice. Who knew he was in trouble with the police? But I do recall now that there seemed to be some gambling going on over there. You just never know about people these days, do you?"

Now I was wishing for a black and white with TO PROTECT AND SERVE written on the side, and a bumper sticker that read: THERE IS NO EXCUSE FOR DOMESTIC VIOLENCE. Turn on the sirens while you're at it. Anything but this!

"Good morning, Mr. Sullivan," Russell said as he leaned toward the passenger window. "Climb in. Your chariot awaits." It was like a clown car at the circus. No telling what would jump out of it. "I've been fiddlin' with this rod since I first bought it from a junk dealer twenty five years ago."

Yeah, bet he saw you comin'.

"I got eight good horses under that hood. They eat a lot of gas, but they get me where I'm going. Check this out!!!" He pointed under the dash.

Oh, my God! It's even got an 8- track player. Scattered about on the dash were tapes by Waylon & Willie, George Jones, and every piece of crap that K-Tel ever put out. In the player, but thankfully not on... yet, was The Best of Box Car Willie. *Oh boy!*

Russell brushed away old newspapers and junk mail from the passenger's seat exposing the foam rubber where the leather had given up years ago.

"Don't just stand there admirin' this beauty. C'mon, get in! Time's a wastin'. After I drop you off I gotta get my fat ass over to Victoria's freakin' Secret. The wife's turnin the big 5-O today, and I'm gonna get her a little somethin'...very little...Get it?... very little?" He mumbled something inaudible under his breath as I failed to laugh at his little joke.

Russell was a big man with short black hair that was graying at the temples. Undersized dark glasses hung on his oversized nose with a bushel of little black hairs hanging out his nostrils. He had on a wide, bright yellow tie with the map of California on it; and wore a brown jacket and pants with black shoes. His mustache was home for crumbs from recent pastries that had missed his mouth. His shoulder holster was visible with a gun snug inside, unlike his shirt which partially drooped over his belly.

The girls at Hooters must really be looking forward to seeing you again!

The reek from his cigar greeted me before I sat down. "I suppose it would be inappropriate for me to ask you not to smoke."

"Yeah. You can ask. It won't do you no good, but you can ask," he chuckled to himself.

"Detective," I suggested, "you might want to take a napkin and wipe your mustache. It's not very appealing."

"What- aya, plannin' on layin' a big wet one on me? You a homo or somethin'?"

His eyes bulged out like Jackie Gleason's on The Honeymooners after getting his hand caught when the window he was yelling through fell shut. "Noton, YOU are a mental case!!!"

"I just thought you might like to know you have food in your mustache, that's all."

"Yeah, how do ya know I'm not savin' it for later?" He laughed as if his hobby was grossing people out. I decided to keep any further remarks to myself. I had enough grief in my life.

The drive to the Airport was relatively quiet for about ten minutes, and then the fashionable detective spoke up, "Ya know, Charlie, may I call you, Charlie?" He didn't wait for a reply. I got the impression that no one has ever managed to get a word in edgewise when Russell had the need to talk. "Charlie, I kinda wanta apologize for bein' so formal, wakin' you up the other night....ya know, not acknowledgin' that I know you, but, hey!...It's part of the job."

"You know me?" I pointed at myself redundantly as my mouth hung open for any nearby fly to pop into, and there were a few hanging around. He couldn't have surprised me more if he said he was on the President's Council for Physical Fitness.

"Well, you probably don't remember, but we met once about four years ago. You had my kid, Mike, in your class and he was havin' problems. My old lady dragged my ass to a meetin' with you to see if we could straighten little Mikey out."

"Yes, Mike Russell. I remember. He was a good boy...just had a few problems with getting his homework in on time. I hope he's doing all right," I said sincerely.

"HA! I wish homework was his only problem. The little snot was runnin' with a bad crowd, stayin' out till all hours of the night and comin' home when he got hungry or needed a few bucks from the old man. I tell ya, Charlie, it was touch and go there for a while. His path was set straight for Juvy where a lot of his other playmates ended up. His mother and me were ready to give up on him, but thank God he got his act together. I gotta tell ya, Charlie, you made a good impression on him. You took extra time with him and helped him out with some of his other subjects. He didn't speak too good about his other teachers, but he always said good things about Mr. Sullivan. He said you were really interested in him doin' good."

"I'm glad he's doing well. That's the only good news I've had this week."

"Yeah, Mikey turned out all right. He's followin' his old man into the wonderful and thankless job of law enforcement. My boy graduates from the Academy next month and will have a shield with L.A.P.D."

"Wow, that's terrific. Please tell Mike I said congratulations."

"I'll do that, Charlie. I'll do that. Thank you." It seemed like the Detective was truly pleased to get that off his chest. I could tell he was really proud of his son and the way things turned out for him. So was I. "Mikey's a good boy, Charlie, a real good boy... Musta got that from his darlin' sweet mother," Russell offered with a degree of sentimentality.

We were nearing the Airport and Russell was about to light up a stogie, then thought better of it. He pulled out a bottle of Pepto instead and took a swig, "This job will kill ya, Charlie. Two years to retirement and then I'm goin' to forget all this shit. I might go private and be answerable to only me. I gotta do somethin'. Stayin' home with the ol' lady will kill me if the job don't." He laughed out loud.

I understood what he meant about *only doing his job*. Barn was only doing his job by not revealing information contained in Andrea's private file, and I was doing my job by helping young Mike with his homework. It was then that the old light bulb lit up in my brain and I said, "Detective Russell, may I ask you a question?"

"Go for it, Charlie! But call me Bob. After all we've known each other for four years," ribbed the Detective as he poked me in the side. I began thinking there was something other than Pepto in that bottle stuffed inside his jacket pocket.

This was my chance to ask for a favor. "Is it possible for you to obtain some information on somebody for me?"

"Who you got in mind, Charlie?"

"Well...ahh...Bob...her name is Andrea Rios. She'll be teaching history this year at Marshall High. I just met her a little over a month ago."

"What's got your curiosity up about this particular broad? Has she got somethin' to do with all that crap goin' on in Maine?" the Detective quizzed.

"No, not at all. She's just a friend, but somewhat of a mysterious friend."

"You warm for her form, Charlie boy?" Again he laughed at his own remarks.

"Bob, you are a good detective. I am a little curious about what she's been doing the last few years. She's mentioned her family to me...like her mother and father and where she's from...but that's about all I really know."

"You think maybe she's got a husband stashed away, or a boy-friend she doesn't want you to find out about? You can't trust any of them, Charlie. Some stud comes along with a bigger wanker or more money and it's *See You Later Alligator*. If I ever catch my old lady messin' around I'll be spendin' time with some of the bastards I put in Quentin."

"I just can't imagine any woman in her right mind leaving you, Bob, especially if they ever get to ride in this fine automobile."

"Yeah...well...maybe you're right." Russell's body language suggested he wasn't sure whether I was kidding him or not.

" So, you think you can help me?"

"Do you have any other info on this Rios woman? Rios is a pretty common name around here."

"As far as I know she's from Ventura. She graduated from Pepperdine. Her father's name is Miquel. He's retired from Cal-Tran, and her mother's name is Kathleen. She has a sister, Denise, who's a dispatcher for the California Highway Patrol... And I should point out that Andrea is *very* beautiful."

"Whoa! Don't leave out the most important part," Russell said, flashing that big Cheshire grin. "Funny though, I know most of the dispatchers for CHP, but I can't recall a Rios. Maybe I know her by her married name. Okay, Charlie, I'll see what I can run down for ya, but I can't spend a lot of time on it."

"Thanks. I really appreciate it."

"Charlie, c'mon, I'm a romantic-type guy, especially if the skirt has some major ta ta's." He said that as if he couldn't be more serious, and then poked me in the ribs again.

"Yes, I'm sure you are very romantic. Your wife is a lucky woman," I said with as much sincerity as I could fake.

Russell reached into his pocket and pulled out a couple of business cards. He told me to write down my cell-phone number and hand it back. I kept one card with his number on it, not to mention what looked like a ketchup stain.

We chatted about a bunch of mundane topics the rest of the way, but Russell did mention that there was a sky marshal on my flight who had my description and seat number just in case I "got any ideas". Also, there would be a Portland Detective by the name of Tony Reza waiting for me at the Portland Jetport. So much for asking Brother Joe to pick me up.

I told him the only idea I had was to clear this all up, and get back to Oceanside as soon as possible.

As we pulled up in front of the Southwest Terminal at L.A.X. I was feeling a little better. Russell may be able to help solve some of my questions about Andrea. Although I was curious about what the cops back home wanted with me, I felt a need to go anyway. Maybe I *could* help.

9

"Ladies and gentlemen, this is your Captain speaking. We have reached our cruising altitude, and I have turned off the seatbelt sign. You are free to move about the cabin, but please be prepared to fasten your seatbelt if I should turn the seatbelt sign back on. We do have reports of some turbulence up ahead. Thank you for choosing Southwest. Enjoy your flight."

Thirty thousand feet up and six hours away from the old neighborhood, I sat next to an accountant from Westwood, California. He was a yaker, talking mostly about the way lawyers, labor unions, and women's organizations were ruining this country. When I did get a chance to get a word in I told him he should meet my brother. They could go steady.

When my seat-buddy got up to use the facilities I saw my opportunity to avoid his comments and bad breath. By the time he got back I pretended I was sleeping. I had one of those wonderfully uncomfortable airline pillows stuffed behind my head with my face against the window. I really couldn't sleep as my mind drifted back over the years searching for memories that were dormant in my brain.

I once heard an infomercial in the middle of the night that offered a memory course. The slick pitch man said, "Your memory is like a giant tape recorder, taping everything....every second of your life. To remember what you want, all you have to do is rewind the tape to the part you want to remember. It's *all* there in your brain, just waiting to be released at your command. To learn exactly how that's done call me now at 800 something something, and get my book and tapes." I thought about calling, but I couldn't remember the 800 number.

As the jumbo jet sailed along I tried to rewind the tape in my head anyway. Jimmy Peters popped up. I first met Jimmy in the fifth grade. We hit it off right away, and for the next eight years we were inseparable. Then came graduation. I stayed in Portland and got my teaching certificate from the University of Maine. Jimmy headed off for Emerson College in Boston. They were famous for their broadcasting courses and by then Jimmy wanted to become a BIG JAB GOOD

GUY, but it didn't work out that way. Life seldom does.

I remember when Jimmy and I were twelve; we talked about all the jobs we wanted when we grew up. Rock-N-Roll singers or professional baseball players were at the top of our list. But, since we couldn't sing or play ball to a great degree of excellence, we decided we would be detectives like the ones on <u>77 Sunset Strip, Hawaiian Eye, Bourbon Street Beat</u> and <u>Surfside Six.</u> We went for a stretch when we thought we could become professional gamblers like Bret and Bart Maverick; but after Joe beat us out of twenty bucks playing poker, we change our minds again. I think it was then we decided....*screw it*!!!...We just wouldn't grow up at all. But of course we did; and circumstances, not wishes, decided what we would do. Jimmy met a cutie named Jocelyn. They eventually married and moved to North Carolina where they both worked in real estate, and did very well. We talked on the phone and exchanged letters frequently over the years, but eventually the phone calls and letters became fewer and fewer, until about six years ago when they ended completely. The last time I called, the operator said the phone number had been changed to a private listing at the customer's request. I sent a couple of letters, but they both came back as undeliverable. We had grown apart and moved on with our individual lives. I could hear Mary Hopkin singing on the radio in my mind, <u>Those Were The Days</u> (My Friend. We Thought They'd Never End).

I am definitely going to look up Jimmy's mom when I get to Portland. She still lives there. Joe told me he ran into her one of her daughters at the grocery store about a month ago. Jimmy's sister said her mom wasn't doing very well and didn't leave the house much. When Joe asked about Jimmy, his sister said he didn't keep in touch with the family. Joe said she acted like she really didn't want to talk about him. I worry about Jimmy. I hope my best friend is okay.

On the tape in my mind I stopped at my 12th birthday. My mom and dad were so pleased to present me with a brand new apple-red Schwinn bicycle. As I took it for its virgin ride on the dirt road behind my house my mom shouted, "You can ride it anywhere except down Cassidy Hill."

Cassidy Hill is the steep street that runs past the old cemetery on the West End. The city used to close it down in the winter. It was perfect for snow sleds and toboggans. Lots of kids had gotten into accidents on that hill. The slope starts out slight but quickly turns down at a sharp angle, sucking you in like one of those Venus Fly traps.

"Okay, Mom, I promise. I'm going to ride over and show Jimmy. I'll be back before dark," I yelled without looking back. I never even said thank you. It's too late now. She sacrificed a lot to save the money for that bike. I really don't need a memory course to remind me about her. Her family was her life, especially her *boys*. She was a small woman with a big heart. She had a quick smile and a pretty face. She rarely raised her voice or lost her temper. I think her greatest enjoyment was just seeing us smile. I feel bad now that, in my childishness, I played little tricks on her...like changing the hands on the big kitchen clock. She would say, "On, my gosh, look at the time, your father will be home any minute." Of course, he would come home at his normal time, but she would think he was three hours late and want to know where he had been. It didn't take him long to figure out who was the responsible party. *Then,* she raised her voice, "Charlieeeeeeeee!"

Jimmy had received a new bike for Christmas the year before. He was sticking baseball cards in the spokes when I rode into his driveway. The cards made a neat clicking sound as the wheels went around. We both thought that was so cool. Who knows how many valuable baseball cards we destroyed back then? That's something I don't want to think about.

"Hey, Jimbo, check this out!" I dismounted and displayed my birthday present.

"Cool. Where did you steal that?" Jimmy asked as he stuck a Mickey Mantle in one spoke and a Hank Aaron in another.

"It's a birthday present. I didn't steal it...My mom did."

"Yeah, and my mom traded my big sister for mine." He smiled, as if that thought would be really great if it were true.

"No wonder I haven't seen your sister around, not since the last time I gave her a quarter to show me her fried eggs."

"You wish!" Jimmy exclaimed as he took hold of my new ride and rode it up and down his driveway, doing small wheelies.

STUNG

"Yeah, she said I could touch them for another ten cents!"

Jimmy climbed down off my new bike and pushed it back to me. "Hey! That's my sister you're talking about, my friend...Nobody touches them but me!"

"Eweee!!!" we both said at the same time and then punched each other in the shoulder. Friends did that back then.

"Let's go for a ride and see how fast that new bike can go," Jimmy suggested. He gave me a couple of baseball cards to attach to my wheels. With Willie Mays riding in front and Stan "The Man" Musial riding in back, we set out.

"First one to the cannon on the promenade is the winner, and the loser has to buy root beer floats at Dudley Weed Drugstore," I bargained as I pushed down on the pedals and rolled out of his driveway.

"You're on!" Jimmy shouted as he cut across his lawn and took the lead.

We raced up Danforth Street, then made a right turn up Vaughn and left onto Pine. We both arrived at the cannon about the same time. I claimed I was first, and Jimmy said he was. Then we made derogatory remarks about each other's mother and called it even. That kind of ritual went along with the shoulder punching of the day. We rested the bikes on the grass and fell down laughing. This continued on for several minutes until we both were completely out of breath.

Once we regained our composure, Jimmy suggested we take our bikes down Cassidy Hill, past the cemetery. My mom's voice echoed in my head, *Don't ride your bike down Cassidy Hill.* I told Jimmy that I had promised my mom I wouldn't do that. He said she would never find out, but I said I better not.

"Boo hoo hoo, does wittle Charlie do everything his wittle Mommy says?" Jimmy taunted.

It wasn't the words he said, but the manner in which he said them, that gave me second thoughts...those damn second thoughts... those, *Oh-yeah,-I'll-show-you-thoughts*. The hill was an inviting challenge, and I gave in to his request as the radio in my head played Johnny Cash, <u>Don't Take Your Guns To Town</u> (Son. Leave your guns at home). I didn't listen to my mom, and the boy in the song didn't listen to his. We would both regret it.

Jimmy and I rode down the promenade, past the prominent homes of Portland's richest residents, until we reached the top of Cassidy Hill. Jimmy started down first and I followed after. The ride was swift and fun. The new bike was steady and sure. The sound of the crisp cardboard baseball players was rapid like a machine gun. The handlebar streamers of red and white were sailing in the wind. My feet could barely keep up with the revolving pedals, and I laughed at the thrill of it all.

Suddenly I heard Jimmy yell, "Check it out. Babe alert!" He pointed to a girl walking down the hill next to the cemetery fence.

I looked to see a long-legged blond beauty with a pony tail in white jeans and a black sweater. As I past by she looked at me and blew me a kiss. She said, "I love you, Charlie." Then she walked through the back gates of the old cemetery and disappeared.

"OH MY GOD!!!" I shouted out loud as I sat up straight in my seat, startling the accountant and the other passengers in the rows in front and back of me. I started to sweat as I remembered seeing that girl, who I now realized looked just like Cindy. But how could that be? She looked like she was sixteen or seventeen, but I was still just twelve and didn't meet Cindy till *I* was seventeen. I began to rationalize that it must have been some other girl or perhaps even a sister. Lots of girls wore pony tails back then and had white jeans and black sweaters. It had to be a coincidence. It had to be. What other possible explanation could there be?

Meanwhile, back on my memory tape, I lost control of my new bike and smashed into the cemetery fence. *Don't ride your bike down Cassidy Hill. Don't take your guns to town, Son.* When I looked up, my bike was not even a resemblance of its former beauty. The streamers were torn from the handlebars. The horn and headlight were busted. The shining chrome was scarred. Willie and Stan "The Man" were ripped to shreds. The front wheel was now permanently bent and facing the crushed back wheel; and I could almost here them say, *Do you believe this dip-shit ruined us on the very first day?*

The only one standing there was Jimmy, saying, "Oh man, you're ass is grass and your mother is the lawnmower. You can hide out at my house for a few days if you want."

My overactive mind, which often circled Cindy moments, had just revealed a new one. Once again I told myself I had to visit Jimmy's mom when I got into town. I had to find him and ask him if he remembered the day I crashed my new bike going down Cassidy Hill, and if he remembered that girl...that *mysterious* girl.

The yaker gave me a nudge and said, "They are serving a snack. Do want yours?"

I turned off the tape recorder in my brain and shut down my memory for a while.

"Thanks. Yes, I'll take mine."

I pushed down the tray in front of me and settled in for some peanuts and a Coke. They never have Pepsi on a plane. I thought of Jimmy again. He would have bitched about that till they made a special landing, and a flight attendant made a special trip to 7-Eleven to get him one. I laughed out loud at the idea, and my neighbor thought it was in response to one of his stupid remarks.

I ate and the yaker talked, "And I'll tell you another thing, if Hillary Clinton ever becomes president, I'm going to shoot myself." All of a sudden the idea of her presidency didn't seem so bad to me. Fortunately, my seat-buddy was getting off in Chicago, but that was still more than an hour away.

Meanwhile, I picked up a copy of <u>Sky News</u> which was located on the back of the seat in front of me. I pretended to read the magazine like I had pretended to sleep before. I saw the words on the pages but ignored them. Instead, I turned my memory tape recorder back on. Next stop, the Halloween weekend when Jimmy and I were accepted into the gang of big kids who were all Joe's friends.

To be totally cool, and keep that status with the group that hung around my big brother, everyone had to endure the same ritual of going through the local *haunted house* on the Halloween before their 13th year.

Actually, it was on the eve before Halloween that the festivities began. On that night...the *chosen*...Jimmy and I in this case, would gather with all those who had successfully completed the mission when it had been *their* turn to enter the condemned premises.

I guess every town has a run down dilapidated house that suffers the rocks and insults of the area kids. Ours was the old house that once belonged to one of Portland's most famous residents. First there was Longfellow, next was John Buckley. Buckley would probably be a rock concert promoter today, but back in his time he promoted more sinister things. Known as, The Old Buckley Place, it was built around 1880 for John Buckley and his *family*. Once it had bright red bricks and the finest imported hard wood. Stained-glass windows, painstakingly etched and painted by the finest European craftsmen, were hung in the big foyer. Buckley spared no expense in making his home the finest in town. But over the years the bricks faded and the wood rotted. The windows were pierced by stones and BB gun pellets to the point that on a sunny day rays beamed through them like natural lasers. The whole structure tilted on it's foundation before it fell during the winter after Jimmy and I had made our journey through its dark and dank rooms. It's no longer there on the corner of Pine and Carlton, but its memory lingers. If you pass by there today, they say you can feel a slight change in the temperature as if there's a time warp nearby.

Joe would tell the story of how it became haunted, and when the newly frightened were ready to piss their pants...that again would be Jimmy and me...we had to enter the old boarded-up palace through a basement window where the wood had been pried apart. Next we would have to climb the three flights of stairs that led to the attic. Once there, we would have to wave through another broken window in one of the gables that surrounded the roof. The rest of the guys would be waiting safely down below and across the street to see if we made it. Some kids would only last about ten seconds in the place before scurrying through that basement window again. At that moment they didn't care about being cool or being part of the gang, they just wanted to get their asses out of there. But, I was Joe's brother and Jimmy was my best friend. *We just had to make it.*

I can hear Joe now telling the story as we all sat in a circle on the grass in the small backyard at 89 Pine. It was about five in the afternoon and already dark. The lights, from the many kitchen windows that surrounded us, reflected Joe's eerie facial expressions as he began speaking in a low, almost whispering voice. All of us had heard the story before, but Jimmy and I paid special attention, as this was *our* night. This is the story, and Joe would always rip off Ripley by saying, "Believe it or not."

Old Man Buckley was what was known as a *show-man*. He collected the weird and the unusual from all over the world and displayed them in circuses and freak shows throughout the country.

Buckley had no wife and family. He would often say that his creatures *were* his family. He built that big house just for them, and there they would stay until their next date with the public who would pay good money to see them.

At first, the family was made up of the crippled and deformed soldiers of the Civil War. There were men without arms and legs. Some had faces that had been almost blown apart by a cannon ball, leaving them without ears and a nose. There was one who was just mostly mouth and not much else. They say Old Man Buckley even had the head of a rebel general in a jar, its skin just hanging and floating in some sort of formaldehyde. Those who saw it say the eyes followed them across the room.

He soon added strange animals to the mix. He had a two-headed python, some African spiders that were the size of a rat, chickens with four legs, and a goat with its heart on the outside of its body. They say that for an extra dollar he would let his customers watch the two-headed snake and those rat-size spiders devour live baby chicks. Even today there are very few pigeons and squirrels near that house. It's said that the snakes and the spiders reproduced, and their broods are still in the house waiting for their next meal to come along.

Tonight that may be you, Charlie...or you, Jimmy...heh heh heeeeeeee.

Jimmy and I sat there looking at each other. Although we had heard the story before, this night it had extra special meaning. We were both holding on to baseball bats and flashlights. We weren't going in there empty handed or unarmed. As the other kids snickered at us, Joe continued:

> Listen up, Ladies. Don't miss a single word. The extra special attractions came next. From some place called Borneo were a brother and sister known as "The Terror Twins". They were joined at the shoulders and could never get away from each other. One was a male and one was a female. Their facial features were so grotesque and deformed that grown men would turn away in horror. The twins hated each other and all who came near them. They would say curse words that even sailors hadn't heard yet.
>
> In the Middle East Buckley found a grown man who was just a foot and a half tall. He was known as Big Harry and some of the mothers thought he was a real live doll. Some wanted to take him home for their kids; but when Harry would reach for their lady parts their husbands would chase him, and Harry would jump up into the lap of the Terror Twins. The irate men would just raise their fists and shout obscenities from a safe distance. They weren't about to get near the twins. And they would definitely stay away from "The Crocodile Man". He was the main attraction and brought in the most money. Buckley captured him in the Amazon with the help of some pygmies. The pygmies were happy to see the hungry monster go. He had made many-a-tasty meal out of a lot of their friends. His body was covered with scales. He had arms and legs just like you and me, but he had the head of a crocodile. They say when Buckley died; The Crocodile Man crawled into the swampy mud in the basement of the old house. You and Jimmy be sure not to trip over him when you go though the basement window tonight...heh heh hee.

The Commies could have dropped an atom bomb right there in our backyard, and Jimmy and I wouldn't have moved. Joe was in top form. I looked at Jimmy; and Jimmy looked at me. Each of us vowed that we wouldn't leave the other behind in case *something* happened to us in the Old Buckley Place. We knew what Joe would talk about next. We knew when he was done with the story of Buckley's greatest find we would have to follow in the footsteps of all the twelve-year olds that had gone before us. Joe went on:

In 1897 old Buckley read the book about Dracula, and was so impressed by the story that he decided to set out on a journey to Old Europe, in hopes that one of the bloodsucking fiends really did exist, and that he could capture one and bring it to America to make a fortune.

He searched and searched and had just about given up. Then an old gypsy in Bucharest told him of a castle where real vampires were buried, but not necessarily dead.

Buckley paid a small fortune to have some locals go with him, to help him capture one of the sleeping monsters. The gypsy told Buckley to make sure he put the vampire in a coffin or box with some dirt from the current burial grounds. That would keep the vampire *alive*...heh heh.

They found the place, and near sundown they discovered five caskets in the cellar of the main castle. There were four large caskets and one small. The family crest of hanging-bats and perching-owls covered the caskets along with huge bulbs of garlic, and Buckley commanded his men to open the coffins and see if they really contained the monsters described in the book. The men refused; but old Buckley, he was a sneaky one. He revealed to the reluctant workers that there were no vampires. That was just a story the family told to protect the gold that was hidden in the caskets. Greed took hold and the men agreed to finish the task.

With steel bars and knifes they cracked open the containers one at a time. As the lid of the first was rolled away, there were no bodies and no gold. Then they opened the second and the third and the fourth...but NOTHING, no bodies, no gold...just empty caskets.

Buckley turned to his frustrated crew and said that it was only reasonable that the gold would be in the smaller casket because there would be no room for a body in there. So the weary men cracked open their final chance for wealth, but again there was no gold. But, there was *something*. The beast inside, comforted by the night, jumped out of his casket and started biting and sucking the blood out of the frightened grave-robbers. Old Buckley was used to the strange and the weird. He kept his cool as he gathered the garlic and wrapped it around himself. The vampire hissed and growled; but Buckley backed him into the casket with a cross, just as he had read in the book. As the monster retreated to his resting place, Buckley threw in the dirt from the burial ground, and nailed the casket shut with the cross and the garlic laying on top.

His crew had been slaughtered not by an ordinary vampire, but by a vampire *child*, ten-years old according to the inscription on the door of the family vault.

Buckley was thrilled beyond belief. A child who was a vampire monster would be even a greater attraction than an adult in his world of side-shows.

Buckley went back to the local village and hired more men to help him with his *treasure*. They put the Boy Vampire on board the cargo ship, SEA DRAGON, and Buckley took his latest find across the sea to America...to Maine...to Portland...to our neighborhood...heh heh heh!!!

Now, no one knows exactly what happened, but the Terror Twins, Big Harry, and most of the strange animals were found dead in the old house when the cops went to check up on Buckley after he had failed to show up for a big 4th of July performance. They found Buckley hanging from the ceiling in the parlor. The room was completely empty, and the ceilings were ten feet high. Just how The Showman was able to hang himself is still a mystery. They never did find The Crocodile Man or The Boy Vampire, but maybe you two will find them tonight...or they may find *you!*...heh heh hee.

When the undertaker went in to take down Buckley's body, it was gone. The town, knowing about Buckley and his strange companions, decided to just board up the house and contain any evil that lived there.

Now, Charlie, you and Jimmy must get up, enter the house and pray that you don't run into Buckley's ghost...or The Crocodile Man...or The Boy Vampire. If you complete your task, then you will be official members of our little group. If you don't, then you can never hang out with us *ever* again.

"Joe, you scare the crap out of me every time you tell that story," John Spiller said.

"I don't dare look inside my shorts," commented Dana Wilson.

"Ya know, that's really a true story," added Bill O'Neal.

"Get outta here!" warned the ever skeptical Tommy Caine. "Me and Mike walked through there and didn't even see a mouse! Ain't that right, Murph?"

Mike Murphy just raised his shoulders and said, "I don't know, Tommy. I had my eyes closed most of the time. It could be true...it could be."

Everyone else agreed it *was* true. Jimmy and I got up and walked slowly toward the Old Buckley Place. The others followed behind us and took their place across the street, making scary sounds as Jimmy and I opened the wrought iron gate and walked through the weeds and tall grass that hadn't seen a mower in years.

With flashlights and baseball bats in hand, we came to the basement window that would let us in. Somebody had written on the pried away boards: All Who Enter Here Will Perish Here. The words were painted red, like blood, and drops of paint trickled down...at least... it...looked...like...paint.

Jimmy and I flipped a nickel to see who would go through the window first. It was heads. Jimmy had tails. Jimmy lowered himself down into the basement and let out an, "OOOH SHIT!" as his feet sank in the mud that made up the floor of the old cellar.

"Jimmy, are you okay?"

"I don't know. My sneakers are gooed up with slime. Wait!... Damn!!!...I dropped my flashlight."

"Let me shine mine through the window and see if you can find it."

"I don't see it. I think it might have sunk in the mud. Charlie, do you think...The Crocodile Man might have taken it?" Jimmy was starting to panic. "I think I hear someone breathing!...Oh man, I'm not so sure this is a good idea. Who wants to hang out with your stupid brother and those other dolts anyway?"

"Hold on, Jimmy. I'm gonna lower myself in. Here, take the bats and don't let them sink. Is there something to stand on besides the mud?"

"There's an old table just to the left of me," Jimmy reluctantly assured me, as he leaned the bats against the wall. "At least I think it's a table."

I looked toward Brother Joe with a face that said, *You better not be going anywhere till we get out of her.* With that I let myself down onto the warbling old table. Jimmy steadied me with one hand and the table with the other. Come to think of it, it was probably Jimmy and me who were warbling.

Now, with the one flashlight between us, Jimmy and I let the beam sweep from one end of the soggy basement to the other. Suddenly, a big bucktoothed rat ran across the back wall and into an open pipe. Giant cobwebs were hanging everywhere with victims still squirming, trying to get free from their sticky silky prisons. In one web was a tiny bat with wings half-eaten away, it's tiny teeth snapping away in lost hope.

"Look at the size of those cobwebs. They must have been made by a really big freakin spider!"

"You mean like the African spiders Old Man Buckley used to have?" Jimmy nervously asked.

"Don't think about it. Just move on." We went about ten feet. Then there was the most foul stench, like something rotting or decaying. "This place smells worse than my socks," I complained.

"Then your socks smell like shit!" Jimmy said as he grabbed onto my arm.

We started on our way toward the first set of stairs with baseball bats in hand and one flashlight. We were walking like prisoners who were shackled together with a ball and chain, but we were just locked together by fear. Somehow feeling Jimmy's breath on the back of my neck was comforting. I would hate to be alone in this hole.

Eweeee...I hoped that was Jimmy's breath.

"I think we should run as fast as we can up all those stairs, wave; and then run back down here and out the window," Jimmy suggested.

"Or we can take it slow and easy and not get lost," I recommended.

As two more rats appeared we both agreed Jimmy's way was best; and we took off, sloshing through the sickening mud.

The worn-out wooden cellar stairs were crooked and creaked like they were alive and in great pain with each foot that fell on them, but at that moment we didn't care if we were stepping on little old ladies. Hell we would have preferred it. We just wanted to get to the first floor as fast as we could.

We soon reached what must have been the kitchen at one time. We passed through without any problem and entered the living room where Old Man Buckley either hung himself or was hung by parties unknown. We gazed at the ceiling as if expecting to see the ghost of the old home owner. We stood there...still, with musty smells that almost made us gag. Suddenly, I felt Jimmy and I weren't the only ones there. I paused and listened.

"Jimmy, do you hear anything?"

"Just my freakin' heart pounding."

"No, listen, be quiet." We were silent, hoping for nothing, but expecting noises or voices other than our own.

"Shit! I hear something now," Jimmy whispered loudly.

"It sounds like someone breathing and moaning, almost like they're in some sort of agony."

"It can't be Old Man Buckley. The dead don't breathe...do they, Charlie?...do they?"

"I don't think so...But a crocodile man or a boy vampire can," I reasoned.

"Charlie, let me ask you one more time."

"Yeah?"

"How important is it that we hang around with your brother and the others? Don't we have the most fun when it's just you and me?"

"It's just you and me now, Jimmy, and I wouldn't call this fun!"

"Yeah, guess there are times when it's more fun with a crowd."

Jimmy looked around slowly, hoping there would be a bunch of friends instead of the unknown terrors we were sensing.

"Right now I don't care if they make us wear dresses to school," I said as I gazed at my surroundings, not knowing what was behind us...or ahead of us. I'm with you, Jimbo, if you just want to make like a tree and leave"

It was then we heard a splash in the basement and then footsteps on the cellar stairs.

"You got it, my friend! LET'S GET OUTTA HERE!!!" Jimmy yelled.

But there was nowhere to go but up and so we ran up the next two flights of stairs to the attic and the broken window where we yelled to Joe and the others down below and across the street. Well, we tried to yell. We opened our mouths, but when we tried to speak only trembling whispers would come out. They couldn't hear us, but they could see us. They waved back and gave us a thumbs-up as if to say, *All right you made it. Now come down so we can go home.*

But we couldn't go back down. We could hear the menacing footsteps on the stairs getting louder and closer. Jimmy and I took our bats and bashed out the rest of the windows and boards, and went out on to the eves. It was the only way Joe would know we were in serious trouble.

"What the hell are you morons doing?" Joe yelled, but we still couldn't answer. It was like our words were trapped in those tiny little clouds of quotations you see in comic books.

There was definitely someone or something on our tails and closing in fast. The footsteps were getting more frequent and the temperature was starting to drop. It became icy cold, and I could see my breath. And then I could see a shadow on the wall, revealed by the streetlight below. It was looming larger as the footsteps grew louder. The silhouette was tall and thin and in the shape of a man, at least it looked somewhat like a man.

Jimmy pointed down and I saw the old fire escape below. It was about a six foot drop We didn't know if it could hold us. I looked behind and saw what seemed like a bony hand reaching for the end of the railing at the top of the stairs. We were more afraid of what was behind us than in front of us, and so we made the leap.

STUNG

The old fire escape swayed and creaked as rusted bolts scraped against thin iron steps, but we were determined to shimmy down it as fast and as far as we could, no matter what. Joe and the others were now yelling for us to run as the figure of an old man was now occupying the window above. He looked like he was wearing a cape and had on a tall hat like the ones in those old Abraham Lincoln photos.

The fire escape ended about ten feet from the ground, but at that moment we would have jumped if it were a hundred feet. We rolled onto the cement sidewalk as we landed, scraping arms and elbows. But we didn't notice and we didn't care. We were out of the house and away from whatever or whomever was the creep in the stovepipe hat.

Joe and the others were throwing rocks up at the window, trying to keep the unknown predator from coming down the fire escape as we made it to safety.

Someone called the police when they saw Jimmy and me out on the fire escape. When the cops arrived we told them what had happened. We stood there, frozen in fear, as the police broke down the door of the Old Buckley Place. They were looking for a fugitive and figured that might have been him we saw inside. The Fire Department arrived shortly there after, and about a dozen of them when in to assist. An hour passed before they all came out.

As they were leaving, Officer Doug Shannon, the cop who walked the beat in our part of town, yelled, "You kids better go home. Everything is all right. We checked every nook and cranny. There was no one in there."

I yelled back, "We were being chased up the stairs by someone!"

"C,mon, fellas...it was just your imaginations playing tricks on you. Like the psycho docs say, 'You were expecting to see something, and so you think you did.' You boys will probably have nightmares tonight." Officer Doug laughed. His fellow cops chuckled along with him.

Jimmy pointed and replied, "But we saw him up in that window."

Joe and the other kids confirmed the sighting.

"There was a coat rack up there with a sweater on it. That's what you saw." They laughed again as they got back into their squad cars.

"What about the tall hat?" I asked, almost in desperation that one of them would believe me.

"What tall hat? There was no hat. Now go home!" Officer Shannon said more sternly than before.

Jimmy and I stood there, friends to the end. We knew what we saw. Then we returned to the safety of our homes.

That was just the first day of an eventful Halloween weekend. The very first time I ever set foot in the old bone yard was on Halloween. It was the night after Jimmy and I had our encounter with *someone* in the Old Buckley Place, someone who wore an Abe Lincoln stovepipe hat, someone who the cops said didn't exist. We had earned the right, and were now trick or treating with Joe and the other *big* kids. This would be their last year begging for candy. Next year, when they entered high school, they would move on to private parties. We would do the story telling and be in charge. We would be the ones to scare the crap out of some unsuspecting *little* kids.

It was getting near dark, and our pillow cases were bulging with Tootsie Pops, lollypops, corn balls, sour balls, corn candy, candy kisses, jelly beans, Bazooka bumble gum, gum drops, Neeco wafers, peeps, licorice sticks, Bit 'O' Honey's Sweet Tarts, Sugar Daddy's, Sky Bars, Good 'N' Plenty; and a huge variety of chocolate candy, not to mention a slug of apples. Nothing pissed us off more than some old lady kissing us on the cheeks and making us sing God Bless America, and then handing us an apple. Joe suggested we step into the nearby cemetery and dump the fruit to make more room for the good stuff.

It was then that Tommy Caine dared Jimmy and me to walk from the front gate of the cemetery to the back gate, about a half mile away.

Jimmy said, "You give us half your candy and Charlie and I will do it."

"Wait a second, Jimmy. I didn't say I would."

"Charlie's a chicken. You were afraid of a coat rack with a sweater hanging on it. Charlie's a chicken," Tommy teased.

"Am not."

"Are too."

"Am not."

"Are too."

"All right. Shut up!" Joe interrupted. "Charlie, if you want to do it, it's up to you. There's still plenty of pickins out there and I'm gonna get all I can."

"Us too," Dana Wilson and Mike Murphy said in acapella.

Jimmy turned to Tommy and asked if he was going with us.

"No way man, I'm the one making the bet...that you won't make it before the boogie man gets you or you turn back," he snickered.

"What a turd you are, Tommy," Jimmy said.

"I'll walk around on the sidewalk, and if you make it to the other gate I'll be there to give you half my candy." Tommy then turned to Bill O'Neal and John Spiller, and winked.

Meanwhile, Joe pulled the old Halloween swicheroo and changed masks so he could go back and hit up the same houses again, the ones that gave us the best candy. Dana Wilson and Mike Murphy did the same.

Knowing Tommy never planned to meet us at the back gate, Joe turned to him and warned, "If you're not there at the other end if Charlie and Jimmy get there, I'll kick the shit outta ya." Joe was not only my hero but the leader of out little gang. Nobody crossed Joe's little brother and got away with it.

Suddenly Bill O'Neal and John Spiller told Tommy to go on his own and that they would head back with Joe, Dana, and Mike.

Tommy, now on the spot, agreed not to stiff us. He said he would go on his own, and if Jimmy and I didn't turn and run back he would hand over half his loot.

I whispered to Jimmy, "I think I am chicken. Last night took a lot out of me."

"Don't worry, Charlie. I got an idea," comforted Jimmy. Last night's experience had a different affect on my friend. It made him feel almost invincible.

"Geez, Joe, how long do I have to wait to see if Charlie and Jimmy make it?" Tommy asked, now wishing he had kept his big mouth shut.

"It will be completely dark by 5:30. Wait till then." Joe commanded.

We all agreed.

Joe and the other mask-swappers headed off. Tommy started on the safe way around the cemetery, and Jimmy and I set out on our journey past the tombstones. There was about twenty minutes of daylight left, but the moon was already showing.

We had gone about one hundred feet, until Tommy was out of sight when Jimmy stopped and said, "Here's what we're gonna do." He started to laugh at the prospect of a perfect plan and I was infected. We fell to the ground, expelling our case of the tee-hees. When the giggles left we got up again.

I gave him my full attention and Jimmy explained, "We have plenty of time to get to the back gate before dark. We'll stay just out of sight till sunset, but we'll be close enough to run if we get scared. We'll scootch down behind one of the bigger tombstones where we'll be able to see the gate and Tommy."

"But why don't we just go right to the gate and get Tommy's candy? Why hide at all?" I asked innocently, not knowing all of Jimmy's devious plan.

"You'll see, my friend." Jimmy smiled an evil looking smile.

I learned over the years that any time Jimmy wanted to make a point he would always say, *my friend*.

We continued walking and soon discovered the big space in the middle of the cemetery that would become our baseball field for the next several years. All of a sudden I wasn't scared at all, even though I felt there was *someone* watching. Jimmy said he felt it too. I guess I wasn't afraid because Jimmy was there. And Jimmy wasn't afraid of anything. At least he didn't let on...not after surviving the trip through that haunted house with its hidden creatures and the unknown creep who chased us up the stairs and out onto the fire escape. We wanted to stay and explore some, but our other task was at hand.

Little did I know at the time that this day would start such an important chapter in my life, and that this old cemetery would truly *haunt* me for the rest of my life.

As we continued toward the back gate Jimmy put his hand into his pillow case sack and pulled out a bandage and some ketchup. It was going to be his second disguise when we hit up the best candy-givers the second time around.

"I'm gonna put the bandage around my head, and douse it with ketchup and rub it all over my face. When it gets really dark I'll run out the back gate screaming that a zombie got you, and was coming after me and Tommy. We'll scare the crap out of that wise-ass."

Another of our silly spells came on, and we sat down till we recovered. It's hard to be scared when you're laughing.

As we got near the back gate we crouched down and out of sight. Jimmy put his plan into action, and it worked perfectly. Tommy went screaming into the night and left his whole pillow case of candy, twice the promised bet. We made ourselves sick eating all those sweets, but it was worth it. Jimmy and I had been good friends from the start, but it was that scary weekend when we knew we would be best friends forever. The next day after school we took out bats, gloves, and ball and had the best time ever in our new *cemetery playground*.

After an hour stop in Chicago we boarded again. Next stop…Boston…and then a shuttle into Portland and my fate.

My seat buddy for the Chicago to Boston trip was a refined looking woman who politely introduced herself and went about her business typing away on a laptop. She looked like a librarian, all prim and proper. For some reason I thought of Mr. Romance, Detective Russell, saying, *She looks quiet, Charlie boy, but those are the ones that are tigers!!!* Again, I tried to sleep and send the Detective out of my thoughts. My memory tape recorder came on, and, as usual, Cindy was there. I thought of her often over the years, almost daily. But mostly it was for a brief moment, and then her image would pass as quickly as it came. It was like she had me on a long leash and could pull me back into her world anytime she pleased. But now, with nothing but time, I rewound the tape to that magical summer to see if I could find some buried moments that I had forgotten of even repressed.

"Hellooooo Baaaaby!" I was back at that first day and my first embarrassing words. I thought in the beginning that it was Jimmy she was interested in, and that she picked me because of his cruel words, "Charlie is the Big Loser."

MIGHTY JOHN MARSHALL

Now, as my memory gets clearer, I can see she was smiling at me before his rude remark. It seemed her green eyes were drawing me in as if possessing me. I had no choice. She *made* me fall in love with her and in a hurry. I wasn't a boyfriend, I was a target. What did I have that she couldn't get from any other guy? Suddenly, and without warning, the plane was going through some turbulence and air masks were falling. Some passengers were eeeking out little screams and then quickly, more turbulence and fanatical shouts of terror as the big bird dropped like a stone.

I could hear the pilot saying, "Ladies and Gentlemen, please leave your seat belts on till we...CRASH!!!..HEH HEH HEH...HEH!" His voice sounded just like Jimmy Peters', but that wasn't possible.

I tried to escape from my trance and shut down that damn tape recorder, but my brain wouldn't let me. It was like being on the outside looking in. I could see some passengers were pressing their hands together in prayer. Mothers were holding tight to their babies. Even old men and young men were crying. Young newlyweds across the aisle were repeating their vows, hoping they would be together in the next life.

She whispered, "I'll love you forever where ever we are."

He pleaded, "If I'm not there when you get there, wait for me. I will find you." Then their lips locked, waiting for the final moment.

Four female flight attendants came running up the aisle trying to calm the passengers, but as the plane continued its destination to death and destruction, their faces melted like hot wax and they were left with just their skeletons. They collapsed into one big heap. Then, their fingernails quickly grew long sharp razors and they slowly clawed their way back up. They started slashing any exposed throat. With savage fury they attacked the newlyweds, plunging their knife-like nails into their backs. Soon they turned toward me, and with an evil laugh started chanting in unison, "FOUR GIRLS! FOUR GIRLS! FOUR GIRLS!!! They are all DEAD except one, and you are responsible, CHARLIE!!!" They started singing the theme from Cops, (Whatcha Gonna Do When They Come For You? BAD BOYS! BAD BOYS!). They repeated it over and over and kept laughing louder and louder until I thought my head would explode.

The turbulence was overwhelming. I was going to die!

79

"EXCUSE ME! SIR! EXCUSE ME!!!" I felt a hard slap on my face and the librarian-looking lady next to me said, "Wake up and get your hand off my leg!...or I'll call the stewardess."

I looked around and saw some passengers reading, others sleeping. Many were just quietly talking, and the newlyweds across the aisle were holding hands, lost in each others eyes. I was a big ball of sweat. I apologized to the lady next to me and she said, "You were really having a bad dream. You should never sleep on a plane."

I apologized again and said, "I don't think I'll ever close my eyes again. Just a suggestion…Never buy a memory course. Never turn your tape recorder on...even if you don't have the course."

She gave me a strange look as if I were the biggest nut on the planet, and then went back to her laptop. It must be nice to have such concentration and not let your mind wander. It's probably a blessing not to know that there's a tape recorder in your head recording every moment of your life. Maybe you are wishing by now that had I never told you. And, by the way, the batteries never run out. There's a little pink bunny banging on a drum in your brain, making sure those bad dreams and memories don't get lost among the good ones.

We landed smoothly in Boston. The turbulence was over, or was it?

I purchased a Stephen King book, <u>CHRISTINE,</u> at a gift store on the Delta concourse at Logan. I didn't want to think or sleep the rest of the way. Maybe King could come up with something weirder than what was going on in my real life and in my dreams. His story was about a car that ran into people causing extensive damage to itself in the process, and then bending itself back into shape. Guess ol' Steve never heard about Old Man Buckley and his *family*, or the thing in the Abe Lincoln hat...or Cindy.

10

Detective Tony Reza was standing at the luggage carousel when I got off the last leg of my flight. He was tall and thin with dark brown hair, matching eyes, and a pleasant smile. Dressed in a perfectly pressed and fitted suit and looking more like he belonged on the cover of GQ, the Detective extended his hand as I approached, "Welcome back to Portland, Mr. Sullivan."

"What, no handcuffs? Are you going to read me my rights?" I asked as if he were too young to understand police procedure.

"That won't be necessary, Sir. You're not under arrest. We just have some questions for you."

The kid was obviously more polite than I was. But it was a long harrowing flight, and I was now getting more nervous. The fact that I was finally back in my hometown was sinking into my thick and mixed-up head.

Reza helped me with my suitcases and escorted me to another unmarked vehicle, one that was not as conspicuous as Detective Russell's baby-blue Camero ragtop with the HOOTERS sticker and loud muffler.

As we exited the terminal Reza explained that the meeting and the questions would take place the following morning at the offices of John Feeney at One City Center. Feeney had gotten heavily involved in the case. His wife, Sandra, was still in seclusion since the death of young Paul, but John was obsessed. He wouldn't rest till he found out who killed their son and the Winchell boy.

"I can't tell you much about why they want to talk to you, Mr. Sullivan, but the case has been assigned to me." explained the smartly-dressed Detective.

"If they know I have been in California all this time, how can they possibly think I had anything to do with the killings?" I had asked the same question to Detective Russell back in Oceanside and got no satisfactory reply. Reza couldn't produce much more.

"Listen, we've tried to get that answer from Mr. Feeney, but he says he wants you there when he turns over his so-called evidence.

He's got a lot of friends in this town including the D.A. and the Chief. That would be Brian DeWolfe and Chief Ray Richardson."

"Do they know the cause of death yet? I understand that there were no signs of foul play. I'm guessing, with no visible marks on the bodies, they must have been suffocated in some way."

"That's another mystery. Our own forensic doctor, Frank Blanchette, says one thing and the State Medical Examiner, Roland Greenier, has another theory. Of course, I'm not at liberty to reveal their findings to you. Not yet."

"Let me ask you, Detective, and I don't want to sound condescending."

He stopped me before I could complete my question, "Why would they assign such a young detective to such a big case? I think Feeney had something to do with that. He probably feels he has more control dealing with a rookie than he would with someone who has more clout. Like I said, he's very powerful in this town."

"How do you feel about that?"

"Hey, I know I gotta pay my dues. I look at it as a great opportunity. I have my own theory as well, and we'll see what pans out."

"And your theory is?" I asked Reza as he opened the passenger door of his vehicle, like he was a chauffeur and I was some important dignitary or celebrity.

Reza just smiled and said, "So, do you think the Sox will make the playoffs this year?"

They were going to stash me for the night at The Portland Regency, an upscale hotel in the Old Port section of town down by the waterfront. There have been a lot of changes in my home town and the Regency was one of the better ones.

As we rode along I couldn't help but notice all that was new and all that remained the same. We drove by Hadlock Field which is now the home of the Portland Sea Dogs, a Red Sox minor-league team. It's located in the same spot where Joe and I had played our little league games for the Knights of Columbus, back in our day. Then we drove by King Junior High School where Jimmy first taught me about *elbow-tit* and where Joanie St. John gave me my first hickey. I remember telling my mother it was a rash, brought on by the crap-

MIGHTY JOHN MARSHALL

pie cafeteria food. "Really, Mom, that's what the school nurse said. I better bring my own lunch from now on, huh?"

As we drove up State Street to Longfellow Square I could see the old poet was still sitting in his bronze chair, waiting for some little kid to jump up into his lap to hear him recite The Children's Hour. There he was in all his glory, gazing down Congress Street, and the pigeons were still crapping all over him. They were relentless critics.

There were certainly a lot more galleries and boutiques on Congress street than when I was a kid. Other than Longfellow, the only stalwart was Joe's Smoke Shop. All the big movie houses had been abandoned or taken over. The marquee bulbs were no longer flashing at The State, The Capitol, The Strand or The Civic Theaters. Even the old W.T. Grant's building had been subdivided into sandwich shops and specialty stores. It was in Grant's Department Store where I bought Heartbreak Hotel, my first Elvis record, and where Jimmy and I bought our first baseball gloves.

I remembered all the fun Jimmy and I had at the old lunch counter where you could get a root beer float for twenty cents. And, if you complained that you found a hair in it, the old ladies behind the counter wouldn't charge you at all. We thought we were putting one over on them, back in that Ozzie and Harriet world. God bless them. Today the counter workers would have called for security and charged us with fraud.

We pulled up in front of the plush hotel on Milk Street which used to be an old National Guard armory and where my high school held basketball practice when I was a freshman. The hoops and the hardwood floors were gone, but if you listened closely you could still hear a basketball bounce from a long time ago. At least I could.

"Mr. Sullivan, I'll pick you up at nine," said Detective Reza as he escorted me to the lobby.

"Thanks, Detective. You've been very professional," I said with a genuine smile for this likable young man.

He smiled back and said, "Nothing's too good for Joe's brother."

It was then I knew I was really home. It gave me a small laugh, if just for a brief moment.

Reza left and a scrawny looking bellboy with MONROE printed on his name tag took over. As he escorted me to my room he asked,

"Have you heard about all the strange cemetery killings going on in this town? It's really spooky, Man!"

"Yeah, I think I read somewhere that there was some sort of serial-killer or something," I replied as if I had been on another planet for the last couple of weeks.

"Serial killer, my ass!...Oh shit!...Excuse me, Sir, I'm not supposed to say 'ass' while I'm on duty."

"No problem with saying 'shit' while you're on duty?"

"Oh fuck!...You're right!!!...What was I thinking? Please excuse me again."

"Yes...well, that's quite all right. So you don't buy the serial-killer theory?"

"More like some sort of creature from another world!" claimed the excitable bellboy as he struggled with the luggage. "My friend, Jeff, says he saw bright yellow and red lights from something hovering over that area. I think aliens have landed right here in Portland, just like the ones that landed in Nevada back in the fifties, Man. The Government is keeping it from us just like they did back then. Ya know Bush and his cronies started that whole war in Iraq just to keep our questions about those little big-eyed creatures in Area 51 off the front pages? Cause there was all kinds of new information about to come out." Monroe then looked to his left and then to his right to see if anyone suspicious was lurking about as he revealed his own theory with a loud whisper, "I think they want to mate with our women because their own race is dying out." His eyes widened as he smiled. "How great is that...going from planet to planet...having sex with every woman they find? Man, it must be cool being an alien." The bellboy stood there, lost in his daydream, until I gently shook his shoulder, afraid that I might never get to my room.

"Monroe, how long have you been a bellboy?"

"Not long, this is just temporary job. I'm going to be a lawyer someday and fight for the underdog, legalization of drugs, and tearing down our borders so the whole world can enjoy the blessings we do. There'll be no such thing as illegal aliens."

"Like the ones hovering over the old cemetery?"

"Yeah," he laughed. That's a good one, Man."

"Aliens, huh? Well, it's as good a guess as I have," I confessed.

"All those people were frightened to death. That's what the tabloids say and they are more honest than the Republicans, Man."

"I'm sure the real truth will come out soon," I assured him as I stood in front of my room door.

"I don't know about that. Now that the MSNBC newsman got his, the whole press will probably be kept away from that old cemetery," Monroe offered matter-of-factly like that bit of news was common knowledge.

I was just about to slide the electric key and turn the handle to my room when my little helper came out with this latest revelation.

"Monroe, what the hell are you talking about?"

"It was just on the TV in the lounge, Man. He was found dead in his trailer just before he went on the air. There must have been over fifty reporters from all over the country up there and just as many lights and cameras, and no one saw nothin'."

I had planned to take a much needed leak as a soon as I got into the room, but I clicked on the TV and forgot my bladder. I sat on the bed and watched in awe as this latest report was repeated again. The bellboy hung around for his tip.

As I watched and Monroe waited, I called Joe.

"Action Central News," said the familiar sarcastic voice on the other end.

"Hey, Asswipe. I'm at The Regency. Have you got the TV on?"

"Yeah, I saw it. It's been a real circus up there. This has been the biggest thing to hit this town since Elvis failed to show up for his final concert. Lay off those jelly donuts, Charlie! Lay off those jelly donuts...heh heh heh."

"Joe, can't you ever be serious?"

"Ya, seriously, don't call me tomorrow before nine. I need my beauty sleep."

"Ya, then you better sleep for a week 'cause you are ugleeeeee."

"Hey, did Reza tell you nothing's too good for Joe's brother?"

"Is that all you care about, you moron?"

"You got it, Charlie. I saw him last night down at O'Toole's and told him to say that. I had him in class about 10 years ago. He's a hot shit. Now get some sleep yourself. We'll catch up tomorrow."

Joe was right. There was nothing I could do tonight. I flipped Monroe five bucks and crashed with my clothes still on.

Like Russell, Tony Reza was right on time. He met me in the lobby and handed me some coffee, "Good morning, Mr. Sullivan. Are your ready for your moment in the spotlight?"

"Thanks, Detective," I said as I accepted his generosity. "Yes, let's get this over with. And by the way, did you know about that newsman getting killed last night?"

"Yeah, it came over my radio just before I picked you up at the Jetport." Then he smiled and said, "If a young detective wants to someday be an old detective he learns to keep some things to himself."

"Do me a favor," I asked. "When you do get to be an old detective, don't wear a brown suit with black shoes and a wide colorful tie with a map of the state of Maine on it. And stay out of Hooters."

"Why do you say that?"

"You're a detective. You'll figure it out!"

"But, we don't even have a Hooters," he exclaimed with a puzzled look on his face.

It was my turn to smile. Reza kept that same look on his face all the way down the outside stairs where his car was waiting, but I asked if we could walk. It was a nice sunny day in the city and Feeney's offices were nearby. Besides, it gave me a chance to notice other changes in the Portland landscape.

The number of bars, restaurants, and coffee shops almost outnumbered the citizens on the street. Everything was quaint, as if they were trying to make everything new look old again.

We arrived at One City Center in Monument Square, the heart of downtown, just before 9:15. The new building, where once stood the old and what we thought was the permanent, Maine Hardware, was full of radio stations and lawyers. John Feeney's offices took up the entire eighth floor. He was a big man in a small town.

The carpets that lined the hallways were thick and comfortable. They made your feet feel like you were walking on air. The mahogany paneling was real, and the paintings on the walls were sea-scapes of various Maine locations by local Maine artists. The place was busy with secretaries and interns, and with computers and fax machines. It even smelled expensive. The entire office worked like a precision watch with everything and everyone in their place, doing their appointed duties without question. At the very end, with a pan-oramic view of the city, was the office of Attorney John Feeney, the man that made it all tick.

Sitting in an oversized black leather chair, he looked way too old for his age. Considering what he'd just gone through, I thought that was understandable. I remember a young John Feeney from our days at Cheverus High. Athletic and handsome in his football uni-form, he was the all-American boy... rich, smart, and handsome. Now fifty pounds heavier and with a thick gray beard that made up for the lack of hair on his balding head, he looked more like one of the Jesuit teachers from back in his glory days. However, his silk suit and lavished surroundings betrayed any vow of poverty.

Feeney's office was like his own personal shrine with trophies from high school and Boston College. His lettered sweaters from both institutions were behind glass and hung on the wall behind him, along with a bunch of legal documents showing he graduated *magna cum laude* from Cheverus and B.C. Assorted pictures of his family were abundant, including one on his desk that showed John and young Paul displaying a big marlin on a father-son fishing trip to Florida. A similar photo with a young John Feeney and his dad, Patrick, was next to it. One wall of pictures was devoted to photos of John and some political big shots, both local and national, including an autographed picture that read, "If I ever need an attorney, I'll call John Feeney." It was simply signed "Bill".

As he recognized me he jumped up with remarkable agility, ex-tended his hand and said with a forcible smile, "Charlie Sullivan, it's good to see you! You haven't changed much. Must be all that Cali-fornia sunshine you have out there."

It was an awkward moment for both of us. We were old school-mates; but his young son was now dead, and for some reason he thought I might know something about it.

"John," I said, as I clasped his hand in mine. "I'm so very sorry to hear about your son."

"Thank you, Charlie. You can imagine what Sandra and I are going through. She hasn't left the house since the funeral."

"Please extend her my deepest sympathies."

"I'll do that." He paused for a moment to gather his professional composure and went on, "Charlie, I want you to meet Brian Dewolfe from the District Attorney's Office and Chief Ray Richardson from my...ah...I mean...our Police Department. You of course know Detective Reza." We all cordially shook hands. "Gentlemen, please take seats."

The D.A. and the cops sat down on the long leather couch, and I took the short hardwood chair set up in front of Feeney's big desk. Suddenly I had a vision of Jimmy Stewart and Lionel Barrymore in It's A Wonderful Life. I felt like I was George Bailey looking up at an intimidating Mr. Potter.

John stared at me from his comfortable chair and called his secretary on his intercom, "Kim, hold all my calls, except of course, Sandra."

"Yes John...ah...I mean Mr. Feeney," said the soft obedient voice on the other end.

He gave me fifteen seconds of silence and then stated, "Charlie, you know a man in my position has a lot of powerful friends and a lot of powerful enemies. Among my good and powerful friends are the Chief and the D.A. here."

The two dutifully smiled in agreement, as if to do otherwise would have been considered an act of mutiny.

"My enemies number more, from that first bastard I prosecuted as a young lawyer up in Bangor, that Chamberlain character who raped and killed a waitress, to those goddamn corporate polluters in some of our biggest industries. They would all like to hurt me anyway they can. Revenge is a bitter and demanding mistress. I should know...I mean...well, you know what I mean"

A flashback to George Chamberlain running and screaming from those bee stings sprang into my mind. I even thought of his father standing like a nose tackle in his doorway, asking Jimmy and me if George had killed another cat. I never thought I would hear that name again. Then again, I never thought I would be back in Portland with some suspicious cloud hanging over me regarding the murder of a young child.

"As you may or may not know, Charlie, there's a victim of the recent cemetery assaults still alive up at Maine Med. She's a college student who was attacked with her three friends. Her name is Kathy Kostenello. Does the name mean anything to you, Charlie?" He sat back in his chair and folded his hands, obviously hoping that I would fall into a trap.

The other three men looked at me as I reacted to the name, first presented to me by Detective Russell back in Oceanside.

Chief Richardson spoke up in a demanding voice, "Answer him, Mr. Sullivan."

"Well, there's a detective back in California who asked me if I knew that name. It was the night he handed me the plane ticket to come back here."

"And do you know that name, Mr. Sullivan?" asked D.A. Brian Dewolfe

"NO!!! I don't" I was feeling ganged up on, but somehow was expecting it. Why else would they drag me all the way back here?

John Feeney leaned forward in his chair. In his hand he was holding a manila envelope. He kept turning it over and over as if to hypnotize me into saying something he wanted to hear.

"Charlie, I'm going to let you in on some facts that, so far, I have kept from my three friends here. Yes, maybe if I had released it sooner, it might have prevented further deaths. But the only death I care about is my boy!!!" he exclaimed as he pounded his fat fists on his highly organized desk, almost knocking over the marlin pictures. He stood up now and faced the view of Portland, all the while holding that envelope behind his back as if taunting me with its contents.

He continued, "One of my friends is a nurse up at Maine Medical Center, who shall remain nameless for the time being. Let's just say I once helped her out in an extremely messy divorce case, but I haven't been fully compensated yet. Well, this very same nurse attended Miss Kostenello when she arrived at the emergency room. She helped get her undressed and prepared for examination. Unfortunately, Miss Kostenello is still in a coma. Yet, in a way, she's been able to give us a big clue. Do you know what that clue is, Charlie?"

he quizzed as he slowly tore open the mysterious container. "I could have shown this to the Chief and the D.A., but I wanted to show you first and see the look on your face. Any guesses?"

"I have no idea, John," I said in anticipation, my heart now racing with the moment of truth at hand.

Then, in a flash, the contents were exposed on his mahogany desk.

"Recognize anything, Charlie!?!" Feeney shouted as if revealing a murder weapon to an unsuspecting killer.

The Detective, the D.A, the Chief, and I all stood up at once.

My racing heart stopped in its tracks, as if the shock of what I was seeing would make me the ninth victim.

There on the lawyer's desk lay a tarnished chain with a locket. Barely visible were the words, LEST WE FORGET. It was the last thing I expected to see. My knees weak, I sat back down.

"Do you recognize that little trinket, Charlie?" Feeney asked, not as my friend but as a prosecutor.

I didn't answer right away. I couldn't answer right away. Meanwhile, the D.A. and the two cops approached the desk to examine what might someday be *States Exhibit A.*

"Go ahead, Gentlemen. Pick it up, it's already been checked for finger prints. There were none found, none at least that could give us a possible match."

Now growing more confident, Feeney turn to me again and said, "Do you know whose picture I saw inside?...YOURS, CHARLIE. YOURS!!!"

Not waiting for an answer, the lawyer continued on in a voice loud enough to be heard all over the suite even with his door closed, "Do you know where that was found? It was tucked tightly in the fist of Miss Kostenello when she was brought into the Emergency Room. I'm betting she took it off her attacker!!!"

The noise was suddenly buried by the silence that followed. Everyone took a breath and then another.

Chief Richardson now took his turn in the inquisition, "Sullivan, we know you weren't in town at the time, but who would have such an item in their possession?"

Before I could explain, Feeney collapsed into his chair. This powerful man, who ruled his realm with little sympathy for anyone but himself, was sobbing like a baby. The loss of his child was too much for him to grieve fully before. Now the process was beginning.

We all sat quietly, respecting his sorrow. Slowly he began to find the strength he needed to go on with a life that seemed to have little meaning for him now. With a voice that was much weaker than before, almost no louder than a whisper, he pleaded, "Please, Charlie help me find my boy's killer. Tell me everything. Don't leave out the smallest detail. Please."

I nodded to him with understanding and told my tale of how I met Cindy and the story of the chain and locket. I explained the erotic encounters with the girl with no last name and no home. I provided all the information about where I bought the locket and the meaning of the words inscribed on it. I revealed the location where I last saw it... by the big old elm tree near home plate. I left it there in the rain. It was gone the next time I went back. I never saw it again until this very moment.

They all listened intently as I went through every detail, and when I had finished Detective Reza spoke, "Mr. Sullivan, if this mysterious young girl didn't come back for it, what's your best guess as to who might have picked it up?"

They all waited for my answer as if nothing else in the world mattered at that moment. The D.A., the Detective, and the Chief were all standing around me while the grieving John Feeney came over and put his hand on my shoulder, as if to say, *You're still my friend and my old schoolmate.*

But I still sensed, if I couldn't be anymore help to him, he would throw me out without a second thought. Maybe it's my years of hearing excuses from students as to why they don't have their homework turned in on time that has hardened me to genuine sincerity. I did feel real sorrow for him because of Paul's death. It was a sad thing for any parent, no matter who they were. Of course I would help John anyway I could. I told him that my first thought, when I didn't see the locket again, was that some bum or hobo had picked it up while looking for bottles or cans.

"Is there anyone else who knew you were going to give this Cindy girl your gift?" asked Detective Reza. "Did you tell anyone that you left that gold chain and locket up there?"

They waited patiently as I began to rewind that old memory tape. All of a sudden I was back there on that windy cemetery hill with the thunder crashing and the rain pouring down. "I see the lighting again and the hornets nest fall to the ground. I see the bees swarming under the tree, paying me no mind. I'm holding that chain and locket to my heart, as if it were Cindy herself. At that moment she was all that mattered, all that I wanted to see...Wait!!! I do see someone. I can't make out who it is. I now remember thinking it was just one of the old bums that crossed through the cemetery to get down to The Hobo Grounds where they could catch a train out of town. I can't see a face, just some shadowy figure, very tall but unrecognizable. I'm sorry, that's all I can see."

Lawyer Feeney listened to the entire adventure with his hand still on my shoulder. "Think harder, Charlie. What happened next?" he asked, as if there were a trap door under my chair and the wrong answer would send me tumbling down to the nether world.

"After she didn't show, I was feeling pretty bad. So I went down to see my best friend, Jimmy Peters. He could always make me laugh and I needed that."

Suddenly I stopped.

"What is it, Charlie?" asked the bereaved father. "Did you tell this Peters kid where you left that chain and locket?"

"Ah...well...yeah, but Jimmy wouldn't have taken it. He was by best friend."

"Where is this Jimmy Peters today?" asked Chief Richardson.

"Do you have an address?" the D.A. inquired.

"I haven't heard from Jimmy in over eight years. He was living down in Charlotte last time I knew. His mother and one sister still live here in town. His mother must still be in the same house down on Danforth Street," I said.

"Danforth Street! That's right near that old cemetery." John Feeney perked up with new information to devour.

"Listen!" I continued, "Jimmy and I were closer than brothers. He wouldn't have taken it," I repeated. "Surely it must be someone else."

As an aside Tony Reza offered, "Ya know, Chief, I'm still not sure that caretaker is being completely honest. Why don't I pay him another visit and see if he knows anything about that locket and chain?"

"That old cemetery has a caretaker?" I asked in total surprise. "When did that happen?"

Feeney spoke. "Why that old place has always had a caretaker. That is when we can find some yahoo to take the job. Sandra handles the trust that was set up years ago by the Friends of the Western Cemetery Foundation. It provides a small annual payment and free lodging in the caretaker's shack. We usually find someone who likes living alone and wants to spend all that time caring for the dead."

"I never saw any shack up there," I stated. Again I was surprised.

"Well, it's not actually on the cemetery grounds. It's just down the hill in the railroad yards, down in The Hobo Grounds."

"Learn something new everyday." I said. I looked at all four of them and nervously asked, "Am I still a suspect?"

They waited for Feeney to speak. "No, Charlie, but we all hope you will stick around for a while. All your expenses are being taken care of; and we may have more questions, especially if that college kid comes out her coma. One other thing, all we discuss regarding this case stays among us five unless otherwise agreed upon."

"What about Joe?" I asked. "He knew there was a girl still alive and that the coroners couldn't agree as to the cause of the deaths. He hears a lot of things. I think we should keep him informed."

"Your brother should work for the freakin' FBI. He knows more about what's going on in this city than I do! I always thought he was a bit of a prick but, hey... he was Paul's favorite teacher, and he was there for Paul's wake and funeral mass. Include him, I've got no problem with that," relented the attorney.

We all nodded in agreement.

"There's one other thing I would like to mention." I said.

"What's that?" the quartet asked in harmony.

I told them of all the weird events and accidents that had happened to our other friends in the old cemetery, and how I never had any problems. I reminded John that it was there that George Chamberlain was stung over and over again. I asked if it would be all right if I paid a visit to my childhood play-land. Maybe standing there, I could remember more.

"I've got the whole place sealed up tighter that a drum," explained Chief Richardson. "Ever since that newsman got killed we've kept them all back. I think for a while there were more reporters and rubber-neckers outside those gates that buried occupants inside. If you want to go in there I'll okay it, but take Reza and a couple of uniform boys with ya. That is, if it's all right with you, John?" the Chief added dutifully.

"It's fine with me, whatever it takes to bring this horror to an end or at least some closure," okayed the *power behind the throne.*

"John?" I asked. "Can you tell me the name of the caretaker?"

The attorney gave a heads up to the young detective, like a base coach giving a runner the steal signal. It was crystal clear that this lawyer was really the man in charge. Yes, they feared him, but they also respected him.

Reza relayed the info, "His name is Wendle Bronson. Have you heard that name before?"

I thought hard. "The name seems familiar, but I can't place the face. Wendle Bronson?" I repeated. "Where do I know him from? I'll have to think on it some more. You might want to check and see if there was a caretaker working those years when Jimmy and I played in there. If there was, he might have been the shadowy figure I saw that night. If he took the locket, you might have your killer or at least a good lead."

Feeney looked at his hand-picked detective, as if to say, *Why didn't you think of that?*

Then the four of us left John Feeney alone with his grief.

11

We had spent almost ten hours with John Feeney, as I relived the summers of my life in that cemetery with Jimmy and the one magical season with Cindy. Coffee and sandwiches had been brought in along with hourly updates from Feeney's pretty young secretary. Each time she would give him a sympathetic look as if to say, *Are you all right?*, or maybe to say, *Do you want to come over tonight?* At least that's how it seemed to me.

A need for the facilities was provided by a spacious bathroom right off the lawyer's lavish office. Its gold plated faucets and pristine interior were another means to impress a client that he or she was in the confines of the most important and successful attorney in town.

As we stepped out into the fading sunlight, Chief Ray Richardson checked headquarters to get the latest developments in what the network newscasts were now calling: THE GREAT CEMETERY SLAUGHTER. What they were really saying was: *The more the dead, the better the ratings.* In the back rooms of sales offices, I could imagine the shouts of glee going up as the body count did. It's not news anymore. It's the Super Bowl. There's a million dollars in new sales with every additional death. That's the world we live in today, not the world I knew when Jimmy and I were at peace within the gates of the now ill-fated cemetery...a place that will probably go down in Halloween history along with Dracula, the Wolfman, Frankenstein, Freddy Krueger, Jason, and the Crypt Keeper.

"No new information and no new deaths," the Chief reported as he put his phone back in his pocket and wiped the sweat from his visor. "Damn, it's still hot! I don't think this drought will ever end...Haven't seen one like this in years."

I walked back to the Regency Hotel along with Reza, Richardson, and Dewolfe. We had formed somewhat of a bond after our experience in John Feeney's office. I was now confident they knew the surfacing of the chain and locket was as big a mystery to me as it was to them. It was no longer me against all of them. I was now one of them.

"Mr. Sullivan, I'll make all the arrangements for us to visit Mr. Bronson and the cemetery. How does nine in the morning sound?" Detective Reza asked as we reached the front steps of the Regency where my little friend, Monroe, was bending the ear of another guest.

"You've heard about Area 51, well I'm calling this town, Area 207...'cause that's our area code. I'm telling ya, the Martians have landed, Man... Right here in Portland...ah...I mean Area 207."

Reza gave me a *who's-that-nut?* look and I said, "Nine is fine, Detective. I'd like to go along as well when you talk to Mrs. Peters. I'm sure she'll feel a bit more comfortable with me there."

"Absolutely," was the Detective's response.

"We've got a press conference scheduled for tomorrow. I've got to release what little we do know before they call for my resignation," The Chief added, his eyes searching the D.A.'s for his thoughts. "Should we check with Feeney first?"

"The whole city is ready to go off their collective rockers if we don't give them something," DeWolfe warned. "I'll give John a call when I get home tonight, but I'm sure he'll be all right with it."

With that, they all shook my hand, and I headed back to my room.

After a thirty-minute nap and a quick shower I called Brother Joe. We made arrangements to meet at O'Toole's on Forest Avenue. It was where Joe held reign as the unofficial Mayor of Portland. O'Toole's was a dark dive where the drinks were over priced and watered down. The furnishings were strictly discount, with a Velvet Elvis hanging above the bar. Somebody had replaced the "first dollar" that O'Toole ever made. He used to keep it taped to the cash register. Now, in it's place, was a faded I.O.U.

The jukebox played nothing but 50s and 60s rock-n-roll, and according to my big brother, not the "crap" the *oldies* stations play over and over again. Joe saw to it that the neon-flashing Wurlitzer was stocked with records that real old-time rockers would appreciate with artists like Gene Vincent, Eddie Cochran, Wanda Jackson, Jack Scott, Charlie Gracie, and the guy with the coolest name in rock-n-roll, Ersel Hickey. A few Ricky Nelson's and Bobby Darin's were thrown in at the request of some of the more regular patrons, but they had to get Joe's approval first.

O'Toole's was the kind of neighborhood joint that was more famous for its camaraderie than its booze, although the pizza was above average. Doused in a fog of cigarette smoke, the place was packed with customers who lived there as much as at home.

As soon as I opened the door I spotted some of the old gang...some that had been in my classes...some that had been outside the Old Buckley Place that night Jimmy and I ran from the creep in the Abe Lincoln stovepipe hat...some that had played ball in my cemetery playground and were part of my lost innocence.

Among them was Dana Wilson or "Disco Dana" as he has been known ever since he opened his first dance club on Exchange Street back in the late seventies. He dropped out of school his senior year to go on the road. He was lead singer with an all-girl back-up group. His little band was known as, <u>Dana & The Debutantes</u>. They had a small regional hit called, <u>Linda, Shake Your Money Maker</u>. Disco Dana took what little money they had made from record sales and live appearances and opened up his night club. He still dressed like Travolta did in <u>Saturday Night Fever</u>. Dana was tall and thin; but his curly red hair was receding, and the freshly implanted *plugs* stuck out like a sore thumb.

I saw Bill O'Neal or "William" as his mother liked to call him. She never did let him go back to the cemetery after something scared him off. Bill sold insurance for Allstate. Joe said people were always slapping Allstate bumper stickers on his back without his knowledge, or teasing him with one of those, "I-got-bad-news-and-good-news jokes" with the punch line about saving a lot of money with Geico.

Bill married right out of high school and now has ten kids. He was always trying to sell insurance, even at O'Toole's where he's known as, "Rabbit", for his prowess at reproducing. I guess with ten kids the best insurance is for Bill not to be alone with his wife. In school they voted Bill: First to most likely get a girl pregnant. He didn't disappoint.

One of the guys I didn't see was Tommy Caine. As a matter of fact, I never did see much of him after that Halloween night he ran screaming down Cassidy Hill, when Jimmy said there was a zombie hot on his trail. I was hoping to buy him a drink to make up for taking all that candy he left behind. He's was probably out politicking. Tommy was after the Republican nomination for Governor while John Feeney was working for the same from the Democrats. Joe said Tommy was slightly to the right of Rush Limbaugh and was campaigning against taxes and welfare. He wanted to stop the latest proposed increase in the minimum wage so businesses wouldn't want to leave the state. That platform was not popular with the blue-collar customers at O'Toole's.

As I made my way to my old friends, shaking hands and reliving "good times", I noticed the picture on the wall next to the cash register. It was Private John Spiller in his Marine dress-blues.

Johnny was a good kid who always tried hard in school, but did poorly. He played by the rules and worked odd jobs ever since he was a freshman at Portland High. Every penny he earned went to help support his widowed mother and his three brothers.

He enlisted in the Marines right out of high school when some slick-talking recruiter painted a picture of travel and good pay. Six months later he was traveling all right, in a Huey helicopter in Da Nang. The chopper set down to pick up some wounded and dead. As John and his buddies put the bleeding and the bodies on board, he heard a voice coming out of the jungle grass, "I'm dying. Baptize me before I die. Please."

John's sergeant told him that it was an old Commie trick. The Commies knew Catholic doctrine better than most Catholics, and they used it to their advantage on naive but well meaning grunts like John Spiller. They were taught that any Catholic can perform a baptism in an emergency, when there's no priest around. "Please, baptize me...please!!!"

John protested that it could be another marine, but his sergeant gave him a direct order to "GET BACK ON THAT CHOPPER!!!" The young marine heard the command but ignored it. He grabbed his rifle and canteen and ran into the tall grass, toward the voice of the pleading soldier. The helicopter left without waiting. His buddies said they saw him fall as they hovered above. As Private Spiller poured the water and made the sign of the cross, two bayonets were plunged into his back. John, who had been part of our little group, who made it all the way through the Old Buckley Place, who had worked so hard to provide for his family was left...dead and alone in a land we had never heard of...when we all hung out together, innocent and happy...back in that Pine Street Neighborhood.

He's a hero at O'Toole's. But, for disobeying a direct order, the military wouldn't even put his name on *The Wall*. But he wasn't forgotten or alone. O'Toole's had its own wall, and Father Mike Murphy saw to it that John's picture was proudly displayed with other local boys who had made the supreme sacrifice. Every night, before last call, the customers at O'Toole's saluted and toasted "the boys on the wall".

Joe arrived shortly after I got reacquainted with my old friends to a cheer of, "Joe, how's it hangin'."

All I could think of was the gang at Cheers yelling, "NOM!"

Right behind Joe was Mike Murphy or Father Mike as he was now known, and the tone of the crowd changed quickly. The how's-it-hangin' shouts faded as the crowd all became little altar boys again. Of all the guys in our neighborhood Mike was the one I liked the best, next to Jimmy. We lived on the second floor and Mike and his family lived on the first.

I remember the night he came upstairs to tell us that he was going into the Seminary. It was Mike's eighteenth birthday. "Joe, Charlie, I just wanted to let you know...I got the calling." He was beaming from ear to ear.

"I didn't call ya," Joe said.

I moved back from the kitchen table, and motioned to Joe to do the same as I teased, "Joe, he's got *the calling*...He's going to be a *priest!*"

"Eweeee, it's not contagious, is it?" Joe exclaimed.

"I don't know. Don't get too close or look into his eyes," I warned.

"You guys are just too funny aren't you?" Mike replied with a smile.

"Is there a cure? I asked, as I pretended I was choking.

"Trust me," Mike joked. "You two guys are immune."

I also remember that night because, just hours before, I had my first encounter with Cindy.

"Good evening, Father. Hello Father, nice to see you. Father, my boy is making his First Communion next Sunday...blah blah blah."

"Take it easy, boys. I'm not here to give a sermon."

"YEA!!!" the crowd shouted and went back to their drinks and conversations.

Joe approached me with that smirkey smile that formed his face, "Hey, Dipwad!" That's the best he could do after not seeing me for all those years. I guess I would have been disappointed with a hug. I liked it that he hadn't changed. It gave me a sense of security.

Father Mike gave me a hug and moved on to the rest of his parishioners, some of whom he hadn't seen in church in a long while.

Meanwhile, I brought Joe up to date on all that had happened at my inquisition, including the fact that the survivor had the old chain and locket that I had given to Cindy all those years ago.

"No Shit! You never told me about that." That's all he had to say and then added, "Too bad about young Paul, but his old man is still an asshole. You know, he's been boinking his secretary for years."

"Really, be sure to mention that to Father Mike."

"I'm sure he's heard a lot worse behind the wicker screen," Joe said as he looked around to see who else he could introduce his little brother to.

"If you know so much, how come you don't know who's killing all these people?" I asked as I looked for someplace to sit. The old joint was really packed that night.

"I have my theory," Joe boasted.

"You have a theory. Detective Reza has a theory. Even the freakin' bellboy at the hotel has a theory. All God's children got a theory... But what are the facts?"

"Once the case is solved I'll tell you whether my theory is right. Hey Nuwell! How about a beer!" Joe demanded.

Nuwell, the bartender, was behind that bar the last time I was in O'Toole's all those years ago. It was comforting to know that some things never change in a world that's full of change, like the music blasting on the jukebox. It was playing Conway Twitty's It's Only Make Believe. I thought that was as good a theory as anyone had. It would have been great to think that the deaths in the old cemetery was just something made up to scare little kids.

Father Mike joined us at the bar only to hear Nuwell ask, "Mike, do you have to wear the collar in here? It's bad for business."

"Ah, but it's good for mine. There are a lot of people in here look-ing for more meaning in their lives. As a matter of fact, I think we'll hold the parish council meetings in here from now on."

The bartender stood there speechless as Mike said, "Nuwell, the look on your face is priceless!"

"For everything else, there's Mastercard!" I added.

"Very freakin' funny...ha ha! All right, Mike, I can't spend all night arguing with you. What can I getcha?"

"Joe's buying, so I guess it's up to him".

"HA! Now *that's* funny," Nuwell laughed. "If Joe's buying you'll be drinkin' water! He's still got the first nickel he ever made."

"You know my brother well," I agreed, and we all laughed.

The door opened to squeeze in one more patron. Joe said it was Frank Blanchette, the Coroner for the Portland Police Department. I remember Frank from King Junior High. He was a quirky kid with thick glasses and lots of zits. The only time he showed any emotion was in eighth grade biology. He was almost orgasmic when it came to slicing open slimy creatures. *Hey, does school get any better than this!?!* He was more than willing to cut open as many frogs as he could, while most of us were having trouble with just one. I think it was the only time any girl ever invited him to join them for any-thing.

Frankie, how you doing? Are you going to the dance Satur-day night?...no?...That's too bad...By the way, Frankie, do you think you can help me with my frog?

Blanchette worked his way to the bar and said, "Nuwell, my usual." The Coroner swallowed with one gulp and said, "Another!"

Frank still looked the same with those thick glasses. His face was pockmarked from years of picking at pimples and blackheads. His shoulders were rounded now, covered partially with long white hair that was matted and unkempt. His frame was frail and looked like a mild wind could topple it. A cigarette hung from his lower lip. No one greeted him with friendliness as they always did for Joe. Frank was a lonely boy who was now a lonely man.

While Joe made the rounds with Father Mike, I made my way

though the crowd and greeted Doctor Blanchette and told him it was good to see him.

"Yeah, Charlie Sullivan, I remember you," He said as he coughed and unintentionally blew smoke in my face. "You never could cut open a frog without gagging," he laughed under his breath.

"I couldn't have done it without you, Frank. If I didn't thank you then, I want to thank you now," I said sincerely as I extended my hand. He looked surprise as if this didn't happen to him very often.

The Cororner put down his drink and snuffed out his cigarette on the bar. He shook my hand with a strength that belied his appearance, "I appreciate that, Charlie. I really do."

"Can I buy you a drink, Frank?"

"Well, no one in here has done that before! Thanks."

"Nuwell, one of whatever Frank is drinking, and a Pepsi for me."

"Pepsi! Charlie you're still a weenie. No wonder you couldn't split open a frog," Blanchette giggled the way the school girls did behind his back all those years ago.

"I still couldn't do it!" You were a hero to all us weenies at King Junior."

Frank did something then that he probably hadn't done in a while. He displayed a genuine smile, as if recognition and appreciation had taken a long time in arriving.

A few more stiff drinks and Frank started filling me in on all the injustices he suffered in his lonely world including how the State Medical Examiner, Roland Greenier, was overshadowing his findings in the latest big case: THE GREAT CEMETERY SLAUGHTER. My new old friend said the State Examiner was now agreeing with him as to the cause of death of all eight victims after disregarding the preliminary results.

"I told that arrogant bastard right from the start what happened. But, no, he just couldn't accept that, not the great Dr. Greenier. Now that he's come around to my way of thinking, ya know what that old fart does?"

"What Frank? What does he do?"

"He called in the findings to John Feeney an hour ago and took all the credit...the prick...after telling me we would present the findings together...the dink!"

"That does suck."

"Life sucks and then you die." Blanchette took another drink. "Isn't that what the kids say?"

I put my hand on his shoulder and asked, "Frank, would you be speaking out of turn if you told me what killed all those people?"

"I don't give a shit who knows. It'll be in the Press Herald tomorrow. I'll tell you how they all died...POISON!!!"

"Poison!!!...You mean like arsenic?"

"*Something much more deadly, in the doses it was delivered.*" He came closer to me now and lowered his voice, "Charlie, they were all *stung* to death." He then nodded his head to confirm his statement.

"What! How can that be? I understood there were no marks on the bodies. With enough bee stings to kill, wouldn't there be all kinds of welts and swelling?"

"Normally, yes, but these ain't your normal bees, Charlie. They're not even your regular killer bees."

"What makes them so different, Frank?"

The Coroner surveyed his surroundings before saying, "These little buggers sting on the *inside.*"

The noise from the jukebox and the crowd was loud and constant, but all I could hear was Frank revealing the details. "How's that possible?"

The Coroner took another drink and lit up another cigarette before continuing. "Somehow they manage to fly into the mouth or sail through the nasal passages. They can slide down your ear drum and find their way right to your noodle. We even found some; I mean I even found some, in the rectum of one of those sorority girls. I don't want to sound crude when talking about the deceased, but they got her while she was taking a dump." Frank took another long drag on his unfiltered cigarette. "That's my well-trained medical opinion anyway"

I listened with almost total belief...almost total. After all I had heard in the last ten days anything sounded like it could be true. Visions of those tiny bees that used to be around Cindy when I was seventeen popped up in my head. I was sure their size was just a coincidence with the ones Frank found doing his autopsies. They never bothered me back then. In fact they seemed quite friendly. I put them out of my mind and went out with our conversation.

"Don't get upset, Frank, but does Greenier agree with you?"

"He didn't want to at first. He was afraid the public would laugh him out of office, but he can't come up with a better finding so he's going along with mine."

"Are you *sure* they were bees?"

Frank seemed irritated with my question. His demeanor suddenly became almost combative. Apparently his nemesis, Roland Greenier, had asked the same thing.

"Those little fuckers are as small as a mosquito, but they are still bees and with a powerful dose of venom...a strain I've never seen before." Frank stared into space, contemplating his own revelation.

I looked around and saw Joe was still busy over by the jukebox which was now playing Bobby Freeman and Betty Lou's Got A New Pair Of Shoes. I wanted to tell Joe about the bees, because with his big mouth, the news would spread fast. But then I thought better of it. Maybe this little detail should be kept quiet for a while. It could cause an unnecessary panic.

I tuned back to the Coroner. "Frank, how was the Kostenello girl able to get away?"

"As I understand it she's a good athlete, and my guess is she outran the bastards. She was the only one found at the top of Cassidy Hill. The other three died inside the place, over by the mausoleum." Frank continued speaking as he looked at his watch. "Charlie thanks for the drinks and the company, but I gotta get my ass home. Next time the drinks are on me." He shook my hand again and walked a little taller on the way out of O'Toole's.

As Joe gave me a ride back to the Regency I filled him in on my conversation with Frank Blanchette. I told him poison was now considered the cause of death. I didn't mention the bees. He gave his normal response, "No shit!"

12

For as long as I remember, Jimmy Peters' mother and father were hand-holders. If they were just walking down the street or shopping at the supermarket they were locked into each other's fingers. I remember spending many nights with Jimmy and his parents. Jerry and Sara Peters would even hold hands while sitting on the couch, just watching TV. When they were apart there were frequent phone calls, even after 30 years of marriage. They took the greatest pleasures in hiding small gifts for each other and always acted so surprised and happy when the gifts were found. They never left each other's company without saying, "I love you." When Jimmy and I were kids we thought they acted so *ickey*. Now, as a grownup, I know they had it all and I'm envious. You would be too if you knew Jerry and Sara Peters and the way they were before cancer came calling in the winter of '81.

Mr. Peters owned a small dry cleaning business on Brackett Street where Jimmy and I would help out once in a while. He always overpaid us while kidding us that we didn't do a good job. "You boys work for fifteen minutes and then take a two hour break. It's supposed to be the other way around." Then he would break into a big grin and say, "Sounds like a pretty good idea!" He was a tall, plain looking man who was gray and balding before his time. He laughed frequently and his sky blue eyes were *always* smiling. Jerry Peters was just one of those guys everyone liked and enjoyed being around.

Sara Peters was athletic and active in school and at church. She was extremely beautiful with short blond hair and eyes that matched her husbands in color and style. She possessed a dancer's graceful body and a TV star's personality. She could have had any rich and handsome guy in town, but she knew what mattered most. She chose Jerry without hesitation. She was so full of life and joy that just seemed endless at the time.

That's what made it so difficult as Detective Reza and I saw her stooped and aged body peering through lacy curtains that hung on the front room window.

STUNG

"Go away. I'm not interested in what you're selling. Go peddle your papers somewhere else," she said through the screen.

I rang the bell one more time and said, "Mrs. Peters, its Jimmy's friend, Charlie Sullivan."

"Charlie Sullivan? Is that really you? I don't see so well any more. Come closer," the old lady commanded, and I obeyed.

I stepped toward the window and she disappeared. Soon the front door slowly opened and Sara Peters beckoned us inside. She embraced me and held on as if it transported her back to happier days. In my thoughts, I remembered the last time I hugged her. It was at the funeral home. While Jerry slept with his rosary beads replacing her tender hands, she said not to cry because we would all see him again. She wanted to believe it because of her faith. She had to believe it to keep from going crazy.

"Charlie Sullivan, I can't believe it's you standing here. Jerry and I loved you like you were one of our own," Jimmy's mother said in a strong clear voice, as she squeezed my hands and hugged me with her head to my chest.

She had always been so good to me, and it pained me now to see this once beautiful woman walking slowly and deliberately. Squinting her fading blue eyes on a furrowed face, now blotched with age spots, she kissed me on the cheek. I introduced her to Tony Reza and she asked us to sit down on that same couch where all that handholding took place those many years ago.

I looked around the homey surroundings that I knew so well. Even so, she was proud to point out the pictures of her children that were everywhere in the living room along with little figurines and statues of religious icons. On and in the huge walnut china closet were plates that reflected vacations spots that she and her husband had visited, and some of the many little gifts that they had given each other over the years. She started pointing to each one, acting like a curator in a fine museum. We listened politely as she relived her memories

"Jerry and I bought this one on our honeymoon when we went to New York City. See, it has the Statue of Liberty standing right in front of the Empire State Building...Course, in reality, they are much farther apart." She took it out, kissed it and put it back.

The Detective looked at me as if to say, *Betcha' didn't know that.*

"Charlie, do you remember this one? We got that one when we took you and Jimmy to Montreal, to the Worlds Fair."

"How can I forget? Jimmy and I got thrown out for standing on each other's shoulders so we could reach up and touch Elvis' first guitar." I laughed as I remembered that day.

"Oh, you boys were awful! We were so embarrassed." She put it back with a small but endearing laugh. "My stars, I'm just carrying on like a foolish old woman, but let me show you just one more thing." She stood on a small step and reached for the plate and saucer on the top shelf. "This is one of my favorites. We got it at Lourdes. You know, the Village of St. Bernadette. When Jerry was first diagnosed, the doctors said he would only last three months. We went to Lourdes and Jerry prayed, asking that he could live five more years...till he got the mortgage paid off...so that I wouldn't have that worry. He didn't pray for the pain to stop, just for time to fully provide for me. He came home and worked as much as he could. The doctors were so mad at him. Then, exactly five years to that very day he prayed for more time, he rolled over in his hospital bed. He kissed me and told me he loved me as I held his hand, and said the Lady of Lourdes had kept her word. He left right then." The old woman sat down on a small chair and lowered her head, shouldering the burden of her loss. "Charlie, could you put it back up on top for me?" she said in a small whispering voice.

Detective Reza and I gave her time to complete this memory. I couldn't help notice on the small table near by was the same black rotary dial phone that had been there when I was twelve. Above the table was the only picture that hadn't been there before. It was a replica of the one that had hung on the wall in Jerry Peters' hospital room. It portrayed doctors and nurses attending a patient while all the time Jesus was standing at the foot of the bed with an assuring smile. His arms were wide open and welcoming.

We sat down, with Sara Peters continually holding on to my right hand.

The Detective let me ask the questions. "Mrs. Peters, I was wondering if you could give me Jimmy's address. I'm ashamed to say we lost touch about eight years ago, and I would love to see him or at least talk to him."

Her old eyes suddenly grew moist again, "Oh Charlie, I should have written to you. You were his best friend, but he begged me not to contact you."

"About what, Mrs. Peters?"

"Oh, I suppose it doesn't matter now, not after all this time." She took her eyes off mine and stared down at the floor. "He had a wonderful life and job down in North Carolina; and then one day, while celebrating a real estate deal with some coworkers, he took a drink. You and Jimmy always drank Pepsi, do you remember?"

"Yes, Mrs. Peters, I remember," not letting her know that I hadn't outgrown that habit.

She looked up at me for a brief moment, gave me a smile and continued on, "At first his wife just laughed it off. She had never seen Jimmy drunk before; but soon his drinking became his new love, replacing her." The old woman stared off into space contemplating it all. In a few seconds she continued, "He entered a number of programs and each time we thought he had gotten better. But he would slip and fall again."

I never would have guessed what I was hearing. Jimmy and I never had any urge to drink back in our cemetery playground days. We were high on life back then.

As I sat there, listening and holding her hand, I had a flashback to the September of our freshman year. Along with some other friends, we were making plans for Saturday night. Jimmy and I wanted to go to the dance and chase girls, while the others said they wanted to get a six pack of beer and go to the football game. The majority voted for the game and so we went. Jimmy and I watched the others as they threw up under the bleachers during half time, and we both decided that chasing girls had to be more enjoyable than that. Apparently, Jimmy had changed his mind.

"Where is Jimmy, Mrs. Peters?"

The old woman was holding on to both my hands now. "I don't really know, Charlie. Each time I talk to his wife, I ask if I can come for a visit. She says he doesn't want me to see him till he gets better. He does call me about once a month and lets me know that he's at least alive, and begs me not to come see him...not yet. I haven't held my baby in years." She broke down and Reza and I give her time to do what was needed. She stopped herself in a few minutes and looked me in the eye again, "He's a proud man, Charlie. My Jimmy is a proud man." She got up and moved to a nearby shelf. She picked up a picture of Jimmy, taken at high school graduation, and held it to her heart.

"He's gonna be all right, I just know it," I assured her as I got up and put my arm around her. "Next time he calls will you tell him I was here? I'm going to give you my cell phone number and he can call me anytime." I wrote the number down on a piece of paper near her old rotary phone "And, Mrs. Peters, you can tell him I love him, and I want to help anyway I can."

She took the paper and squeezed my hand again, "I know Jimmy loves you too. You were just like brothers. Do you remember the time Jerry and I took you to the Worlds Fair in Toronto...no, Montreal...oh land sakes...no that's where we went on our honeymoon. Did you know Jerry and I once went to Lourdes, the village of St. Bernadette? Did I show my plates from that trip?"

"I'll see them next time Mrs. Peters. And remember Jimmy and I are still brothers. We always will be," I guaranteed her.

Sara Peters seemed to perk up as she knew I would do anything for my best friend. I told her to call me anytime if she needed to talk.

She waved good-bye at the door with a hanky in her hand. "Next time you come over, Charlie, bring your mother. Lord, I haven't seen her in years."

Not since her funeral, Mrs. Peters, not since her funeral.

As we got back in Reza's car he said, "She sure is a sweet old lady. Do you think Peters will call you if she gives him your number?"

"I don't know, I hope he will...I hope she remembers."

"I hope he's sober if he does," the Detective said. "Sounds like he couldn't give us any help unless he's lucid. With the shape he's probably in, he most likely couldn't remember last week, let alone a chain and locket from when you guys were seventeen."

"Detective Reza, I'm positive Jimmy didn't take that locket back then. I'd bet my life on it."

Reza turned on the radio as he asked me to call him Tony. And I said I would like it if he called me Charlie. The horror of this summer had brought us together as friends.

We sat out in front of the Peters' home on Danforth Street and listened to the press conference now in progress.

Chief Richardson was speaking, "According to the reports from the State Medical Examiner, all the autopsies revealed that all eight victims were poisoned."

"What's that, Chief? What kind of poison?" came unknown voices from a sea of reporters now growing more anxious.

"We are not revealing the type of poison at this time. Suffice it to say it was lethal enough to bring down an elephant. Doctors, Roland Greenier and Frank Blanchette, are still running tests as to the exact chemical breakdown."

I turned to Tony and said, "If he says the poison was a result of bee stings there will be panic in the streets."

"Bee stings!?! How do you know that?" The Detective reacted like I had just shot holes in his well kept theory of how the victims died.

"Tony, you gotta know the right people to talk to. I have my sources," I said with a smirkey smile, the one that Joe uses frequently

"Yeah, another reason I'm sticking close to you till this is over." Tony tuned the radio up a little louder.

The press conference went on with the next question, "Do you have any ideas who the killer or killers may be?"

The Chief answered, "There are no suspects yet."

"Did the dogs with the canine unit sniff out any clues when they went through the place?"

"Nothing that could give us any indication that there was anyone hiding in there."

"Chief, some are saying there is some sort of beast living in that cemetery. What do you say?"

"That's crazy, pure speculation! There is no proof whatsoever of any monster or alien, and I want those kinds of foolish rumors to end right here," Richardson demanded.

"You're saying you know the killers are human?"

"I'm saying you should be reasonable and leave the conjectures and theories to the professionals." I liked the Chief, but I could tell he had a short fuse when it came to dealing with the media. "Spreading idiotic rumors is not going to get us anywhere."

"Chief, how long are you going to keep us away from that cemetery?"

"That's still a crime scene up there, and we don't want you compromising any evidence that still might be in there. So anyone trying to get pass the police barricades or caught up there without my personal permission will be arrested."

I could hear the frustration in the Chief's voice growing stronger.

"He's about to blow," Tony said. "He's a good man, but he has no tolerance for anyone getting in the way of official police business."

"As soon as we have anything else that requires us to inform the public we will call another press conference immediately. Now, if that's all, we have work to do."

"One more question, Chief, "What's the status on the victim still alive at Maine Med.?"

I could just imagine the mob of reporters scribbling on their note pads and shoving their tape recorders closer to the podium. A blend of voices was now screaming for more on this new revelation...that there was a *live* victim who could shed some light on the situation.

"Everybody please be quiet!!! I can't answer a question with all this noise."

Listening on the radio I could hear the Chief covering the microphone as he probably turned to D.A., Brian Dewolfe, for consultation and advice. After about thirty seconds the muffled microphone was clear again.

The crowd quieted almost to a hush as the Chief answered, "I don't know who gave you that information; but, yes, we have what we hope is an eye witness...But she is still in a coma. If and when she is able to talk we will pass that information on to the press. Now please let us get on with our jobs."

"Chief, you say, *she* is in a coma. Does that mean it's one of those sorority girls from the other night? Do you have a name, Chief?"

Richardson didn't answer.

"He's probably upset with himself for revealing the sex of the survivor," the Detective guessed as he stared at the car radio.

You could hear the crowd yelling to get his attention, "Chief! Chief! Chief!", but he had obviously stepped away from the podium.

Tony turned off the radio and said, "Richardson is going to roll heads till he finds out who talked about the Kostenello girl. Let me ask you something, Charlie. If the Kostenello girl was attacked by bees, who did she grab that chain from?"

"I've been wondering that myself. Does it click with any part of your theory?"

Gazing out the car window and looking toward the bottom of Cassidy Hill the young Detective quietly said, "I'm afraid to say that my theory is continually changing, but obviously that old cemetery isn't the peaceful playground you once knew."

Dispatch interrupted our conversation with an urgent message that we meet with Chief Richardson at John Feeney's office.

With sirens screaming, Tony sped through the familiar streets of my youth. We raced down Danforth, up Emery, down Pine past my boyhood home and straight down Congress to our destination. The only thoughts that played in our minds were fears of more dead, or a suspect in the case. We hoped for the latter, we got neither.

After a brief update to Feeney, Richardson, and DeWolfe on our meeting with Sara Peters, the big attorney introduced Tony and me to a shabbily dressed man with a patch over his eye. He appeared nervous in the plush surroundings of Feeney's office, and the smell of alcohol stuck to him like a cologne. He kept smacking his gums where teeth used to be, giving the appearance that he was chewing on something. It was hot tee-shirt weather, yet he had on a winter parka while sporting a dirty Sea Dogs baseball cap. He was obviously not a member of the country club, nor likely to be playing golf with Feeney and his friends any day soon.

"Gentlemen, this is Mr. Theodore Wheeler. He is a friend of Mr. Holt and Mr. Nelson. They were the two unfortunate men who were the first victims in the deaths up at the old cemetery. Mr. Wheeler, please tell us again why you wanted to speak with us today."

"First of all, I'd like it a whole lot better if you gentlemen would call me One Eye. That's what I'm used to answerin' to. Only my mother, God rest her soul, could call me Theodore." The raggedy man sniffed and blew his nose on a nasty-looking napkin with a Dairy Queen logo on it.

"All right, One Eye, if that's what you prefer. Now please continue." Feeney returned to his oversized chair. Sitting behind his big desk and looking down on Wheeler, the lawyer looked more like a judge about to render a decision of perjury if Wheeler didn't tell the truth, the whole truth, and nothing but the truth.

I knew that feeling of intimidation from my turn in Feeney's hot seat. One Eye's need for a few extra bucks gave him the courage to move closer to the desk and say, "Well sir, I heared tell down at the shelter, you was offerin' a big ree-ward for information about the goins' on in this here cemetery slaughter thing. Now, I'm not here for just the money mind ya, but I could use a couple of bucks if there's some comin' my way. No sir, mostly I want to do my, whatcha call it?...my civic duty."

"We appreciate your civic-minded concern, One Eye. Now tell my friends what you told me and the D.A. earlier." Feeney leaned back in his big chair waiting for the answer that would shock us all.

One Eye rubbed the stubble on his chin as he explained, "Me and Holt and Nellie have been hangin' out together for a long time. We're thick as thieves... not that we're really thieves mind ya," he pointed out nervously as he quickly looked at all of us one at a time. "Those guys are my friends and I want to see that they gets the justice they deserve for bein' done in, but I gotta tell ya , they don't really need no justice"

"Why do you say that?" Tony asked.

One Eye stood and pronounced loud and clear, "Cause they ain't dead!...I seen 'em with my own good eye...walkin' down St. John Street last night, just fancy as ya please. I was dinin' at McDonald's, lookin' out the window, and there they was...both of them! I ran out and yelled to them. They looked right at me, but they didn't say a word. They just kept walkin', and after all we been through together...the snooty bastards!"

"Tell me, Mr. Wheeler..."

"One Eye!"

"Tell me, One Eye," asked Brian Dewolfe, "Were you drinking last night?"

"HA! I drink every night. You would too, if you'd done two tours in Nam...But I wasn't so blotto that I didn't recognize those two foul-weather friends walkin' so high and mighty...lookin' like they had broom handles stuck up their heinees."

"You do realize that Mr.Holt and Mr.Nelson were *buried* over a week ago in Potter's Field?" offered Chief Richardson

"All I know is I seen what I seen." The witness vowed with more force in his scratchy voice. He then sat down with authority, as if proud he knew more than the cops. He looked at each of us and nodded as if to say, *Don't ever doubt Ole One Eye.*

"One Eye, will you let us put you in protective custody down at the jail until we can check this out?" the Chief asked.

"Why not? A brief stay at the Cumberland County Hotel means three squares and a soft bed. But I want my own cell...I don't want no bunkies!"

Richardson called for a black and white to escort One Eye Wheeler to his new accommodations at the jail located just behind St. John Street where the alleged sighting took place.

After he left Feeney's office on the arms of two uniformed officers I asked the Police Chief, "Why do you even listen to that guy? Does he have any credibility?"

"Let me tell you two things, Mr. Sullivan. One Eye has been a reliable stool-pigeon in the past, with tips on robbery suspects and drug deals. Secondly, we are just assuming the identities of those dead winos from the shelter I.D.s found on their bodies. There was no fingerprint verification. The homeless are known to swap I.D.s for one reason or another...."

Before he could finish, his cell phone interrupted him. After listening for about twenty seconds, the look on the cop's face, which was usually red in a state of constant blush, turned deathly pale. The Chief clicked off the phone without responding to the caller and sat down in a thud, squishing the air out of Feeney's expensive leather couch.

"For God's sake, Ray! What's wrong?" asked the attorney.

Richardson just stared at the floor as he slowly said in a voice void of emotion, "Mike Smith, the grave digger over at Potter's Cemetery just called the station. Somebody dug up the graves of Holt and Nelson. They're...gone!"

As we all took a breath in disbelief, John Feeney picked up the phone and called over to Mt. Calvary. Three long minutes went by before he got the answer he wanted. The graves of his son and his son's friend had not been disturbed.

"Ray, I want guards over by my boy till we find out what the hell's going on!" Feeney began sweating heavily, as anyone would, at the thought that the final resting place of a love one might be disturbed.

The speechless Chief just nodded.

"It's probably just a bunch of wild teenagers," the District Attorney noted. "Cemetery vandalism has become a real problem, but it's mostly turned over stones and monuments. Kids these days! It's that damn rap music!!!"

The Chief struggled to his feet and said, "I better run a check on the graves of the other victims in this case, the three girls down in Massachusetts and the newsman. As I remember, his body was sent back to Atlanta."

Feeney barked another order, "Keep that stooly locked up until we can get some answers. Could be he's running some kind of scam. He may have been a reliable informant in the past, but that doesn't mean he's not cooking up something here to make money."

Richardson agreed, as was his custom in dealing with the most powerful man in town.

As Tony and I left Feeney's office along with the D.A., I heard the stressed-out attorney say on his intercom, "Kim, call Sandra. Tell her we've got to work late tonight and not to wait up."

"Yes, Mr. Feeney, whatever you say." She grasped his meaning. *Whatever gets you through the night is all right.*

13

Tony and I made a quick trip to Yarmouth to pick up some protective gear from local beekeeper, Skeeter Grizzard. Similar gear had been ordered for all involved when Frank Blanchette's findings were revealed to Richardson, Feeney, and Dewolfe. We ran the risk of the snooping press seeing the bee suits and asking more questions, or forming more opinions as to "just what the hell was going on up there in that old cemetery?" But it was decided it would be a greater risk for those involved not to be protected as best they could.

Our next plan was to grab some burgers and fries at Mickey D's on St. John Street, and to see if anyone else at the fast-food joint had seen One Eye Wheeler yelling to his two friends last night. We planned to visit the caretaker Wendle Bronson as well. I should know by now that nothing in my world goes according to plan...not anymore.

There was one fry-cook who remembered seeing Wheeler, but he said One Eye was in there just about every night. He didn't recall Wheeler yelling to anyone across the street but it was possible. The cook said One Eye did have a couple of buddies he used to hang around with, but he hadn't seen them with One Eye in a couple of weeks.

As Tony and I finished up with our eats and interrogations he checked for messages on his voice mail.

"Get this message to Charlie Sullivan. Don't go near or into that cemetery during the day. Call as soon as you get this," was the warning on Tony's pager.

Puzzled, he looked at me and asked, "Do you recognize that voice?"

"Sounds like Frank Blanchette." I then conveyed the conversation that had taken place the night before at O'Toole's.

"He's the original absent minded professor," Tony commented. "He didn't even leave his name."

"He's got a lot on his mind...like we all do."

I called the number left on the caller I.D. "Hello, this is Mr. Warren Blanchette, can I help ya?" said the voice with a very heavy Down East Maine accent.

"Mr. Blanchette, this is Charlie Sullivan. Is Frank available?".

"Oh, Mr. Sullivan, Frank said if you called ta tell ya he was goin' to the hospital to check on a patient and wants you to meet him ther'a if you can. Now, what did Frank say her name was?" he asked himself."

"Kostenello?"

"Ayah! That's it, and he said it was impo'tant you didn't go into that cemetery until you talk ta him."

"Thank you, Mr .Blanchette."

"Mr.Sullivan, Frank said you two were old friends and ya treated him to some drinks last night. I don't remembah him mentionin' many of his friends to me. Seems we don't talk as much as we used ta since my Anne past away. Frank's mothah was a good woman...ayah, ayah...She was his best friend too."

"Well, I'm sure he has a lot of friends, probably doesn't have time to mention them all," I said as I tried to break off the conversation.

But Frank's dad just wasn't ready to hang up. "No, he has time, lotsa time...just not many friends. You should come by for suppah sometime. I know Frank would like that. I can cook up a *wickid good* beef stew that would burn the roof off the mouth of the Devil. It was one of my wife's secret recipes. That fella on the TV with the cookin' show, that Emeril guy ther'a, he'd killed to get his hands on my Anne's recipe file."

"I would like come by sometime. I look forward to it. Thank you Mr..."

"You know Frank does have a few female friends. He talks to them on the computah...complete strangahs! Now, I ask ya, is that how the young folks are gettin' togethah these days...and he opens right up and tells 'em how good lookin' he is and that he has a new Mercedes automobile...I ain't nevah seen it though...guess he keeps it at work. Oh well, I guess computah friends are bettah than none... gets lonely for man, not havin' a woman around." Mr. Blanchette paused and then laughed before he delivered his next words. "Maybe I'll learn that computah too...find me a good woman...ayah ayah...None out there like my Anne though...No...None like her. So long Mistah Sullivan...now you stop by sometime...bye now."

The old man said goodbye with a strength in his voice that hadn't been there when he first answered, and I wondered to myself if Mr. Blanchette would like to *hold hands* with Sara Peters someday. I think his Anne would approve.

We stashed our trash and made our way to the hospital located just up the hill.

Flashing his badge, Tony was able to get us right into the security area where two uniformed cops were on each side of room 1401, the room where the Kostenello girl was being cared for. They were talking with Frank Blanchette as we approached.

Frank waved to us to come his way and then took us aside, "I'm glad you two are here. Listen, I know you guys are going to that cursed cemetery. It would be better if you go in after dark while those bees are most likely to be inactive. It would also be a good idea to suit up in protective gear and not to wear any strong cologne or after shave. Bees are attracted to perfumes of any kind."

"Frank, do you think those two winos, Holt and Nelson, were wearing "Obsession"? Just doesn't seem likely they would be hanging out at the perfume counter at J.C. Penny's," I reminded him.

"There's a lot of sugar in alcohol. They like that too ya know, Wiseguy!"

Tony looked at me for my thoughts. "You really think we should go into that cemetery after dark, Charlie?"

"No problem with me going in there at night. I think I know my way around that place with my eyes closed. But, Frank, I thought you said these weren't ordinary bees."

"Their size and the potency of their venom are different, but they probably have all the other characteristics of their more normal cousins," he suggested.

Tony reminded Blanchette that we had already taken precautions, and had put two special beekeeper suits in the back of the Detective's trunk. We should be completely protected. The state boys surrounding the area would be getting suits as well.

"Let me ask you something, Dr. Blanchette. That newsman was killed at night. Shouldn't those bees have settled down by then?"

"Good question, Detective. From riga mortis and lividity levels, I would say that all the other victims died either before sunset or just after dawn. I'm guessing that all those bright lights the media was using at night confused the little bastards' senses...but that's just a guess."

The Coroner then walked us farther away from the guards. "I have some new information," he said in a loud whisper.

Acting more paranoid, Frank suggested we go out side and take a walk on the promenade where there were no lurking ears; and, I thought to myself, where he could have a cigarette.

It was a breezy summer day; and we were all concerned about any size bee or hornet we might come across. But all the bees we saw were on their best behavior, no close relations to the evil insects that had caused all the misery. Frank mentioned that we were far enough away from their home territory. *Run two blocks away, George, and you'll be safe. Run, George, run!*

What is it you wanted to tell us, Frank?" I asked as we walked across the newly-mowed grass. The sweet smell was pleasant but attracted more bees. They remained friendly. We remained on guard.

Frank stopped, pulled out his lighter, lit one up, clicked the lighter shut, continued walking and said, "I just got the final blood work back on Kostenello and there is no sign of any venom. I mean not a trace! If she was with those other three girls she didn't get stung. That's my opinion, but I can't open her up to search for stings unless she croaks."

The Coroner puffed his cigarette rapidly and stared into space, as if the idea of doing an autopsy on her excited him. Suddenly, I had an image of Frank back at home sitting at his computer in the dark, logged into a chat room: **Hot Coroners Over 40**

> **CadaverMan** : Hi Sylvia, what do you have on to-night?

> **SylForAThrill** : Just the radio, Frankie baby! Just the radio

"Croaks? Is that one of your frog jokes, Frank?" I asked as I came out of my vision of Frank chasing the ladies in cyber space.

"Cute, Charlie. That will cost you more drinks at O'Toole's."

"Anytime. We'll let my brother buy." We high-fived each other. My old biology buddy managed a small chuckle, followed by that irritating cough that most smokers have in common.

Tony looked at us as if to say, *Are you both ready to grow up now?* Then he asked, "Just what caused Miss Kostenello to go into a coma."

Frank didn't hesitate, "In a word...SHOCK!!! Something or someone scared the hell out of her. Something went 'BOO!' in the night...Something out of the ordinary. I just checked her chart. Her heart rate and blood pressure are still way out of whack."

"Have you told John Feeney or the Chief yet?" Tony asked.

"Hell no! That bastard, Greenier, will start to second guess the cause of death on the others, and try to ruin my findings and my reputation."

"Well, the Chief has to be told. He has to make a decision on what to tell the public. Killer bees are one thing; but something else, something that could scare someone into shock is knowledge he needs to have."

"I suppose you're right, Detective" begrudged the Coroner as he field-stripped his cigarette and let the wind take the last of the ashes.

Tony turned to me and asked again if I still felt we should go into that cemetery, knowing now that bees may not be the only danger.

"For some reason I feel safe going in there. I always have, and, as long as you are with me, I believe you will be safe as well," I reassured my companion.

"If anything happens to me you will have to answer my mother." Tony smiled.

"Yeah, she gonna kick my ass?"

"Worse, Charlie, much worse. She's not sweet-little-old Sara Peters. Mom is like a tiger when it comes to her cubs and since I am the only cub, watch out!"

"C'mon, I'll just turn on that old Sullivan charm. That can make any tiger purr like a little soft and cuddly kitten."

"Oh, brother!...Opening up a stomach with all it's decaying contents couldn't make me gag like that!," Frank said as he took out another pack of cigarettes, removing the cellophane like a surgeon at his finest.

"Well, Charlie, you come over to the house tonight and we'll see how charming you are," the Detective wagered.

With that we parted company with Blanchette. He went back to the office to report his findings, and Tony and I went back to our original plan. Our next stop would be the caretakers shack and a meeting with Wendle Bronson. Tony had felt all along that Bronson knew more than he was letting on, and I was still thinking about his name. I knew I had heard it before, but just where or when was the question. Maybe Mr. Bronson knew me and could refresh my memory. But as usual our plans were about to take another detour.

The direct approach to get to the shack down at The Hobo Grounds took us by the old cemetery. As we approached the top of Cassidy Hill we were stopped at the police road block. After a brief conversation with two State Troopers, authorization was granted for us to continue.

Tony's unmarked police car rolled slowly down the hill at my request, just as my apple-red Schwinn had done all those years ago. *Don't ride your bike down Cassidy Hill. Don't take your guns to town. Don't drive that car down that hill today.* The windows were put up and the doors were locked at his request, ever mindful that we were now entering the territorial home of some very menacing bees and maybe *someone* or some *thing* else. I had hoped the Kostenello girl could have described her attacker. But she was still sleeping and we couldn't wait for her to come out of her coma. Time was marching on. People were dying.

There on the left, as the car inched its way down the hill, were the back gates of my old playground. It had been years since I had been there in person, although I hung out there numerous times in my thoughts. I could see the grass had grown taller and the stones seemed to lean at shaper angles than before. Other than that, it still called to me as it always had. The unusual odor in that place, that I was so used to when Jimmy and I were young, invaded the air filtering through the car vents. With the windows rolled up it seemed stronger than usual. It was hypnotic in its nature.

Hello, boys, why don't you stop in for a quick game of flies and grounders. The stadium is full and the spectators won't be leaving before the game is over...Because in here, the game has been over for a long...long...time.

As we passed a little further, I could see the top of the old elm tree that had meant so much to me. I could smell the peppers, pickles, olive oil and onions from Italian sandwiches. I could hear Jimmy hurling insults my way as I dropped a fly ball. His laugh was loud, clear, and infectious.

Oh, Man! That was an easy one. You suck, Charlie. You couldn't even catch a cold.

All of a sudden, the strawberry fragrance that Cindy used to captivate me was *all* I could smell. I was seventeen again. Mom was home baking bread. Dad was cracking jokes. Jerry Peters was happily working down at his dry cleaning business and thinking about a gift for Sara. Warren Blanchette and his wife, Anne, were going out for dinner and a movie. John Spiller hadn't heard of Viet Nam. Disco Dana was just starting his all-girl band. Bill O'Neal only had one kid. Yastremski was still hitting fast balls over the Green Monsta'. Elvis hadn't left the building for the last time. My heart had yet to be broken. I was happy again. I was home. Bob Fuller was on the radio, saying "The BIG JAB loves you people. BIG JAB average area temperature is 80 BIG JAB degrees and the time...time for the BEA—TLES!"

My mind started to wander deeper and deeper, and although Tony was talking to me I was too far away in my dreams to hear him. I had images of the sirens, or the *furies* as they were called in Greek Mythology. They were irresistible beauties whose enticing songs lured lust-filled sailors from the sea and onto the rocks, to their doom. The sirens in that cemetery were calling to me to join them in their eternal sleep. And there, sitting on top of the biggest mausoleum, was the queen of them all. Her long blond hair was resting over her bare breasts and her arms were reaching for me. I could hear her soft voice caressing my ears. "Come to me, my Love, my Charlie. Come rest and be at peace."

"Cindy." I whispered in my trance.

The jolt, as Tony slammed on the brakes, brought me back to reality. It almost brought me through the windshield.

"Did you see that!?!" asked my companion as he latched his fingers around the steering wheel, like it was a security blanket from his teething years. "What the hell was that?" He was sweating profusely and his tanned complexion was fading. He was trembling as if the car was out of tune and making his body shimmy and shake. But the car was stalled, dead on the hill.

"Tony, I didn't see anything. I was thinking about something else. I was lost in a daydream."

"How could you miss it? It ran right across the street. He or *it* was all dressed in black and moved more like he was flying than running."

"Wish I could help you out but I saw nothing." I looked around. There was no one all dressed in black. There was no one sitting on top of the mausoleum. There was no ball game and no visible spectators. Everything was still...and quiet.

"What are you, *fucking* blind!?!" he screamed.

"Easy, Tony, calm down." I had never seen this cool Detective so bedeviled.

He took a deep breath, "Charlie, his face was...was ..."

"Was what?"

"I don't know, but it didn't look human. It was horrible. Charlie, get me back to the hospital. I feel like I'm going...to...pass...out." He collapsed onto the wheel he had been holding so firmly.

I grabbed his police radio and called back up to the Troopers at the top of the hill. They arrived in a flash and rushed the unconscious Detective back up to Maine Med. I turned his car around and followed behind.

I waited outside the Emergency Room for the results on his condition. His mother had been called and soon she was there pacing the floor, a bundle of nerves and fear. I introduced myself and brought her up to date on what her son and I had been doing. I was careful not to reveal the scarier parts of our mission. In her anxiety she didn't need anymore to worry about. I'm not sure she heard any of the words I said, except for, "then he passed out and collapsed onto the steering wheel."

She continued pacing, shooing me a way like I was a pesky fly. But, I gotta tell ya, Maria Reza was more than attractive. Her long black hair was pulled back in a long thick pig tail. Her huge baby-blue eyes were tired but pretty. Her dark skin and white teeth were framed by bright red lipstick, and her hair dresser's smock failed to conceal an alluring figure. I was amazed at how much she reminded me of Andrea Rios. I was about to learn the similarity was only in appearance. Her son had warned me. *Mom is like a tiger when it comes to protecting her cubs, and I'm the only cub. Watch Out!* I thought he was kidding...WRONG!!!

"Mrs. Reza, you have a fine son and he's a good cop," I said without knowing I was about to set her off on a tirade.

She stopped cold in her tracks and turned my way. "Yeah...his father was a good cop too...a good *dead* cop!" she said angrily with a temper that was apparently never far from the surface.

"I'm sorry to hear that. I'm sure..."

"Everybody's sorry, but sorry don't make the pain stop when your sixteen, knocked up and alone. Sorry don't help feed the baby and pay the rent. Sorry don't make the world go away when you hurt so bad you just wanna die, *Sorry* is one sorry freakin'word. Don't talk to me about, *sorry*," she snapped while fumbling for a cigarette.

I gently reminded her that she couldn't smoke in there, and she quickly gave me a *go-to-hell* look. But soon she patted my hand and said she didn't mean to take out her frustrations on me. She warned, with a small smile, that it didn't take much to piss her off. She didn't know I had already been warned that the Sullivan charm was impotent when it came to winning her over, but I just had to try. It's one of my character flaws.

"Better to be pissed off than pissed on, I always say." I hoped that would make her smile.

She stopped her pacing again. "Tony said you were a History teacher from California. Do you say that kind of shit to your class?" She scolded me in the Brooklyn accent she grew up with.

I think I could be afraid of her under other circumstances...Hell, I'm afraid of her under *these* circumstances. I then sat there quietly, waiting for the news to come.

Maria Reza was silent for a few minutes, maybe in prayer, and then came over and sat next to me. "After my husband was killed...he was only twenty four...Tony and I moved here from Brooklyn to start over. I begged him to go to law school but, no...He wanted to be a cop like his father and here he his in the hospital. His father died in a hospital just like this...He was stabbed fifty-six times when he stopped to help an old man who had fallen down in the subway. They wrote PIG in his own blood on the wall. I thought if we moved far enough away, we would be safe from that kind of insanity. But nowhere is safe today. I still can't close my eyes till I hear him come in through the front door at night and walk up to his room and say, 'Mom, I'm home,' before he closes the door."

"He's a good man! We have become pretty good friends despite the fact that there were some initial doubts as to my innocence concerning the mysterious deaths at the old cemetery where I use to play as a boy."

"You *played* in a cemetery? You must have been one weird kid!"

"Well, I guess you would've had to known me back then, and the way things used to be in this town before all hell broke loose."

"I'm not sure I like knowing you now," she said with total indifference.

"Tony did say you were an...interesting woman."

"I'm a woman with her only baby laying in there with tubes and needles stuck in him. And by God, they better fix him up good or they'll hear from me. I have a bad temper and you'll see it if they ain't out here soon with some answers."

I didn't have the guts to say, "You mean I haven't seen it already? You mean, there's more?" I just kept my mouth shut, which in this case would be more effective than the Sullivan charm. Soon thereafter, with no relatives or friends there with her, she turned toward me and used my shoulder to cry on. I think she sensed that I had come to think a lot of her only son, and that made me seem less like a stranger.

The doors to the emergency room opened and a nurse with Kelly Beane on her name tag asked," Is there a Maria Reza or a Charlie Sullivan here?"

Maria jumped up immediately and I followed after her.

"First, let me tell you that Mr. Reza should be fine. It was his appendix. His seat belt must have irritated it, but it would have burst on its own sooner or later. Luckily he was so near the hospital, otherwise it could have been more serious. The doctors are finishing up now and he should be in the recovery room in about a half-hour. I'll let you know as soon as you can see him."

Tony's mother cried harder now than before; and then she punched me in the shoulder, the way Jimmy and I used to do.

"Ow!!! What's that for?"

"I'm crying cause I'm happy, you idiot! I punched you to release some anger. You're a man, you wouldn't understand."

I quietly said, "P.M.S." Then she gave me a look and said, "You wanna get whacked again?"

That song by Jim Croce, <u>Don't Mess Around With Jim</u>, went through my head. Only I changed Jim to Maria. I was definitely afraid of this woman, and yet I was attracted to her. Maybe I should have checked myself into the Psychiatric Ward while I was there.

14

"I *hate* math, Sister Mary Margaret?"

"You just have to apply yourself, Charlie," advised my 5th grade teacher.

"I *hate* applying myself," I replied from my front row desk. I always thought she kept me in the front row because she liked me. When she said she wanted to "keep an eye on me" I just figured she found me cute. What did I now, I was ten-years old.

"Maybe you need more homework, young man." Sister Mary Margaret's face was growing sterner as the old nun pushed back from her desk and picked up her yard stick, slapping it gently against her side.

"I *hate* homework. There isn't supposed to be homework in the 5th grade," I protested.

"Well there is now!"

"Then I *hate* the 5th grade!"

"Charlie Sullivan, I don't want to hear that word again!" she exclaimed now banging the yard stick a little harder and louder.

"Which one?...Math, 5th grade, or homework?"

"HATE!!! You little Wisenheimer! The word, *hate*, should not be in your dictionary!"

I sat back in my chair and she in hers. We were both quiet for about five minutes, and then I slowly raised my hand.

"Yes, Charlie, what is it?" she reluctantly asked while leaning her elbows on her desk and rubbing her forehead with her fingers.

"Sister, look...Right here in my dictionary is the word, hate. It's on page 262...But you shouldn't say, Wisenheimer...'cause *that's* not in here."

She mumbled something under her breath, reached for a little bottle of aspirin and asked Shirley Wiles to please go get her some water from the fountain in the hall.

Good old Sister Mary Margaret. If she were here today I would tell her that I *hate* cell phones. One thing we didn't have back in the "good old days" was cell phones. Somehow we managed to get through the day without them. Appointments were kept. The school bell rang on time. The trains ran on schedule. The downtown bus passed my house every hour at twenty three past the hour. Huntley and Brinkley were always there exactly at 6:30 PM with the news we needed to know. Everything worked just fine, and there were no damn cell phones. But now you are naked without one. The one I wore had one major flaw. You had to charge it continuously. Of course it could be that I was the major flaw. I'm sure that would have been Sister Mary Margaret's guess.

Those of us who grew up in the Elvis and Beatles eras don't seem to take to change too well. We would have been happy frozen in time if that was something God would allow. Maybe if we make it to the next life we will be given a choice of what time warp we want to live in for eternity. I'll pick one without cell phones. Sister Mary Margaret will probably pick one without me.

As the doctors worked their wonders on Tony with their new technology, I tried to make my cell phone come alive, but it was dead. So I did what anyone else would do...I pounded on it! The lights came on but only briefly and then...nothing.

While we visited with her son in his hospital room, Maria Reza offered to give me a ride over to the old house where Brother Joe still lived. Tony assured her he was just fine, but she's one of those mothers who needs a lot of convincing. The doctors said he would have to stay at least one night and then could go home and rest for about a week. I had a feeling he didn't mind the one night, but being babied by his mom was probably going to be a strain. She must have kissed him twenty times before finally letting go of his hand and leaving the room. In a rare moment when she took her eyes off him, he shot me a look as if to say, *I want to talk to you when you get a chance*.

I nodded in understanding as I left his room.

The throng of media reporters was continuing to swell as we left the hospital and made our way to Maria Reza's Honda Accord which she had parked in a "no parking" zone. Things like illegal parking don't concern a mother anxious to get to her son when he is hurt.

I recognized some of the bigger names from the networks plus local reporters like Pat Callahan. They were all jockeying for positions closest to Maine Medical Center's main entrance. All were ready for any recent scraps of news that could be thrown to their hungry audiences. While just down the Western Promenade, less than a mile away, was something *unnatural*.

Evil had come to town and was planning to stay for a while, or perhaps take up permanent residence. When One Eye Wheeler sees something out of the ordinary you have to question the source. When a bright, young, sober detective sees something strange and inexplicable, then you know that something's not right.

Maria Reza took the freshly written parking tickets from under her wipers, tore them up, threw them into the air like so much confetti, and then unlocked the doors.

"I hate these freakin' cell phones," I said as I tried to make another connection to Brother Joe. Four numbers pushed and then nothing. I wondered if Barn or Detective Russell had tried to call and couldn't get through. I wrote a note to myself on the back of the ketchup stained business card that Russell had given me: Call Barn and Russell, ASAP.

"When you have to write things down that means you're getting old," commented Tony's mom as she passed by the corner of Carlton and Pine...the corner that used to contain the Old Buckley Place. I looked over where the house once stood. I felt a chill.

"Yes, Mrs. Reza, I'm getting very old, so go easy on me before I have a heart attack right here in your front seat...I guess I should be grateful I'm still on solid food," I said sarcastically.

"You can call me, Maria...It's the least I can let you do since you'll soon be pushing up daises, Old Man!" She mimicked in an elderly voice.

"You're all heart, Maria."

"What are you writing down on that card? Are you reminding yourself to call your wife?" She took her eyes off the road as if trying to read it...making me very nervous at the same time

"I'm not married," I said as I put the card and pen away, then nodded and pointed to her to look where she was going.

"What a surprise!.. And a fine catch like you!" she teased as she gazed around my old neighborhood.

"Well, are you married?" I asked right back.

"No, I'm not. What about it?" she snapped.

"Gee what a surprise!!! How fortunate for the male population of Portland...Uh uh, that's not the finger where a wedding ring would go."

I could see that any relationship I was going to have with this woman would be built on wise cracks and insults. Maybe I had met my match. We were developing a friendship; not only built on smart remarks, but also because of Tony. She said to check in on her son at anytime. I would have anyway. I really liked that kid.

Maria pulled up in front of 89 Pine, and I was immediately infected with more memories. They came flooding in like a tidal wave. I felt myself falling into the same kind of trance that had grasped me when Tony and I took that cruise down Cassidy Hill, just before his attack. But for the moment I was distracted by my pretty but pugnacious driver.

"Here, take my card too. Since you are spending so much time with my son, you should have it. And call me if you need a haircut...that is if you trust me with a pair of scissors in my hands." She smiled viciously.

"I'd probably be safer with the daughter of Dracula," I teased back as I exited her Honda.

When I crossed in front of her car she honked at me. I jumped and dropped my useless cell phone.

"What a putz!" she shouted and laughed as she drove away. I was definitely afraid of this woman.

As my eyes surveyed the familiar surroundings of my youth, I thought of that Tom Jones song, The Green Grass of Home, except there was no longer a mama and a papa there to meet me or a girl named Mary(with hair of gold and lips like cherry). There never was a Mary...but there was a girl named Cindy with hair of gold and lips like honey. And somewhere in the back of my mind I felt someday I would see her again...and soon. There never was much green grass, except the tiny patch in the back yard where we would sit and Joe would tell the story of Old Man Buckley and his family. The white paint on the red bricks was still peeling the way it always had. The cold granite stairs, where we use to sit on warm summer nights and play the radio, showed more cracks but remained sturdy. The front door bell still stuck when you pressed it, and the big front door still fought you as you forced yourself against it when the buzzer sounded.

I looked up the hall stairs and for a minute I thought I saw her standing there, smiling sweetly. *Did you have fun with your friends today, Charlie?*

"Yes, Mom. We played ball until four, then went to Jimmy's house to watch <u>American Bandstand</u>. The Everly Bothers were on today, singing <u>All I Have To Do Is Dream</u>."

That's such a nice song. What would you like for supper, Sloppy Joes or fried chicken?

I thought I saw him too, standing next to her and joking. *Hey, Son, which would you rather do, go fishin' or go swimmin' with bow-legged women?*

"Either one is fun...as long as I'm with you, Dad."

Well, come on up and have your supper. You know, Sloppy Joe's, were named after your brother...hee hee hee!

The aroma of fresh baked bread greeted me and then faded quickly as I heard a strong voice yell, "Hey, Pea Brain, don't forget to wipe your feet." If Joe had said anything else I would have thought I was in the wrong house. They all looked alike on my old block.

Joe was sitting at his computer which now occupied a lot of his waking moments. He had gotten into genealogy and loved to regale me with the exploits of long-dead relatives from centuries ago. "Did you know your great, great, great uncle robbed banks in Ireland?"

"Ooooo...Wow! Is there still a reward for his capture?" I asked.

"Sit on it and rotate," came the reply. That was one of Joe's favorite sayings, a real oldie but goodie. I wondered to myself how he would get along with Maria Reza. I'd pay money to see that battle.

To his students and to his friends he was a gentleman, tall and thin, with a friendly wave and a quick smile. I guess I liked him best the way I knew him best, teasing and acting like he was king in his world. He was always there to protect or speak up for his little brother. To my face he would be gruff, but when he was with his friends he was always bragging that Charlie did this or Charlie did that.

He had grown to look more like my dad, while I favored my mom. His hair had been brown and mine had been blond, but now we share the same gray. Of course mine is premature. He always complained that he got our grandfather's hair genes, because his was receding and forcing the very attractive "comb over".

I filled him in on all that had happened since we spoke last, and he just grunted a reply while lost on the computer...checking out the lives of relatives, long gone and buried. But they were alive to Joe.

"Look, here's your third cousin, Michael, on Dad's side. He was shot, but not killed, when his best friend caught old Mike fooling around with his wife. Her name was Maureen O'Malley. She left her husband when he went to jail for shooting Michael...and then she married Michael...heh heh...this is freakin' cool."

His TV was showing the footage from the funeral services for the three sorority sisters as relatives and friends were saying how they would remember them. Some were crying and some were angry, and demanding the police do a better job of tracking down the killers. Then came the announcement that Greta Van Sustren would be talking to the parents of the dead girls tonight at ten in a FOX exclusive "brought to by blah blah blah and your local blah blah blah dealer."

As Joe continued his search on the computer for more dead relatives from the middle ages, I stepped into the other room to see if I could get a hold of Barn. It should be about sundown in Oceanside.

"This is the Allen Residence."

"Yes, Mrs. Allen, this is your credit card company. We are calling to verify that the charges for those 900 sex numbers were placed by a Mr. Bernard Allen."

"Charlie, will you *ever* grow up?" Georgia laughed into the phone.

"Would you want me to?"

"No, I might not recognize you."

It was good to hear her voice. Georgia Allen just had a knack of making me feel safe and secure. She was like a second mother to me.

"Is Barn around?" I asked as I looked at my own mother's picture on the table by the phone. It was one of her holding me when I was about a year old. That's the good thing about pictures like this one of her. They stay just the way they are. They don't get sick. They don't grow old. They don't...die.

"Yes, Charlie. He'll be happy to talk to you. It seems every five minutes he's asking if you've called. MR. ALLEN!...CHARLIE'S ON THE PHONE!!! He should be here in a second. When are you coming back?"

"Not sure, but at least they know I had nothing to do with it."

"Well, that's good news. Hold on, here's Mr. Allen. I love you, Charlie."

"I love you too."

"Charles, it's about time you called," gruffed the old man.

"I've been busy, Barn. As soon as I got off the plane women were throwing themselves at me."

"Charles, Charles, you are one of a kind."

"Thanks, Barn. Now tell me, have you heard from Andrea?"

"Yes, she called this morning. She said she had phoned but couldn't get a hold of you. I told her what had happened with you being called back to Portland, and she seemed very concerned."

"Oooh. That's a good sign."

"She's coming over when she gets back, and I'm going to talk to her about clearing up all the questions you have. I would like her to tell you herself when you get back, rather than over the phone; but now I just want get it over with."

"Barn, if you're trying to drive me crazy, you're doing a hell of a job."

"That's my mission in life, Charles. By the way a Detective Russell called asking questions about her."

"Well, finally I'm getting some action for my tax dollars. What did you tell him?

"I told him all that I know. She's going to teach English this semester at Marshall."

"Ya, but that's not *all* you know."

"That's all I know as far as he's concerned. I'll be glad when the fall gets here, and you'll be teaching History and I no longer have to play, <u>I've Got A Secret</u>! I'll be scheduling faculty meetings and you'll be...heading up the debating team. Won't that be great?"

"You're a lot like me, Barn."

"Stubborn?"

"Very Stubborn!"

We laughed, wished each other well and hung up. Joe was still working on his computer. I couldn't wait till he got his phone bill and saw the charges. Now, that will be a Kodak moment. Might as well have two Kodak moments. I took out Russell's business card and picked up Joe's phone again.

"Sheriff's Office."

"Detective Russell, please."

The phone books for the last ten years were piled on top of one another under the table. Joe never threw anything out. I gazed into the kitchen and noticed he still had a toaster that only had room for one slice of bread; and I thought, except for cell phones, maybe progress is a good thing.

"Russell here."

"Detective, this is Charlie Sullivan calling from Portland, Maine."

"Yo, Charlie. I tried to leave you a message, but I couldn't get through on that cell phone number you gave me."

"Sorry about that. Did you have any luck finding any information on Andrea Rios?"

"I'm not sure I would call it luck. I called Captain Marc Stitham at CHP and he informed me that Denise Rios and her mother and father were killed in a car crash six years ago. He did say there was one survivor who just walked away without a scratch. He believed it was your friend."

I guess it's true what they say, *When it rains, it pours.* I was sure that Andrea said she was going to visit her parents. Why would she lie to me? Why didn't she tell me her parents and sister were dead? Was this part of what Barn was keeping from me? Did *she* have something to do with it?

"Charlie...Charlie, you still there?"

"Yes, Detective, I'm still here. Is there anything else?"

"Not much. I ran a check on her. She doesn't show up in our computers; no arrests no warrants. I called a few of her known neighbors after I talked with Captain Stitham, and they said she moved away after the accident leaving no forwarding address. All of them made a point to say she was a wonderful young lady who was always helping out in the neighborhood. But, let me tell ya, from my years of experience, you can't always rely on neighbors. They may live close by, but that don't mean they know what goes on behind closed doors...I hope they don't know what goes on behind my closed doors when me and the old lady play nurse and patient...and when I put the cuffs on her when we play cops and robbers. Woo Ha!!! I'm glad the neighbors don't know that! Know what I mean, Charlie Boy?"

Not exactly, Bob...not sure I want to know. I would like to know why Andrea didn't tell me her family had been killed?"

"Hey, Charlie, who can figure out what goes on in a broad's head?"

"Maybe it was too painful for her to talk about," I suggested.

"Ya, that's probably it. At least you know she's not a serial killer...not that we know of anyway. I gotta go. If I find out anything else I'll give you a call, if your cell phone is working."

"Yeah, God only knows. Thanks, bye."

Joe was still at his computer with no idea I had just run up his phone bill. I could hear him cackling in the other room, "Hey, Charlie...you're great, great aunt on Mom's side was placed in a looney bin for walking though town naked, protesting the higher taxes placed on whisky. We got a regular Lady Godiva in the family...Wait till I tell this one to the guys down at O'Toole's...Charlie...Charlie, you listening to me?"

"Ya, whatever," I replied with no concern. I sat down at the kitchen table and strained by brain to see if I could remember Andrea saying anything about an accident. Fresh strawberries that Joe had picked from his tiny garden were on the table, and the fragrance reminded me of Cindy and Andrea, my mystery girls.

15

No news is good news, so the saying goes; and there has been no bad news, or at least no new deaths in the GREAT CEMETERY SLAUGHTER since that network anchor felt the wrath and bites of those venomous bees. Chief Richardson and his men, along with the State Police, had done a good job in preventing any unauthorized personnel from getting within stinging distance of the old cemetery on the Western Prom. But how long would it take, I wondered, for the word to get out to the nervous and unsuspecting public that it wasn't a mad man, but rather a bunch of bees that were doing all the dirty deeds.

It was good getting the local paper on line, but back home I could hold it in my hands and read it wherever I wanted. I tucked today's edition under my arm and walked from my hotel down to Becky's Diner on Commercial Street. The place was packed with rugged fishermen, businessmen, salesmen, secretaries and tourists. I finally found a single stool at the counter and placed my order with Missy. That's the name the pretty waitress had printed on her apron. The smell alone of bacon, steaks, and eggs jumping on the grill was worth the long walk from the Regency.

I finished the front page with stories about the killings, the funerals, and the condition of the girl in the coma at Maine Med. There was nothing there that I didn't know. There were also quotes from the national media saying how much they enjoyed the beauty of the Maine Coast and the lobster dinners at the numerous restaurants on the docks, as if that was the only reason they were in town. For some reason I guess the locals like to hear outsiders tell them things they already know. "Martha, did ya see what Geraldo said 'bout the Chowda' down at DiMillo's."

I flipped to the sports section and saw that the Red Sox had lost another heartbreaker in the 9th inning despite the fact that Pedro pitched went seven, striking out fifteen. But the bullpen couldn't do their job. I know the first thing Joe will say when I call him today, "They suck!"

Missy placed a tall glass of freshly squeezed orange juice in front of me along with a smile. No extra charge. As I reached for the juice I folded the paper and placed it on the counter, and that's when I saw it, buried on the back page: INMATE MISSING, BELIEVED ESCAPED.

DATELINE Thomaston: Warden William Dudman announced last night that a full search has begun for inmate George Chamberlain who was not in his cell at bed check. At first it was believed that Chamberlain had special permission to watch a movie in the prisoners' recreation room. When others who had attended the movie were found back in their cells, the guard on duty sounded the alarm for an in-house search. Chamberlain was serving a life sentence for rape and murder of a Bangor waitress, but for the last ten years had been given more privileges for good behavior. Warden Dudman wanted it known that he had not agreed with prison psychiatrists who said Chamberlain was not posing much of a threat and may be rehabilitated in time. Bangor police were immediately informed. The convicted killer still has family there. Dudman also stated that the escape would not interfere with the annual prison picnic, where the warden was expected to make his announcement that he would be seeking the Democratic Nomination for Governor.

I reread the small article, as if on a second reading it would say the prisoner had been captured and was back in his cell. Not the case. George Chamberlain, who was never supposed to see daylight again, was out there...somewhere in Maine...ready to rape and kill again.

"You look like you either won the lottery or seen a ghost, Mister," exclaimed Missy while stifling a yawn.

"Not the lottery, but sort of a ghost from my past," I replied. "A guy I once knew may have escaped from prison." I pointed out the article to the sleepy waitress.

Her ebony eyes bulged as she saw the name, George Chamberlain. She was sleepy no longer. "Oh my God! That's the maniac who killed my mom's friend at Mooney's. My mother was a bartender there at the time. I've got to call her and tell her. Oh my God!!!"

Missy took off running, and left my toast and scramble eggs burning black. While a replacement waitress took over, I grabbed my cell phone. Information gave me the office number for Attorney John Feeney in Portland, Maine.

"Feeney, Finnegan, and Fields, may I help you."

"John Feeney please. Charlie Sullivan calling"

"Mr. Feeney is out of the office. Would you like his voice mail?"

"Is his secretary, Kim, available?"

"Just a moment please."

"This is Kim Jenkins."

"Hi. This is Charlie Sullivan. Can you get a message through to John?"

"What's the message, Mister Sullivan?"

"Tell him George Chamberlain may have escaped from Thomaston."

"Yes, he found out this morning when Chief Richardson called to say the victim at Maine Med. was coming out of her coma. He left for the Hospital about fifteen minutes ago. As a matter of fact I just left a message at your hotel that he would like you to meet him there."

"Hell's bells! Thanks, I'm on my way." I left my breakfast and a ten dollar bill on the counter, and flagged down a cab.

When we pulled up in front of the Hospital it was like a circus outside. The word was out. The girl in the coma would soon be talking. Outside, all the networks and cable-news channels were checking wires and microphones. The info babes were putting on their make-up and hair spray. The local station anchors were there too, seemingly more concerned about impressing the network big-shots than the well-being of a young college girl.

I spotted Chief Richardson and he waved me in past a row of reporters who were now wondering who I was and why I had privileges. Numerous questions were being hurled.

"Chief, who is that? Is he a specialist?"

"Are you bringing in outside help, Chief?"

"Is that the psychic we heard was coming?"

"Is he a relative of the girl in the coma?"

"Chief, at least give us the guy's name!"

The Chief answered all their questions with two words, "No comment!"

We took the elevator to the 14th floor. When the doors slid open there was another circus. All on the local list of characters were waiting outside room 1401 for the moment the doctors would give the word that the girl inside was ready to talk.

There was Brian DeWolfe, the District Attorney, standing with John Feeney who was nervously tapping his fingers on the wall. Frank Blanchette was managing to carry on a conversation with Roland Greenier, the State Medical Examiner. Doctors and nurses were scurrying among them. Even Detective Tony Reza was there in a wheel chair, his mother on guard to make sure no one bumped into him.

I was happy to see Tony feeling better so quickly. "Only a weenie uses a wheel chair," I teased.

He laughed, but before he could speak Maria Reza said, "You call my son a weenie one more time and your weenie will be in a cast before you leave here."

"Yes, Mrs. Reza! I certainly don't want to get on your bad side... not that you have a bad side."

"Ya...well...you're lucky my son likes you," she said with a small smile.

"Don't let her scare you, Charlie. She likes you, too."

"Tony Reza!!! You want me to push this chair down the stairs?"

"No, but push me toward that lady sitting over there by herself. That's the Kostenello girl's mother."

Mrs. Kostenello had been spending every waking and sleeping moment at the Hospital since she arrived from Lynnfield, Massachusetts. She had a cot set up in her daughter's room and up till now hadn't left the young girl's side. But this morning the doctors asked the mother to wait outside the door. Apparently Mrs. Kostenello spent all her time in prayer, but not silent prayer. The doctors wanted quiet while they made final preparations to try to coax her daughter to full awareness. The girl had opened her eyes and was moving her extremities, but as of yet she couldn't talk.

The mother looked out of place. It was the middle of summer, but she was covered from head to toe in an all drab-green wool outfit with a skirt that reached her ankles and black shoes that were laced and uncomfortable looking. There was a bible in her hand and an oversized crucifix around her neck. Her face was barren of make up and her complexion was almost alabaster white. She appeared as if she was in a world of her own, not aware or at least not caring about all the commotion outside and inside the hospital.

Tony approached the woman as if he needed a permission slip to do so but had left it home. "Mrs. Kostenello, I am Detective Tony Reza...and if you feel up to it, I would like to ask you a few questions."

"What kind of questions?" she snapped.

"Did your daughter have any old boyfriends or acquaintances that were upset with her?"

That question animated the woman. "I ll have you know my Katherine is a good Christian girl who knows the Devil's ways and doesn't have anything to do with boys. Those other three girls with their heavy make-up, tight sweaters, and short dresses are the Devil's hand maidens. That's why *they* are dead and the good Lord spared my Katherine."

The indignant woman folded her arms like a proud Indian Chief who had just proclaimed, after making a decision on whether to go to war or not, "I have spoken!"

"I'm sure she's a wonderful young lady, but we just want to find out if there is anyone who might have wished her harm," Tony tried again.

Mrs. Kostenello reprimanded the young detective. "Just as the Lord protected Daniel in the lion's den, He protected my Katherine. I don't know who attacked her, but I'm praying whoever it was will spend an eternity in hell with those three harlots. PRAISE JESUS!!!"

Becoming frustrated the Detective felt this wasn't the time to press the woman and said, "Well, I certainly wish your daughter all the best. Maybe we can talk again later if you have time."

"If that's what the good Lord wants," the woman stated as a matter of fact.

Maria Reza rolled her eyes and whispered in my ear, "That poor kid in there might be better off in a coma."

I didn't have a chance to affirm her comment before the door to 1401 was opened and three doctors stepped out into the hall way. Doctor Ronald Hamilton spoke, "Miss Kostenello is still weak but her vital signs are much improved. She should be fine, but she's not able to speak yet. We will monitor her constantly and in a few hours I think she may be able to talk. With the permission of the authorities we will hold a press conference when that happens and give an update on her condition."

All through his remarks Mrs. Kostenello kept repeating, "Praise Jesus!"

Doctor Hamilton then turned to the girl's mother and said in a low voice, "Mrs. Kostenello, I do have some other news for you. If you would join me in my office I will explain. It's just down past the nurses' station."

"I am not going anywhere, except back into my daughter's room. Tell me here and now, Doctor," commanded the righteous woman. "The Lord is my shepherd. I have nothing to fear and nothing to hide."

"Please, it might be better to discuss this privately," suggested the doctor as he placed his hand gently on her shoulder.

The woman removed his hand promptly. "Dr. Hamilton, I allowed you, and the other doctors with you, to have your privacy with my Katherine. Now, if you have something to say be quick about it. I want to return to her side immediately!" demanded the strong willed woman.

Feeling the same frustration that Tony Reza had experienced just minutes before, the doctor conceded. "Very well, Mrs. Kostenello, I am very sorry to have to inform you that your daughter lost the baby she was carrying."

You could hear a pin drop. And then you could hear Mrs. Kostenello drop. She fainted and fell to the floor. She was attended too immediately by the staff while the rest of us shot glances at each other, as if to say the same thing that Maria Reza had just whispered in my ear.

John Feeney, seemingly unconcerned about the woman's plight, was on the phone to his secretary and confidante, canceling his appointments for the rest of the day. He would remain at the Hospital waiting for the first chance to speak to the girl in room 1401. With that he turned and invited me to grab some coffee in the cafeteria. I accepted and told Tony I would drop into to see him later. He gave me a nod, as did his mother.

While the lawyer and I sat at a small table near the window in the hospital cafeteria, storm clouds were gathering and not just outside.

"Charlie, this whole mess is going to be the death of me. What with losing my son, my wife no longer interested in anything except a bottle of sleeping pills, not being able to give full attention to my clients with trial dates coming up, and now Chamberlain's on the loose."

"Is there any new information about his whereabouts?"

"No, but I'm betting he's not headed for Bangor."

"Why do you say that, John?"

The lawyer dumped a full pack of sugar into his black coffee, and then explained, "Every month since I put that punk away he has been sending me notes saying someday he would get out and make me pay. It's not unusual for any prosecutor to get those kinds of threats. What *is* unusual is a lifer breaking out. I'm paranoid enough to think that chicken-shit warden let him escape. He knows I want that Democratic nomination too. He might think that Chamberlain being on the loose is the straw that will break my back. Well if he does, he doesn't know John Jacob Feeney as well as he might think." There was almost insanity in the lawyer's eyes as he spoke.

"John, do you really think the warden would stoop that low, or that he would take the chance that Chamberlain might rat him out?"

"Rat him out? Dudman doesn't worry about that. Who's going to believe a killer and a rapist over a well-respected law enforcement official, one who may be the next Governor?...Over my dead body of course." The insanity look grew in his eyes.

"It's still hard to believe that a politician would be *that* devious," I commented.

The lawyer took the last gulp from his second cup of coffee. He put down the cup and stuffed the cellophane wrapping from a pack of Twinkies into it. "Charlie, politics ain't pretty. That's all I can say about that."

Have you told the cops about the threats?"

"Not till this morning. Richardson has a couple of uniform boys watching the house. I feel pretty safe at the office. Tell me what you know about Chamberlain. I remember you mentioning him the other day."

"Hell, John, I only met him a couple of times, and that was when I was seventeen. The last time I saw him he was ringing wet and cursing those bees, the cemetery, his father, Jimmy Peters, and me.

"The firemen doused him pretty good, huh?" The lawyer smiled a revengeful grin.

"They almost drowned the bastard. In the end it was hard to tell whether he was madder at the bees or at the firemen," I said as I recalled the moment.

"I wish they had drowned him, Charlie. I wish they had." Feeney crushed the two paper cups in front of him as if he thought of them as necks he'd like to squeeze.

We sat quietly for a long time just sipping coffee and staring out the window. He with his thoughts and me with mine.

I can't exactly say what occupied his mind; but in my head, circulating through my brain, was a mysterious girl from long ago who stole my heart in that old cemetery. And a mysterious girl I had just met a few weeks ago in Principal Bernard Allen's office who was stealing it again.

Feeney's cell phone rang and he sprang to his feet, "She's talking, Charlie. Let's go."

We arrived at the Kostenello girl's room as she was asking the doctors to please keep her mother away from her. The mother was on her knees in the corner, wailing away and pounding her bible on the wall as if to emphasize to the heavens that they need not punish her wayward daughter. The young woman would taste the wrath of God's servant on earth.

Dr. Hamilton said to all of us that we could ask her questions, but not to get her overly excited or he would put a stop to it.

The lawyer was granted the first question. "Miss Kostenello, my name is John Feeney. I am so happy that you are going to be all right. We all are." We all shook out heads in agreement. "Now, take your time and tell us everything you remember about that night you and your friends spent in the old cemetery."

Kathy Kostenello was a pretty blond-headed, blue-eyed all-American girl. She reminded me a lot of a young Sara Peters. Jimmy's mother had many of the same features.

"Are my friends all right? Did they make it out of there?" asked the still frightened girl, hoping for one answer but expecting another.

She could tell by our silence and the look in our eyes that she was the lone survivor. She took a moment to grieve and blow her nose.

John Feeney, with years of experience in questioning crooks and witnesses, knew the best way to make her feel comfortable around him. He could be ruthless if that was needed, and he could be gentle and sincere as he was now.

"Kathy, we know you thought a lot of your friends. I lost my son, Paul, in that cemetery too." He didn't fight the tears in his own eyes as his son's name came to his lips. "The best thing we can do for them now is be brave and help find their killers."

The young woman felt immediate empathy for John Feeney and was able to continue. We all listened intently. Even her mother stopped her wallowing as Kathy began.

"We arrived there just before sundown. We had to stay until dawn, and then someone would come and pick us up and take us back to the sorority house. They gave each of us the name of a person buried there, and we were supposed to find their headstones. To prove we did, we had to return with the birth and death dates printed on the stones. We all kept together and helped each other find the names. We had flash lights and plenty of food. There was a big field in the middle and a big old elm tree where we put down our sleeping bags and a blanket."

Of all those gathered at her bedside, I was the most familiar with just the spot she was talking about. Oh the tales that tree could tell if it could talk.

"We knew going in that we wouldn't be able to sleep, but we just felt more secure with our sleeping bags. We were glad we brought them too because by midnight it was getting pretty chilly. We started a small fire. One of the girls, Julie Alcala, had been in girls scouts with me and we were showing off our camping skills. By the time we settled down for the night we had found three of the names and decided we would search for mine at sun up. We read magazines and listened to the radio and talked about boys and...sex...and stuff like that for most of the night"

Her mother frowned with disapproval at the mention of boys and sex, but kept silent as if her faith had been shattered.

Kathy now appeared more nervous than when she had started her story. "Then, about five in the morning, Mary Foley had to go to the bathroom. She went over behind this big mausoleum, and after about thirty minutes we got worried when she didn't come back. We yelled for her over and over. When there was no answer my friend Julie and the other girl, Jill DeFranco, went to look for her while I cleaned up the area."

The Kostenello girl was now crying profusely, and the doctors monitoring her heart rate cautioned that we should stop for a while. She protested and said she wanted to finish. Feeling compassion John Feeney took the young lady's hand, something her mother wouldn't do. Kathy looked into the eyes of Portland's most powerful lawyer with thanks in her own eyes. She sensed that he wouldn't be judgmental.

"After about ten minutes, Julie came running toward me yelling and crying that Mary and Jill were dead. I thought she was saying something about little bees had attacked them, but her words were kind of garbled. Julie fell about fifty feet from me, and when she didn't get up I began to run for help."

Doctor Hamilton interrupted and insisted that we stop, but again Kathy protested.

Then the horror in her eyes helped convey what she would say next. "I was about ten yards from the gates and this monstrous looking creature jumped out from behind an above ground crypt. He grabbed me and started dragging me back toward the mausoleum. His face was grotesque like you would see in a horror movie and his eyes... his eyes...were burning red!...His breath smelled like decaying fish. I know it sounds crazy, but that *fucking* prick wasn't human!!!"

Kathy's mother then interrupted. She just couldn't hold her tongue any longer. After all, it was the obligation of God's servant on earth to speak for Him. She approached her daughter's bedside with the finger of righteousness pointed directly at her.

"You are no longer flesh of my flesh. You are a fornicator with a filthy mouth." With that tirade ended, the mother left in a hurry. Her daughter looked hurt but somewhat relieved.

Each of us used our own words to reassure her that we really cared about her, and not to pay attention to her mother at the moment. Feeney told Kathy her mother was distraught and didn't mean those words.

Feeling she was truly among friends Kathy finished her story. "As he was pulling me toward the mausoleum I looked around on the ground for anything I could use as a weapon. I picked up a water bottle that we left there and hit him with it. The water splashed on him, and he howled in pain and let go of me. Can you believe this bastard was wounded by water?"

She paused as if to ponder her own question.

John Feeney asked, "What happened next?"

The young woman looked at her new friend and said that was all she could remember. The lawyer then pulled out the chain and locket and asked if it meant anything to her.

The girl examined it carefully and said she liked the inscription, but had never seen it before.

Feeney explained that she was clutching it in her fingers when she was found outside the cemetery.

Kathy said she didn't even remember getting out of the cemetery, and didn't know how she ended up with the golden trinket. She said she was sorry she couldn't be more helpful.

The lawyer pattered her on the shoulder and said not to worry about it for now, and if she remembered later she could let him know. What John Feeney wanted at the beginning of her story was the answer to who killed his son. Now, although he still wanted that, he had found her pain and her apparent hard life at home had truly touched him, or so it seemed to me at the time. It was like he was given someone else to care about. He got up and told the doctor to take good care of her, give her anything she wanted, and to send all bills to him. Then he kissed her on the forehead and left the room quietly, promising to return soon.

The D.A and the Police Chief followed behind the lawyer. I started to leave with Tony Reza and his mother. I was about a foot from the door when I asked Tony to let me know when he would be ready to call on Wendle Bronson.

It was then Kathy Kostenello spoke up. "Excuse me, Sir. Can you tell me the name you just said?"

I explained to her that the Detective and I wanted to question the cemetery caretaker, and that his name was Wendle Bronson.

Suddenly, she sat up in her bed and covered her mouth with her hand. She slowly removed it and said, "That's the *name*!"

"What's the name?" I asked.

"Wendle Bronson!" That's the name I was given to find...the name on the tombstone."

I looked at Tony and Maria Reza who were now just as stunned by this news as I was. A chill ran down my spine, and then in a flash, I was back there in my early years.

It was a very hot summer day and Jimmy, Tommy Caine, Bill O'Neal, Mike Murphy, Dana Wilson and I met at Harvel's corner store and bought a case of cold Pepsi and a mess of junk food. Then we made our way to the elm tree near home plate in the old cemetery. Tommy hadn't spoken to Jimmy or me since the autumn before, when we had conned him out of his Halloween candy with that story about the zombie. We decided to rectify the bad feelings with a little party in the old bone yard. Actually, it was Mike Murphy's idea. Guess we should have known then that Mike was on his way to the Priesthood. Mike was such a "do-gooder"...and a real teacher's pet.

("Pssst. Hey, Charlie, I think Ellen is wearing a bra today"

"Let me see...yeah, I think you're right, Jimbo."

"Charlie Sullivan and Jimmy Peters!!! I know what you are doing back there. Come down and sit here in front," demanded Mrs. McDonough. "Michael, would you and Gary switch seats with those two immature young men?")

We got to the cemetery about ten and played ball for a couple of hours, until the hot noon day sun and all that sugar and carbonation caught up with us. Dana, Bill, and do-gooder Mike had other things to do in the afternoon. They left. Jimmy, Tommy, and I were about to leave as well; but Jimmy and I stayed behind to pick up the trash, as we had always done. After all, this was *our* home away from home. Tommy needed to relieve himself and headed for the taller grass. We promised to wait for him.

I remember now commenting on the number of little bees that were crawling all over the many cellophane wrappers of Devil Dogs, Ho-Ho's, Ring Dings, and the rest. A lot of them were making their way around and down into the soda bottles too.

"Hey, Jimmy, I ain't pickin that stuff up until those little bastards are gone."

"We *gotta* get the bottles. They're worth 3 cents a piece!"

"You get 'em then! You can have all the money," I promised.

It was then we heard her. "Boys, don't be afraid. They will do you no harm"

"Shit! Lady, don't sneak up on us like that," Jimmy exclaimed as we both jumped.

She was dressed all in black and covered from head to toe. Except you could see her eyes...her big *green* eyes! She waved her arm and the bees left their treasure and swarmed up on a branch above. I remember thinking at the time, *that's one strange lady*.

Jimmy and I scurried to pick up the wrappings and the empty bottles while we had the chance. But, before we could pick up the first one, we heard Tommy screaming, "Snake! Snake! I think it's a rattler!!!"

When he came running over with pee all over his pants and sneakers, Jimmy and I forgot everything else and started laughing uncontrollably. That's when Tommy swore at us and vowed he would *never* come back to the cemetery. By the time Jimmy and I caught our breaths again, Tommy was gone. The bees were gone, and the lady was gone.

Could that have been Cindy that day...a day when I was barely 13 years old? I now wondered as I stood there in room 1401 thinking about the name that the Kostenello girl had just mentioned...Wendle Bronson.

Jimmy and I didn't give much thought to the lady back then, other than to comment that it was lucky for us she came walking by. As Jimmy picked up the bottles he kept me to my promise, that if he picked them up he could have the three cents a piece.

While Jimmy gathered his fortune, I decided to check and see if there really was a snake over by the tombstone where Tommy pissed all over himself. I approached with caution and baseball bat in hand. Geez! There was a snake, but just a rubber one that someone had left there. It was then I noticed the name etched on the stone: GEN-ERAL WENDLE BRONSON. I knew I had seen that name before. It was there all along, on my memory tape.

16

The caretaker's shack was not a big part of my childhood memories, although I do recall the shabby wooden structure located in the Hobo Grounds. It was across the street and down the hill from the Western Cemetery. I thought it was property of the railroad yard at the time and had nothing to do with the cemetery, but apparently I was wrong. There was a dirt lot that was big enough for a baseball game, just not as enticing to Jimmy and me as the open grassy field up on the hill. The homeless were more commonly known as hobos back then, and that's how the place down by the tracks got its name. It was where they congregated. It was where they *lived* while in town.

The name now occupying my mind was, Wendle Bronson. I'm still somewhat stunned to find out it's the same name that was on Kathy Kostenello's list...the name she never had time to find...the same name I did find all those years ago. Sure, there's the possibility that this guy is a descendant who's just looking after dear old great, great granddad. But on hearing the name, John Feeney and Chief Ray Richardson decided we couldn't wait for Tony Reza to recover before we called on the current Mr. Bronson. Tony agreed, and I promised to fill him in on our findings as soon as I got back.

It was near sunset when we three arrived in the Chief's squad car. A steady rain was falling, and it seemed the long summer drought might soon be over. The wind was gustier down in the railroad yard than up the hill on the promenade, where it was blocked by the massive mansions that belonged to Portland's high and mighty.

There was no paved walkway down the hill, just a well-worn dirt path. Empty railroad cars along with empty cans and bottles decorated the landscape. A train was slowly passing by as if sneaking out of town. When we were kids we always stopped to watch them like they were part of a parade, but today they seemed to have lost their wonder. For the most part they go unnoticed. They've gone the way of the circus and the drive-in movies. They now wear the label of "who cares". We made our way down the narrow path, the Chief in front with the snap on his holster popped for easier access. His radio was velcroed to his shirt and his nightstick was riding on his belt. As he jaunted down the dirt path the hand cuffs on his belt loop jingled like the spurs on a cowboy's boots. He was prepared for whomever or whatever was in that run down shanty. At least that's what he thought at the moment.

The shack itself looked to be a two-room structure that obviously never felt a paintbrush. The windows were dirty to the point of disgust. The whole building looked like it had been covered by a giant spider web. *They say, Old Man Buckley, even had giant African spiders and for an extra dollar he would let you watch them eat live baby chicks.* There was lingering smoke coming out of a stove chimney. A small light outside the only door was broken, but the bulb still burned as if down to its last watt. Inside there was little light, but I could hear music playing. I recognized the sound of Dion and The Belmonts and (Why must I be) A Teenager In Love.

The Chief tapped on the door with his night stick, and then again, harder. The only reply was a growl from what sounded like a real big animal. The Chief banged the door even harder. The growl from the other side grew even louder. Richardson put away his stick and hauled out a can of pepper spray. Slowly, he removed the gun from his holster. The lock on the door looked fairly new and sturdy, and the only thing keeping us from the beast within. The growls were getting more sinister and closer to the other side of the door.

My heart rate was climbing, and all I could think of was Red Foxx on Sanford and Son, holding on to his chest. "Lizebeth, Darlin', this is the big one!!!"

"Break it down!" commanded John Feeney in a voice barely audible against the sound of the roaring wind, which had picked up considerably down here in the low lands...blowing in right off the water with little resistance.

"John, I can't do that without a search warrant!" the Chief shouted back with a heavy rain bashing against his face.

"Don't worry about that small detail. Trust me; I can get one predated that will hold up in any court. I've done it before and I can do it again."

Both the Chief and I knew the attorney wasn't just bragging. He could do it all right.

"Well, at least let Charlie break it down. If anyone finds out we broke in, it might go over better if the culprit wasn't the freakin' Chief of Police," insisted Ray Richardson.

Feeney just smiled, pulled out a pistol of his own and blew the lock apart. We didn't need to open the door; the wind took care of that.

There in the faint light we saw it. On guard with snarling white teeth, like a mummy protecting the pharaoh's tomb, was a dog the size of a small rat. We all looked at each other and managed a light laugh in relief. The Chief holstered his gun and put away his pepper spray. The lawyer tucked his pistol back in his pants, and I let go of a big rock that I had picked up outside the door.

The little dog moved slowly backward as the Chief crouched down to pet it. On the small radio sitting on a crooked wooden table I heard the DJ say, "Good times and great oldies, here's Sam the Sham and Wooly Bully."

It may have been a great oldie, but now the times were turning bad again. There in the entry way of the back room, the growl we heard before was growing louder and more menacing, drowning out Sam the Sham. Huge yellow eyes now appeared in the blackness and were wincing in madness. The floor boards creaked as its weight came forward. The terror of it all took us by surprise. Then with a great roar the beast lunged for the chief. Canines, the size of a man's finger, were snapping and clicking near his face. The massive creature opened its jaws and secured the panicking cop's throat.

John Feeney was struggling for his gun as I was searching for that rock that I had dropped to the floor. It was nowhere to be found. Then I looked up and in the doorway, silhouetted against the darkening sky was a stranger who simply said, "Brutus!" The beast let go of the Chief's pulsating throat and backed off, still growling and slinging spit. Richardson scurried back on his legs, holding on to his throat and gasping for air. The lawyer moved over to the frightened cop; and I just stood there, paralyzed by what had just taken place.

"What's the meaning of this?" demanded the stranger.

"Are you Wendle Bronson?" I managed to ask, with one eye still searching for my missing rock. It seemed to have blended into the filthy surroundings.

"Maybe." was the reply.

Brutus was now laying down with his huge face on the floor and his eyes looking up at his master, ready at a moment's notice to follow an order to kill. The little dog sat at the big dog's side reminding me of that Looney Toon where one dog is a hero to the other and keeps saying, "Hey, Spike, you're my friend. Huh? Right, Spike? Right?" The bigger dog swats at his admirer and says, "Aww, shat up!"

The Chief was now standing and slowly reaching for his gun. Brutus growled and the Chief thought better of it.

The lawyer in John Feeney now stepped forward and said, "This place should be condemned. I'm in a frame of mind to call the Board of Health and have it closed. Those animals will be put to sleep."

The stranger laughed in criticism and said, "Thanks. Guess I'll have to move in with you. When you try to take out Brutus, you better call up the National Guard."

"Sir, would you please tell us, are you Wendle Bronson?" Feeney asked, like he was in court and Bronson was sitting in the witness stand.

"What if I am, so what?"

"Well, Bronson, if that's who you are, you owe your job to me. My wife Sandra handles the trust that pays your salary and provides the free housing you have here."

"Oh, I can see the headlines now: **Lawyer Condemns Client's Property**", the stranger mocked.

The Chief, forgetting his recent brush with death snickered, "He's got a point, John. It wouldn't look good for a man seeking the Democratic nomination."

Feeney cursed under his breath and threw his hands up in disgust. I couldn't help but think that the rich and powerful bowed and scraped at Feeney's feet; but this guy, with no bargaining power and even less money, had stopped the lawyer in his tracks. I admired that without saying so.

Bronson, pleased with his remarks, acknowledged he was the caretaker. He stepped forward and lit a hurricane lamp, shedding a little light on his *free* surroundings and saying, "You will pay for that lock,

Rich Man. And that's Mr. Bronson to you." His sarcasm continued on. "As you can see I have a lot of valuables in here. I would offer you a chair but that massive trust fund apparently can afford only one." Then the caretaker laughed loud enough to startle the big attack dog now taking refuge over by the small stove. His little friend followed behind.

As he drew closer to the light, I could see a man who was pale and thin. His shoulders were stooped, as if carrying a great weight. His head and upper body were covered with a poncho, exposing very little of his face, but I could see his eyes were steel gray and bloodshot. He wore motorcycle boots and he reeked with the smell of alcohol.

"Mr.Bronson, please forgive us," I said. "We are a bit unnerved. We are concerned with the killings that have occurred in the cemetery you look after."

I asked John Feeney to show Bronson the locket and chain. He complied and gave it to the caretaker. "Have you ever seen that before?"

Bronson grabbed it and sat down as he took out a pair of dirty eyeglasses. The caretaker studied the chain and locket carefully, and then held it tight in his palms. He rolled his head back on his neck and uttered a sigh. Then he stood up, held it closer to the light and clicked it opened, revealing my young face from long ago. He removed his glasses and slowly sat back down again, and asked in a less demanding voice, "Where did you get this?"

"It was found clutched in the fingers of a girl who was attacked in the cemetery," the Chief said.

"A very special girl," added John Feeney, now taking a less arrogant tone.

Bronson said he wasn't sure if he had ever seen it. The accuracy of his memory all depended on the level of alcohol he had consumed on a particular day; and this day, that was at least a six pack of beer and maybe a bottle of wine. He couldn't say for sure.

"Please, Mr. Bronson, think as hard as you can," I asked again.

He got up and moved over toward his dogs, checking the water in their dish. "Well, since you say please, my friend...I guess I can take another look. Bronson brought the trinket closer to his weary-looking eyes.

"What did you say?" I interrupted.

"I said I would take another look," snapped the caretaker. "Quit crowding me."

"No, not that. It was the way you said, *my friend*."

I grabbed the lamp and moved toward him, and pushed down the poncho covering his head. In the flickering light of that old shack, more like a mirage than a memory, was the aging face of my dear old friend, Jimmy Peters.

I broke into tears and hugged him, "Jimmy, I can't believe it's you!"

The caretaker slowly pushed me back, took the lamp from me and held it to my face. Taking a real good look at me for the first time on this dark and stormy night, his mouth dropped in nervous surprise. He wiped his tired eyes that were now welling with tears, and then reached to resume the hug. "Charlie!"

For the next ten minutes we just held on to each other, laughing and crying at the same time. I kept repeating, "Jimmy" and he kept repeating, "Charlie." Finally we broke our embrace and he said, "When I saw your ugly mug in that locket, I put on my best poker face. There was no way I was going to say it was my best friend."

"I appreciate that, but I've been cleared of all suspicion."

"I'm surprised you recognized me in the dark light with my head covered," Jimmy said.

"I almost didn't, but I remembered how you use to always say...*my friend*."

Feeney and Richardson had given us our space. They were captivated by the turn of events. The attorney then suggested we go out for coffee, and carry on the investigation and the reunion some place warmer.

"And some place with additional seating and away from that...that...*dog*!" added the Chief.

A half-hour later we found ourselves in a back booth at The Village Cafe. With hot food and hot coffee we were ready to hear how and why Jimmy Peters became Wendle Bronson, and what he knew about the weird happenings in the cemetery.

Before we started I told him of my visit with his mother and how she desperately wanted to see him. Jimmy put his face in his hands and said he just couldn't do it, not till he could beat his demons. He went on to say the reason he came back was to be near her, and that someday he would find the courage to go home. He took the job when he saw it advertised in the paper. It allowed him to be alone in a place where no one would come to see him. He picked the name Wendle Bronson to hide his true identity.

"Charlie, do you remember the time Tommy Caine got frightened by a snake and pissed all over himself?" Jimmy managed a small laugh as he asked the question. Even in his current state he couldn't help himself.

"I was just thinking about that today! You know, I remember, and there really was a snake there."

"Ya, a rubber snake. I put it there! I was hoping sooner or later he would have to take a leak, and when he did, I told him everyone used that old marker with Wendle Bronson's name on it. Man, I fooled him again. Un-freakin' believable!" Jimmy smiled at his victory from so long ago.

"And that's how you became Wendle Bronson?

"Ya...guess Tommy gets the last laugh. Now the whole world pisses all over *me*."

"Not anymore, Jimmy...not now that I'm back in your life."

He took a big gulp of coffee and broke down again. Feeney and Richardson were moved by my old friend's story, and the bond we had was growing deeper. Slowly Jimmy stopped his tears and asked for another cup of coffee. With a deep breath he was ready to tell us what he knew about the GREAT CEMETERY SLAUGHTER.

My friend looked at Chief Richardson and said, "I wanted to call the cops and tell them what I'm going to tell you now, but I was afraid they would think it was just a wild story made up by some drunk. And if they did believe me, they would fingerprint me as a suspect and find out who I was. Some young detective did come by a week ago. I told him I didn't know anything, but I don't think he believed me. After he left I went out and got the lock that you guys busted tonight. I relied on Brutus up till then. He was just an old stray that I started to feed about five years ago. He became my new best friend...my lock and my protector too."

"And a damn good one!" commented the Chief. "And the other one, he's a pistol too."

"The little dog was left up at the cemetery a few months ago and so I took him in. They have been great company for a lonely man."

"What's the name of the small one?" I asked.

"Never got around to givin' him one," Jimmy said as he stared at his cup.

"Jimmy, it's time to tell us...It's time to tell me...about the chain and locket. Did you take it?"

Jimmy looked at me to confess that he did go up to the cemetery that day I left the gift for Cindy. "I don't know why I went up there, Charlie. I just did. It was about sundown. She was sitting under the big elm, holding it in her hands. I was about a hundred feet behind her and yet she knew I was there. She told me to come to her. But there were all these bees surrounding her and I was afraid of getting stung. She said they wouldn't bother me in the kind of voice someone says not to worry about their dog. *He won't bite*." He smiled at the thought that he couldn't say that about Brutus. "It was really weird, man. She just waved her arms, and those bees all left like they were obeying her. Charlie, she was crying and holding on to the locket and looking at your picture. And...now I'm only telling you what I saw...but it appeared to me like there was steam coming from her face...as if the tears were burning her."

The waitress asked if we wanted more coffee about three times before we acknowledged her. We were oblivious to all around us. We hung on to Jimmy's every word as he took us back in time. This is how Jimmy remembered it.

"How come you didn't meet Charlie today? He's really bummed."

"Charlie must be free of me to live the life he was born for. I didn't know how to tell him what I'm going to tell you. I summoned you here so you would know. You must promise to keep my secret or a great tragedy may come your way. It's not that I want to harm you,

Jimmy. It's just that Charlie means the world to me. I know now *he* is my one true love, the one I have waited for over all these centuries. He's the only one who can set me free, but he's not ready... not yet."

"What do you mean?...you *summoned* me. How could you do that? What kind of a tragedy? What do you mean, you're not free? Is someone holding you against your will? And you say you've been here for centuries? I don't understand what you're talking about."

"I summoned you because I can. I have many powers you can't understand...but you must accept. If not, you will join me and another one here...the *undead*."

"Cindy, you are really freakin' me out!"

"Then listen carefully...and obey."

I was like in her power. She stood up and put the chain around her neck. Then she waved her arms again, and all those bees came back and swarmed on her chest. At first I thought they were too small to be bees, but they were bees all right.

"I called back my little playmates to show you a sign of my power."

"You've got me convinced...but I still don't understand."

I thought I was dreaming at first but it was real, all too freakin' real.

"Charlie Sullivan is very special to me. I haven't loved anyone in a very long time. I know he wonders how old I am and where I am from. I didn't know how to tell him...that I have been here in this place for almost 150 years...and over 100 more years somewhere else."

"Ah...Cindy...ah...I think I have to get home before dark."

I had never been so scared in all my life. She grabbed me by the shoulders and peered right into my eyes.

"Jimmy, you are his best friend and I will not harm you as long as you keep my secrets. Do you know why you and Charlie have never been fearful of this place?"

"No. Why?"

"You, and especially Charlie, truly loved this place and always treated my home with respect and I respected you back. You cleaned up after your ball games and your lunches. Over the years, many who came here disrespected these grounds with trash, and by relieving themselves on the resting places of the innocent ones here. I saw to it that they weren't harmed, but I did frighten them off."

"Cindy, I think I might *relieve* myself right now. I am really frightened too!"

"There is one here who would harm you if I am not around. He has killed many over the years. There is no way to destroy him. My power is greater, but in the past he has found ways to cast me into deep sleeps for short periods of time. It is during those times that he commands the bees to kill all who come near."

"Well, you weren't here when Charlie was here earlier. Those bees could have attacked him"

"Jimmy, please understand...I have always been here. The bees can never hurt Charlie. I spent a great deal of time filling his body with the venom that I and my little friends possess. He is immune. He thought so much of my special kiss.

"Cindy, why are you scaring the shit out of me? Why don't you just keep your secret to yourself?" I wanted to run but somehow she had a hold on me. I couldn't move.

"Jimmy, there are other secrets I will hold back. But I am telling you this so that you will know, if the day comes when someone brings more horror to this place by summoning the bees to kill, it is not me. It is my enemy and he has great power. Soon he may have more power than I. If that time comes, you may tell Charlie what I am telling you now. And if you ever come back here, Jimmy, always bring fresh water with you. The bees and the Evil One will flee from it, as will I. It causes us great pain but cannot destroy us." She looked me right in the eye when she reconfirmed, "Jimmy...we are already... *dead*."

She took the chain from around her neck, as the bees made room, and kissed it. Then she put it back.

"It will be a sign that the Evil One is growing more powerful if this chain and locket is ever found in anyone else's possession but mine. It is then that Charlie will find the strength to do what he must do...he must destroy me and set my soul free."

With that she slowly walked toward the big old mausoleum and disappeared.

"When the dead bodies started showing up as this summer I started drinking more and more. Damn it if I don't need one right now!"

"Damn if we all don't!" Feeney said.

"Amen!" said the Chief, as we all sat in silence.

Feeney, Richardson, and I were in awe of the story Jimmy had just told. We just stayed there till closing time, almost helpless to move.

Jimmy words and the account of his meeting with Cindy were swimming back and forth in my mind. I felt stunned, sad, happy, confused, and almost...relieved.

Stunned, because I never realized that Cindy was some kind of *unnatural* being.

Sad, because I felt bad for all that she's been through, confined in one place waiting for someone...me...to set her free.

Happy, because I know now that she did love me all along...that she *still* loves me.

Confused. Who wouldn't be with the account Jimmy just gave?

Relieved, because I am getting closer to understanding why my life has never been the same since the sunny summer days when we, that is, when *I* was seventeen.

I needed something to help me get through this night, even if only a wisecrack made in the silence of my mind. *To think, all this time, I've been in love with an older woman...a much OLDER woman.*

17

Chief Richardson was approaching the current press conference a bit easier than the first. Speaking in public had always terrorized him. He had taken a Dale Carnegie course when he first became Chief; and, up until now, it hadn't seemed to help much. But after last night and what he had heard from Jimmy Peters, he seemed more seasoned this time around. Talking to the media couldn't compare in panic to having a two-hundred pound dog latch onto your throat, or learning there was a three hundred-year-old woman and some other kind of weird creature just a few miles away. No sir, this was a going to be a piece of cake. So he thought.

I had come to respect and like the Chief very much. He was a good cop and more importantly, a fair one.

Tony said that the Chief has been threatening to retire for a few years and spend more time with his wife and grand kids. The Chief grew up in Bangor and, as Tony tells it, Richardson was just a young rookie when he found the body of a waitress, the one George Chamberlain raped and left for those rats to finish off in that abandoned warehouse. Young Ray first met young John Feeney when the lawyer called on him to testify for the prosecution. When an opening came up in the Portland Police Department for a sergeant, it was Feeney who recommended Ray Richardson. Ray had just gotten married and the promotion and the pay raise meant a lot to the newlyweds. So, they packed all they had into their old Ford pickup and moved to Portland. Of course, Feeney was just looking to make a grateful ally. He was building his unwavering power base and Richardson was just another step. The lawyer's motives may have been totally selfish, but Ray was thankful just the same.

The Chief stepped up to the podium. Flash bulbs clicked and the murmuring voices grew quieter. The number of microphones and the number of reporters had doubled since the last time the Chief stood before the public.

"Ladies and Gentlemen, before I take your questions, let me give you an update. The young lady who had been in a coma has thankfully awakened and seems to be doing very well. We had a chance to talk to her, but she doesn't quite remember all the events of that night...except to confirm that there are a number of bees in that cemetery that are obviously quite deadly. That coincides with the lab reports from Frank Blanchette and Roland Greenier. The bees are apparently the culprits. Their venom seems to be a new strain that up till now no one was familiar with. Now I'll take your questions."

Fifty questions flew through the air all at once. The feeding frenzy was on. There was fresh blood in the water, and the sharks in the press could smell it.

"One at a time, please! One at a time!" The Chief shouted over them and then picked one he knew by name. "Miss Ibrahim from The Herald."

"Chief Richardson, are you telling us than a bunch of bees killed *all* those people? Are you saying they were all *stung* to death?"

"We didn't know for sure at the beginning, but both my department's Medical Examiner and the State's Medical Examiner are in agreement that the venom from this particular species is very, very lethal. Now, let me caution all those here and those listening on the radio or watching on TV; if you stay away from that area you should be completely safe. They won't leave their territorial boundaries...and you shouldn't leave yours," the cop added, trying to be amusing in a tense situation, as if some part of that Carnegie course had kicked in.

"Chief, just when are you planning to do something about those bees?" asked Pat Callahan from NewsCenter 6.

"We plan to go in there with some very heavy pesticides as soon as the wind conditions allow. As you know we have had some gusty winds the last few days, and we have to wait for a calm day so the pesticides don't spread into the surrounding neighborhoods. Just keep the hell away from there till then. After about three days from the time of spraying, and we feel it's safe, we will remove the barricades."

Before he could choose the next questioner, a nameless voice called out, "Chief, can you tell us the name of the girl who survived and how she managed to do it?"

"We are keeping her identity quiet for the time being. Luck is my best guess as to how she survived. She apparently was separated from the others during the attack and was able to get away. Hopefully she will remember more later, but we don't want to press her at this time. She's still in fragile condition."

"But what caused her to go into a coma?" came another unknown voice from the unsatisfied press.

"I would say it was the shock of seeing her friends drop like flies in front of her face. One minute you're laughing and carrying on with your friends, and the next minute they are all dead but you. You too would probably lapse into a coma from the horror of it all," argued Ray Richardson as he grew more impatient with the questions being hurled at him like so many darts at a dart board. And he was the bull's eye.

The next dart hit its target square on. "Chief, there are rumors that she saw some strange being in that cemetery...some...monster!"

The sound of the restless press and the surrounding citizens grew more excited. Neighbors and strangers were looking at each other with that *could-that-be-true* frame of mind.

The Chief raised his hands to quiet the crowd and then warned, "I told you the last time not to listen to these crazy rumors. Please, just go about your business. Stay away from that area and let us do our jobs. There have been no more incidents since we restricted access to that part of the West End. I feel it's safe to say that most of the danger is over, and once we spray we will be able to bring this whole incident to a close."

"Chief, I heard one of your own detectives saw something out of the ordinary and ended up in the hospital," came the next unexpected voice. The sharks were no longer willing to wait for the Chief to pick and choose among their numbers.

Again the crowd grew more alarmed and the Chief grew more agitated.

"I can confirm we have one of our own in the hospital but as a result of an attack of appendicitis, not from being assaulted by some... Creature From The Black Lagoon!!! That's all for now. We'll call another press conference when and if we receive any more pertinent information."

A small groan went up among the nervous crowd and they dispersed. The Chief stepped off the podium and performed his ritual of wiping the sweat from his visor.

John Feeney and I watched the press conference from his plush office. Somehow the pleasant and secure surroundings helped give the illusion that nothing was wrong in my world. (Ozzie and Harriet were happily helping out at the church rummage sale, and Ricky and David were down at the malt shop. And there's their friend, Wally, laughing and giggling with the new waitress. Ricky sure looks sharp in his cardigan sweater. Of course, they'll all be at the dance tonight when Ricky performs his new hit, Hello Mary Lou.)

"Richardson is getting better at keeping secrets and he's turning into a regular Rodney Dangerfield," stated the lawyer as he clicked off the TV. Sitting on his desk, he snapped elastics back and forth over his wrists, as if it helped him to think and make plans. "Charlie, do you think that story your friend gave us last night was true? The fact that I haven't discounted it completely is because, with all the weird shit that's gone on, it doesn't sound that far fetched. Killer bees...Wheeler saying he saw two dead guys walking down the street...your old friend using an alias from a tombstone...Kathy frightened into a coma by some big ugly bastard...So what's so strange about you having a *three-hundred-year-old* girlfriend?!?"

"I haven't seen Jimmy in a long time, but I believe what he said. At least I believe he believes what he said. I always felt in my gut there was something about Cindy that was out of the ordinary. I loved her so much I didn't worry about it at the time. And one other thing, John."

"What's that?" Feeney asked as he was shooting the elastics off his big thumb, aiming at some of the pictures on the wall. "Take that Baldacci, I'm gonna have your job when your term is up. You can go back to serving spaghetti to those rubes up in Bangor."

I went on as he continued his target practice. "When Detective Reza had his bout with appendicitis, he had just seen something or someone who matched the description given by the Kostenello girl. I didn't see anything. My mind was somewhere else, but I don't think Tony would say he saw something if it really wasn't there. He's a trained professional and that makes him a reliable witness."

Feeney agreed as he pushed back from his desk, flicking all the remaining elastics around his wrists to the floor for someone else to pick up.

"I want you do to me a favor, Charlie. See if you can get Peters sobered up, and go over that story again, just to see if he tells it the same way."

"If you think it will do any good?"

"It's just an old lawyer's trick. Come back a day or two later and ask the same question, and see if the defendant responds the same way. Give it a try."

I agreed, shook his hand and told him I would be in touch.

Jimmy was outside *his* plush surroundings as I made my way down the hill. The skies were still cloudy and the onshore winds were just as active as the night before. He had shed his poncho for a torn brown sweater and an old Red Sox baseball cap. The big dog was by his side, gnawing on a bone that looked like it might have belonged to a small dinosaur. I'm sure it was just a big soup bone that Jimmy had gotten for him, but I decided not to ask. The little dog without a name was yapping and chasing one of those slow moving trains, as if at that speed he could actually keep up with one. Jimmy waved to me with his cap, to assure me that Brutus was not going to be a problem.

As I got closer I was struck by how much Jimmy looked different and yet still the same. I guess I saw him both as he was and how he is now. The quick pace of a young man had been slowed by time and the effects of alcohol. We were always the same height but now with his shoulders stooped he looked shorter. He still wore those same Elvis-type sideburns from when we were in high school, only now they were grayer and thinner. The same unruly hair that had plagued him in his youth was still causing him trouble as it stuck out and flared up in a totally random manner. His mind was just as quick as back in the day, and his infectious laughter still made me lose control. Despite the hell he has gone through the last several years, he still manages to crack us both up.

It's strange and wonderful at the same time, that when you meet up with someone that meant so much to you in your childhood, you revert to the silliness of those times.

"How did you get here, on that bike your mother stole for ya?" Jimmy teased as I approached with my eyes on Brutus. The small dog had now tired of chasing trains and would lick the bone any time his big friend would let him near.

"That reminds me I still owe your sister a quarter," I shot back.

"It's a dollar now...you know, with inflation."

"A dollar!?! For that price, they better be inflated too."

We laughed and sat on the ground till the silliness passed. Some things never change and that's good, but the times change and you never know whether that will be good or not.

Jimmy invited me inside and all that he had now saddened me. There was no TV or any kind of modern appliance. The cast iron pot bellied stove was his means of warmth. An old Amana refrigerator was small but working. There was no bathroom as such, just a cracked and chipped porcelain sink and toilet about four feet from the stove, separated by a sheet of plywood. A mattress and a cot occupied the back room. The rest of the decor was stacked cans of beer and bottles of every kind of liquor the local store had to offer. There was the table and chair, and the small radio was now playing I'm Henry VIII, I Am by Herman's Hermits.

"Ya know, Jimmy, there's one thing the oldies stations here and in California have in common. They play the same sucky records over and over."

"That does rot. There will never be another BIG JAB."

The music was such a part of our world back then, and there were the girls who came in and out of our lives. Mostly for Jimmy back then it was a girl named Cheryl or "Frenchy" as he liked to call her...but that's another story for another time. And for me, of course, there was Cindy.

"How often do you go up to the cemetery now?" I asked as the reminiscing faded.

"Rarely when I'm sober. I put small flags by the military men before Memorial Day and the 4th of July. I pick up trash and try to mow that grass about every two weeks. That's about it. The rest of my time is Miller Time." With that he opened the refrigerator door and cursed that there was one beer can left. "Shit!...Ya want a Pepsi?"

"Yeah...and you have one too," I urged.

My heart was heavy for my old friend. "Jimmy, if I help you, will

166

you try again to get into a program?" *My Jimmy is a proud man, Charlie. He's a proud man.*

"Believe it or not I do have days where I think I can give it up; but then the memories of all I had and all I lost come calling, and I just give in. Meeting up again with you, Charlie, sure will help me try." He smiled and I saw him as he was.

"Jimmy, what do ya say we take a walk up there, just you and me?"

"If you want. I haven't been able to get in there since they threw the road block up around the place. I have never been bothered by those bees...probably Cindy had something to do with that...and, if what Cindy said is true, you have nothing to fear. Besides, with the clouds and drizzle, they should be inside their nests."

"I got prior approval that can get us through," I said as I showed him the document Feeney and Richardson had given me. "And," I added as I reached into my jacket, "I have a bottle of water just to be on the safe side."

"Uggg, water!" That stuff would kill me too!" he joked.

It was good to see him laugh and smile. If nothing else, this trip back to Portland was worth it to have Jimmy back in my life.

For the first time in a long time we set out on a trip together to our cemetery playground. I flashed my papers to the State Cops, and they allowed us through with a comment that we must be nuts to go into that place. Maybe we were, but Jimmy had not been bothered while doing his job and I have never been afraid there. I have no explanation of why I felt that way, I just did. And now, after hearing last night from Jimmy that Cindy had made me immune with her "special kiss", I felt more confident than ever. She really did touch my tonsils all those years ago. At least I didn't imagine *that*. I wasn't completely crazy.

The front gate had a yellow police banner across the wrought iron bars, but we easily went under it. The light rain continued to drop as my heart rate went up. I was back, not in my thoughts, but for real. There were no bees that we could see, but that didn't mean they couldn't see us. What is it in our senses that tells us that someone is watching when we can't see anyone? Whatever it is, it was alerting

Jimmy and me that we were not alone. The radio was back on in my mind, most likely triggered by the fact that it usually was on for real back when Jimmy and I were playing flies and grounders in the big open field. I heard the Cadillacs singing, <u>Peek-A-Boo</u> (I'm Watching You).

We walked slowly across the old baseball diamond toward home plate I looked up at the tall old elm tree, its branches drooping with a rich abundance of leaves. It could easily have concealed dozens of nests.

As my eyes took in the familiar surroundings, I turned to my best friend. "Jimmy, it's just the two of us. Was that story you told last night really true...or something you made up to scare away the kids?"

The current caretaker looked at me with honest eyes and said, "Every word was the truth, and I'm not certain that it is *just* the two of us. It's like we're back in the Old Buckley Place. Remember that Charlie?"

"Yeah, don't remind me."

Jimmy knew every nook and cranny in the cemetery, and I remembered most of them.

It hadn't slipped my mind, if by some chance Jimmy was right about Cindy and her powers; she could very well have been just a stones throw away. And she might not be alone.

The unique odor of that old cemetery that I remembered from long ago was still there. For the first time I realized that there was the smell of strawberries mixed in with the grass, the salty air, the dirt, and the death. Strawberry was *her* fragrance. It was Andrea's fragrance too, and for a moment I wondered if there was any other connection between the two. Other than their scent, they held mystery and beauty in common. I wondered...

Standing at the base of the old tree we surveyed the area around it. The memories of me with Cindy were overwhelming, including the first meeting...the other meetings...the last meeting. As I relived that summer in my mind, I asked Jimmy to retell the story of his last encounter with Cindy, and all she had said and done.

Jimmy brought along his poncho and spread it out on the ground under the tree. We sat with our backs against the old elm and he began again, repeating what he had told John Feeney and the Chief last night. It was the same story with the same warnings, the same bees, the same power over them, the same Evil One, and the same Cindy.

Suddenly, he sat up straight and said there was one other thing. "She mentioned that she and some others were banished from some place in Massachusetts in 1820. I didn't pay much attention to it at the time. I was still trying to digest the facts that she said she was over 250 years old and could command the bees to do her bidding." Jimmy grew more excited and stood up now. "There's something else, Charlie. She said she was a mind reader. If you had any kind of thought she could see it. She said that's how she knew your love for her was true, or at least your love for who you thought she was."

"Yes, I know. I thought it was just some kind of trick, like those gypsies did on the pier at the beach. You know...the kind that has such an obvious answer you can't see it...and when you find out how it's done, you feel like such an idiot. But it wasn't a trick with her...It was part of her nature. That's how she knew about the fried eggs and all the other impure thoughts I was having when I was around her. It was really embarrassing."

"I'll be jiggered! I'm embarrassed for you!"

"Thanks a big freakin' deal, Buddy. And you were the one that said beauty was only skin deep and we should *skin* her. She probably saw that on *your* mind."

"Cripes! I never thought about that. Let's come back some other time. If she's here, she might not be in a good mood."

"I'm not worried, she loves *me*," I teasingly bragged.

"Yeah, well just keep *thinking* that I'm your best friend, *my friend*." Jimmy smiled.

We punched each other in the arm. Cindy couldn't help but know that I loved Jimmy. He was as safe as I was as long as her power was stronger than the one she spoke of, the one she feared...the Evil One.

The drizzle halted and the sun started breaking through. Strangely the new light brought no new heat, just the opposite. Jimmy had finished telling his story again, and we sat there under the big elm quietly pondering it all. The chill in the air continued.

Then, over by the mausoleum where Bill O'Neal had thrown his soda bottle years ago and said there was someone chasing him...where one of those sorority girls lost her life while going to the bathroom... where her friends died too when they went looking for her...where young Paul Feeney and Steve Winchell had shot there BB guns...where just days ago I thought I saw a bare-breasted beauty beckoning to me...yes, there, by that massive burial mound I saw something.

"Look!" I whispered to Jimmy.

"What the frig is that?" he whispered back.

The figure, dressed all in black, wore a long cape and reminded me of the pictures of pilgrims we had seen in out elementary school history books. Only this wasn't Thanksgiving and we weren't at Plymouth Rock.

The evening sun, despite the cooling temperatures, seemed to be steaming the freshly fallen rain. It created a cloudy mist that covered his feet. The creature looked more like he was hovering rather than walking. He slowly moved back and forth in front of the tomb but took time to gaze our way. His facial features looked beastly from a distance. We weren't close enough to describe them in detail. Soon the normal odor turned foul like dead fish, just the way Kathy Kostenello had remembered it. The unknown being raised his hands, and an opening to the great crypt revealed a scarlet light as he stepped inside. The light and the stranger disappeared at the same time.

"I saw it but I'm not sure I believe it," said my best friend. "He must be the Evil One that Cindy was talking about, the one commanding the bees to kill."

"That's got to be the same thing that shocked Tony and the Kostenello girl. Hell, if he had grabbed me the way he grabbed her, I might have gone into a coma too," I fessed up.

We stood there, scared and curious. I realized that if Jimmy's story was correct, that *thing* was probably there during all those summers, all those ball games, and all through the lovemaking days with Cindy. He had been there since that Halloween night when we first came upon the grassy ball field. He might have watched us that night, but thanks to the power of Cindy, he was unable to harm us. When Jimmy ran out yelling to Tommy that there was some kind of zombie chasing him, Jimmy didn't realize how close to the truth he was. I didn't realize, as I sat behind a stone watching Jimmy play his trick, that something dead *and* alive could have grabbed me at any moment. Had we known he was there, Tommy would have gotten all *our* candy. We would have never gone back. I would have never met Cindy...had we known.

"Why doesn't he attack us like he did that college girl?" Jimmy asked.

"Why don't you go over there, knock on the door and ask him?"

"I'll be right behind you, Charlie." Jimmy patted me on the back.

"Why don't we get your sister? She'll do anything for a quarter." I said as I did a 360 degree turn around, looking for more surprises.

"Very funny, *my friend*, but she would probably scare him!"

We joked, but only used it as a crutch to help us through the moment. We huddled together and moved slowly like the time we were heading for the basement stairs in that haunted house on Carlton and Pine, just after Joe had warned us to be on the lookout for the Crocodile Man and the Boy Vampire.

"Well, we made it out of the Old Buckley House and we'll make it out of here." I said with wavering conviction.

Jimmy shook his head in agreement. "If that guy over by that crypt had on an Abe Lincoln hat, I would have been long outta here by now...and pissing my pants all the way"

"We better leave before we both do, and let Feeney and Richardson know that we indeed have a bigger problem up here than just bees. I have a feeling that bastard we just saw isn't going to be affected by pesticides."

"Shit, he's a poster boy for pesticides," Jimmy joked as we turned and hurried back to the front gate.

The sunlight was fading and the night wind was now calm. The chill in the air was leaving as well. When we got to the front gate we looked over at the mausoleum in the far distance, but nothing seemed out of place. All was quiet on the hill except for a faint buzzing sound.

18

The hotel room message center was flashing *urgent* when Jimmy and I arrived back at the Regency, and I thought to myself that nothing in my life was more urgent than anything else. Not anymore, not after all I've seen and heard these past few days.

I had talked Jimmy into staying with me. I not only wanted to keep an eye on him and help him with his problem, but I just enjoyed being back together with my old friend even under these weird and scary circumstances. Maybe I should say, especially under these weird and scary circumstances. Anyway, for Jimmy, it was like a trip to paradise to be here and not down at that dump by the tracks.

We had stopped by to leave enough food and water for Brutus and the little dog. It should last them till our next visit. With the lock busted on the shanty door they could come and go as they pleased.

Jimmy crashed on his bed and I checked my message. It was from Bernard Allen back in Oceanside. I felt like I was on a roller coaster with everything in my life now going faster and faster and another big dive was coming up. Hold on!

Nervously, I dialed. Quickly, he answered. "Allen residence."

"Barn, what's so urgent?"

"Charles, I'm glad you called. Are you okay?"

"I haven't lost my mind completely, but I'm getting close."

"Well, maybe I can help put you over the edge. By the way Mrs. Allen sends her love. She's sitting here watching over me like a mother hen to make sure I tell you that."

"Give her my best, Barn."

"I will. Now listen. Andrea dropped by today and we had a long talk. She feels terrible that she's given you the wrong impression. I told her how you felt, and that I hadn't told you her real reason for coming to Marshall High."

"Barn, if you knew everything that has been going on here that's not in the press, you would know that nothing could surprise me now. I can't wait to tell my class what *I* did on my summer vacation."

"Charles, I look forward to hearing you give that talk. But hold on to your hat, because I think I *can* surprise you...Andrea is flying to Maine the day after tomorrow."

"Holy Toledo, Ohio! I was wrong...that *is* something that surprises me...I'll be jiggered!"

"Why do you say that?"

"Oh, it's just something my best friend says when he hears or sees something totally unexpected. He picked it up from some old movie."

"Little Lord Fauntleroy."

"What?"

"'I'll be jiggered'! That's what one of the characters says a lot in that movie."

"Thank you, Roger Ebert! Now tell me why Andrea is coming to Portland?"

"She says it's something she feels she has to do. She doesn't want to tell you over the phone. She has a month before classes start, and she's not going to be talked out of it. You know, she reminds me of you in some ways. You can't talk her out of or into anything when she has her mind made up."

"Cute, Barn, is there anything else you want to tell me?"

"Yes, did you know she has some friends in Portland and she is going to stay with them?"

"Friends...here? She never told me that. You'd think she would have, knowing this is where I'm from. Geez! That girl is a puzzle! Did you know that before? Is that part of the secret you are holding back?"

"Charles, that's the first I've heard of it. Her friends will pick her up at the airport. She said she will call you when she gets into town. I gave her your cell phone number and the name of the hotel where you are staying."

"Barn, you are just a fountain of surprises."

"Ah, Charles, there is one other thing. I wasn't going to mention it, but I think maybe I should."

"Oh, tell me she's gone cruising with Bob Piconne in his little Corvette!"

"No, nothing like that. It's just that I have a feeling in my gut...

maybe it's from years in this job...but I feel there is something else she's holding back...even from me. I don't want to add to your anxiety, but there's something, Charles...something. I just don't know what. Be careful."

"Tell you what. I'm going to take a shower and bury myself under the covers, and just make the world go away...if just for a few hours."

"Sounds like a good idea, Charles. I think when you discover Andrea's *big* secret you'll be more at ease, and that will help you get some peace."

"How big? How much peace will I get?" I asked, hoping for a hint.

"Charles! Go to bed."

"What about that feeling in your gut? I wonder if that will give me peace when I find out about that?...if it proves to be reliable."

"I don't know, Charles...I hope I wasn't wrong for mentioning it."

"I'm glad you did. You're pretty observant for an old man. To tell you the truth, my gut has been telling me the same thing. There's something about her that just doesn't fit. Night, Barn. Kiss Georgia for me."

Wait! Who's an old man? We'll see who can run a mile the fastest when you get back here, Wiseguy...and call us when you've had a chance to speak with Andrea...and, Charles...we...ah...oh, you know"

"I know, I love you too."

I put down the phone and looked at Jimmy. He was already sawing wood and very loudly.

I crashed on my bed and stared at the ceiling till my eyes were feeling heavy, and I knew the dreams were not far off. I feared they wouldn't be pretty, not tonight. The radio in my mind was playing In Dreams by Roy Orbison and (The Candy-Colored Clown They Call The Sandman) sneaked into my room, sprinkled his freakin' star dust and told me everything was going to be all right. The lying little bastard!

There I was in the old cemetery playing ball with Jimmy. It was just getting dark. I hit a long fly ball and Jimmy chased it till he was out of sight. I was waiting and waiting for him to come back. When he finally did, he was all dressed in black; not like Johnny Cash. Cash never wore a cape and a tall stovepipe hat like Abe Lincoln did. As he got closer I could see it wasn't Jimmy He stopped near the pitcher's mound and said in a low sinister voice, "Hello, Charlie, my name is John Buckley and I've come to fetch you and Jimmy home. I'm going to cut him up into little pieces and feed him to my friend, the Crocodile Man. He does need his protein."

The fiend laughed so loudly that the lights from the surrounding houses all came on. It was then I could see Jimmy, and he was in a cage screaming for me to get him out.

"Don't pay any attention to him. He will soon be quiet," Buckley said in that low monotone voice that seemed to resonate among the tombstones.

"What are you going to do to me?" I asked as my heart was playing ping pong with my chest.

"Why, Charlie, I wouldn't harm you. I have special plans for you. You are going to be part of the *family*...Won't that be nice?" he said softly as he smiled through his rotted teeth. It was then I could smell dead fish and decay. He came closer, and I could see his face was gaunt and his flesh was peeling away and hanging loosely.

"You know, Charlie, I really didn't hang myself. That was just a wax dummy. My children thought of that one...the little devils."

As he laughed again I could now see two figures standing on each side of the cage that Jimmy was in.

"Come, Charlie, meet my children. Of course they are really not *my* children, but oh...how it does please me to think of them that way."

Standing to the right of the cage was a vicious looking little vampire with his fangs exposed and his face strained, as if contemplating his next victim...me!!!

"Calm down, Rudolph, Charlie is for your sister."

"Joe never said anything about a girl vampire when he told us your story," I said as if that would win me a get-out-of-cemetery-free card and we were playing a Transylvania version of Monopoly.

"Joe's an asshole!!!" he yelled and his grin grew more menacing.

Suddenly, I was back in the Old Buckley House on the corner of

STUNG

Pine and Carlton, and Jimmy was screaming, "CHARLIE! CHARLIE!!!" as they put his body through a giant meat grinder. His legs were ground like hamburger as his torso and head were slipping slowly toward the blades.

Behind him I could see my brother and some of my old friends.

The Crocodile Man had Tommy Caine in one claw and Bill O'Neal in the other. Joe's head was in the scaly monster's mouth, and he snapped it off like it was a green bean from Joe's own garden. The beast tossed Joe's head into the air with his teeth, caught it and swallowed it whole when it came back down. It wasn't long before he coughed Joe back up and spit him out, saying, "You taste putrid...ughhhh!"

Then he bit Bill's head off and repeated the procedure. O'Neal lasted a little longer in the Crocodile Man's gullet, and then he too was heaved as unceremoniously as Joe.

Tommy Caine was next and as Tommy's head sunk into the belly of the beast, the monster smiled. It was like watching Goldilocks and The Three Bears. Joe was too hot. Bill was too cold, but Tommy was just right.

In the corner was Disco Dana. He was covered in a giant cobweb and those huge African spiders were munching on his eyes like they were hor'deourves.

I stood helpless, like I was frozen solid and couldn't move. Suddenly I could smell strawberries. I was free of my bond and she was before me as Buckley smiled his evil grin and said, "Charlie, this is Andrea, one of my greatest treasures. She is from Crete and she is an illusionist. In other words, Charlie...what you see is *not* what you get." His fiendish laughter seemed to go on forever.

There was Andrea just as I had seen her last with her perfect face, her perfect smile. She was beautiful.

Jimmy was screaming in anguish as he gave up one organ after another. Finally he yelled, "Skin her, Charlie! Beauty is only skin deep!...SKIN HER!!!"

"Yes, Charlie, take this knife and see what I really am...your sweet little Andrea."

"Andrea, I could never hurt you."

"You're so pathetic. Let me show you the *real* me and she waved her arms and...

Jimmy started yelling, CHARLIE! CHARLIE! CHARLIE! Wake up! Wake up, Charlie! You must have been having a nightmare."

My eyes opened and there was Jimmy shaking me with a very concerned look on his face. "Are you all right?"

I gave myself time for my lungs to start breathing normal again, and then I looked at Jimmy and said, "Screw the Sandman!"

"What does that mean?"

"It means I ain't closing my eyes for the rest of the night."

Jimmy gave me a puzzled look and went back to sleep. I have no idea why his snoring didn't keep me awake anyway.

I clicked on the TV to see a replay of last night's Red Sox game. Why a Sox fan would want to watch a repeat of them getting their asses kicked again is beyond me but, hey, like I said before, "Whatever gets you through the night is all right."

Jimmy got up early and we took the walk down to Becky's Diner. I had a lot on my plate, and not just scramble eggs. There was the continuing mystery of Cindy, the eight deaths in the cemetery, those tiny killer bees, that *thing* near the mausoleum, getting Jimmy to visit his mother and checked into AA, a visit to Tony to fill him in on the latest happenings, and Andrea coming here to lay another bomb on me. And I hadn't forgotten that George Chamberlain was still on the loose. Hell, if he knew Jimmy and I were back in town, he might forget Feeney and come after us. We're probably just another two cats as far as he's concerned. *ONE 's an accident! SIX is goddamn cruel*!!!

As we sat at a booth in the corner, quietly eating our breakfast, a tap on my shoulder was followed by, "Hey, Mr. Sullivan, if that's your real name."

I looked up to see the smiling face of Monroe, my bellboy buddy from the hotel. Next to him was a bearded man wearing an army fatigue jacket with peace signs all over it. He had on granny glasses like John Lennon used to wear.

"Hey, Monroe, I haven't seen you around lately...And what do you mean, if that's my real name?"

"No offense, Dude. I ain't workin' for the man no more. Me and Jeff (he points to his friend) are in business for ourselves. We are uncovering the truth about the great mysteries of the world."

"Yeah, Man...great mysteries," added Jeff.

"You mean like flying saucers and little green man?" I asked. "You still think we are being invaded by aliens from outer space?"

"That ain't all, Man. There's Bigfoot, the Loch Ness Monster, those crop circles over in Europe, and all kinds of ghosts. And there was once even a haunted house right here in town. It was located on the corner of Pine and Carleton, but one night it mysteriously toppled over. They say the owner and occupants are still *alive* even to this day and..."

Before Monroe could finish with his list, Jeff interrupted, "And don't forget E.T...He's based on a real dude. Spielburg just didn't make that shit up, Man."

They nodded to one another in affirmation as Jimmy and I looked at each other, as if to say, *Who the hell let these two out of their rubber rooms?*

"So, Monroe, you still haven't told me why you think my name isn't Sullivan."

"Cause I seen ya on TV when you were up at Maine Med., being waved through that bunch of reporters like you were really important."

"He's important to me," Jimmy quipped. "He's buying this breakfast."

"Very funny, Dude, but me and the Jeffster here think you may be a government agent, sent to find out if there are really aliens in that cemetery up there."

"Yeah, secret agents wouldn't use their real names," said the man with the granny glasses.

"Tell me guys, if there are little green men up there from Planet Zenon, do you think they want their pictures taken? Do you think they are going to pose next to their spaceship waiting for you to set the proper exposure? Are you going to ask them to say, *CHEESE*?"

"Hey, Man, don't laugh. They probably want their story told, but no one's been brave enough to sit down with them and listen to them."

"Yeah, and maybe they'll give us a ride and teach us all kinds of neat things," Jeff said.

Monroe now blushed as he added, "And they might take us with them from world to world when they have sex with all the women. Jefferoonie and me, we can help them with that."

"Ya, women. We'll help get them women...yeah...Whatever we can do to represent our country."

The two were now just staring up at the ceiling lost in thoughts of fame and debauchery.

"You boys have quite the imagination," I said loudly, kicking them out of their trance.

"Huh...ya...well...you have to use your imagination. All the dirt ain't out in the open, Man. That's why ya gotta look under the rocks."

"Yeah," said Jeff, "And that's why if you see two dudes behind ya don't worry. We won't get in the way, but we got our camcorder (he taps oh his back pack) and if we can capture those space guys on film, no one will say we're are imaginin' nothin'." The two would-be ghost busters high-fived each other.

"You two just be careful messing in things that are going on around here," I warned.

"YEAH!!! Only a secret government agent would talk like that," Monroe exclaimed.

I looked at Jimmy and he said, "They got you, Double O-6...ah...Charlie. Better call the Bureau and tell the big boss there are two guys in Maine that are on to us."

I left a twenty on the table and our two friends behind with their mouths wide open, frozen in their tracks.

As we got to the door, Jimmy flashed them the Vulcan sign and said, "Live long and prosper."

They saluted back in the same way, their mouths still open.

When we arrived at John Feeney' office, Chief Richardson and District Attorney Brian DeWolfe were with the lawyer. Dewolfe was not buying the story that Jimmy had told.

"Do you expect me to believe a 300-year-old woman is *above* ground in that cemetery, and that she talks to the bees and they do her bidding? And now add to this fantasy that there's some monster grabbing innocent young girls when they stumble across his path! Be reasonable man. Only a small frightened child would believe such drivel."

"Of course it's hard to believe," said Feeney. "Detective Reza confirms the same sighting as the Kostenello girl. Now, granted, it may be some asshole in a Halloween costume, but he obviously has something to do with this whole mess."

"I'm sorry, John. I know your son was your life, but you are just grasping for straws trying to get some closure. If this crap gets into the press, you and the Chief will be locked up in the looney bin, and I just may give them the keys!"

"Brian, you are a good friend and a hell of a D.A., but if you get in my way while I'm tracking down Paul's killer, I'll have your license to practice revoked!" the lawyer promised loudly with the veins in his neck pulsating.

"All right, let's calm down," suggested the Chief as he stepped between them. "This whole thing is making us all upset. We all have the same objective. Let's not make threats that we would never say under normal circumstances."

Feeney and Dewolfe looked at each other and sat down, knowing the Chief was being reasonable.

The brief silence that followed was broken when Feeney's secretary ran into the office.

"Kim, what's going on? Never come in here without buzzing me first. You know better than that! When that door is closed, it's closed for a reason," lectured the lawyer.

"Quick, John, turn on the TV. There's a news bulletin on Channel 6."

There on TV was the next shoe to drop. News anchor Pat Callahan was about to interview Abigail Kostenello, the bible-thumping, scripture-quoting mother of the surviving sorority girl.

"Ladies and Gentlemen, we are here in Monument Square talking with Abigail Kostenello whose daughter was one of the girls attacked in the cemetery and left in a coma. She has come forward to reveal her daughters name, and to give us new details about the events in and around the Western Cemetery."

The reporter turned to his informer and asked, "Mrs.Kostenello, can you please tell us how your daughter is doing?"

"My Katherine is coming along fine. She is still under a lot of medication and is not a hundred percent yet. But, with the help of the Lord and with my care, she should be coming home soon and away from this evil city."

"Did she say who her attacker was or give a description?"

The righteous woman looked directly into the camera and raised her bible, "I am here, His voice in the wilderness, to tell you people to repent and set your path back to the Lord. Here in this town there is an unnatural evil sent directly from the bowels of Hell. He or it attacked my Katherine...not realizing she is protected by ME and Almighty God!"

Callahan tried to get in another question but Abigail Kostenello was in her moment, "I give you fair warning, Citizens of Portland. These could very well be the final days. This may be your last chance. You vile non-believers are in danger of losing your immortal souls. Turn away from lust and greed, and hear me! Get down on your knees because the evil is coming for you and your children."

The newsman was trying to interrupt, as he realized he had lost control of the interview, "Mrs. Kostenello...Mrs. Kostenello... Mrs...Please let me ask you if you can describe your daughters attacker?"

"He is one of the *undead*, all dressed in black. His breath smells of decay. He spits fire and he has the strength of a thousand horses. And if you look directly into his eyes he will stop your heart from beating. He..."

The TV screen went black and the station put up a company logo.

We looked out on to Monument Square through the lawyer's open windows. There were already people running in the streets. Crowds were heading for the police station to demand action, *now*. You could hear others saying they were going home to get their guns. Abigail Kostenello was urging them to march on the cemetery and help her defeat the beast that lives there. We could still hear her yelling, "Re-

STUNG

pent, you heathens!!!"

Feeney snapped a pencil in two and threw it out the window at the ranting woman. "Chief, you better get back to the Station and call up every available man you have. That stupid bitch has just ruined all out attempts to keep the town from panicking. Have her locked up for disturbing the peace before she can do anymore damage."

Brian Dewolfe, now falling in line behind Feeney, suggested we call the news outlets with an official press release that refuted what had just been broadcast.

Police sirens began wailing as reinforcements were sent to help the State Boys, guarding the perimeter around the old cemetery, maintain the peace.

"What about the plans to spread that pesticide?" I asked.

As he left Feeney's office Chief Richardson said we would have to put it on hold till we were sure the area was secured.

Within an hour Feeney had the Kostenello woman arrested. And by the time the six o'clock news came on, the Chief was on all the channels explaining that she was not well. He said as the result of almost losing her daughter, she had been given medication that had a bad reaction with other medicines she was already taking for schizophrenia. The lies mixed with some truths did put a lid on the panic in the city, and by sundown the level of excitement was almost back to the way it was before Abigail Kostenello grabbed her fifteen minutes of fame.

19

I could hear Tony Reza laughing as Jimmy and I approached his hospital room. Upon entering we found him out of his bed, dressed and ready to go home. The pretty nurse, who was in the Emergency Room when he was admitted, was now trying to explain to him that he had to sit in a wheelchair as he left the Hospital. "It's Hospital policy."

"Charlie, glad to see you…Ah…This is my nurse…Ah…Kelly Beane."

The nurse nodded in recognition. "Can you help me convince Mr. Reza to use the wheelchair until he gets outside the Hospital?" There was a look of frustration mixed with a flirtatious smile on the nurse's pretty face.

"I think you'll just have to shoot him. It looks like a perfect case of justifiable homicide," I said as I introduced them both to Jimmy.

"Hey!...That's the cemetery caretaker!" exclaimed the Detective.

"He's also my best friend." I surprised him. "If you can stop fooling around with the nurses long enough, I'll fill you in on all you've been missing."

"Ah…Miss Beane, you have my number. If you have to get in touch with me for *any* reason don't hesitate to call," Tony said in a voice void of emotion but with a look that said, *Maybe we could get some coffee sometime.*

"Oh yes, I think I have your number all right," chuckled the nurse as she motioned for her patient to sit his ass down.

It was then that Maria Reza walked in, just in time to hear the flirtation going on. "I guess you are feeling much better young man!"

Nurse Beane saw her chance to take advantage of Maria's presence. "Maybe you can talk him into the wheel chair so I can release him properly,"

"Tony, get in that chair now!"

My young friend argued no more. He knew who the boss was.

"Can you teach me your methods?" laughed the nurse as she wheeled her patient out of the room and toward the elevator.

Outside. Detective Reza asked if we could meet him over at his house and catch him up to date on the things that weren't in the news. I looked to his mother for approval. I knew who the boss was too. Approval was granted.

The Reza house was on Melbourne Street in the Munjoy Hill area of the old city. It was a working-class neighborhood where neighbors usually had been the same neighbors for a very long time. Chances are they knew your business and you knew theirs. It reminded me of the lower half of Pine Street where I grew up. It wasn't pretentious but it was friendly, a good place to settle down and raise a family. The Reza's shared their small white clapboard home with a golden retriever by the name of Riley, who just continued lying on the coach as we entered. His eyes gave us a glance as if that was his normal greeting to strangers. His senses told him we meant no harm to his family or surroundings. Either that or he was just too lazy and comfortable to give a rat's patuti that strangers were entering.

"Get your fat ass off that couch! How many times do I have to tell you? You want your dinner, you better move now, Dog!!!" Maria commanded.

The dog jumped up like he had been laying on a hot plate and ran like a greyhound as he left the comfort of his former surroundings. He also knew who the boss was.

He's a real tiger," I said to Jimmy. "Let's bring him by to meet Brutus and the little dog when we feed them next time."

"We won't have to feed my bad-ass dog. He'll just eat that lazy bugger."

"Naw, Brutus can't be that mean!" I said as Maria busied herself brushing Riley's long golden hairs off her small but comfortable looking couch.

"I'm not talking about Brutus. I mean the little dog!" Jimmy punched me in the shoulder.

Having him with me made this whole ordeal seem much saner.

"You two just keep teasing my dog and I'll take a bite out of you," warned Maria Reza as she vacuumed up the remaining dog hair.

She would have done it too. I thought to myself that you didn't need a watch dog with Maria around. Pity the poor bastard who tries to break in her house, a place that was filled with pictures of her only child plus citations from the Department and trophies from his days playing baseball for Portland High. It was obvious that she took pride in her home. Simple as it was, she tried to keep everything looking showroom new. On the table by the TV was a young picture of Maria with a smiling policeman who must have been Tony's father. A small American flag stood on each side. I thought of the inscription on Cindy's locket and how appropriate its meaning would have been for Maria and the man she had given her heart to back in Brooklyn. *Lest we forget.*

The rest of the home had furniture that was a mix-match of different colors and woods, some cherry, some pine, some maple. It wasn't furnished like the elegant homes nearer the water, but I'm betting none were cleaner of more homey-feeling. She scared me to death, but I had come to like and respect Maria Reza more and more with each passing day.

Having changed into some comfortable clothes Tony settled in a big old recliner, while his mom brought us ice tea and home made cookies.

"Did you frost the glasses first?" I asked, as I thought of Georgia Allen, *I always frost the glasses first. That's what makes my lemonade taste so good.*

"Frost the glasses? You want your glass frosted? Go stick it in the freezer along with your head! I'm not a waitress, although this one doesn't know it." Maria said as she pointed to her son who had that *why-are-you-picking-on-me* look on his face. "Frost your glass...You're lucky I don't frost you ass!" She smiled, pleased with her remarks.

I didn't bother to ask if she had *bought* the cookies herself. Maria didn't seem to have Georgia Allen's sense of humor. Jimmy and I sat on the couch next to the friendly golden retriever who had slowly crept back into the living room. He was now on his back on the hardwood floor with his legs in the air just waiting for anybody, even a complete stranger, to rub his belly. So I obliged as Maria pulled up a chair next to her son.

I began first and told them how Jimmy became Wendle Bronson and of his seeing the chain and locket when he met with Cindy on that Saturday evening so long ago. I let it all hang out, telling them about her powers, her age, and her warning to Jimmy—that if the locket was ever found out of her possession it meant a great evil had been unchained. Tony and Maria listened as intently as had Feeney and Richardson. The story was hard for me to tell and maybe harder for them to believe.

Maria finally said, "Geez! What a bitch to have stood you up like that! She should at least have written you a note."

Jimmy spoke, saying Maria probably wouldn't want to say that to Cindy's face.

"Bring her on. I'll kick her ass," said the defiant woman as she refilled our glasses.

"Mom, you ain't back in Brooklyn anymore." said her only child. "And remember, everything you are hearing about this case is not for public knowledge. Don't go blabbing to your customers down at the shop."

"Well, Maria, if what Jimmy says is true, you may have a chance to take her on if you go up to the old cemetery," I added.

"Hey, if she is up there, I'll do it...if she comes near my Tony. Besides it should be much easier to kick a 300-year-old ass." She cracked herself up.

Tony then stood up in a way that conveyed something important was about to be spoken. "Charlie, do you remember I said I had a theory?

"I remember. Does any part of what I just said fit anywhere in your theory?"

We listened closely as he went on, "I thought there may be a tie in with the history of that cemetery. I did some checking with the news-paper archives to see if there had been any other deaths in or around the place. Let me show you what I found on microfilm."

Tony showed us a copy and read the account of an old newspaper story:

Dateline: August 1,1858: The city awakened yesterday morning to find that a third body has been discovered in the Western Cemetery. Like the others, there doesn't seem to be any wounds or bruises on the body. The young girl has been identified as Helen Pruitt, the daughter of businessman Michael Pruitt and his wife Agatha. The bereaved parents said their daughter often cut through the cemetery to get to a friends house on Danforth Street. Police Chief Ed Grotto has warned everyone to stay out of the cemetery until his men have had a chance to investigate these matters more thoroughly. Young Miss Pruitt will be buried in that very same cemetery on Thursday after a small graveside service.

Detective Reza theorized there might have been earlier deaths under similar circumstances, but the archives didn't go back any farther. However he had found two other articles, one from a newspaper in 1900:

Portland Police located the bodies of two Portland High School students in the Western Cemetery yesterday. The boy and girl were seniors and reported sweethearts. Joseph King and Annie Simpson had been thought to have run away to get married over the objections of the Simpson family. It is now feared that they made their way to the cemetery where they took their own lives by swallowing poison. Police arrived at this conclusion as no wounds or bruises were found on either Mr. King or Miss Simpson. Their nude bodies were found embracing each other. A letter was found next to the bodies where apparently young Annie had started to write a note. Police revealed the only word written was "Bee". It is assumed the poison took hold before she could complete her words.

We all looked at each other with strengthened beliefs as Tony continued, "The third story was in the July 16th, 1927 edition of the Portland Evening Express."

STUNG

The rash of mysterious deaths that have plagued the West End continued yesterday as two transients were found dead in the old cemetery. This brings the total to six in the last three months. The first two were runaway teen boys from Houlton. The second and third were the two elderly ladies from the local garden club who were said to have gone looking for rare flowers. Police Chief Thomas Savail said the only thing all six had in common, other than being found in the cemetery, was the lack of cause of death. None of the bodies had any wounds or cuts that would have been caused by a gun or a knife. There were no visible marks on the necks to indicate any kind of strangulation. It is thought that the killer might have suffocated all six, possibly by putting a cloth or bag over their heads and holding it tight. A thorough search of the cemetery has turned up no clues. Savail theorized that the killer probably was a bum who rode the rails and got out of town by climbing into an open boxcar down by the busy railroad yards. The Chief said the Boston and Maine Railroad had been asked to check their cars more thoroughly in hopes the killer would be found, or at least convinced to move on when he felt the tighter security.

"That's very interesting, Tony, but the conclusion of the police in those last two stories might be accurate." I stated. "The letters on that so-called suicide note left by those two kids might have been part of another word."

"Well, the conditions of the bodies and the location in that cemetery don't sound like a coincidence to me. Surely it must be considered as some kind of tie-in," concluded the Detective.

"Is it too late to have the bodies exhumed to find out for sure how they died?" Jimmy asked.

"It wouldn't hurt to ask Frank Blanchette, "I suggested.

"There are two other things." Tony added. "I cross-checked with the police archives and the exact locations of the bodies in 1858,

MIGHTY JOHN MARSHALL

1900 and 1927 were found around the big mausoleum."

"Do we know who's buried there?" I asked.

I could tell Tony was not comfortable with the answer he was about to give. He looked at his mom with that *now-don't-get-scared* look. "I did some checking with the Maine Historical Society. That entire big structure is the tomb of Cynthia Manchester. It was built in 1820. She was not from an extremely wealthy family, but that big structure was built to inter just *her* body. I had a theory that old cemetery held the clues, but I never thought the major clue would be a 300-year-old girlfriend of yours, Charlie. But after hearing your story and what your friend Jimmy says, I don't mind telling you I am becoming a believer in your fantastic tale."

We all said quietly, thinking about Tony's findings.

Maria Reza spoke, almost hesitantly "So, Baby, you are saying that Charlie's lost love, Cindy, might be Cynthia Manchester?"

The Detective just shrugged his shoulders and said, "Could be."

"Tony, you said there was one other thing?" I reminded him.

"It may be just another coincidence but I asked Joe Kupo, the Weatherman over at Channel 6, to check the conditions during those time frames. Just like June and July of this year, there was a long drought in 1858, 1900 and 1927 just before the killings."

"You are one hell of a detective, my young friend. You better tell Feeney and the Chief about your findings."

"I wrote it all up and gave it to them and Brian Dewolfe this morning." Tony confessed.

"Well, where do you go from here?" Jimmy asked.

"Richardson said they'll try and spray again tomorrow," the Detective answered. "The question is, what are you going to do next, Charlie? Are you going up there again?"

They all looked at me in anticipation of my answer.

"I'll go with you, Charlie," Jimmy offered.

"Thanks, Buddy. I've got to try to see if she is really there...just one more time before they spray the pesticides. I want to get as close to that mausoleum as possible. There might be some kind of writing or inscription on there that could give us some answers."

"But what about that beastly-looking character we saw guarding

189

that tomb?"

"Hey, that's probably what I saw too when we were driving down Cassidy Hill," Tony added. "Maybe I should go with you."

"You ain't going near there, Tony! You are supposed to be resting for the next few days," insisted his mother.

"Charlie, you guys should wear those bee keeper suits I have in the trunk."

"No, I don't think so. If something goes wrong and I have to run I don't want to be slowed down by one of those clumsy suits."

"Me either," Jimmy added.

"I will take some bottles of fresh water. The Kotenello girl said when she threw some water on her attacker he let her go. When she said that, I remembered how Cindy would never come out in the rain. It seems to tie in with your theory, Tony. She or they are active during a drought and have an unusual fear of water Cindy even told Jimmy that. Why that is I'm not sure yet, but it won't hurt to be bring some along."

Maria jumped up, scaring the lazy dog now sleeping at my feet. "Hold on! I've got an idea. I'll be right back."

Tony's mother disappeared down the basement stairs and soon we could hear boxes crashing and things breaking, and above the noise Maria's voice yelling, "What the hell did I do with that shit?"

Within a few minutes she was back with a big smile on her face and two giant toy guns in her hands.

"Tony, do you remember these? They are your G.I Joe Jumbo Bazooka Squirt Guns!"...You know...from when you were a kid?"

"You kept those all this time?"

"Oh, Baby, a mother doesn't throw those childhood mementos away."

Tony's mom shoved one in my hand and one in Jimmy's "Fill those suckers up with water and bring them with you...Isn't that a good idea?" She searched our faces for approval.

"I think that's a hell of an idea, Mrs. Reza," Jimmy said.

"You are a friend of Charlie, you call me Maria."

"Not a bad idea, not a bad idea at all," I inserted as I squeezed the trigger to check mine out.

· "You better think it's a good idea too, Tony, or I'll bring out your baby pictures."

"No, not that!" he protested with a blushing face. "It's a great idea!"

The mother smiled, pleased with herself that her plan had been accepted.

"And take a walkie-talkie and keep in touch with the perimeter cops," Tony insisted. "They can be there in a flash. We'll tell them when you go in."

"Well, tell them I'm going in this evening. I have another important personal meeting tomorrow with a friend from California."

"Is it your girlfriend coming to see you, Charlie?" asked Maria Reza with an unusual quiet voice, the beam now off her face.

"To be honest with you, Maria, she's coming all this way to tell me why she can't be my girlfriend."

"Oh that's too bad," she smiled.

"See, Charlie, I told you my mother liked you."

"You keep quiet and go to bed and get some rest," his mother said now in her normal tone.

"Do me a favor," asked the Detective who had become such a good friend. "Be careful...and call me, or come see me afterwards, no matter what time it is."

"Yes, Charlie, be careful," Maria said as she gave me a hug."

20

Brutus had an appetite that was unusual even for a dog his size. He would eat anything from Spam to corn flakes. He didn't like anything that was nutritionally recommended by a veterinarian. He was a lot like Jimmy and I were when we were kids...junk food junkies. Okay, like I still was. Brutus especially liked chocolate bars, and Jimmy would always keep some on hand for those times when Brutus was not in the mood to obey. Flash a Baby Ruth or an O Henry his way and the Big Brute would do any trick in his repertoire. He was a force to be reckoned with, but he was a slave to his sweet tooth.

After feeding the little dog, which still had no name other than, *here boy*...Jimmy, Brutus who was chomping on a Snickers Bar, and I made our way to the cemetery. With our jumbo bazooka squirt guns filled with Poland Spring's best water and a police walkie-talkie clipped on my belt, we were ready for whatever would come our way in the old stomping grounds of our youth. At least, that's what we thought.

We made contact once again with the perimeter State Cops, and, once again, they told us we were nuts. But they would be standing by if we called. They had each been issued special protective gear to keep the tiniest bees from getting in. When we told them of the potency of water, they looked at each other as if none of them was going to be the first to trade in his sidearm for a squirt gun. They did agree to take it under advisement as they tried to contain their giggles and guffaws.

"You got a license to carry a squirt gun that size?" one of them joked.

"Did your Mommy buy you that for your 50th birthday?" screeched another.

"Better be safe than sorry," Jimmy said as he fired a test squirt at Brutus who barked in protest. "Besides, if the water doesn't work there's always my puppy here."

"If he's a puppy, I'd hate to see his mother," another of the State Troopers shouted after us as we headed for our destination.

Jimmy replied in a barely audible voice, "He probably weighs a lot less than yours."

With that little remark we continued on with the cop yelling, "Hey!!! What did you say about my mother?"

For two best friends who had spent so many days in that place there was now apprehension, but nothing you could really call fear. Of all those concerned, only Jimmy and I could understand how we each felt. You might say we were going home and home is usually the safest place of all. We were like two kids trying to explain to our parents that we did know the dangers out in the world, but parents never quite believe it...and we can't quite believe the level of their concern. *Don't ride your bike down Cassidy Hill.* It's just the way it is. This time their concern might have been justified and home might not be all it's cracked up to be.

I had also noticed that Jimmy had not had a drink for about two days, at least not that I had seen. Maybe all the excitement had taken his mind off his personal demons. We were both caught up in this strange mystery and the girl, woman, or *thing* that was the center of it all.

We were now passing by the very spot where I had first seen Cindy walking by...her tan legs, long and lean...those bleached white shorts and that bellybutton-revealing black tank top...her blond ponytail swishing back and forth like a hypnotist with a slowly swinging watch. *Your eyes are getting heavy...sleepy...soon you will be under my power.*

The temperature was getting cooler and the skies were clear as we entered through the front gates on Vaughn Street. It was just after six, but it was eerily quiet. The wind, which was fairly gusty, didn't make it's normal whistling sounds through the maples, oaks, and elms that shared the grounds. Jimmy remarked that even for a cemetery it seemed very still. Brutus plodded his way next to us with his nose to the ground, stopping now and then to scratch away at a piece of turf. My memory was doing the same. The whole place seemed much smaller than I had remembered it. I guess, as I thought of it over the years and of the joy it had brought me in my youth, I made it bigger in my mind because of its importance. We do that with those we love too.

STUNG

When I was a kid, I looked up at my dad and thought he was ten feet tall. We were on eye level when I became an adult. Yet as he lay in his coffin with his old army outfit reciting, "So long, My Buddy", he looked tiny, withered down by old age and emphysema. But in my memory he was still ten feet tall...maybe taller.

The sweet scent of strawberries, *her scent*, was growing stronger as we neared the big crypt. I had never really paid much attention to that mausoleum back in our baseball days. Other than Bill O'Neal using it as a dumpster, I never gave it much thought. *I think I woke it up. Run you guys. Let's get outta here.* It was just something I was aware of but didn't check out. Built mostly of brick and heavy metal, it had heavy vegetation hanging over it's sides and entrance. The archives said it was built for just one, and yet, the huge iron door covered with long gnarly vines suggested that the builders were making it ready for other relatives when their time came.

We were about twenty-five feet from the entrance when Brutus started to growl down deep in his throat. His big ears shot straight up and his fur began to bristle. His barks followed, quick and sharp. Then he sank down on his heavy paws and started slowly crawling. His panting was growing faster as if his instincts told him danger was near. The huge dog looked at Jimmy and me as if to say, *You sure you two assholes know what you're doing*?

Jimmy and I didn't speak. Our body language was perfectly clear. We both readied our water guns at the same time in anticipation of the hulk that looked like a giant pilgrim. But as of yet there was no sign of him or should I say, *IT*.

Hopefully we wouldn't panic the way Tony had. To be fair, no one would have been prepared for such a fright. After all it was the middle of the day under a sunny sky when the Detective was surprised by horror. Birds were singing, and in the nearby neighborhoods the sound of children's laughter carried down the hill. No one would expect to see the boogieman under such conditions. Maybe that's why it was so scary. It was so unexpected. Usually monsters like to hide in the shadows of night...but this thing just didn't give a sweet shit.

I had never been so close to the mausoleum before; and now, about a foot from reaching out and touching it, I could see the words on the rusting plate. I stepped forward as Jimmy brushed leaves, twigs, and dirt to the side:

> HERE LIES THE BODY OF
> CYNTHIA MANCHESTER.
> RE INTERRED 1820.
> MAY GOD HAVE MERCY ON HER SOUL
> AND PROTECT US FROM HER KIND.

I read the words over and over, out loud at first, and then quietly to myself as I attempted to digest their meaning.

Jimmy broke the silence. "Charlie, why does it say that?...*from her kind?* Are there others like her or just that big creep we saw the other night?"

"I...don't...know," I said slowly as I ran my fingers over the words. As if my doing so would help me glean more meaning. "Why does it say *re-interred*? Was she buried someplace else and then reburied here?"

"I've mowed the grass around here for the last several years, but I've never paid attention to these inscriptions. I guess the leaves and vines made them go unnoticed. Of course, in my advanced state of inebriation, I didn't even notice or give a second thought to the whole creepy building."

Brutus was now crying like a bear caught in a steel trap, yet he was perfectly free. The growl and quick sharp barks had gone and fear had now gripped him. It was if he knew what was on the other side of that iron door. He began running in circles like he had gone mad. He was shaking his head back and forth, tossing slugs of sloppy spit into the still night air. Jimmy grabbed him and started pulling him further away from the crypt. With each step back, Brutus seemed to get quieter and less anxious. Both he and Jimmy headed for the old elm tree. The big dog settled down under its branches as Jimmy cradled his head. I could hear an occasional half-hearted bark and then nothing. Brutus had surrendered. It was just me and my trusty squirt gun now.

Suddenly I heard it. The voice came from nearby, perhaps behind the tomb. But if Brutus was right, it may have come from within. It was loud and deep, in a Darth Vader mode. "You would be wise to leave now. She who protects you will soon not have the power to hold me and my followers back. Then we will destroy you and all those who come against us."

I tried to yell to Jimmy, but my words failed to leave my throat. It was like being back on the eves of the Old Buckley Place on that Halloween weekend when that mysterious creature chased Jimmy and me up the stairs. We had tried to yell to Joe and the others but the words just froze in the air. It was the same now...I was helpless to speak.

The strawberry fragrance that had been so pleasing to me was now replaced by the stink of rot and decay, like dead fish decomposing in the hot midday sun.

Before I could take a step back, thousands of tiny bees came streaming out of some invisible hole in the giant crypt. The buzzing sound grew as they hovered in front of me. I was having trouble breathing. For the first time in memory I was no longer comfortable in my cemetery playground. This was not the same place where Jimmy and I had our most fun, playing an innocent game of "flies and grounders" and eating Italian sandwiches on those routine Saturdays of long ago...Not the same place where I fell in love with a strange and beautiful girl. I was as frightened as a child lost in the woods, and darkness was descending.

Again the warning came, but it was much more personal and frightening. "Charlie Sullivan, I could have killed you years ago if not for that wench. Soon she will be powerless against me, and YOU will DIE!!!"

When he said my name I felt a weakness in my whole body, and I was cloaked in fear. Slowly, and with great difficulty, I started stepping away from the bees and the sound of that terrifying voice. My finger didn't even have enough strength to pull the trigger on the jumbo bazooka water gun. As for the walkie-talkie, it might as well have been home. I wouldn't have been able to make it work, not then...and if I could, the cops on the other end would have only heard... static! Fear was totally in charge now.

I looked toward Jimmy again. He was still comforting the nervous beast that had become his pet. The fact that Brutus had been equally scared was no comfort to my manhood. The old elm was about five hundred feet away and I slowly crept toward it. Jimmy waved me on in encouragement. I tried to run but my legs wouldn't hear of it. It was if they were saying, *You're lucky that we will even walk.* But ever so gingerly I moved forward. I must have looked like Boris Karloff with that Frankenstein strut.

Suddenly, I could see someone coming up the other way in back of Jimmy, Brutus, and that big elm. It was a girl all dressed in white with long blond hair flowing in the evening breeze which had picked up with her presence. The smell of strawberries was coming back. I couldn't see her face yet, but my heart was praying it was her. I still couldn't get any words out so I pointed to Jimmy to look behind him. All of a sudden Brutus jumped up and almost knocked Jimmy over. The giant dog started running toward her as if to attack, but instead stopped in front of her. Quickly, he laid down with his tail tucked between his legs in submission. She bent down and patted him gently. I looked back and the bees were following behind me as if to remind me that danger was just a wave of the hand away. I felt safe as far as they were concerned, but Jimmy was not immune. His life depended on how much power Cindy still had against the big creep in the crypt.

Jimmy was speechless as I joined him. My voice was now coming back as I reached the spot that once had been home plate. I could see her clearly now. The fear I had just known was leaving and the love I had always known was returning.

She was still magical. She was still beautiful. She was still seventeen. She *was* Cindy. I wanted to run to her and hold her, but so much had changed since our last meeting. I stood there with Jimmy waiting for fate to make the next move.

Brutus was now facing our way with Cindy by his side. He seemed to have found his missing courage, as if he just returned from Oz. Cindy's new protector started barking warnings, but it was not at Jimmy and me. It was directed toward the shadowy black figure which was again outside the big tomb, and walking back and forth throwing menacing glances our way.

Cindy approached, and, with a wave of her hand, sent the bees toward the big old crypt. They obeyed like loyal servants and disappeared inside. The Evil One followed behind to fight another day. Then Cindy walked slowly toward me.

Even though I knew in my gut this day and this moment would come, I was still trembling in disbelief that it was finally here.

With the evening sun bathing her in bright rays, her hair shone...as if under a halo. She looked like an angel. It's funny the things that can go through your mind when your senses are out of whack, at least the things that can go through my mind. For a second I thought about looking around to see if I could spot Della Reese while the radio in my head was playing Bobby Vee and <u>Devil Or Angel</u> (Whichever You Are, I Love You).

She was within my reach again and she beckoned me closer. "Charlie, I knew you would come. I knew you would."

I didn't speak right away. What do you say to the love of a lifetime when you haven't seen her in a lifetime? Jimmy nudged me and moved me forward with a reassuring pat on the back.

I approached slowly, soaking up that rare beauty that was hers. "Cindy...I don't know what to say. I've waited for this moment for so long. My feelings are all mixed up...but I know I still love you."

She took my hand and pulled me to herself with an amazing gentle strength. She looked into my eyes and studied them as if reading a message. She smiled. "Charlie, yours is a true heart and my heart will always belong to you."

She kissed me long and deep and held me tight. I took comfort in her arms and said, "I feel like *I* am seventeen again."

Jimmy stepped back as if he were not part of the moment. He finally whispered slowly and loud enough to make me hear, "Charlie!!!...your hair...is blond again...There are no wrinkles on your face. You look like you did in high school...You *are* seventeen again!"

Cindy turned and gave a smile to Jimmy. He had been told many years ago of her powers and had kept his promise. She was pleased with him and told him so. Jimmy developed an awe-shucks attitude as he kicked his leg back and forth. He was now completely at ease, but gave two old loves their space and took Brutus back toward the front gate. The big dog looked toward Cindy as if asking permission to leave. She nodded and Brutus nodded back. She didn't need a candy bar to control him. She just naturally had that way about her with man or beast. I could never say no to Cindy. Brutus and I had that in common too.

Soon, Cindy and I were alone in the same spot where I left her my gift all those years ago.

She gave me another hug and a kiss, and smiled to herself. "Charlie, I know what you're thinking now just as I always knew what you were thinking the first time I kissed you in the summer of your seventeenth year. There's still a lot of little boy in you."

With that I felt myself returning to my current age. It was if she had the power to make me seventeen forever, but not the authorization.

"Charlie, live your age as God has planned. Life is long enough. When you try and alter that, you can only bring sorrow upon yourself. I know that now."

"Cindy, I have a million questions; but first, please tell me...did you put me in some sort of trance back then, or did I really fall in love with you of my own free will?"

"Charlie, you were a young boy with raging hormones. I didn't need to put you in a trance, but let's say you were the first boy in a *long* time to put *me* in a trance. Yes, I really loved you and I always will. I had watched you from the first day you came by here. You probably don't remember, do you? You must have been about eight years old. You were with your schoolmates and your little girlfriend. Her name was Donna. Do you recall?" Cindy closed my eyes with a kiss and instructed me with a whisper, "Remember."

I thought back. Suddenly the lights dimmed as I retreated into the past. Showtime!

I was back in the fourth grade, my last year before I would go to parochial school and cause Sister Mary Margaret to question her vocation. I was at McLellan School just a few blocks away from the old cemetery. It was spring. I know because our teacher, Mrs. Emmons, said that crocuses were the first flowers to bloom in the spring. Every April she took her class on a walk up to the Western Promenade to see the new flowers display their pretty colors. Sometimes they popped up right through the melting snow.

Mrs. Emmons made each boy pair up with a girl and walk in formation, hand in hand. She thought it was cute. The girls liked it too but the boys hated it, mostly because Mrs. Emmons chose the partners.

"Charlie Sullivan, take the hand of Donna Lawson."

If there was one girl the boys *wanted* to holds hands with, it was Donna. She was the only girl we didn't think was gross. She reminded me of Darla Hood, Alfalfa's heartthrob on <u>The Little Rascals</u> ...same short dresses and pleasant smile. She even smelled good, rare for girls in my fourth grade class.

Donna and I were up front. Mrs. Emmons and the rest of the class followed behind. When we walked down Cassidy Hill all the boys held their breath as we passed the cemetery.

Mrs. Emmons said, "All right, boys, act your age. You are little gentlemen."

No we weren't... as was revealed by Brad Sturgis when he said, "If you don't hold your breath when you pass the cemetery, the boogie man will get you."

All the boys went; "OOOOOOO" and the girls all started screaming. Mrs.Emmons' yelling scared them all the more. Donna ran into the cemetery and I chased after her, calling her name. When I reached her there was a great big stranger all dressed in black walking toward her. She thought it was the boogieman Brad Sturgis had been talking about. Donna screamed and ran back to the rest of class now reconvening on the hill. Before I ran back I made a snowball and heaved it at the guy. It hit him right in the head and he howled in pain and...

"Oh my God, Cindy!!! Was that the goon over by the mausoleum?" I asked as I opened my eyes. I had completely forgotten about that.

"Yes...I was watching nearby and I thought you were so brave. The moisture from that snowball was extremely painful to him. I read your young mind back then and I was charmed. I never forgot you. I saw you frequently over the years..."

I interrupted. "Then that *was* you I saw when I crashed my bike on Cassidy Hill that day!"

"And when you came through here on the Halloween night when you were twelve, I was watching. I also rarely missed one of your baseball games when you and Jimmy spent your Saturdays here."

"Why did you wait so long to speak to me?"

"Those were not my bees that attacked your other friend that day.

I had no control over them, but I decided then to make my presence known to you. I wanted to make sure that little episode didn't frighten you away. I needed you...so I could leave this world. I waited all that time, and when you reached my age I willingly gave myself to you. What you didn't know then, you couldn't have understood then. I have been seventeen for a *very* long time."

"Jimmy told me all you said to him. Is that all true?"

"Yes...all true." She looked more serious and less playful. She was sad now and I felt the same. She took my hand and held it tightly, the way she had that day when she told me she was going away. "I'm so glad you are here. I placed your locket in that girl's hands hoping that it would bring you back. I had to see you and talk to you. No one else would understand. No one else can help me find everlasting peace."

"Cindy, did you cause the death of all those people?" I had to ask. I had to know.

"No, Charlie. I tried my best to save them. Over the years I have prevented a lot more people from getting stung, but with each passing year my enemy grows stronger and the day may come when I will have no control over him."

"You mean that freak over by the tomb?"

"Yes. He is very powerful and very dangerous, but the bees can never harm you. I filled you with their venom slowly over that summer so that you would be immune."

"With your *special* kiss?"

"Yes, with my *special* kiss."

She began to walk me slowly toward the front gate. "Charlie, I must go...but beware of the Evil One you just saw. Warn the others! He is getting more and more powerful with each passing season."

"What the hell does he want and why does he send the bees to kill?"

"He wants to rule the world with an army of slaves who will do his bidding. He experiments on the bodies after the bees have done their mission. He pours different potions down their throats in hopes of finding the perfect spell."

"What kind of spell?"

"Through the centuries he has failed, but this season he has succeeded on the first two to die. They are *undead* with supernatural strength and they can do the one thing he cannot. They can roam beyond the boundaries of this place. As of now they too can be destroyed with water, but if he succeeds in finding the ways to make the water harmless, no one will be safe. And there's more."

"More?"

"He is working day and night to find a way to make those buried here...rise up out of their graves and join his army of slaves. He must not succeed, Charlie."

Her words were almost more than I could bear. There was no joke or wise crack that could get me through this night.

"Cindy, what about the two boys, the three young ladies, and the other man who were killed recently? Will they come back to life?" I asked, hoping and praying the answer would be no.

"Charlie, it is *not* life. The first two men are still dead but they will not find peace until they are destroyed again and their souls are freed. As for the others, I don't know. It might be wise to have their bodies soaked in water."

"This is *such* a nightmare. I don't know if I will be able to convince their families to dig up their remains, especially my friend John whose son, Paul, was a victim."

"You must try, Charlie. I have my own gift to help you do that. I had thought of showing it to you back then, but I sensed you needed more time to be ready to handle it. That time has come."

She reached into a small sack that she was carrying, and produced a book that looked as if the wind could easily blow away its fragile yellowed pages. It was bound in cowhide and on the cover was the name, Cynthia Manchester.

"Charlie, take this and read it. This is the account written during the time between my sixteenth and seventeenth year, just before the time I was condemned to die. It has never been out of my possession...till now." She pressed it into my hands and kissed me. As we neared the gates she gave me one of her gentle hugs that I had come to enjoy so much.

"Come back after you have read it. Just remember, I love you."

"Cindy, one more question, are you...ah...are you...ah?"

"Am I really over 300-years-old?"

"I have to know before I go completely crazy."

"The answer is yes...and no," she said in her most soothing voice as if she was bracing me for another shock. Her eyes were comforting too and she continued, "I was born in 1683, but was buried alive at seventeen-years-old in 1700. I died at seventeen but my soul is still bound on earth. My body can't age until my soul is free. Then I can rest. You can help me rest, Charlie. You must. But first I must find a way to destroy the Evil One before he destroys you and all those around here."

"Maybe that will happen tomorrow, that's why I was hoping to see you tonight. The police are going to spray deadly pesticides to kill the bees."

"No poisons can destroy the bees. You have to drown them with pure water just like the *undead*. Just like me. After my enemy is destroyed...you must set my soul free by pouring water on my heart while saying the Lord's Prayer."

"I can't do that!"

"You will when the time comes. I want to sleep in peace. Help me join my family. I have been away from my mother and father and my two brothers for too long."

"But Cindy..."

"Would you want to stay within the confines of this place for eternity as your friends and loved ones pass on to their final reward, never to join them?"

"You are asking an awful lot from someone who's waited so long to find you. How can I destroy you now? You know I still love you."

She smiled that sweet smile, the same one I had seen on Andrea's face. "Then you will do as I ask, and when your time comes we may be together again."

"I'm still not sure I can do it. I ...."

She pressed her fingers to my lips and squeezed the diary in my hands. I watched her walk away with sun rays following her. The bees were returning, keeping her company.

21

How do you tell a grieving father and mother that their only son may not be resting in peace, that he soon may be joining the *undead*? You don't, not yet. I decided for the time being to let only Chief Richardson know what Cindy had said was possible, that *all* the latest victims may soon be walking the streets like Mr. Holt and Mr. Nelson. Discreetly, he would keep a black and white in constant surveillance of Paul Feeney's resting place, as well as that of Paul's friend, Steve Winchell. Looks like One Eye Wheeler may be credible after all. Where and what his two friends were doing with their new found *life* was not known, not yet.

We gathered back at the Reza residence around nine that night to read the old book that Cindy had given me. There was Tony, with his mother at his side. Jimmy hadn't left my side since we were reunited down at the old shack. Chief Richardson was there, as well as the D.A., Brian Dewolfe.

There was one new addition to the usual group. Attorney John Feeney had brought along his personal secretary, Kim Jenkins. She was striking, a long and lanky platinum-blonde whose over-sized breasts were not in proportion to her tiny waist. Kim was the kind of eye-candy that was built for a rich and powerful man. On the radio in my mind I could here Little Richard singing, <u>The Girl Can't Help It</u> (She Was Born To Please.)

Cindy's book was written in a lot of Old English with many of the pages rotted away. John Feeney asked if our newest member could read the journal aloud. He said she was familiar with this type of writing and could translate it more easily. The beauty had brains. She was a graduate of Boston University, and somehow Feeney wanted that known. Their relationship was the worst kept secret in his office; but if people were going to talk, he didn't want her labeled as a bimbo. No one knows what Sandra Feeney thought about the young secretary. Probably, at this moment, she didn't really care.

Kim Jenkins began to read Cindy's own words.

MIGHTY JOHN MARSHALL

It is the 16th of July 1699, my 16th birthday and Mother has given me this book of writing paper. I am so happy to have it as I can write down my thoughts and some of the potions mother has taught me. I will save it for important dates and events.

July 26, 1699: Father is very ill and I am praying for him. He is no longer able to hunt or care for his bees. His experiments are difficult for him to perform. He says that science is a gift from the Almighty, but he is afraid the people will think he is a wizard and Mother is a witch. He has kept most of his work quiet since the troubles over in Salem Village. His friend, Giles Corey, was among the 19 killed. Father says Rev. Samuel Parris and the others like him were superstitious fools.

August 10, 1699: Father died this morning. I want to cry forever but Mother needs me more than ever. I must be strong for her. She is feeling so badly because the potion she was working with, gathered from the bees, was not ready to save Father. Their work has consumed them ever since the twins died at seven years of age. Now Mother must carry it on alone. She says we must keep our faith in the Lord.

September 1, 1699: Mother and I have crossbred the bees again. The new generations are getting smaller, the way Father had hoped, so that everyone would know his bees from all other species. Mother has great power over them. She says she has a potion now to keep us from being stung. We drank it today.Mother says we must say the Lord's Prayer now everyday in the event jealous neighbors say we are practicing witchcraft. She says a bad witch can never say the Lord's prayer correctly. We must always have it memorized.

September 12, 1699: The bees have killed their first rabbit. It is the first fresh meat we have had since Father died. We found some of the bees inside the rabbit. It made mother smile. She said father had hoped for that. He wanted other hunters to know his bees killed that way so they couldn't lay claim to his prey.

September 21, 1699: This is truly a blessed day. The bees brought down a big deer. They will hibernate soon. This kill will last mother and me through the winter. We finished cleaning it and put it to the salt. That should keep it till the freeze which should be soon.

October 12, 1699: John Wallace from the next farm over came by today. He bought some honey and candles from us. He is so handsome. His family is very wealthy with many horses and cows. I don't like it that they have so many slaves. Mother says everyone should be free. He has invited me over to ride a horse. I haven't asked Mother yet.

October 30, 1699: I am feeling so happy. I visited John Wallace again today. I told Mother I had gone looking for fresh kills from the bees. She still does not approve of John. She doesn't trust wealthy land owners like the Wallaces. Mother is especially concerned about one of the slaves. She has heard from relatives still over in Salem Village that this one slave had a great influence over some of the potion makers that were hung there on Gallows Hill in 1692. It is said he learned their magic and then claimed they were evil witches. His name is Lubuka. Mother says he is from Barbados where they practice the black magic.

November 10, 1699: Mother and I visited father's and the twins' graves today. Mother said it was all right if I spoke to them out loud. I told them how much we loved them and missed them and looked forward to the day when we could all be together again. On the way home I confessed to Mother that I had visited John Wallace at his farm. She said she knew and was glad that I finally had told her. We hugged. I love her so much.

November 21, 1699: John came by today and Lubuka was with him. I could tell Mother was not happy to see him. The big slave didn't speak unless John gave him permission. Lubuka wore no shirt even though the frost was heavy on the morning grass. He stood almost seven feet. His head was shaved and his look was intimidating. His eyes were as black as coal. His teeth were clenched behind a strong jaw. John once made him bite off the head of a chicken, even though I begged him not to. When John gave him permission to talk Lubuka asked Mother how she controlled the bees, but Mother refused to answer saying it was a family secret. He offered to share some of his magic with her in return for her secret, but she refused again. He grew angry and John told him to be quiet and respect Mother's wishes. They left and I felt bad that John did not give me a smile as he went out the door. The slave left behind John and looked back at us with a face that seemed to have grown ugly and monstrous. After they left, Mother said he was more evil and dangerous than she first thought. We must be on our guard and never trust him.

December 1, 1699: The first of the heavy snows came last night. John brought some firewood over by wagon. Mother was grateful, but refused to take it without paying him back in honey, candles, and some fresh baked bread. My heart beats faster when John is near. I don't dare tell Mother I hope to marry him someday. I am unfamiliar with the new feelings in my body. They are pleasing to me and make me want to lay with him. I don't know how to tell Mother.

December 10, 1699: I awoke this morning in time to see the big slave from the Wallace Farm standing outside the fence. He was dressed all in black just like John and his father would dress. I thought for a slave he was given much freedom. When I would visit John, I always noticed that Lubuka was treated much better than the other slaves, almost with respect. He did not come inside the fence, but spoke some words I didn't understand. He drew a circle in the snow and poured what looked like blood from a big jug. He said some more words as he spread his arms over the circle. In a flash it was on fire. It burned quickly and made a great smoke. When it cleared there was no one there. I'm afraid to tell Mother. She will never let me go over to the Wallaces to see John again.

December 25, 1699: Today is Christmas Day, our first without Father. I can tell Mother is hurting but we celebrated just the same. I gave her a blanket for her bed that I had made over the summer. She is truly pleased with it. She gave me a beautiful clasp for my hair. It had belonged to her mother. I am so proud to wear it. I was hoping John would come to visit. I guess he is busy with his family. This evening Mother said she had another gift and began to teach me the secrets for reading minds. I can keep no secrets from her. She can read my mind as quickly as the thoughts come. Soon the thoughts that John has I will know. Mother says this gift must only be used for good and never to hurt an innocent. We talked about the feelings of lust that are overcoming me. The feelings I have in my body are natural according to Mother, but I must pray that I have the strength to control them till I can share them with my husband. I am hoping so that it will be John.

January 17, 1700: The snows are heavier than usual. Mother is working almost tirelessly on a potion to prevent diseases like small pox. It was Father's life's ambition to rid the world of suffering. After the twins died he became almost obsessed with nothing else. He said the bees with their deadly venom would do his hunting for him so he could devote all his time to working on his many experiments. At first Mother said he was trying to play God, but Father said if God gives us brains to find such things, surely He would approve. Now Mother carries on his work, and I fear for her as she tries different potions on herself. Today she taught me more about reading thoughts and I'm getting good at it. Sometimes Mother and I don't talk. We just communicate silently with our thoughts.

January 21, 1700: John came by today with Lubuka. He brought us more firewood. Mother must have read Lubuka's thoughts as did I. He is evil, and we both could see that he wants to learn Mother's potions and secrets. He is planning a revolt and hopes to have all slaves follow him in his quest for power. He has put a curse on our house and is troubled that we are still alive. His thoughts are curious as to how we survive. I can see it also makes him afraid of us as well. I am happy that John's thoughts are on me. I blush to write that he wants to make love with me. Somehow I must find a way to warn John about his slave, but Lubuka is rarely out of John's sight. John's father bought Lubuka to look after John and has threatened the big slave with his life if anything ever happens to John.

January 29,1700: Mother has great hopes that her herbs and bee venom will combine to make the formula she has hoped for. Already there are bees in the hive who have lived longer than any others, but they are in their winter sleep so mother continues to experiment on herself. The fever that has swept the village has spared us so far. Mother is happy that her herbs and potions are working. She has offered them to the neighbors, and many claim they have had a miraculous affect. In gratitude they have brought us much food and clothing for the cold days and nights.

February 5, 1700: I find myself thinking of John almost continuously. I can tell Mother is concerned. I have become as good as Mother at mind reading. I can tell

STUNG

she is also worried that the neighbors will think she is practicing witchcraft. Last night her medicines cured the the young daughter of the Danvers family. Elizabeth had a bad cough for weeks, and now she is laughing and fever free. Mother continues to experiment with new medicines on herself.

February 12, 1700: It is unusually cold. The firewood is burning fast. If it weren't for John bringing us the kindling I think Mother and I might freeze. She is so involved in her work. She probably wouldn't notice if there were no fire at all. Her fame continues to spread and a family from Boston made the long trip in the snow to ask about a cure for their five-year-old son who was deaf and still has not spoken since his birth. Mother rubbed a potion on his ears and lips. He struggled as the odor was quite offensive until mother opened a bottle and a lovely strawberry smell permeated the room. The young boy stopped crying and called for his mother and then his father. The parents were overcome with surprise and joy and began to cry. The father, who appears quite wealthy, offered Mother a great sum of money. She told him to give it to the poor in Boston.

February 28, 1700: Mother gave me a small bottle of the strawberry fragrance, and I put some on my face. The scent is now always with me. She says it will help calm the bees when they awake this spring. I hope John finds it alluring. I ache for him and the time I can be alone with him. I hope that his slave will leave us alone. The winter continues. It is dark and cold. I don't think mother knows the day or month. She works so hard, and I am worried as she seems to be growing thinner. I look forward to suppers when we sit and communicate with thoughts and words. I love her so much.

March 2, 1700: Rev. Morse and an elder from the local church stopped by today. They have come to see for themselves what others are whispering. Mother told them that we are God-fearing people who would never practice the black magic. We both could read their minds. Rev. Morse is a kind man with a loving heart, but Elder Frederick Miller seeks more power in the community. We can see his mind has many dark thoughts. His ambitions drive him to expose us as witches. Mother glanced at me to make sure I knew his mind. I did and I am afraid. I must speak to John. His powerful family has much influence. Mother had given John some special herbs for his sister's fever on his last visit, and she was fine by the next day. Surely the Wallace family will speak well of Mother if trouble comes.

March 12, 1700: John came by today to invite mother and me to dine with his family on his 17th birthday coming up this Saturday. Mother still does not like John much. She knows that he wants to make love with me. Some thoughts are easier to hide than others. She will not deny me as she knows I so want to go. She did not really want to, but she accepted the invitation for both of us. John said he would send Lubuka with a wagon to fetch us. Mother asked if someone else can come for us. It was then I told John that his slave is a great danger and that his whole family should be careful. John does not believe us. He laughed and said Lubuka is harmless, but said he will have his sister Lucy come along as well. Mother agreed. She knows the evil slave will not try to harm us in Lucy's presence.

March 16, 1700: This has been a special day. Mother gave me a drink from a small cup. She says that no harm can come to us now. Mother drank from the cup and said her work was complete. She took to bed and was asleep in moments. I watched her until my eyes grew weary. She seems to be at peace and my heart is gladdened.

March 18, 1700: This is a most eventful day. We have just returned from the Wallace Farm and John's birthday celebration. It was a wonderful feast. Even mother seemed to laugh and forget her sorrows. The Wallace family is so nice, and John's father told mother not to pay much attention to the rumors of witchcraft. He even said he would like to help Mother bottle her potions and sell them around the colonies. Mother and I could tell he was a sincere and fair man. The slave was quiet on the ride to and from John's home. Lucy and John both took us back with Lubuka. He is very powerful though and realizes that we can read his thoughts. Mother thinks he may have the gift too and has ways of blocking some of his thoughts from us. We can also block our thoughts from him.

April 1, 1700: The snows are starting to diminish as the weather turns warmer and brings the rain. Mother says there is much to do to prepare for the return of the bees in about a month. Mother seems more content these days. She says that soon she will tell me a great secret, and that I must not be afraid. We continue to say the Lord's Prayer daily now that the accusations of witchcraft are getting more common. Most of the neighbors and townspeople don't pay much attention. They know and appreciate all that Mother has done for their families. Mother says we have a lot of wonderful friends, but Elder Miller and some of the other church members are jealous that God has favored her with gifts not given them.

April 7, 1700: This day we have learned of a massacre at a farm over in Falmouth. The owner's slaves have killed the family of Edmund Budway and burned his house and barns to the ground. It is rumored that the slaves drank the blood of those they killed and cut out their hearts. Mother thinks Lubuka had something to do with it.

April 15, 1700: Today was a most unusual day. Mother sat me down and held my hand as she explained that she felt that no earthly harm could come to me. She said that even in death my body could not be corrupted. She explained that the potion she had given me to drink was what she and Father had hoped for, and that I should live for a very long time. She then said she had to do something and I must understand. She had to prove her potion was correct. Last night before bed she had swallowed some poison. It should have killed her at least before dawn but when she awoke she was fine. My heart was fearful that she will take more chances and I begged her not to. She said the only way to prove her new potion was absolutely perfect was for a loved one to pour pure water on her heart while saying the Lord's Prayer. That should release her soul from her earthly body, and she would be with Father and the twins in Heaven. Mother says a long life is wonderful, but nobody wants to be away from their loved ones forever. I have learned so much from her, but I could never give her such a remedy. I don't want to live without her. I am crying now and must end my writing for today.

April 25, 1700: John came by today with his father to talk with Mother about a business opportunity. Mother did not tell him of her potion for immortality, but did offer to make up some batches of healing medicines and a special one to survive all bee stings. Mr. Wallace was pleased and said we must visit his family again. He mentioned how John would like that and smiled at me. Mother smiled at me too. I'm sure my face was red with the blush. This has been a happy day.

April 29, 1700: The feelings burn inside me when I think of John and I know his feelings make him want to bed with me. I cannot really tell yet if he wants to ask for my hand. There are potions I know I could use that would make him want to marry me, but I want him to use his free will. I know my strawberry scent already has an affect on him. Mother knows my feelings, but does not press me. She says she remembers how badly

STUNG

she wanted to be with Father. She says a body should never lie or use unnatural means to obtain a desire.

May 1, 1700: Mother seems so content with herself. She is laughing more and singing silly rhymes. She says that spring is here and all is well. I think she may be losing her mind, but she says she is happy and again talks about being with Father and the twins. She has promised me that she will no longer tempt the fates with deadly poisons. I am feeling much relieved to see her this way. It's the way I remember her most when I was a little girl and we would all go out in the fields and play. I can see the joyous thoughts in her mind, although I do continue to worry that she will see the thoughts I have on my mind for John. We are going horseback riding in a few days. I am thinking of telling him that I love him.

May 12, 1700: I do not know what to write. I feel if I put my thoughts down on paper they will leave my mind and mother won't see them. John and I went riding in the warm sunshine. Then, back in the barn as we put the horses in their stalls, John chased me up to the hay-loft. I could see the thoughts of love and lust on his mind. I could not be upset with him as I confess I had such thoughts as well. He kissed me so gently at first and then harder as we lay down on the hay. I think the strawberry fragrance on my cheeks intoxicated him. He seemed driven to complete the act of love. His hands reached for my breasts. I was afraid at first but slowly I began to help him remove my garments and then his own. There, in his barn, we lay in our nakedness. I could read his mind and knew where to touch him and kiss him as he secretly desired. I cupped my breasts in my hands and brought them to his lips. I soon felt an emotion take over me as I have never known. I teased him with the thoughts he was thinking. I feel most of the responsibility is mine. I know his desires more than he could ever know mine. I felt like a temptress with great power over an innocent being. I confess I enjoyed this part of myself. Mother says we all have weaknesses like it says in the bible, and now I know mine. I must fight this feeling as I truly want John's love given freely without tricks or magic. I know now I can make him love me, but I must let him choose me of his own free will. I don't think I will sleep tonight. I have much to think about.

May 19, 1700: John and I made love again today. I told him I loved him and he said the same. I haven't been this happy in a long time. Mother is happy with her garden and her bees. They are even smaller now than before. I wish Father could be here to see them. Mother no longer needs to call to them. She waves her arms and they assemble nearby, and sometimes right on her chest or back. They are her protectors. She is teaching me how to control them.

May 25, 1700: This has been a terrifying day. The big slave went to Elder Miller and said that Mother and I were practicing witchcraft. They came by today with a minister other than Rev. Morse. His name was Rev. Charles Foster. He said that Rev. Morse was quite ill with the fever and Lubuka said Mother had put a curse on him. Mother offered to visit Rev. Morse and take him some healing medicine, but Elder Miller said the minister would be cured by the prayers of the faithful and not by black magic. Mother was hurt. Then she grew angry because she knew the big slave was the cause of Rev. Morse's sickness, and that he was responsible for turning the new clergyman against her. Mother is no admirer of lies and injustice. Without thinking she set the bees on Lubuka. He screamed in pain and ran over the field toward the Wallace farm. The bees returned and settled on mother's shoulders. Elder Frederick Miller and Rev. Foster were horrified by the attack and by the way the bees obeyed Mother. I was glad the evil slave suffered from her wrath, but tonight

STUNG

I fear this will bring even more trouble for us.

June 1, 1700: The happiness I have known is gone. A great sorrow has befallen us and the Wallace family. John's sister and my friend Lucy was found dead this morning in her bed. Mother knows that Lubuka has poisoned her, but Lubuka said it was Mother's bees. The big slave had managed to capture some and put their stingers in Lucy's neck. Mr. Wallace is greatly saddened, and John has said that Mother and I should be questioned by all the elders of the church. Many of our friends and neighbors, who have experienced mother's wonderful cures, are now saying they think she may be a witch. They are afraid the elders will accuse them of the same if they don't support Elder Miller and Rev. Foster. I am very afraid for Mother.

June 5, 1700: More bees have been born. Mother now has all of them assembled around the outside of our house. She says we must use them to protect us in hopes that Rev. Morse will get well and speak for our innocence. She says Lubuka has more power than she thought. He was able to survive the bee stings. I have much fear. I pray that John will surely realize that Mother would never have done anything to harm Lucy.

June 9, 1700: Elder Frederick Miller has assembled a great crowd around our home. They have torches and are yelling vile language. Mother says to write down all that is happening in my book. If we have a chance we can show all that has gone on to Rev. Morse. Other than John, he is our only hope. They stop their noise as Rev. Foster raises his hand. He yells for Mother to come to the door. Mother tells me in her thoughts not to be afraid. Mother goes outside and Rev. Foster says that Rev. Morse is dead. Bee stingers were found in his neck. I see Lubuka smile. He senses Mother and I know that he is responsible and he takes great joy in it. Elder Ferderick Miller yells for Mother and I to leave the house as he and the others will lay their torches to it and kill all the bees. I urge Mother to send the bees to save us, but she says there is too great a chance that many of our old friends will be killed. She instructs me to keep writing. Surely someone will read this and realize the true evil is Lubuka. The big slave has the power to influence the crowd. He steps forward and asks Elder Miller if he can talk with Mother alone. Rev. Foster nods his approval as well. Lubuka comes to the front door where only Mother and I can hear him. He tells us that he will see that we are left alone if Mother shares the secret he has always wanted, the power to control the bees. Mother says she will consider it if he sends the crowds away and comes back tomorrow with John. She wants John to witness his word to us, that he will keep his part of the bargain. Lubuka agrees. He convinces the crowd to put out their torches and go home. Quiet has returned if just for a day. I am so frightened.

June 10, 1700: Lubuka returned today with John. John has changed his feelings for me. My heart is breaking, but I must be strong for Mother and myself. Lubuka told Mother in front of John that he knows Mother had not sent the bees. He said his good magic showed that her heart and my heart harbor no evil. John seemed somewhat relieved. John's companion has become a trusted servant to him. It almost seems like John is his servant. He told John he should return and tell his grieving father that the Manchesters are innocent. John left without looking at me. I pray that soon we will be together again. Lubuka insisted that Mother now tell him how to have power over the bees. Mother is fearful of his intents with such power, but she kept her word and showed Lubuka how to summon the bees. He was pleased and went outside to try his new gift. The bees swarmed to him as he commanded. He laughed in a menacing way as he walked back toward the Wallace farm. Mother told me she has taught him how to summon the bees, but not how to make them kill. When he finds out it will be too late. By then John would have told his father of our innocence. I find hope for the first time in a longtime.

June 13, 1700: I take pen to hand today only because Mother says I must. Word has reached us that the escaped slaves from Falmouth have killed all in the Danvers family, and then Mr. Wallace and any of his slaves that would not join them. There is no mention of John and I am praying that he has escaped. The Sheriff has asked for volunteers to track down the killers. All the men over sixteen have gathered at the church to make a plan.

June 14, 1700: The Sheriff and the elders of the church led by Frederick Miller came to see Mother. They have asked her to send the bees to help quell the insurrection. They have now come to believe that Lubuka is the leader and is planning more killings. He has taken over the Wallace farm and is promising freedom and riches for all those who follow him. In their fear the town has turned to Mother. Mother said she will send the bees in hopes of scaring the escaped slaves but not to kill. Elder Miller turned to me and said that Lubuka was holding John Wallace as a hostage. My heart is relieved that John is still alive. The elders asked me to convince Mother to send the bees to kill. She communicated to me that would put John at a great risk, as the bees could very well attack him too. Mother refused. Frederick Miller said he will deal with Mother when the rebellion is over. He is an evil man but has much power over the church members.

June 20, 1700: The Governor has sent men from Boston and Plymouth to help put down the slaves led by Lubuka. Those who returned from the Wallace farm said there was much blood shed, but they have overpowered Lubuka and some of his followers. It is said that besides Lubuka there are six others who have been captured. There is no word of John and I continue to hold out hope that he is still alive. Mother is preparing potions for the wounded who have stopped by seeking remedies. She said that tomorrow we will go look for John.

June 21, 1700: Mother and I have spent the day looking for John, but all at the Wallace farm have perished. Mother thinks that the evil slave knows where John may be. We went to the jail to see Lubuka. We thought we might read his mind, but he is very powerful and is able to block many of his thoughts. The Sheriff agrees with Frederick Miller and Rev. Foster that Lubuka is a wizard and they will soon hang him and his followers.

June 23, 1700: Rev. Charles Foster came by today with news that Frederick Miller's elderly mother has died. She was attacked by the bees. Mother knows Lubuka must have commanded them from his cell, but without the knowledge to make them kill they wouldn't have stung the old woman. Mother said she must have died of fright. Her heart couldn't take such a startling event. Lubuka was counting on that. Frederick Miller blames mother. I am much afraid that soon they will take Mother and try her as a witch. I hope that these writings will be read some day if anything should happen to Mother and me.

July 1, 1700: The trial for Lubuka and the others captured with him is over. He has been sentenced to death by hanging. The other six have been condemned to the same fate. Lubuka has requested that Mother and I visit him. He told the sheriff that he knows what happened to John and will only tell Mother and me.

July 2, 1700: We have just returned from the jail where Lubuka is being held. He told Mother he would tell us where John was if Mother finished the secret of how to make the bees kill. She gave him a potion to drink first.

STUNG

The big slave drank it and mother smiled. She then told him how to command the bees to kill, but her power over them is greater and she can counter his commands. She turned to Lubuka with joy in her voice and told him the potion she gave him will bind his soul on earth, and he will be undead until someone who loves him pours pure water over his heart while saying the Lord's Prayer. She said no one will ever love him, and he will be condemned to live in and around his grave forever with no peace. The big slave cursed her and refused to say where John was being held. Mother said she was able to read his mind this time while he was not guarding his thoughts. I asked to go to John, but mother said we must wait for the morning. I yearn to go to him but mother told me to be patient. She says he is alive and well in the cellar of the house of Frederick Miller. Mother said it will be easier to help him escape in the morning. Again I will not sleep well.

July 3, 1700: Mother and I have rescued John and he is with us. He is so confused over all that has happened, but I am hoping that time will deliver us from these troubles and that my John will give his heart to me again. I am so tired. I must sleep tonight.

July 4, 1700: We were awakened this morning by a great crowd. It was Elder Frederick Miller and Rev. Foster leading the people. They were calling for Mother and me to come outside. John went out to quiet them, but someone threw a big stone and John was hit. I can write no longer today. I must go to John.

July 4, 1700: This night as I write is very difficult. The Sheriff and his men are in the control of Elder Frederick Miller. They have taken Mother, John, and me. John has recovered from the attack. We were allowed to take some possessions with us. I have my book with me. Mother says to continue to write down as much as I can. We are to be tried tomorrow for practicing witchcraft. I am so afraid, but Mother and John are a great comfort. Lubuka and the other condemned prisoners mock us with their laughter.

July 10, 1700: I have not had the strength to write my thoughts for the last several days. Mother and I have been condemned as witches. John has been given his freedom in return for his testimony against Mother and me. Mother always sensed his weakness, but had hoped he would never have a chance to show it. In a week I am to be hung with Lubuka and his men. Mother is to be burned at the stake in the town square. There is no hope.

July 12, 1700: The horror of this summer continues. Mother frightens me as she tells me she really died the night she took the poison, but the potion she made from the bee venom has kept her body from corrupting. Mother has requested a cup of water and has asked me to send her soul to be with Father and the twins. She says that even after I am hung I will be undead and must find someone who loves me to pour pure water over my heart. Surely John will do that much for me. Mother says he is weak, but he has enough love for me to complete the task. She says I must be strong and always keep in mind that soon we will all be together again in the next life. Lubuka laughs as he knows that he too will soon be undead. The thought of it now makes him glad. Mother says I must destroy the bees so that Lubuka will not use them to kill. She tells me to drown them by commanding them into the river. After that I will ask John to pour water on my heart. I want to go with Mother now. I want to be dead, but I must obey her and follow her wishes.

July 16, 1700 : This is the first day of my seventeenth year. All that has happened has overwhelmed me. This is the day of my fate. This is the day Mother will be with Father and the twins. This is the day Lubuka and I will become undead. Elder Frederick Miller had never given us a chance to say the Lord's Prayer at the trial, but as I poured pure water over Mother's heart I repeated it slowly and perfectly. She grasped my left hand as I tilted the cup of water with my right hand. She smiled so sweetly and gave me brief comfort. A bright light dashed from her heart to the heavens. I felt a strange peace knowing now she would be happy forever with our family. The big slave watched in amazement as she left this world. I cannot hold back my tears. And now I will write no more as the most terrifying news has reached me. John is dead. Lubuka sent the bees while I was grieving for mother. I must remain on earth and under the earth until the day a true love will find me.

As Kim finished reading the account we were all silenced by the amazing words we had just heard. I was not the only one to have watery eyes. Cindy was truly a remarkable person, and the bond of friendship for those gathered in the room was strengthened by her words. Even John Feeney realized that Cindy had not sent the bees to kill his son. She was trying with all her power to fight the evil commands of Lubuka.

"Just how did she and that bastard come to be buried in that cemetery and not down in Massachusetts?" asked Brian Dewolfe.

Tony said that he planned to visit the Maine Historical Society tomorrow and check further into their records and to contact the Massachusetts Historical Society as well.

"Well, at least we know that big creep can't travel far from the cemetery. The rest of the city should be completely safe," Feeney offered.

I looked at Richardson who caught my eye. We were both thinking the same thing. Holt and Nelson, the first two victims, had no such boundary limits. And there was the possibility that young Paul, the Winchell boy, the sorority girls, and the newsman may join them. Who knows what kind of hell that could bring. We could only hope the potions Lubuka gave them will not have the same effect as it apparently had on the friends of One Eye Wheeler.

"Meanwhile, we'll begin spraying the cemetery tomorrow with the pesticides. It may not do any good, but we've got to show the people we are doing something before that Kostenello woman can stir them up again," Chief Richarson reasoned and then added, "I can only hold her for 24 hours...Funny, but she seems like the real witch."

"And, Ray, I don't care how silly it seems or how much shit you take, I want you to see to it that all your men have water guns," instructed the powerful lawyer.

As Jimmy and I returned to our hotel room, we didn't talk. We both played reruns of our lives in our minds. I'm sure for Jimmy, as for me; there were many happy memories that surrounded the sad and painful ones. I wondered what kind of memories we would have years from now when we looked back on this summer...or would there be *no* looking back.

While staring at the ceiling and waiting for the Sandman, I not only thought of Cindy and all she had meant to me, but also of Andrea Rios. I thought maybe the bad news I was expecting from Andrea wouldn't seem so hard to take with all I had just learned. My last words as I surrendered to the Sandman were, "Well, at least now I know who John was." Cindy's words of, *Oh John, it's been so long*, were a mystery no more.

22

The phone rang at the same time the alarm sounded. Startled, I jumped up and slammed my fist down on the clock radio. A quick look at Jimmy in his bed told me that it would take more than an offensive ringing to wake him.

"Charlie? It's Andrea. I hope I didn't call too early."

"Andrea! You can never call me too early. It's so nice to hear your voice."

I never realized before how much she sounded like Cindy. If it were Cindy on the phone, I would have believed it. Or maybe in my mind I wanted her to be another Cindy. I wanted her to be that other chance at happiness that has eluded me.

"I've been reading all about the strange things going on here in your hometown. Are you doing all right?" Andrea asked in that soft and comforting voice.

"The short answer is...no! I can give you the long answer when I see you."

"I'm staying with friends on Broadway in South Portland. Do you know where Willard Beach is? I'm not far from there."

"Yeah, sure. I spent a lot of time there many years ago, chasing girls. Do you want to hear about it?" I teased, as if there were the slightest possibility I could make her jealous.

"If you want to tell me," she said without the least bit of irritation in her voice.

I could never break that congenial mood of hers, no matter what I said. She didn't seem to have a hateful or jealous bone in her body. It just added to her charm.

"Cindy...ah...I mean, Andrea, why didn't you ever tell me you had friends back here?"

"I'm sorry, Charlie...but I'll tell you everything today... And who's Cindy?...A friend you didn't tell *me* about?...Guess you don't tell me everything either," she laughed.

"She's just someone you remind me of...someone from my past."

"Well, she must be mysterious too. I know that's how you think of me," she replied dead on.

"How? How do you know that's the way I think of you?"

"Oh...just a guess."

"You mean like how you guessed I was a Pepsi Man?"

"Yes, something like that. You know, woman's intuition."

"Yeah, I'm not so sure I know anything anymore. Guess I'm getting old. Time to pin a note on my jacket with my name on it and send me out to the feed the pigeons."

"Oh, don't be such a fuddy-duddy! Can you meet me at noon by the big rocks, where the steps go down to the beach?"

"I'll be there." I guaranteed her. "Should I bring an inner-tube to play with in the water?"

"Better not...I might not be able to tell you from the other little kids," she said in her playful way.

"Yes you will. I'll be the one that's six feet tall...Sure you don't want me to pick you up?"

"It's just a short walk for me. I'll be waiting when you get there. See you then, Charlie."

"See you then, Andrea."

My emotions were having a field day. My love for Cindy and my feelings for Andrea were racing around with my concern for Jimmy and my fear of what might happen if Lubuka gained full control over the bees, and also if the *undead* added to their numbers. I am a full-believer in all that Cindy wrote in her journal, and so are those who heard her testimonial as read by Kim Jenkins at the Reza house last night.

The Sunday paper was waiting when I opened my hotel room door. The headlines said it all: **PESTICIDE SPRAYING BEGINS TODAY AT WESTERN CEMETERY.**

There were a number of warnings and suggestions to the public to stay at least three blocks away. Nearby residents were asked to leave before nine and to make sure that all windows were closed. Area citizens were reminded to secure all pets and property. It was noted that the local police would beef up patrols to prevent potential break-ins while the homeowners were away.

STUNG

The paper ran various stories recapping all that had taken place since the first two victims were found. There were pictures to accompany the facts. Somehow, seeing the photos of the dead along with quotes from their relatives about how much they are missed and how special they were, made the whole thing seem so much worse than reading each individual story as the deaths occurred.

Reporter Lisa Ibrahim even found some people who had come forward saying they were close cousins with the winos who started the whole ball rolling when they stepped into the cemetery to share a bottle. They traveled with the One Eye Wheeler crowd, but it seems only One Eye knew the God awful truth...that Holt and Nelson were not in their graves. That hasn't made the paper yet, but the panic in the streets will indicate if the news gets out.

This could be one of greatest events in history, and all the hangers-on want to be part of it.

("You know that cemetery where all those weird killings are taking place? Well, I have a cousin who has a friend who actually walked by their once.")

You know the type. They were the kind who would have said they were at Woodstock when they weren't even close. They were on the grassy knoll in Dallas when a young president was slain. They were at Fenway Park when Ted Williams hit a home run in his last turn at the plate. They were outside the gates at Graceland when a king fell off his throne. They were on the *next* flight into New York after the Towers fell. Fame by association is a common ailment now taking hold here in Portland.

After a hot shower and a quick breakfast I called Joe and updated him on the latest events. With a little prodding I convinced him to come over and stay with Jimmy while I kept my destiny with Andrea. Jimmy was doing pretty well with his demons, but if left alone, they might become good friends again.

I parked my rented car in the lot near the beach. The walk to the rocks where I was to meet Andrea was about a half-mile away. I hadn't been there in years, but the memories were fresh and good. The salty air and seaweed just added to the moment. The sand was deep and fought against my foot steps as if it were an aerobic exercise. The waves crested against the shore with no great threat. Above, the seagulls searched with peering eyes to nab any unsuspecting crab or clam. Children ran down to the water with pails and shovels as there parents shouted after them to, "BE CAREFUL!!!" Sun worshipping young babes were laying face down with their bikini tops undone. Nearby, young boys tossed a football which they somehow managed to land near one of the pretty girls. "Hey! Watchit!" And the boy would mumble some kind of apology while checking her out more closely. Times change but teenage tricks remain the same.

All on the beach seemed oblivious to the horrors that were just miles away. On that shore everything was the way life should be, fun and innocent...the way I was...until that summer...that cemetery...and that girl. If wishes could make it so, I would be back in my teens tossing that football and chasing those bikini babes on the beach. Of course Jimmy would be with me. No time for shenanigans today. I couldn't wait to see Andrea, and at the same time I was hoping to put it off. I don't think the reality of seeing Cindy again has fully gripped me. I'm sure under ordinary circumstances I would be so happy I couldn't stand myself. That feeling that God had given me more than my share of happiness was not to be mine...not with Cindy...not in this lifetime.

I continued on. I walked past two lovers holding hands and playing with their barking dog. There was a group of young kids about to take snorkel lessons, and their instructor was trying to be heard above the dog, the radios, the screams of fun, and all the other normal sounds on a summer beach...But normal wasn't the way it was for me and I felt jealous of their ordinary lives. I had one once.

I was getting closer to the big rocks. Yes, there she was. Her silhouette grew larger and her features became clearer with each sand-fought stride. The small cross around her neck glistened in the sunshine and shot rays of white light into my eyes. Even with sunglasses on, I winced against the brilliance. She waved to me like Cinderella on a float at Disney World. But Andrea's float was a big rock. She was dressed in Old Navy shorts and an oversized white tee-shirt with a big yellow smiley-face, and a caption that said: DON'T WORRY. BE HAPPY. Her skin was flawless in the sun and her beauty could not be tarnished by the brightness of the day.

"Hey lady, are you lost? I'm here to rescue you," I teased.

"Isn't this Malibu, and aren't you Harrison Ford?" she teased back.

She extended her hands toward me and gave me one of her gentle hugs. The strawberry fragrance that surrounded her affected me like smoke on a bee. It helped put me under her spell, but there was no *magic* spell cast by Andrea, just a genuine caring that was so appreciated.

"Andrea, there's so much to say, I don't know where to start." Then it hit me like a bolt out of the blue, I had said those exact same words to Cindy just last night.

"Well, please let me start and then I'll be happy to listen to everything. First of all, let me apologize for being so mysterious."

She smiled sweetly as she took my hand and asked to go for a walk along the shore. The sun was bright in a cloudless sky, but I had this uneasy feeling that the clouds in my own life were about to get darker, if that were possible. We walked quietly for a while and then she spoke.

"Charlie, this isn't easy for me. I actually have two secrets to tell you, one that even Mr. Allen doesn't know...one I didn't know myself up till a few years ago. Please be patient with me and let me explain. I wanted to tell you that first day you showed me around the school but..."

"But?" I asked, as I waited for the invisible wallop up-side my head and heard the old Principal's words, *Charles, I just have a gut-feeling that there's something about her that she didn't even tell me.*

She turned and looked toward the sea as if gathering just the right words. Her fingers twirled the silver cross that hung around her neck. The serious look on her face was new to me. Up till now I had only seen the one with the almost constant smile.

"Andrea?"

She put her fingers to my lips, just the way Cindy had done last night.

"Please, Charlie, let me finish. Here, sit down on the sand with me."

With those beach noises all around me, I could only hear the soft voice of Andrea Rios. She continued looking toward the sea while her hand gently reached for mine. Her touch reminded me of Cindy's just as her voice did. With the scent of strawberries, I could have closed my eyes and not have known whether it was Andrea or Cindy sitting on that beach with me. If she had told me she was three hundred-years-old too, I would have gone straight down to O'Toole's and gotten tanked.

Andrea began and I held my breath, "Charlie, I came to Marshall High to teach for two special reasons. The first reason is not as important as the second. You see, I wanted to find out what it would be like to teach children who accepted me for being just a regular teacher and not someone who they had to respect for what I was wearing. What Mr. Allen refused to tell you, is that I'm a novitiate with the Sisters of Mercy…I'm a nun, Charlie…Charlie?

And Liston is down for the count. Cassius Clay is the new heavyweight champion of the world. They are bringing out the smelling salts now. The State of Maine has made sports history. Who thought anything like this would happen here? Sonny never saw that punch coming!

"Charlie, are you all right? Please say something." She shook my arms.

I couldn't speak. It was just like last night when that fiend talked to me from inside his tomb. Gradually the shock eased and I could finally answer this beautiful young…nun!

"Well, I could just walk into the ocean and drown that way or just lay here and let the ocean come to me with the on coming tide."

Andrea punched me gently in the shoulder, "Stop that! Don't make me feel any worse than I do for not telling you sooner."

My mind was working overtime as I looked for a loophole that could make it possible, that she could be my girlfriend and not just a girl who could only be my friend.

"Let's see, if I remember correctly from my catechism classes at Sacred Heart, a novitiate is not a full-fledged nun. You can still get out of it!!!" I said as if I had just discovered the secrets of the universe.

She gave me another one of those gentle hugs that were her trademark. "I don't want to get out of it! I take my final vows in a year. It's all I have ever wanted to be ever since I was a young child. I love the Sisters, and I love teaching and helping children learn...and I love God, Charlie."

I knew then I would feel guilty forever if I tried to change her mind.

"Well, at least, I did lose out to a better man, not too many guys can say that and mean it," I said in defeat as I searched for something to get me though *this* night.

"Andrea, why did you tell me you were going to visit your parents? Aren't nuns supposed to tell the truth?"

"I did tell the truth. I did visit them...at the cemetery. They were killed several years ago along with my sister, Denise. It was shortly after the accident that I decided to join the Sisters of Mercy. I have never regretted it."

Andrea stood up, walked down to the edge of the outgoing tide and dipped her toes into the water. It gave me time to be alone with my thoughts and to comprehend what cards had been dealt me by the fates. In a few minutes she was back at my side. We sat together for a while just gazing at the ocean. We both needed a respite to consider all we were thinking. But she had more on her mind.

Andrea broke the silence. "There is that one other thing, Charlie. I'm afraid it's a bigger shocker, but it might make you feel better that I'm a nun. Do you think you can take another jolt or would you rather we talk more later? I *must* tell you, it may be harder to accept than my first *BIG* secret."

"Oh Man!!! Now I know why Jimmy drinks," I pronounced as I laid back on the sand gazing up at the heavens, wondering who had it out for me up there.

"Who's Jimmy?" she asked, still watching the tide ebb and flow.

"He's was my best friend growing up and we were just reunited about a week ago. I was also reunited with my *300-year-old* girlfriend. You think you can top that?!?" I exclaimed.

Andrea held my hand tightly again, and I told her all that had gone on in that cemetery from when I first met Cindy to the latest encoun-

· ter just yesterday. I told her about my 17th summer, the little golden locket, and all the mysterious deaths that had occurred in the Western Cemetery over the years. I told her about all the police and I had learned, and I revealed the contents of Cindy's journal.

Andrea listened intently, but her demeanor was not one of someone who had just seen a ghost, but of someone who believed and understood everything that was being said. She repeated the name "Cindy" to herself and squeezed my hand even harder. She took a couple of deep breaths and smiled at me again. I had just told her Cindy's unbelievable story, and she accepted it without question or even surprise.

"You've certainly been through a lot these last few weeks, Charlie. I hope you are pleased with what I'm about to tell you."

"I can see that there is nothing that's going to surprise *you*, so hit me with your next best shot."

"Charlie, are you sure you are ready to be shocked again. This is a BIGGIE. I don't want you to go into cardiac arrest," she said in her playful way.

"Go for it, Sister," I said sarcastically, not really ready for another jolt. But you just can't hear someone say they have a secret they want to tell you and then resist the temptation of hearing it.

Andrea reached into her pocket, pulled out a plastic baggy and slowly handed it to me. Tears came to her big blue eyes, and it hurt me to see sadness in her face. She said that before I look into the bag to remember that she loved me very much. I smiled and assured her that she would always have my love no matter whether she was a nun or not. She was pure goodness and I truly wanted her to be happy.

As I opened the little container, Andrea stood up again and went back down to the shoreline. Inside was a weathered piece of paper. It was like the kind Cindy used in her journal. My heart began pounding in my chest like a jack hammer. It *was* Cindy's handwriting. The words jumped at me as if escaping from a prison.

My Dear Little One, I love you very much. I hope and pray that someday you will understand why I can not be with you. I want you to know that you are a precious gift. Your father doesn't know about you, but when you are grown you can decide if you want to contact him. His name is Charlie Sullivan. He is from Portland, Maine and his high school is called Cheverus. Tell him I loved him very much but didn't know how to tell him about you. Please forgive me, My Darling Andrea.

> Mother,
> Cynthia Manchester

By the time I regained my ability to think and to put two words back to back, Andrea was holding me. She was crying. "I wanted to tell you that you were my real father, but I just didn't know how. Please forgive me. I am so glad I found you. I searched the records at the church and found the note that you just read. It was in my file along with a lock of Mother's hair. It smelled like strawberries and so I wear her scent as my own. I searched and was able to find that my Charlie Sullivan was now a teacher at Marshall High in Oceanside. I had to meet you and see for myself who my real father was, and what he was like. Charlie...are you all right?"

"Andrea. You are my *daughter*?" I asked coming out of my shock.

"Yes, Charlie...yes, Father. The Sisters of Mercy took me in and placed me with their orphanage in Santa Monica. I was adopted by the Rios family when I was six-years-old. They were wonderful people and I was so happy being their daughter."

"You...are really...*my* little girl?" I remained dazed.

"Yes, Father, I am *your* little girl." She hugged me tighter.

"You mean...*my* Cindy is your mother?" I continued in a fog.

"Yes, and you must bring me to her. I want to see her so badly."

"Andrea Rios is also Andrea Manchester Sullivan?" I finally accepted. "I'll be jiggered."

"Yes," she laughed and cried at the same time. Are you okay with that?"

I waited for my mind to clear completely. I was glad I was lying down. My weak knees surely would have given way if I were standing. I wiped my eyes and held Andrea closely. She cried again...and so did I.

"Andrea, I am so all right with that. But please call me...Dad... not...Father. People will think I'm a priest!...And that could cause cardiac arrest!"

"You got it...Dad."

We both continued laughing, crying and holding onto each other, neither of us concerned that everyone within shouting distance was watching and wondering who those two oddballs could be.

I walked Andrea back to her friends' place on Broadway. We talked constantly about all the things that came to our minds. I told her about her uncle and her grandparents, all about Jimmy, and again how much I had loved her mother and still do; and about the unnatural life Cindy has had for over 300 years.

When we arrived Andrea invited me inside to meet her friends. They were so welcoming and intrigued about Andrea and her new *Dad*. One of the older nuns was the one who had found Andrea under the old Elm by home plate. The Sisters often went up there to pray for the dead. They figured the mother knew and had left the baby there for them to find.

I asked Andrea if she could come with me to the Reza residence tonight. We were all getting together again to discuss the spraying, and to see what further information about the old cemetery Tony had been able to gather. I was quick to tell Andrea that the pesticides were not a threat to Cindy. She understood that her mother was not in danger from earthly harm.

She also knew that Cindy wanted me to free her soul by pouring pure water on her heart while saying the Lord's Prayer. I told Andrea that I didn't think I could do that. It would be murder.

"I have prayed for her all my life. I will be with you when the time comes. You will not be taking her life...she is already dead. Her soul must be freed. She has suffered long enough. I love her too...Dad."

23

The contrast of joy and terror that was going on in my life was overwhelming, especially after all the ho-hum years that had passed. All in a period of less than two weeks, I was plucked from my comfy life in Oceanside and confronted with horrible deaths and unbelievable terror. As of this moment there were two...maybe more...*undead* on the streets of the town where I was born. I was reunited with the love of my life only to find out that she's some sort of unnatural being who was over 300-years-old. I had found my best friend from my childhood days for whom life had changed so much and of course, Andrea...my new found daughter. I began to think, *what if*. What if Joe, Jimmy, and our friends had never stumbled into that graveyard on that Halloween night when I was twelve-years-old? What if Jimmy and I hadn't taken Tommy Caine up on his dare to cross through that cemetery? We would have never found our baseball field. I would have never found Cindy. I would have never known the thrill of loving her or the pain of losing her. I would have never heard the bone chilling threats of the evil Lubuka as I stood outside that big crypt. I would have never been the father I am now. Yet, if I had a chance to turn back the hands of time, I don't think I would. Life is like that old Clint Eastwood spaghetti-western. You have to take <u>The Good, The Bad, & The Ugly.</u>

The *good* was by my side as I returned to my hotel room. The look on Joe's face as I introduced him to his niece was priceless.

Jimmy was totally surprised as well. "I may never drink again. You have shocked my system...I'll be jiggered."

"That's what my Dad said!" exclaimed Andrea.

"Oh he did? Did he tell you he stole that from me?" Jimmy teased.

Joe then went off to inform the whole town that he had a niece who was nun. "They ain't going to believe it down at O'Toole's when I tell them that one. They're gonna shit their pants. Only my brother, Charlie, would pick up girls at a family reunion...ha ha ha."

"Andrea, this is why I left town and moved to California," I apologized. "Its times like these I wish I had been like you...adopted!"

"Not to worry. I hear a lot worse in the school yard." She hugged my arm and gave her uncle a kiss on the cheek. Joe was cackling to himself all the way down the hall to the elevator. He never could keep a secret and this was a *doozy*.

Andrea, Jimmy, and I left for the Reza house. The pesticides had been sprayed and Tony had done more research on the old cemetery. It was time to make the next plans and coordinate our actions. It was time for everyone to meet my daughter, Cindy's daughter. It was time, if just for a break, to have some fun with Maria Reza. I asked my new-found daughter to go along with the joke I was about to play. She reluctantly agreed as long as I didn't take it too far.

I was flattered that Maria cared for me. I hadn't really let her know that I was feeling the same way about her. I had Cindy and Andrea occupying most of my thoughts and owning most all of my feelings.

It was eight in the evening when I rang the buzzer. Maria opened the door and her immediate gaze fell on Andrea. Before I could do the formal introductions Maria went into action, and I decided to let her have all the rope she needed.

"So, is this the girl who came all the way from California to see you?" Maria's Brooklyn accent was more noticeable than usual. The tone in her voice was pissed off.

"Yes, this is Andrea." Andrea extended her hand but it went unnoticed.

"Have you told her how you go on and on about her and that you love her?" Maria's voice was getting louder and louder.

"Yes. She knows I love her very much."

I was having fun and being mischievous. I hadn't had much time for such things in my life since the day I saw online that two unidentified men had been found dead in the Western Cemetery. I just had to take advantage of this opportunity.

"And I love *him* very much," Andrea inserted.

"Well whoopy shit! Loves makes the freakin' world go round. I am happy for both of you," Maria said, not looking at either of us, with her explosive mood bubbling under each word.

Andrea looked at me through those big blue eyes as if to say, *Dad, it's time to stop teasing this woman.*

Maria was feisty, and I was really attracted by her *moods*. I was still afraid of her, but there's never a dull moment when she is in the picture.

"Well, don't just stand there on the porch where all the neighbors will wonder who's the young babe with her grandfather. Come in. Come in." Maria slammed the door behind us.

Andrea, Jimmy, and I joined the others already gathered. There was Tony Reza, reading some new found information. District Attorney Dewolfe had just arrived along with Chief Richardson. We were still waiting for John Feeney.

"So, Charlie, are you going to introduced your cute little girlfriend?" asked Maria, as she sat down in her chair and folder her arms like a teenager who just found out she wasn't going to be allowed to stay out past eleven even if her friends were.

"I'd be happy to. Tony, Brian, Ray, and *Maria,* this is Miss Andrea Rios."

Everyone shook hands with Andrea and welcomed her, well almost everyone.

"I am very happy to meet you all, especially you Maria. May I call you Maria?" Andrea asked with respect.

"No skin off my nose. Call me whatever you like," Maria said in a huff

"I'm hoping we can become very good friends," Andrea said with total sincerity.

"Oh sure. We can be just like freakin' Laverne and Shirley. We can shop at the mall and have our nails done while we talk about all the guys with the cutest asses." Maria was on a roll and Andrea was giving me that look again that said things had gone far enough.

"Maria, I can see why Charlie likes you, and I can see why you like him. If you want to go out with him, that's okay with me."

"Girl, what the hell are you talking about?" Maria barked.

"I'm afraid we have been having fun at your expense, and I for one want to apologize...unlike someone here who likes to aggravate people," Andrea noted as she nodded my way with that scolding look. Her expression was saying it was time for the child to act like the parent and time for the parent to "grow up." I looked at Jimmy, my only ally who would understand my immaturity. He was enjoying the moment, but said I'd better listen to Andrea.

I took the admonishing and the queue, then put my arms around Andrea and said to the fuming woman, "Maria, there is something I want to tell you. I was going to tell you when you opened the door, but you didn't give me a chance. You know how you are."

"No, Charlie, how am I?!?" she asked directing her wrath at me.

"Why, you are a sweet, loving, understanding, mild-mannered woman...and very pretty too."

"Cut the crap, Laughing Boy. What is it you have to tell me?"

I sat down on the couch and took a deep breath. Everyone waited to see how I got myself out of this mess. "The truth is, Maria, I love Andrea more today than ever before."

Maria's voice was softening but still irritable as she looked into my eyes. "Just a wild guess, Charlie. You never did any counseling in that school of yours?"

"Maria, just shut up and listen!" The words leaped out ahead of my thoughts.

Tony and the others looked at me as if to say, *Do you want to live to see another day?* Maria looked at me in total surprise but she conceded as I continued.

"Let me introduce all of you once again to Andrea Rios...my *daughter*. She has found me after all these years." There was stunned silence as everyone turned to look at Maria. "Maria, are you all right?"

"Oh!!!...You are Charlie's daughter! I am really happy to meet you!" Maria jumped up and shouted. The two ladies hugged and laughed. Then Maria pounded me in the shoulder the way she had done that day Tony had his appendicitis attack, and a lot harder than the way Jimmy and I use to do when we were kids. "Payback is a bitch, Charlie. Just you wait."

"And, I would love to go to the mall with you sometime and maybe even get my nails done; but as for checking out the boys, you'll have to do that for both of us," Andrea cautioned sweetly.

"Ha!!! You mean your daddy wouldn't like that!? Us, a couple of good lookin' babes out on the town, trollin' for some beef-cakes?

Yahoooooooo!" Maria looked my way as if she had already set her revenge in motion.

I felt Excedrin Headache Number 62 coming on. I slowly backed away, closer to Tony. When Maria finds out the next secret, I could be on my way to the moon.

"Well, not only him...but I think my boss would frown on that as well. You see, Maria...I am a nun with the Sisters of Mercy."

The silence was deafening. Tony looked at the Chief. The Chief looked at the D.A. Andrea looked at me. Maria looked at me. I looked at them both.

The seconds ticked by and then Maria reacted. "Oh, Sister!... Oh!!!...Oh, I am sorry for acting so badly."

Andrea comforted her new friend by saying it was my fault for being such a jokester.

"YOUR FATHER is going to need a Sister of MERCY when I get done with him!" Maria scowled my way.

Andrea laughed and we all joined in, including Maria. As for me, I stepped further back to avoid getting punched again.

For the moment I lost the arm of my new found daughter as Maria took it. They both sat down as if they were the ones just reunited after all this time. Andrea had such a special way about her. She was full of love for all she met. How could anyone not want to be around her? I loved being the proud dad.

I continued telling everyone of how Andrea was found in that cemetery and brought up in the orphanage by the Sisters. Andrea showed everyone the letter from Cindy. All were moved by Andrea's story and by her mother's love.

The Chief then spoke and said that the spraying went off without a hitch. In a few days his men would be go in there along with some of the boys from the Environmental Protection Agency and see what the results were. Like the rest of us, Richardson held out little hope that the bees were now dead, although the E.P.A. boys were convinced otherwise.

Tony spoke up next. He had discovered new information about the old cemetery...And how Cindy and Lubuka ended up in Maine.

We all took seats as Tony explained that the cemetery was established in 1829, and it was built near a mausoleum that had been constructed almost ten years before. The big crypt was originally on the outside of the boundaries; but over the years, as new fences were constructed, it became part of the property.

According to the archives, when Maine was brought into the union in 1820, Massachusetts had insisted on many concessions. Some were made public and others kept secret. One of the concessions was that Maine must accept the remains of a well-known witch and wizard who had been buried just outside Plymouth in 1700. The locals had insisted that the many unknown deaths and disappearances that occurred over the years in and around their community were the results of a powerful wizard and witch who remained alive after being buried. And who came out of their crypt to spread terror with the killing bees they controlled.

Tony offered more proof by showing us a copy of a small newspaper from 1700 that was included with the treaty agreement among the federal government, the State of Massachusetts and the newly formed State of Maine. It read:

> Yesterday in our town we witnessed the power and evil of witchcraft first hand. Miss Cynthia Manchester and the slave known as Lubuka were hung in the town square, but the rope failed do it's job. Elder Frederick Miller called for the torches but the flames failed their mission as well. Many in attendance ran in fear while others called for drowning. The young girl protested her innocence, but the black slave cursed at the crowd and warned them that he would get free and kill us all. Both were brought to the sea and weighed down. The water did make them howl in pain but could not destroy them. With each try the weights wouldn't hold. They broke their shackles with ease and amazing strength. It was then decided by Reverend Foster and Elder Miller that the two should be buried alive. They were nailed in their coffins while a countless number of small bees swarmed on them. The big crypt that had been recently constructed for the Wallace family was used to inter the pair while the Wallaces were buried in the more

common area of the cemetery. Reverend Foster then prayed that the evil that has come to our town will never escape the heavy solid wood and stone structure. By the end of the day many families were seen moving out in search of more peaceful surroundings.

"So, you are saying that the Manchester girl and the slave were brought all the way to Portland 120 years after they were buried outside of Plymouth?" Chief Richardson asked.

"It looks that way, Sir," Tony replied.

"There's no mention of him on the mausoleum up there now," I said.

"I think I can explain that." Tony continued, "A slave back then would have no legal rights. He would have been considered just property. He would have never been given any status, not even his name on a tomb."

"You've done good work, Detective Reza," the Chief remarked.

"Thank you, Sir. But there's more. I called the Massachusetts Historical Society earlier today to see if they had any info on strange deaths near Plymouth in the 18th Century. A nice lady, Miss Elizabeth O'Brien, faxed me some reports about an hour ago."

The first item was from the Boston Gazette in 1725:

Word comes today from Constable Richard Hale in Plymouth Plantation that a madman has killed all six members of the Justin Smith family. All met their fate near the cemetery located just outside of town. It is reported that Mr. Smith and his three sons were bludgeoned to death with a huge knife. Betsy Smith and her 16-year old daughter were found inside the cemetery. No visible means of death was determined, but the Smith girl was heard to whisper something about a big slave and a huge amount of bees just before she succumbed. That started rumors again about the slave known as Lubuka, identified as a great wizard who was buried alive along with a local witch twenty-five years ago, has returned from the dead. Local school children have used his name to scare their little friends for years. Constable Hale said such talk was pure superstition and that he and his men will find the real killer in due time. Meanwhile, all in the town are warned to stay away from the cemetery until this matter has been resolved.

"A month letter there was a follow-up story." Tony continued:

The strange killings going on in Plymouth Plantation grew more mysterious yesterday when the murderer was cornered near the cemetery. Constable Hale shot the man several times but without success. His men failed in their attempts as well. The killer, thought to be a runaway slave, was grotesque, standing about seven feet. A local Indian-Guide working with the Constable then fired a flaming arrow into the big slave's chest and his whole body lit up in flames. As he continued walking the flames went out. All ran in horror and the rumors persist that it was the evil wizard, Lubuka, out of his grave and carrying out the killings he had promised just before he and a young witch were buried alive in 1700. Many residents are reported to be moving their families out of the area.

"The last newspaper clipping faxed to me was from The Plymouth Courier. It's from August of 1750:

A great tragedy occurred Thursday last when four members of the Plymouth Militia were found dead near the cemetery. The men had just completed training and at first were thought to be drunk or asleep as no visible signs of an attack could be found. One of the men, Ralph Webster, was found two hundred yards from the others. Sheriff Owens suspects they were suddenly put upon by thieves without warning. It's assumed that young Mr. Webster had tried to run for help. How the four were killed remains a mystery. Local historian, Curtis Hirsch, reports of similar mysterious deaths in and near the cemetery dating back fifty years. Webster leaves behind a wife and a six-month old boy-child. The other three have been identified by Captain Wellman of the Militia but names are being held until family members have been contacted. Adding to the mystery is the fact that a small number of tiny bees were found dead inside the mouth of one of the victims. This fact gives credence to the information provided by Historian Hirsch, that the area may again be plagued by a dead witch and wizard reaching out from beyond the grave to cause evil in the land. Sheriff Owens wants it known that superstitious talk will only add to the problem and that the populace should put such thoughts out of their heads. Both Sheriff Owens and Captain Wellman agreed that the killers were alive and will be found. Curtis Hirsch said he would keep an open mind.

We all gave Tony our attention as he read one more fax. He told Andrea before he read it that he thought it was about her mother, and if she wanted him not to go ahead with it he would stop.

Andrea asked the Detective to continue. She was eager to hear all she could about her mother.

"This was from a local Plymouth resident who wrote a letter to her sister up in Salem Village. It was dated July 26, 1790."

My Dear Pauline, I hope this letter finds you and your Benjamin well. We are all in good health. My youngest, Matthew, is feeling so much better. The fever has broken and he is happy and hungry thanks to a strange young girl we met in the cemetery while we were paying our respects to James' parents. It was near sunset on Monday last. We had just placed flowers on their graves when I noticed a young lady walking with a great swarm of bees on her back. She walked toward the big Wallace crypt without any regard to the very tiny bees. Suddenly and quickly she turned and walked our way. She waved her arms and the bees flew into the crypt. I immediately thought of all those stories and rumors about a pretty young witch who had power over bees. You remember when we were young we would tell the cousins about the big evil slave and the witch who returned from their graves to walk among the dead. Remember how Mother would say those stories were not true and then punished us for telling them. I'm not so sure, Dear Sister. When she came toward James and me we wanted to run, but some strange force kept us there. She approached and warned us that it was dangerous for us to be there. When she turned to walk away I asked her if she was the witch in the stories that children tell. James was horrified that I even asked, but I had to know, hoping she may have a cure for Matthew. She kept walking but said for us to wait. She entered the Wallace crypt and soon returned. I can't explain it, but I wasn't scared, not like James. She smiled at me and handed me a small vile with liquid in it and said to rub it on Matthew's chest. I asked how she knew he was sick, and how she knew his name. She said it wasn't important, just to be sure to rub it all on his chest. When I asked her if she was a witch, she said she was not. But those bees came back and settled on her, and she returned to the crypt. James said we should never go back to that cemetery again and that I was not to tell anyone about what happened. All I know, Dear Sister, is that the potion worked and my son is well. Please write when you can,

Your Loving Sister,
Helen

We were all captivated by the letter, but the Chief was still thinking about the news reports about Lubuka. "Good God!" Richardson exclaimed. "If hanging, fire, bullets, and drowning couldn't kill him, what in the hell are we going to do?...And where in the hell is Feeney? He should be hearing this." The Chief began pacing the small living room like a general contemplating his next move.

"Why were they buried in that spot on the Western Prom when there was no cemetery there? Why weren't they re interred in one of the established cemeteries?" the D.A wanted to know.

Andrea spoke up, "This is just a guess but the Manchester's may have been Catholics, and according to the church history that I have studied, Catholics were discriminated against in Maine in the early part of the 1800s. Several of the churches were burned and the local bishops and priests were forced to leave town. Catholics were probably banned from burial in the normal places."

The Chief's frustration continued. "Charlie, if you know how to destroy them, you're going to have to do it?" His training had not prepared him for the task

I looked at Andrea and replied, "I think I know what Cindy wants me to do."

"You mean that mumbo-jumbo she talked about in her journal?" The D.A. inquired.

I nodded as I kept my eyes on Andrea. She knew what needed to be done. She might even have to do it.

"But how the frig do we destroy that big bastard in the black coat, that Lubuka character?"

"I'm not sure, Chief, but obviously from what we heard from the Kostenello girl and the accounts we just found, we can hold him off and cause him great pain with water."

"I'm going to have every fire truck and anything else that can haul water brought up there to surround the place. Those boys at E.P.A insist that the pesticides will kill anything, but they don't know the full story. I'm going to have to give them their three days to prove them wrong. Meanwhile, it will give me time to get the fire departments coordinated." The Chief ran his fingers through his hair as if that would help him make his plans. "Where the hell is Feeney? It's not like him to be late for anything. You can usually set your watch by him"

Andrea than asked if she could read her mother's journal. I handed it to her, and Maria let Andrea have her arm back as she got up to make some coffee. We all sat quietly, letting my daughter have time alone with her mother's words. I took time to reread the accounts that Tony had just gone over.

Chief Richardson took the opportunity to use the phone in the hall to call the Station for any new developments. There was nothing to speak of. The black and white unit sent to keep an eye on Paul Feeney's grave site reported nothing out of the ordinary. They did say a woman, presumed to be his mother, stopped by to visit.

As he hung up and headed back toward the living room there was a pounding on the door. The Chief opened it to find John Feeney standing there with sweat pouring off his forehead.

"John, what's wrong? Where have you been?"

"He's got Kim," Feeney blurted out in horror.

"Who's got Kim? What are you talking about?"

"Chamberlain! George Chamberlain!!!" shouted the attorney.

"John, come in and sit down and tell us about it," the Chief prodded as he escorted the excited lawyer from the Reza porch.

The attorney stumbled into the living room and plopped into the La-Z-Boy. He looked at Jimmy as if he would be the quickest source for a drink, but settled for the coffee Maria had just made. Feeney drank it quickly and then bounded up out of his chair, and nervously started pacing as Chief Richardson had done earlier.

Still out of breath, Feeney spelled out the facts. "Just before I started on my way over here, I checked my messages. There was one from Chamberlain saying that he had Kim...That bastard of a warden must have told him about Kim and me...He let him escape I tell ya...That prick!...If Chamberlain harms her, I'll kill him with my bare hands!"

"Easy, John, easy", pleaded the Chief. "Now, tell me exactly what he said."

"He says he's going take her up to the old cemetery, tie her up and leave her there for the bees to do their thing. I rushed over to her apartment to see if she was home, but all I found was this note."

The Chief took it from Feeney's trembling hands and read:

> I got your girlfriend, Feeney. I'm going to have some fun with her. Is she very playful? Don't worry, I'll find out for myself. After I'm done with her, I'm going to have her write down everything you two have been doing behind your wife's back. Bet she even knows of some shady dealings that you've done over the years

too. The papers will give you some nice headlines. Guess you won't be Governor after all, you arrogant bastard. Maybe you can save the bitch. I'll leave her tied up but still breathing in that damn cemetery where the bees rule. I understand they can now kill. If you hurry you might find her in time. It all depends how good she is to her "Uncle Georgie" HA! You know what I mean? I haven't had a real woman in a long time and I don't give a shit if those bees get me too. I want out of this world anyway.

"C'mon, Ray. Get your men. We've got to get to her before anything bad happens."

"John, we can't go near that cemetery now. It's too dangerous. They just sprayed the place with deadly pesticides," explained the Chief.

"Well, we just can stand here. We've got to do something!" Feeney insisted.

It was then that Jimmy picked up the note that the Chief had put on the table. Something on it had caught his eye. "Hey, you guys, this is the kind of paper I had in the shack. See, it has the logo of the Boston and Maine Railroad."

Feeney's eyes glistened at this tidbit "That shithead must have her down there. Probably thought that it was abandoned. I bet he hopes to jump a train if he makes it out of that cemetery."

"How did he get by that goddamn killer dog that tried to eat me?" wondered the Chief.

"He must have shot him...or Brutus might be off hunting for a meal," Jimmy pondered. He sighed and sat back down. "I hope he got away. I love that big mutt."

Andrea sat with him and took his hand. Being a comfort was not just part of her job, it was part of her nature.

The Chief called for back up. The D.A. went with Richardson and Feeney. Tony, Jimmy, and I went in Tony's car. Andrea stayed with Maria.

"Be be careful, Tony. You're just getting your strength back," his mother warned. She lived with the fact that he was a cop and the uncertainty that any cop's family has to live with. Would that be the last time she has a chance to say, "Be careful?" She prayed not.

"You be careful too, Dad," Andrea said.

"Yes ,Charlie, please be careful," Maria added in a more comforting voice than her normal tone.

You all be careful. That means you too, Jimmy," Andrea insisted.

Jimmy looked at me, "She's a gem, my friend."

"I know, Jimmy, I know."

24

The perimeter around the cemetery had been extended two more blocks for safety reasons just before the spraying took place. More of the neighbors complained that they had to leave the premises for a few days, even though it was to help save their lives. Hearing threats of, "I'm gonna have your badge for this" or "I'm going to call my councilman" are just part of the job for those who put their lives on the line for very little pay and no gratitude. "Don't forget, I'm one of those citizens that helps pay your salary." One of the perimeter cops said that line was one of his favorites, a real "oldie but goodie."

Tony's and the Chief's cars arrived at the Danforth Street blockade at the same time. It was a hot night with high humidity. The extra protective gear proved necessary but cumbersome. Brian Dewolfe stayed behind at the road block. He was an obese man with a slight limp, the result of a high school football injury suffered at the hands of none other than John Feeney. The situation could have been more serious for DeWolfe if we had to get out of there in a hurry. He looked relieved as he wished us well. The Chief carried an extra mask should the Jenkins woman still be alive. The look in the lawyer's eyes was that of a man obsessed. If he got his hands on George Chamberlain one of them would not come back alive, maybe both of them.

Tony, Jimmy, Chief Richardson, John Feeney, and I started the four block hike up Danforth Street, It was eerily quiet as we made our way past St. Louis Church or "The Polish Church" as it was called by the ethnic population that surrounded it back when I was a boy. The lights were out at the posh and upper-crust Waynefleet School as we passed by. You could always almost always hear the sounds of young girls playing soccer under the lights on the field in back of the school, but not now. The lights were out. No one was home. All we could hear was an occasional night hawk and our own labored breathing. The ever-present song of the crickets was over. Maybe they saw us with those big ugly masks and lost their will to sing. Finally, we reached the dirt path that would take us down the hill to the caretaker's shack.

MIGHTY JOHN MARSHALL

The Chief and Tony were armed with their standard-issue service revolvers. John Feeney had his 350 Magnum, but Jimmy and I were still considered just plain citizens and not allowed to carry firearms. We went along, not only as interested parties, but for what we could contribute. Jimmy could control Brutus, if the big dog were still alive; and I could keep a watch out for any unwanted activity from the cemetery. I would have no problem with Cindy, but that was not the case with Lubuka. Let the perimeter cops laugh; I carried one of the bazooka squirt guns. It was our other weapon and we just might need it.

I was amazed at the athletic ability of John Feeney. He wasn't as over weight as Dewolfe, but he was close. I guess it was the adrenaline that pumped him up. The rest of us had trouble keeping pace with the fast-walking lawyer. He was pissed off not only at George Chamberlain, but at the Warden who was his rival for the Democratic nomination. I had learned that Warden Dudman and Feeney were friends at one time, working on statewide campaigns together in Maine. Both had explosive personalities and often clashed in public. Each was accused of stealing the others thunder in taking credit for successes and placing blame for losses. The final straw came when a young intern, fresh out of college and working on her first campaign, came between them. It was Dudman that brought her on board and developed a more than passing interest. When Feeney saw her he turned on the charm and offered her a job as a clerk in his office, paying twice the going-salary and paying off her student-loans. It was more than Dudman could offer. Today that girl is Feeney's very private secretary and the same girl that has been abducted by convicted killer and rapist, George Chamberlain.

From the top of the hill we could see candlelight flickering through spots in the dirty windows of the caretaker's shack. One lonesome whistle echoed through the night as one of those unnoticed freighters moved on down the line. There was no sign of Brutus, but we could hear the little unnamed dog yapping at someone inside the shack. As I quickly adjusted the mask on my face I could make out the odor of something that spelled danger. The night air around the place was still, and it hung on to the smell of gun powder that lingered there. Someone may be dead.

STUNG

We started down the hill single-file, Feeney in front. When the Chief suggested he go first, the lawyer's stare convinced him otherwise. *She's my secretary. I run this town. You owe your job to me. I pulled you out of that shit-hole, Bangor.* Feeney didn't need to say the words. The Chief understood his look and acquiesced. We could communicate through the masks although our voices were muffled. But it was best to keep quiet and blend in with the noiseless night.

With gestures and hand signals we made our way to the shack that had been Jimmy Peters' home for the last several years. Now inside was chubby, cat-killing, bubble gum-chewing, bee-stung George Chamberlain. He was a bad kid who was all grownup and still bad, an escaped convict filled with hate and revenge for the man who put him behind bars. It was John Feeney who convinced the jury that the only buzzing going on in George's head was his conscience telling him that he was guilty as sin for kidnapping that waitress from Mooney's Country Bar. It was John Feeney who said Chamberlain raped the waitress repeatedly, despite her cries that she had two young babies at home who needed her. It was John Feeney who reminded the jury over and over that the helpless woman was left at an abandoned warehouse with no way to escape the vermin that would finish her off.

"Chamberlain showed this young mother of two no mercy and you the jury must do the same. Return a guilty verdict and send this inhuman *thing* to spend the rest of his days rotting in jail."

It probably didn't take much coaxing from the Warden to make George *run for it*, just a reminder of the trial and his treatment at the hands of then young lawyer, John Feeney.

It was decided that Tony, dressed in street clothes, would approach and knock on the door, pretending he was lost and looking for directions to the highway. Richardson, in uniform, would cause Chamberlain to start shooting first and asking questions later. And if the escaped convict saw John Feeney he wouldn't even ask questions. He would just blast away. If he happened to recognize Jimmy or me, the memories of the day we invited him to play ball may flood his demented brain and that could spell our quick demise. *Georgie Porgie, puddin' and pie. Miss a meal and I bet you cry.*

Richardson and Feeney took their positions under the left-side window while Jimmy and I went around to peep through the back room window.

We could see the Jenkins woman on the cot. Her hands and feet were tied down...her panties stuffed in her mouth. Her blouse had been ripped open and there were deep teeth marks on her breasts. The blood looked fresh. She was staring straight up at the ceiling and the look on her face was pure terror, not just for all the perversions she had suffered at the hands of George Chamberlain; but we could see what she could see. Hanging from a ceiling pipe was a netted bag with two rats trying to gnaw themselves loose, their bucktooth overbites tearing at the thin rope that separated them from their next meal.

Chamberlain was guzzling beer in the front room and throwing empties at the little dog. The frightened animal was cowering near the front door, doing his best to escape from Chamberlain's vicious version of dodge ball. Through his fear he continued barking in defiance, hoping for his big buddy to come home and tear his tormentor to shreds. *Hey, Spike, you and me are friends, right, Spike?* There was no way of telling if the little dog knew what Jimmy didn't know. Would his pal and protector be coming home again? Had Brutus licked his last face and eaten his last candy bar?

Jimmy stayed by the bedroom window while I went over to tell Richardson and Feeney that the Jenkins woman was in there and still alive. No need to tell the rest of the story and make Feeney go over the edge. He was a stick of dynamite now.

The Chief threw a small rock toward the front of the shack, the signal for Tony to knock on the door and go into his act.

With the sound of the knock the little dog started yapping even louder. It almost sounded like a plea of, *Help me! Help me!*

Suddenly, there was a voice from within. "Who's there!?!" It wasn't granny asking if it was Little Red Riding Hood knocking. The voice was gruff and sounder more like the Wolf himself.

We were a fair distance from the most heavily sprayed areas and so the young detective took a chance and lifted his mask, "Ah, my name is Tony and I'm lost. I'm looking for directions to the highway. Can you help me out?"

"No I can't, so get the hell outta here!!! I shot a big fuckin' dog earlier tonight and I don't like people any better," Chamberlain warned.

Reza pushed his luck a little further. "Sir, do you think it would be all right if I used your bathroom? I've been on the road a long time and I really need to go badly."

"Look around, Asshole. The whole area is a toilet. Just drop your trou and take a leak or a dump...wherever you want...and then get going before I call the cops."

"Well, do you at least know of a good hotel around here that would have a safe? I'm carrying a lot of cash! I want to make certain it's under lock and key for the night."

I looked at the Chief who acknowledged without speaking, *That kid's got balls.*

Suddenly, you could hear the creaking of a fast-opening door. The Chief rose up to peer through the window. He could see a silhouette of a man with a gun.

Tony was surprised by the quick move of the convict. Before he had a chance to react, he was looking at the barrel of a Saturday-Night-Special.

"Get in here, Copper!" Chamberlain demanded as he pulled Tony forward with his free hand. "Just how stupid do you think I am? I bet you're not alone, are you?"

"SHIT!!!" Richardson shouted, loud enough to be heard through his gas mask. "I can't get a clear shot through that filthy window and I can't see well enough though this damn mask. I might hit Reza."

"FEENEY, I bet you're out there too!" the killer hollered from inside the shack. "Gotta tell ya, Johnny boy, your girlfriend is real friendly...REAL friendly...She loves rubbing those massive melons of hers all over Georgie's face." Then he laughed in the most sinister manner. "She's got real good PENMANSHIP too!!!" His laugh grew more evil. "I can see it in the papers now. Hell, maybe they'll print a picture of the actual note. It's VERY clear. I even think she enjoyed writing it, took extra care to make sure it was VERY neat and VERY accurate. You're gonna be VERY sorry for jailing my ass!"

The Chief and I had all we could do to calm John Feeney down.

"Don't answer him, John. That will only give him more satisfaction," Richardson urged in his muffled voice.

"FEENEY!! I know you can hear me, you shithead! Well listen up, I got a new deal for ya. Now that I've gotten me some, I decided I like it enough to make me wanna live. That bitch is THAT good!!!" he teased and laughed again. "Tell you what, Feeney with the teeny weenie..." He giggled, pleased with this latest insult. "I'm gonna give your slut back to ya, but I want a million dollars cash and a car. Me and your girlfriend here will drive down 95 for a day, and then I'll kick her ass out...sound good to you?"

"John, tell him yes. That will give us time to get the tear gas I sent for," the Chief said. "We'll fill the place and rush him. Kim will be all right. He won't kill her. Chamberlain's got a taste of freedom now, and he wants to live."

"FEENEY!! I CAN'T HEARRRRRRRR YOU!!!

The big lawyer lifted his mask and yelled, "All right, but I need a couple of hours to get the money together. I don't have it on me, you numb shit!"

"Uh uh, temper, temper...no need for that kind of talk. After all Feeney, we have something in common now, but next time you kiss her, just remember where her purty little mouth has been." Chamberlain was enjoying having the upper hand and he was going to play every ace in the deck. He laughed that same kind of smoker's laugh that his father had when he sprayed Jimmy and me with nicotine spit all those years ago. "You want more time, no problem. Meanwhile, I'm gonna send this dickhead detective back to ya...without his gun of course. Let's just say it's an act of good faith on my part. Besides, I'm gonna have another two-hour go-round with that big titted wonder of yours...and we want our privacy." Chamberlain howled with satisfaction and then added, "By the way, the Warden sends his love!!!" George had just played another ace.

"I'm gonna KILL that BASTARD!!!" Feeney shouted as he stood up.

The Chief pulled him back down. "No, John, we can't take a chance. He ain't going nowhere. We'll get him. Let's go back and see if the tear gas is ready. We'll lob it in. It might irritate Kim for a while but she will be fine."

"Wait!" Feeney instructed, his face still red with rage. "Send back Charlie. At least we'll be here with guns if that idiot decides to go out in a blaze of glory. Before he does we might be able to save Kim."

"What about the money?" I asked.

"Charlie, that's just a waste of time. If we let him out of here he'll just kill her when he gets out of town anyway," Richardson stated matter-of-factly. Feeney agreed.

Tony came out, and I went back to let Jimmy know what was going on. He stayed his position in hopes that Brutus might show. He hadn't heard that his companion had already met his fate, and I didn't think it was the right time to tell him. I then made my way back up the hill and started for the blockade on Danforth Street.

As I got to Vaughn Street I heard my name. I turned and saw her yellow hair shining in the soft breeze. There was a dark sky but the orange moon was bright, providing a natural spotlight for her. She was standing by the wrought-iron fence, and for the first time I realized she was a prisoner to her surroundings. With all her powers, she was stilled trapped by her destiny. She beckoned to me and I went without hesitation.

"Charlie, do not be afraid. He is busy with his monstrous plans."

"Cindy, are you all right? Did the pesticides kill the bees?" I asked in a muffled voice.

"They are fools to think they can harm us or the bees. You must warn them to drown the bees. It's the only way to destroy them. But there is no need to kill them if the Evil One can be destroyed. The bees will die when I leave this world. That thing on your face, is that to protect you from the poison?"

"Yes, it's called a gas mask."

"You can remove it. I inhaled all the poison so that you and your friends would be protected.

I did as she instructed. "But, Cindy, how can Lubuka be destroyed?"

"I see you have read my papers. You know his name. Now you know everything. I am so glad. I will do my best to destroy him. I will find a way...I must."

Seeing her the way she looked...still wanting her the way I always had...made me want to grab her and run away to a far off island where it could be just the two of us.

"Cindy, I still love you so much. How can I possibly do what you ask? How can I destroy you? There must be another way."

"There is no other way. Now you know who John was. He was a good man, but he was weak. You must be strong, Charlie."

"It's just that you mean the world to me and thought of...killing you...is too much to bear."

"Charlie, you won't be killing me. You will be setting my soul free, and I will wait for you in Paradise."

"Was that what you wanted me to do back when we were...I mean...I was seventeen? You wanted me to pour water on your heart?"

"Yes...but then I found out something you need to know." Her face grew serious, almost if she was actually aging. "I just couldn't tell you back then, I just couldn't." She lowered her head as if afraid to look me in the eyes.

I tried to make it easier for her and put my hands over her fingers, still clinching the fence. I whispered, "You were pregnant?"

Her eyes grew larger as if it was the one thing on my mind she couldn't read. "You knew, but how?"

I pushed myself against the fence to get as close to her as possible. "Cindy, there is something else you must know." I was so pleased to give her the good news. "Andrea is *here*, in Portland."

"Andrea?...My baby!?!"

"Our baby, Cindy...Our baby."

Cindy looked so fragile now as she absorbed the news. "Charlie, I *must* see her!!! Please, bring her to me!"

"You know I will. She wants to see you as much as you want to see her."

"Tell her not to be afraid. I filled her with an anecdote as I did you. The bees cannot harm her." She then backed away from the fence, as if afraid to ask her next question. "Charlie, does she know *everything* about me?"

Yes, Cindy...she knows. She even wears your scent. I'll let her tell you all about herself and you will be so proud of her. She is very beautiful and so good."

"Oh, Charlie, this is the most wonderful news! I can go to my final rest in peace." The woman I had loved for so long fell to her knees and cried tears of joy. Though they burned upon her cheeks she didn't seem to notice.

I wanted to stay with her but time was not on my side. I then told her of the current dilemma down at the caretaker's shack.

She got back up on her feet and wiped her eyes. "Let me read your mind, Charlie. Look right into my eyes and think of everything about the situation and everyone involved."

I did as she asked. Cindy closed her eyes and then spoke, "Tell Jimmy to open that back window. I will send the bees in fifteen minutes. Tell the others not to be afraid. They will attack only Chamberlain."

We kissed though the fence and I was seventeen again.

"Now go. Hurry! Tell your friends about our plan...and, Charlie... be sure to tell Andrea that I love her."

"She knows." I comforted her as she walked away.

Cindy didn't look back, but raised her hands and the bees began to swarm around her.

Back at the shack I told Richardson, Reza, and Feeney about my meeting with Cindy. I explained how it was now safe to remove the masks and about her plan to help us. I then went around back and told Jimmy. He opened the bedroom window slowly, just a crack. We sat down and waited.

"Did you see Brutus anywhere?" Jimmy anxiously wanted to know.

I could honestly say I hadn't.

The buzzing sound was low at first and then louder and louder with each passing second. The invaders poured through the window opening, steady and sure. Kim's eyes began to bulge wider and wider. She had no way of knowing these little creatures were her rescuers.

Suddenly, George Chamberlain began to scream in terror as he recognized the bees. He dropped the gun and ran out the door and into the night.

Jimmy and I went in through the bedroom window and untied the terrified secretary. The Chief, Tony, and John Feeney rushed in through the front door.

MIGHTY JOHN MARSHALL

The Chief sent Feeney to comfort Kim, while the rest of us went outside to make sure the bees finished off Chamberlain. The murderer/rapist was running for an open boxcar that was slowly moving down the track. I began to worry, if he made it, he could make his way out of the bees' territorial boundaries. With one giant leap of desperation the frightened convict jumped up and inside an open boxcar. He cursed and mocked his attackers. The Chief and Tony fired their weapons but missed their target.

As they lowered their guns in disgust, there was a great commotion inside the slowly moving train. Chamberlain's screams became louder and we thought some of the bees had gone that extra mile and found their prey.

Like a man being shot out of a cannon at the circus, Chamberlain came flying back out of the boxcar, his neck split and bleeding profusely as it gave way to the mighty jaws of his executioner. Brutus was a mighty force to be reckoned with. The giant dog tossed Chamberlain about like a rag doll. Jimmy gave the command for Brutus to back off, but the dog wasn't as obedient as the bees. Chamberlain was on his own and with one last curse from his bloody lips his life was over. Brutus, filled with blood lust, was panting heavily. He gave a look to Jimmy as if to say he couldn't help himself. Jimmy understood and gave his companion one last hug. The earlier bullet wounds from Chamberlain's gun showed gaping holes in the big dog's chest. Brutus warbled off into the night...to die.

Feeney came out with Kim who was still in a state of shock. He had covered her with a blanket from the cot and we made our way back up the hill and safely to the barricade. An ambulance was waiting to take her to Mercy Hospital just down the street. Feeney jumped into the back.

Before the attendants closed the door Portland's most powerful lawyer said, "Charlie, tell her thanks."

I nodded and he smiled.

As the ambulance pulled away with sirens blaring you could still here the yapping of the little dog with no name. He had made his way behind us. No help from us, just guts and determination.

"Jimmy, it's time to give that little guy a name," I said.

"How about...Little Brutus?" my friend whispered, still feeling the pain of his loss.

"Sounds good to me," I replied. "How does it sound to you, Little Brutus?"

The little dog yapped with approval and jumped up into Jimmy's arms.

25

John Feeney stood on the sidewalk outside the hospital doing two things he hadn't done in a while. One was smoking, and the other was reflecting on his life and the choices he had made. The rest of us politely listened as we waited for the doctors' diagnosis of Kim Jenkins' physical and mental state. John started talking about his wife, Sandra, and how much he still loved her.

My mind flashed backed to the high school football games at Portland Stadium when John was the Captain of the Cheverus Stags and Sandra cheered him on from the bleaches. I made most of the games, but Sandra was there for all of them...rain, snow, whatever. She was a tall, sandy-hair beauty with the kind of smile, innocence and personality of a Miss America contestant (*Mr. Parks, when I finish college, I want to work for world peace and stop hunger.*)

John had those boyish good looks like you might have seen on your Wheaties Cereal box featuring an all-American hero. Other than their physical features, they were as different as night and day. It was a clear case of opposites attract. John's family was wealthy and ran in the highest social circles, while Sandra's family was blue-collar workers whose social events including things like bowling and church activities. The Feeney's would host big parties at the country club and work on political campaigns. Sandra's family was more comfortable with back yard barbecues and just hanging out in the neighborhood with their own kind. They even had second thoughts about taking John's offer to pay Sandra's tuition to Boston University. But their pride took a backseat to their gratitude. It all boiled down to what was best for Sandra. They didn't know then that they should have hung on to their pride and Sandra.

In public, in his presence, Sandra could be quite shy while John told the jokes and bought the beers. Her listening was genuine and polite. Whenever there was small talk, John never heard a word, other than those in his head plotting and planning whatever it was that could benefit his hero, himself. If you had taken the time to notice, you would have seen that Sandra had eyes for no one but

John, while his eyes were sizing up every young female that crossed his path.

Sandra was a regular Tammy Wynette, standing by her man. As I thought of her, thanks to Detective Russell and his 8-track tapes, I could hear Waylon and Willie on the radio in my mind, She's A Good Hearted Woman (In Love With A Good Timin' Man)

But now outside the hospital, with his girlfriend in great stress and pain inside, the reflective lawyer said if he had his life to live over he would do so many things differently. "When this is all over I'm going to take Sandra on a trip, maybe to Europe, to that same little hotel where we had our honeymoon." His eyes were tearing up.

"I think she would like that," said Brian Dewolfe, not quite believing that Feeney had turned over that proverbial new leaf.

"Dewolfe, you Old Bastard, you always had a thing for Sandra didn't you?" the lawyer replied with a half-smile.

"I still do and if she ever comes to her senses and drops your sorry ass, I'm gonna make my move," the D.A. said in a teasing yet respectful way.

"HA! She would never leave me. She should, but she won't...not even after all I've put her through," Feeney boasted as he reminisced. "By God, I am going to make it up to Sandra. Kim is a wonderful girl and she's deserves more than spending all those weekends, Christmases, Thanksgivings, and New Year's Eves alone... and being talked about behind her back. She certainly deserves more than what that prick Chamberlain did to her."

Almost as an afterthought Feeney added that he didn't think his girlfriend/secretary would have written that tell-all note. It was as if he expected her to swallow a poison pill and take her own life before giving him up to the scavengers. "She's always been my good little soldier...you know, just name, rank, and serial number and nothing else." Feeney looked down, giving himself time to digest the betrayal.

"John, I don't think anyone could be expected to take the torture Chamberlain put her through," remarked the D.A.

"Dewolfe, you would have given me up for a good cigar," Feeney said, just half in jest.

"Hell, John, I'd give you up for a *bad* cigar," Dewolfe answered back, making one wonder how much truth was in his little shot at humor.

The lawyer held back any reply to the D.A. He threw down his cigarette and obliterated it with a few quick turns from the toe of his shoe.

"That's it, boys, I've made my decision. I'm gonna straighten up and fly right. Shit, I don't even care about the nomination. Let that bastard of a warden have it."

"Don't worry about that, John. We all heard Chamberlain say the Warden let him escape," assured the Chief.

"Ain't that a kick in the butt cheeks," Feeney laughed. "Now I don't want the nomination and that ass-wipe can't get it. You run for it Brian, I'll back you all the way. You deserve the headaches that go with that job. From now on I'm gonna stop and smell those goddamn roses everyone is always talking about."

"John,...Tony, Jimmy and I are going to head back over to Tony's house. I have to pick up Andrea and Tony's mom will want to know he's okay."

"She'll want to know you're okay too, Charlie," Jimmy teased as he held Little Brutus in his arms. "Do you think she will let me leave my dog with her till I get settled?"

"Not to worry," Tony replied. "Riley will love having a playmate."

"Charlie, who is Andrea? I noticed some pretty young thing when I rushed in on you guys earlier tonight." Feeney wondered out loud.

"That pretty young thing is my daughter and Cindy's daughter." I surprised him.

"And she's a nun!" Tony added.

"Oh man! This is unbelievable! Charlie, you should write a book about this. No one will believe it except maybe those of us here. Hell, I'm right in the middle of it and I don't believe it." The lawyer shook his head as he walked back through the emergency room entrance to check on Kim Jenkins.

"I'm not sure Feeney will ever smell a rose unless there's a vote in its pedals," the District Attorney said in a low voice as we watched John disappear into the hospital.

"Don't you believe a man can have a change of heart?" I asked.

DeWolfe chuckled sarcastically and said, "Maybe some men...but not that one. He may be feeling melancholy at the moment, but that's just a detour on his road to power."

"You may be right, Brian," conceded the Chief. "Only time will tell."

"Ray, please keep in touch with any new developments," I requested.

I was still worried about Paul Feeney. Hopefully he was resting in peace, but I still wondered. Richardson was the only one who knew of the possibility it could be otherwise, but this again was not the time or place to worry John Feeney with news that no parent would want to hear.

"I'll do that, Charlie," granted the Chief. "And you guys call me too if any other weird shit happens."

Weird shit, that seems to sum up the last two weeks of my life.

As we approached the bottom of Munjoy Hill, on the way back to the Reza residence, weird shit was happening again. Tony slammed on the brakes, seizing up the engine, as two pedestrians walked in front of his car. They were paying no attention to the hazards of the road, but these two were no ordinary citizens out for an evening stroll. I recognized their faces from the pictures in the Sunday paper. It was Holt and Nelson, the first two victims in the current round of slayings. One Eye Wheeler had gotten it right. He had seen them walking as they were now, long after they were laid to rest in their graves. Lubuka had succeeded with his formula this time around. It took three hundred years of trial and error and lots of killings, but the evil wizard has prevailed. Holt and Nelson were *undead* and walking around Portland.

With the car stopped, Little Brutus leaped out of the window before Jimmy could hold him back. Brutus had whimpered and cowed at the smell of the undead, but his namesake ran full throttle toward Holt and Nelson. The two continued walking down the Eastern Promenade toward the heart of the city. The dog jumped and sank his teeth into Mr. Holt's right hand. Holt made no noise but shook the little dog off. To our horror, the dog flew through the air with a big hunk of flesh still in his mouth. The bony hand of Mr. Holt was totally exposed and yet he made no sound. Little Brutus joined us in our shock, and spit the dead man's rotting flesh onto the ground. The feisty dog jumped back through the car window and buried himself behind Jimmy, finally acting the way his old partner and hero did. Pardon the pun, but Little Brutus had bitten off more than he could chew.

Tony tried to start the car, but like Holt and Nelson, it was *dead*. I tried the police radio without success, and then, as if sensing a command, the *undead* turned and walked slowly toward the car. Their hands were outstretched, ready to grab their victims at first touch. Their yellow rotting teeth cradled ominous looking fangs; and their bites were almost mechanical, snapping at anything in their paths.

Losing my ability to speak had become a common ailment in the last two weeks. I heard myself say the words, "They are coming for us," but Tony and Jimmy couldn't hear me. Tony was still fighting with the car, coaxing it and cursing at it as if it could actually hear.

Jimmy was still comforting Little Brutus as I started pounding on the top of the front seat, trying one more time to issue the warning. Soon they got the message anyway when Holt and Nelson ripped off the driver's side door. With a cop's reflex, Tony pulled out his service revolver and fired six shots into Nelson's chest. The blasts scattered great chunks of rotting flesh and knocked the *thing* on his ass. But soon Nelson was back up again, resuming his mission and reaching for the nervous Detective. Tony's face turned pale, the way it did when he saw Lubuka speeding across his path on Cassidy Hill.

I sat there helpless as Jimmy tried to save his little dog. Acting like a protective parent, he shoved back Holt with his legs. Bits of Holt's flesh flaked off his body like a bad case of dandruff, but like his old drinking buddy, Nelson, he kept coming. Both of them had their mouths wide open. Their yellow teeth were dripping with some kind of gooey liquid. In an instant I realized it must be the venom from the bees that Lubuka had pumped into them.

Nelson now had his hands around Tony's throat and lifted the Detective out of the car and into the air, high above his head. That smell of dead fish and decay invaded the front and back seats. Fighting anyway he could, Tony latched onto Nelson's ears and pulled them off. We were further sickened as gasses poured forth from the holes now opened on the ghoul's head. The sewer smell intensified.

STUNG

With a natural reaction I covered my mouth and nose.

It was then I inhaled the smell of strawberries and heard Cindy's voice as clear as if she were sitting in that deathtrap with us. "Water, destroy them with water."

I turned around, poked Jimmy, and pointed to the bazooka squirt gun on the floor of the back seat. With a barely audible voice, I begged, "Water gun!"

Jimmy's eyes lit up as if salvation were at hand. He tossed it to me just as Holt took hold of his legs. Little Brutus, forgetting his fear and loving his master, lunged for the throat of the rotting beast. Startled, Holt let go of Jimmy's legs. Jimmy slipped out the door on the other side of the back seat, as I exited the front.

Tony was now gasping for air as Nelson's teeth were inches away from the Detective's heart. I pulled back and forth on the pump action squirter and blasted Nelson in the eyes. He howled with pain and dropped Tony to the pavement. Then Nelson reached for his eyes and tore away the burning flesh from his face. It peeled off like an avocado. Soon there was just bone. Everywhere there was water, whether on flesh, bone, or clothes; there was smoke from the burns it made. Nelson was smoldering before our eyes.

Similar squirts to the face of Holt caused the same results. His screams echoed against the big apartment houses on the block. Both of the *undead* were walking in circles like robots that had been short-circuited. Jimmy pulled Tony backed to our side of the car. Little Brutus, now spitting out more chunks of flesh, made his way back too.

It wasn't long before Holt and Nelson were facing our way again, ready to resume their orders to kill. Tony was barely conscious and couldn't run. It was there we had to make our stand. Jimmy had found the other bazooka water gun under the seat and the battle continued. As the two approached again we fired as fast as we could. Their faces soon turned to nothing but skulls, void of all skin except for their fiery red eyes. The smoke from their burns made a heavy haze and soon they took cover in it. It was so thick that Jimmy and I couldn't see through it. We sporadically fired our weapons, sometimes hitting but most of the times missing. It was like playing a kid's game of BATTLESHIP, sometimes you sink an enemy sub and most times you don't. *B-4...Enhhh, you missed!*

We decided to move back toward the grassy hill on the other side of the street, dragging Tony with us. As Holt and Nelson moved toward us, the haze began to thin, and the silhouettes of the two creeps became clearer.

In my barely audible voice I said to Jimmy, "Wait till they get closer. Aim for their hearts."

Jimmy said, "You got it, my friend."

Holt and Nelson, now walking slowly on almost nothing but their skeleton frames...their rotting clothes hanging off them...were about five feet away when we fired recklessly. They kept coming. They were now about four feet from us, howling in anger and pain as the water splattered all over them. The smoke began to thicken again. Jimmy and I stopped firing. We were running out of water and couldn't see a thing.

All at once a bony hand reached through the smoke and grabbed, Jimmy by the throat, knocking his water gun down over the embankment. My old friend disappeared into the thick cloud, and Little Brutus ran in after him. I panicked and fired what water was left in my gun. Loud Screams mixed together and I couldn't tell Jimmy's yells from those of the *undead*. I fired again, but the big bazooka water gun was empty.

Suddenly, the limp little dog came flying out of the haze and landed...still...in the middle of the street. It was all over for Little Brutus. The faces of Cindy, Andrea, and Brother Joe flashed in my mind as if for the last time.

"In the car," said the raspy voice. It was Tony coming back to consciousness. "Water bottle...Under driver's seat."

Quickly, I ran around the cloudy haze and found a big old bottle of Poland Spring, right where Tony had indicated. The smoke was thinning and Holt and Nelson were walking in one of those robotic circles again. The water from the guns was not enough to destroy them. It had messed them up and fried their brains, or whatever the hell it was that made them function out of their graves.

Almost without thinking, I quickly rushed into the misty mixture and poured the water all over them. Their great strength weakened as the water burned into them, and within seconds they lay on the ground in a big heap of broken, smoky bones. They were dead for the second time...hopefully, for the last time.

I almost took time to feel sorry for them. They weren't responsible for their actions, but they had killed Jimmy and Little Brutus. I went back over to sit next to the recovering Detective, and buried my face in my hands to grieve my great loss. It seemed like an eternity had gone by when I heard the familiar voice.

"What a couple of maroons!" It was the voice of Bugs Bunny. No, it was the voice of Jimmy Peters imitating Bugs, the way he used to do when we were kids. My friend was alive and sitting on the curb across the way. I jumped up and ran over to him.

"Jimmy, how did you get away?"

"Those two idiots dropped me when you hit them with more water, and then they started choking and biting each other. I just ran out of the smoke and came over here figuring you were safe enough with those two goobers going after each other."

"Well, I'll be jiggered," I said, mocking my friend.

"I saw you get the bottled water out of the car and I knew you'd finish them off. Besides, all my strength was gone and I wouldn't have been much help."

I helped my friend up and we went back over to check on Tony.

"I do have some bad news, Jimmy," I said as we crossed the street.

"What's that?"

I'm afraid Little Brutus...is dead."

"He better be. That's the way I trained him."

I stopped in my tracks, absorbing another jolt of surprise.

Jimmy whistled and then yelled, "All right, boy, wake up...C'mon"

The little dog yelped, jumped up, and ran to Jimmy's side.

"After he followed me into that smoke when one of those bastards grabbed me, I told him to *play dead* and they tossed him out. I had a lot of time in that old shack to teach him tricks. Playing dead is one of his favorites. He's a smart little guy."

Little Brutus jumped up into Jimmy's arms and began licking his face.

"My face and his balls! Those are his two favorite things to lick,"

Jimmy said.

His joking was comforting. I had been through hell tonight, but I had to laugh. A best friend like Jimmy is priceless. I knew that, and thank God, so did Little Brutus.

26

The next morning Maria and Andrea offered to cook breakfast for Tony, Jimmy, me, and any others in our current circle. We had all become close, almost like a real family, in just a short period of time. We were brought together by circumstances and fate, and we bonded. We sat around Maria's dining room table talking about the recent events. The table was covered with a lacy cloth that had belonged to her mother. Tony had mentioned how few times over the years she had brought it out. It was for special occasions and special people. It certainly made Andrea and me feel closer to her and her son.

We were joined by Chief Ray Richardson and District Attorney Brian DeWolfe. John Feeney had gone home to be with his wife, to picking up the pieces of their broken lives. We hoped, for Sandra's sake, that he would succeed. The D.A. said he had his doubts. My gut told me the same thing. The Chief seemed a little quieter and more subdued than usual, but I figured that was natural after a tough day's work. The rest of us may have felt the same way, but we had to put on a smiley-face so that Maria Reza wouldn't know that her only son had almost been killed the night before.

As Riley and Little Brutus fought over the same chew toy under the table, we brought the Chief up-to-date on last night's confrontation just down the road. Tony and I had agreed to make his mother think it was just a fender-bender accident. We said it was so insignificant that we would *never* be hearing from those two again. I knew, by mentioning the names of Mr. Holt and Mr. Nelson, the Chief would read between the words, and realize that the two were now dead for the last time. But the possibility that the others would rise out of their coffins was still something to worry about.

"Well, now that I've checked on all my patrols and all is quiet, I am really going to enjoy this fine breakfast," the Chief proclaimed as he tucked a napkin under his chin.

It seemed to me that Richardson was trying to fake a contented emotion. I had an uneasy feeling that he was holding something back, something that would spoil our meal if not our day. Something best not mentioned at the breakfast table.

"Tony, you should be more careful! You always drive too fast!" Maria warned as she poured coffee for everybody.

"You taught me to drive, Ma," Tony said sarcastically in his defense.

"Did I teach you to have a smart mouth too?" she snapped back, and then blushed as she realized she probably had. I decided not to add my two cents. What good would it do?

Andrea gazed at me as if to say, *that's right, better to keep your opinions to yourself.*

I smiled at Andrea and thought again how frantic Maria would be if she knew her son had almost been killed twice last night, once by a demented convict who had pointed a loaded gun two inches away from his face. And once by two guys who had been *dead* for two weeks. Some things are on a strictly need-to-know basis. Besides, Maria Reza would have locked the poor kid in his bedroom and thrown away the key had she learned the facts.

Andrea was now looking at me in that same way Cindy did when she wanted to read my mind. I could tell that my daughter knew we weren't exactly telling the whole truth, but she understood and asked, "How do you like your eggs, Dad....fried?" Then she gently laughed under her breath.

The thought that my daughter had inherited some of her mother's uncanny abilities startled me and embarrassed me. And I thought of that saying that the apple doesn't fall far from the tree.

Maria spoke before I had chance to respond, "Charlie probably likes his eggs scrambled, just like his brains!" Her shoulders shook as she giggled to herself.

"Charlie, this is my mother at her best."

"Well, if that's her best, I'd sure hate to see her worst."

Maria stifled her laughter and fired back, "Well, you just keep on making a fool of me like you did last night, making be think Andrea was your girlfriend and not your daughter, and you will see the worst of me."

"That's enough you two. You act like children...No...You act like you're married," Andrea teased.

"Bite your tongue!" Maria and I responded at the same time.

Everyone laughed. That was good. It was the medicine that we all needed, but I had come to realize that the laughter doesn't last long, not like it did when Jimmy and I played ball in our cemetery playground. Take it while you can. Let it help you through the night, and the night was about to get longer and darker. I could just feel it in my bones.

"So, Chief, where do we go from here?" I asked, still sensing that he was holding something back.

"Those boys at the E.P.A are sure hard to get along with, and I have no choice but to give them their three days to see if the pesticides do any good. We'll hold another press conference then and let the public know everything we know."

"*Everything*?"

"Yes...with all the uncertainty in this case the public has a right to know so they can make an informed decision on whether or not they want to get the hell out of Dodge."

"But, Chief..."

"Ladies, will you excuse us? I'd like to have some shoptalk with the guys."

Maria cleared away the dishes with Andrea's help. "Sure, push us off to the kitchen where we belong. One of these days, Andrea, women will rule the world and it will be a far better place."

"I thought we already did, we just haven't let the men know yet," my new-found daughter joked as the two went off together.

Tony, the Chief, the D.A., Jimmy, and I took our coffee and went out to sit on the front stoop. It was about nine in the morning and already hot and muggy, just the kind of conditions when all the killings take place in that old cemetery.

The colorful sails on the big and small boats, quietly drifting through the waters of Casco Bay, added to the tranquility of another summer day in Vacationland. The innocent scene cast doubts that the end of one age was at hand and the beginning of a new age was just ahead... an age where the dead walk and evil rules.

Richardson's face grew serious as he gave a quick glance around to check for prying ears. The Chief breathed in some morning air and began. "After you left the hospital, even after you went home, Brian,

I stayed behind with John. You know how reflective he was last night. I just felt it was the right time to tell him that his son may not be *resting in peace*."

"What the hell are you saying?" asked the District Attorney.

Tony and Jimmy silently asked the same question as indicated by their furrowed brows.

"You and Tony, and Jimmy here...and even Feeney didn't know; but Charlie's old girlfriend up there told him it's possible that Paul, his friend Steve, the dead newsman, and those three sorority girls may be like Holt and Nelson...*undead*."

I explained further as the others listened, spellbound, "That old slave or wizard, or whatever that Lubuka character is, was trying different potions on the victims after the bees had killed them to see if he could bring them back to life. He wanted to make an army of the *undead* and take over the world, or at least Portland. We know he succeeded with Holt and Nelson, but we are just not sure about the rest."

As our little audience listened in stunned silence the Chief continued, "I've had a black and white doing constant surveillance over at Calvary Cemetery, checking on the areas where Paul and the Winchell kid are buried. I've also sent out warnings to the authorities in Massachusetts and Georgia where the other victims were laid to rest. I told them there may be some grave robbers trying to cause trouble as they had with Holt and Nelson. I didn't tell them that Holt and Nelson were seen out of their graves...and walking around town."

"Not anymore, Chief," Tony added. "They can be killed by dousing them with water." The Detective then gave his boss the harrowing account of last nights fight to the finish with the two winoes from the dead.

"Well, that's two down, but just how many more there are we just don't know," Richardson said as he wiped the morning sweat from his visor. Sometimes I noticed he would do that just before he had more startling news. It was like in JAWS when they would play that dunt dunt dunt dunt music, signally that it was feeding time and a big bite was coming up.

I continued, warned by the visor wiping that another monster may be out of the closet and heading for the innocent victim asleep in her bed.

"And Cindy said Lubuka is working feverishly on a potion of some kind that will bring everyone buried there out of their graves, no matter how long they have been dead. That could spell the end for all of us." My friends sipped on their coffee, contemplating only things that would be personal and relevant to them. Then I added, "The major problem, as far as I know, is that big bastard can only be destroyed by pouring water on his heart while saying the Lord's Prayer. Now, that part may be possible, but it must be done by someone who *loves* him. And that's impossible."

"Is that the way for Cindy too?" Tony asked hesitantly.

"I'm afraid it is, and I guess that's where I come in. That's what she requested. If Paul Feeney and the others are out of their graves, it just takes water till they lose their strength and die again...but for Cindy and Lubuka it takes two more steps.

The district attorney spoke up. "Why say anything to John until we are sure?"

DUNT.

"Brian, let me tell you and the others here what happened in that hospital room last night."

"You mean when he told Kim he was going back to his wife? I was wondering what she would say about that. She's a pretty strong-willed person herself. She's not the kind to go without a fight, or at least causing a whole lot of trouble for being cast aside. Like they say, 'Hell hath no fury like a woman scorned'," stated Dewolfe.

DUNT DUNT.

"No chance of that happening now." Richardson sighed as he continued his update. "Kim was laying there with all those tubes in her arms and up her nose. Her eyes were open and she was looking at Feeney. John was by her bedside and I was sitting in a chair in the corner. I don't think he even realized I was there. At first I thought I must have dozed off and was having a bad dream. But I was awake all right. I just wish I had been dreaming. John just sat there, holding her hand and saying how sorry he was for everything that had happened to her, and that someday she would find the right guy and live happily ever after."

"That's not all than strange," DeWofle responded.

DUNT DUNT DUNT.

"It's what he said next," Richardson cautioned as he sucked in some more dewy morning air. John said, 'You may even have a fine boy like Sandra and I do with Paul. I was just saying to Paul last night that we had to go on another fishing expedition down in the Keys and see if we can catch an even bigger marlin. Sandra said this time she was going along too. She doesn't ever want to be out of Paul's sight again...now that we have him back. Things are really going to be different from now on. It's not every family that gets a second chance to have their son back'."

"Chief, are you saying that Paul *is* like what Holt and Nelson were!?!" Tony asked in horror.

Richardson put his cup and saucer gently down on the concrete step as if it were a piece of fine china. The clinking sound it made was the only noise we heard, as we were all mesmerized by the Chief's story.

"When I heard him say that I almost crapped my pants. At first I just thought he was having some kind of breakdown; or was doing some wishful thinking out loud, not realizing anyone could hear him. I got up, slipped out of the room, and contacted the black and white on duty over at Calvary. I had them take a closer look at the grave site. They were back on the radio within ten minutes."

"And?" we all asked.

"Other than some new flowers, everything was in order."

"Thank God for that!" the D.A. exclaimed.

DUNT DUNT DUNT DUNT.

The Chief took a big breath. "Now, hold on to all that keeps you from going insane. When I slipped back into the room, John was on the phone. He was crying. 'Paul, you know how much I love you. Yes, I'll be coming home soon. Sweet dreams, My Boy. Please put Mommy back on the phone. No, she can't come to the phone? Is she still afraid of her own little boy? All right, I'll be right along. I've finished up here and soon I'll be back with you, Paul. Tomorrow we'll take a drive up to Augusta and check out the Governor's Mansion. Soon it will be our new home and someday you may be

Governor...or maybe even Senator. Yes, I think I can swing that. I have a new plan. Just wait till I tell you'."

DUNT DUNT DUNT DUNT...DUNT !!!

"He hung up, took one last look at Kim, squeezed her breasts, and said, ' Honk honk, you Bitch, you'll never tell on me again.' Then he left and I stood in the shadows. I could barely move. Slowly I walked toward Kim. Her eyes were closed and her face was blue. Her hands were cold and clammy. The tubes were out of her arms and nose. I checked for a pulse, but there was none. She was dead."

"JA-EE-SUS!" exclaimed the D.A. "Did you see him take the tubes out or harm her in any way."

"If he did, it must have been when I was out of the room. I called the nurse and doctor on duty, but they couldn't say for sure how she died. The doctor said the shock of what Chamberlain did could have killed her. Sometimes a trauma like that just makes a body want to give up living. There'll be an autopsy sometime today and we should know more. I called Blanchette and told him I wanted the report as soon as he had it ready."

"Maybe Feeney's telling her he was dumping her was enough to send her over the edge," DeWolfe suggested. "That sneaky prick with his crocodile tears had me feeling sorry for him. That was all an act last night...saying how he wanted to straighten up and fly right. All these years I've worked with him I have never really liked him, but I never saw *all* his dark side...not like this."

"I can't believe it," I said. "He seemed so genuine in his concern for Kim and for Jimmy, even for Cindy. Sandra is who I feel sorry for...I feel like such an idiot!...I think of how he was with the Kostenello girl, so tender and caring. He couldn't have cared less, other than what she had to say regarding Paul's killer. He had me completely fooled."

"Not me," said Jimmy. "Anyone who would let someone live in filth and squalor, the way he let me live in that run down dump, is a first class A-hole."

"Why didn't you say something to me before?" I asked.

"He was grieving for his son. It didn't seem like the time to call him on it," Jimmy replied.

It was then Tony spoke, "Ya know it just hit me. When I went back in to check on Kim after Chamberlain was finished off, Feeney was looking all over the place trying to find that note that Chamberlain made her write. He didn't go to her first to see how she was...That heartless selfish SHIT!"

"What do we do now, Ray?" the D.A. asked the Chief?

"Other than wait for the Coroner's report, there's not much I can do. If it looks like foul play he'll probably worm his way out of an arrest. With his connections it's going to be tough making a charge stick, especially when there are no witnesses."

"Yes, you're right, I know." The D.A. agreed. "He might even plead insanity and make you say you heard him talking to his dead son on the phone. Hell, he'd more and likely say he was trying to help her, giving her mouth to mouth when she stopped breathing (*There was no doctor or nurse handy. I did my best trying to save her. She was such a wonderful woman. This is such a shame. Please remember her in your prayers and at church this Sunday*). Shhh..it!...They would probably give him another commendation to hang on his wall right next to the picture of him and Al Gore...the one that says, 'Best wishes, John. Maine is lucky to have you'."

"There's just one other thing, Chief." I had to ask. "What if Paul really *is* at home? If Feeney is that far gone, he might have dug up the grave on the chance that One Eye Wheeler wasn't just blowing smoke out his ass."

"Charlie, I don't even want to think about it, but I know we'll have to check it out. First thing I'm gonna do is drive over to that cemetery myself. Feeney has enough suck to make those patrolmen I have over there take a hike while he does what he has to. I'll check the grave myself, and if it looks the least bit disturbed, I'll grill those two in the back and white till I squeeze the truth out of them. Now that I think about it, they seemed more nervous than usual last night."

Without notice, Andrea was at the door. Her usual smiling face was sad as she handed me my cell phone.

I have to say I didn't see this coming. There was no warning. I didn't hear the JAWS music this time.

"Hello, this is Charlie."

"Charlie, when are you coming back?" asked the weeping voice of Georgia Allen.

"Georgia, what's wrong?"

"It's Mr. Allen. He had an attack last night. They think it's his heart, but they're not sure what it is. They are running more tests now."

It was the last thing I expected to hear. Barn was getting on in years but he was as strong as a horse. "I'm so sorry, Georgia. What's his current condition?"

"He's stable...but I am *so scared*, Charlie!" Her voice was panicking.

Andrea was holding on to my arm with genuine concern, and I knew from the look in her eye what I had to say. "Listen, Georgia, I'll call the airlines and book the next available flight to L.A. I'll be there as soon as I can."

"Thank you, Charlie. I am so sorry to call you, but Mr. Allen loves you like a son and so do I. I'll feel so much better if you are with me." Her wavering voice seemed to steady with the news I was on my way.

"I love him too, Georgia, and I love you. I'll call as soon as I get into town." We said our goodbyes. I clicked off the cell and went inside to look up the number for the Portland Jetport.

As I made my reservation for six o'clock Andrea tugged on my arm and said, "Make it two tickets, Dad. I'm going with you." I was hoping she would.

Other arrangements were made. Jimmy and Little Brutus would stay at the Reza house till I got back. Chief Ray Richardson, District Attorney Brian DeWolfe, and Tony would keep in touch with me on any new developments. Maria would drive us to the airport. She insisted and you don't say no to her.

Something else I was learning fast is that you don't say no to Andrea either. I knew without asking...with several hours before the flight...my daughter wanted to meet her mother. She insisted. I agreed...It was time.

What can I say? Mother met child. Child met mother. There were lots of tears, kisses, and hugs. It was a private *family* affair, but I know *you* want to know all the details.

With the Chief's help we passed by security. We took the gas masks as they insisted and removed them when we were out of sight. I took Cindy at her word that the pesticides would not be a problem. I had a fully-loaded bazooka water gun just in case Lubuka or any of his army were lurking about, but I knew in my heart and in my gut that we would be fine as long as Cindy had all her powers.

We walked through the front gates and onto the old ball field toward home plate. We sat under that old elm that had witnessed so much over the years. It had seen me play all those ball games with Jimmy Peters, eat all those Italian sandwiches, drink all that Pepsi, and listen to all those songs on our transistor radios. It hung onto my clothes and kept my encounters with Cindy a secret...back when we were *both* seventeen. It was watching as Jimmy and I made our way past it for the very first time, when we tricked Tommy Caine out of all his Halloween candy. It might have even seen me hit Lubuka in the head with a snowball when I was in the fourth grade and Donna was my damsel in distress. It also stood helplessly by when young Paul Feeney and Steve Winchell shot their BB guns for the final time. It could do nothing when four young sorority girls sat beside it, talking about boys, school, clothes, and their dreams of someday having a great career while balancing a family at home. But their dreams would never be realized. Their fate had been sealed that night when three would die.

That old tree had seen so much in the last hundred years, and now it would see a mother reunited with the daughter she had left under it branches when that baby was three months old. With the sun beating down the old elm shared its cooling shade while we waited. The next moment in time belonged to mother and daughter, Cindy and Andrea.

Suddenly from the east she came, quiet, like a kitten searching out her prey. She was radiant in a white robe. Here hair was up and held together by that antique-looking clasp I remembered so well. Her strawberry scent matched her daughter's.

As Cindy approached, Andrea stood up slowly and began her habit of twirling the little silver cross that was her constant companion. Their eyes locked and would not turn away. Even though I loved them both, I felt out of place sharing their moment.

Almost on cue they extended their arms toward each other. Their smiles broadened and their tears fell. They gently moved closer as if a false step would ruin everything. The first embrace was magnetic; and they clung to each other, and the entire world was a better place if only for a while.

I heard Andrea softly whisper, "Mama."

I heard Cindy reply, "My baby...My Precious One."

That, along with their embraces, smiles, and tears said it all.

Cindy ignored the pain the tears made on her cheeks.

The only real noise was the caterwauling made by me, the proud dad. I was glad that big old elm couldn't talk. It might have reported, "It was a wonderful moment, but you should have seen Charlie blubbering like a baby."

Eventually we all sat under the tree and held hands as Andrea told her mother everything she had done since she could first remember...the orphanage...the other kids...the Rios family...the Sisters...finding me. They laughed and cried some more, and as Andrea continued I could feel Cindy grasping my hand tighter...her way of saying to me without words, *aren't you proud of our daughter?*

Cindy was amazed at how much Andrea looked like her mother, the same auburn hair and big blue eyes.

"My mother would crush grapes and stain her hair so that it looked like wine. All the ladies in the town called on Mother for her beauty secrets...until they accused her of being a witch. No matter how much they turned against her, she would be there for them if a child or other loved one needed a cure. I wish you could have known her. You were named for her...my mother...Andrea Manchester."

Minutes turned into hours. Although the whole time we spent together seemed like seconds. Soon it was time for Andrea and me to leave for our trip back to California. Cindy understood the need for us to go, but asked us to return as soon as possible. She said with the hot dry conditions the evil wizard's powers were growing stronger. In one way it was good that he was busy with his experiments. That would keep him in the crypt, at least for a while.

Cindy watched as we left; and hundreds of bees surrounded her, almost like they were hand maidens and she was a princess. In reality they were tiny little assassins, but she *was* a princess...my princess...my Cindy...and it would always be so.

27

The big Delta jet roared into the evening sun, heading west with Andrea and me and a lot of the network biggies. THE GREAT CEMETERY SLAUGHTER was cooling down. There hadn't been anymore cemetery deaths for a while and interest was fading, ratings were sagging. Sixty second commercial rates were falling; and, after all, the news business is just that, a business. When a story isn't worth more than thirty seconds on the evening news, Brokaw, Rather, and Jennings move on. Time to find the next big story. Maybe, if they are lucky, there will be a serial killer in Florida, or a little girl missing and kidnapped in Texas, an entire family bludgeoned to death in Idaho, a baby deep down in a well with time running out in Kentucky, or if they are *really* lucky, World War III!!! *Oh, man, this is great! Tell the ad boys, nothing less than a million dollars a spot.*

As I sat there holding my daughter's hand, I thought how the news boys and babes would high-jack the plane and make the pilot turn around immediately if they had seen or heard about the *undead*, or had their hands on Cindy's journal, or Tony's findings about all the previous deaths over the years. If they had known Portland's most likely Democratic nominee for Governor had just killed his mistress and had dug up his dead son to take him on a fishing trip, there would have been a group-orgasm.

It was then I had a vision of Detective Robert Russell back in Oceanside saying, *Hey, Pal, I'm only doing my job.* I guess these people were only doing their jobs too. It's just that they seemed to do it so callously. Everything was just names and numbers with no concern about the pain behind the statistics.

Then Andrea smiled and said quietly, "Dad, don't be so cynical about people and their motives. Look for the good in everyone."

I'm sure the look on my face was as easy for her to read as was my mind. "Andrea, are you just guessing what I was thinking, or could you really tell? Do you have your mother's ability?"

"Ain't gonna tell ya!" she teased as she kissed me on the cheek and then followed it up by saying, "You know the apple doesn't fall far from the tree."

"All right, Kid, now you are freaking me out! I'm not going to think of *anything* from here to Los Angeles. You're not going to be able to read any more of my thoughts."

"You can't do that. It's impossible for anyone to go more than eight seconds without thinking about something." She smiled. "Now, if it's six hours to home, how many minimum thoughts will you have?" she asked like I was one of her students?

"I stink at math. That's why I'm a history teacher," I stated in frustration. I thought for a minute and then asked, "What's the answer?"

"See, now you have something else to think about from now till then," she teased again.

"Why do all the women in my life drive me crazy?"

Andrea flashed her winning smile as she laid her head on my shoulder, while her fragrance created visions of her mother in my head...and my mind drifted back. I spent ten years in Portland after that stormy Saturday when I left that LEST WE FORGET locket under the old elm tree. If you're thinking I went back to the cemetery during all that time, you're right. On sunny days, especially Saturdays, I would find myself walking and later driving up there. It was just me. Jimmy and I never played baseball there again. As the winters melted into spring and the springs lapsed into summer and the summers surrendered to autumn, I made the cycles with them...always hoping that I would turn and she would be there.

Over the years I even sat under the shade of that big elm eating an occasional Italian sandwich, drinking a Pepsi, gazing at the old ballfield, and listening to the last days of the BIG JAB. Great radio stations are like General MacArthur's old soldiers. They just fade away.

Somehow I always felt she was there or nearby. And now my feelings have been confirmed...She was. But I never knew or even thought in my wildest imagination that on one of those days in the following spring she would leave a baby...our baby...under that tree. And I could never have possibly known back then that our baby would be sitting next to me now with her head on my shoulder.

Don't ever try to figure life out, or think tomorrow will be just another day. Fate is just waiting to jump out of the closet and yell, "SURPRISE!!!"

STUNG

Portland changed a lot during those ten years. It was like the city was growing up, setting its sites on the future and not looking back. But I was always looking back, thinking of the good times that were left behind. During that time the city tore down the majestic and magnificent Union Station to put up fluorescent- blinding super-discount stores.

The town got stung again when whole neighborhoods were cast aside in the name or urban renewal. Families were moving out. Crime was moving in. Ozzie and Harriet were leaving town. Ozzie and Sharon would be writing the next gospel.

Playgrounds were shutting down. Parking lots were going up. Apartments were becoming condos. It was the same address, but with the name change the cost went up. Quaint little brick buildings that once served as neighborhood schools were closed. Regional monstrosities were constructed to take their place. You couldn't walk a couple of blocks and be in school, not anymore. Now you had to take a bus. As for the convenient little neighborhood schoolhouses, Ooops! There goes another condo complex.

The big old movie theaters with their huge balconies and even bigger screens, and with their plush seats and magnificent smells, were giving way to tiny screens, tight seats, and higher prices at the Cineplex.

The Christmas lights on Congress Street seemed dimmer as did the business of the downtown merchants. The MALL was rising out of the dirt and grass of the formerly ignored marshlands. Shopping would never be the same. Mom and Pop stores were fading along with the nickel candy they sold. Chain stores were taking over. Prices were going up. Nameless clerks behind the electric cash registers didn't know your name the way Mom and Pop did. What's more, they didn't care. More fluorescent lights, more blinding headaches.

"What? You want me to pump your gas? What are you, crazy? Get outta here before I call a cop."

Then the tragedies that always kick you up to life's next level occur. Dad dies...Mom dies...Much of you dies.

I heard Cindy whisper in my ear on the tenth anniversary of the day I left her the locket, *I love you, Charlie...Move on*. In the other ear I could hear Horace Greeley and so I went west to California and took up teaching. Mrs. McDonough, Sister Mary Margaret and the others must be tuning over in their graves at the very thought.

"I think they would have been very proud," Andrea whispered as she kissed me on the cheek.

"Stop reading my mind before I lose it all together!" I exclaimed. "Geez!!! I have no privacy when you or your mother are around." I grinned and she knew I would have given up all hopes for privacy if Cindy could have always been with me...if we could have had a "normal" life.

I had seen so much and felt so much in the last several days that I didn't really want to sleep. I remembered the dreams and the tape recorder in my mind that had caused me such stress on my flight to Portland. I didn't want to go though that again, but my eyelids were heavy and my body craved slumber. I was use to the normal eight hours of sleep back in Oceanside, but during the last several nights I hadn't slept for more than four at any one time. Besides, I didn't have a yakety accountant or a smug librarian next to me. This time I had my daughter, *our* daughter.

I saw the flight attendant with her push cart of beverages coming down the aisle. By the time she said, "Sir, would you like anything to drink?" I was gone...back to my teenage years with Jimmy.

"Hey, Ralphie boy, do you see what I see? VA VA VA VOOM!!!"

"Who are you, Jimmy...Ed Norton?"

"Yeah, that's what they call me down in the sewer," Jimmy mimicked in his best Art Carney voice.

"Hardy harr harr harr!! Does that make me fat or a bus driver?"

"It could make one of us very happy. That chick walking down the hill is going to be my Trixie or your Alice. But you have a very slight chance...So don't get your hopes up. It's a matter of which one has the most charm...and that would be *me*, my friend."

"Did you find all that confidence in the sewer, Noton?"

"Quick, before she disappears, let's go talk to her. Geez, what a fox! Would you look at those long legs and long blond hair? I bet she's from California, a real live Little Surfer Girl like the Beach Boys sing about." Jimmy was beginning to hyperventilate.

STUNG

The girl was walking past the front gates of our cemetery playground with her head in the air and her chest pushed forward when Jimmy said, "Hey, Crazy Legs, where have you been all my life?"

"Avoiding jerks like you!" was her quick reply. She just kept walking slowly, never looking back.

I liked her already, even if she didn't speak to me. Zinging Jimmy like that was worth being her next target. He was lying on the ground pretending he had just been stabbed in the heart. "Ow ow ow! That knife cuts deep."

"Don't be too hard on my friend," I said. "Every time he sees a beautiful girl his mind turns to mush. And with someone as lovely as you he may never get his mind back." I didn't mean it a flirtatious way, but it came out that way. I was just telling the truth.

Beauty stopped and turned, "Why, that's the sweetest thing anyone has ever said to me. My name is Cindy Manchester. What's yours?"

Jimmy stabbed himself again. "His first name is Lucky...and his last name is Bastard."

"Please ignore my crude friend. My name is Charlie Sullivan and I live down on Pine. Are you from around here?"

She pointed up the hill. "My family just moved into that big brick mansion up there, the one with the little red sports car in the driveway. Daddy gave it to me last week for my seventeenth birthday. Would you like to go for a ride with me sometime? I've got to go buy a new Itsy Bitsy Teenie Weenie Yellow Polka Dot Bikini and you can drive me if you want." She was now moving closer to me.

"Sure! Anytime!!!" I exclaimed as Jimmy drove his dagger in deeper, but this time there were loud groans thrown in with a couple of *why-him-and-not-me, Lords*.

"What does your family do?" I went on.

Well, Mother, is the Regional Sales Manager for Drake's. You'll have to come up to the house. We have one room filled with Devil Dogs, Swiss Cream Rolls, Crum Cakes, Yodels, Ho Ho's, Ring Dings...all the junk food you could possibly eat. Best of all, it's as much as you want and it's all free!

I just stood there with my mouth open. I looked around to see if

Alan Funt was hiding anywhere with his Candid Camera, but I couldn't see anything. I couldn't say anything either. But Jimmy was now choking himself, and it looked like it was for real.

In a barely audible voice he was now begging me, "Please, Charlie...Don't ask her anymore questions. I can't take anymore."

His pain was my pleasure and I continued, "Cindy. May I call you Cindy?"

"You can call me anything as long as you call me *yours*." She was about a foot from me. Her small but perfect breasts were rising and falling with each breath.

"AHHH! You're killing me. Stop!!!" Jimmy was now gasping for air.

I had no sympathy for my friend and said, "So, Cindy, what does your father do?"

She put her arms on my shoulders and locked them behind my neck. She smiled devilishly. "He owns a whole chain of movie theaters. Anytime you want to make out with me in the back row, I can get us in for free."

"*PLEASE, CHARLIE, NO MORE!!!*" pleaded my friend on the ground with his face contorted with every conceivable pain. Jealousy and envy were torturing him, giving me even more pleasure.

Cindy looked at the Rolex watch her mom had given her for her birthday and said, "I have to go now, Charlie. Come see me anytime. Make it tonight if you can. I want you to meet my grandfather. He's so nice. He's going to give me a million dollars on my 21st birthday. He's coming up from Boston. He owns the Red Sox and, anytime you want to go to a game, we can fly down in his private jet. You can even sit in the dugout if you want. You know what? I bet I can get him to let you play. Would you like that, Charlie?"

" Wha...huh...who...wha...whe" I couldn't say anything other than babble, so I just gave her the okay sign. I looked at Jimmy. He now had a rope around his neck and his tongue was hanging out.

I turned to watch her walk away...All of a sudden she was coming back toward me, pushing a cart and saying...

"Would you like a drink?" She gently shook my shoulder when there was no reply. My eyes fluttered and she said, "Sir, this is your last chance to have a beverage before we land in Chicago. Sir?"

"Ah yes, thank you...You don't happen to have any Devil Dogs or Ring Dings, do you?" I asked the attendant while trying to prolong my dream.

"DAD! You shouldn't be eating all that junk food. We'll get some sunflower seeds and soy milk when we land. That will make you feel better."

"Wow, Andrea, you *can't* read my mind after all if you think I'm going to eat that sh...ahh...that...sugarless stuff," I said as I pulled my seat into it's upright position.

"I take it you were having a pleasant dream?" she inquired.

"Let's say it was a lot better than my last one."

Dreaming is a crap shoot. Sometimes you get a bad one and sometimes you get a good one and once in a blue moon you get the one I just had. The worse part is you can never go back and pick up where you left off. It's a lot like life itself. You can try, but it's just not going to happen.

From Portland right into O'Hare, I watched in amazement as Andrea made friends while she did *her* job. There was a retired couple in front of us who had been married for fifty years and this was their first time on a plane. He was more nervous than his wife, but Andrea kept them busy by asking about all the wonderful memories they shared together. At first the man didn't say much; but by the end of the flight, husband and wife were trying to talk at the same time. They didn't even notice when the plane touched down.

Andrea's natural ability to get along with people was genuine and unguarded. I thought maybe she could see the *good* in others, but where was the good in John Feeney, George Chamberlain or that fiend, Lubuka? Where was the justice in the tragic end for two twelve-year-olds who went to shoot their BB guns in the old cemetery? What was the reason those young sorority girls who had studied so hard to get to college had to die, only to leave their dreams unfulfilled? Why did Private John Spiller who spent most of his growing years caring for his siblings and widowed mother have to lose his life in a true act of charity in the jungles of Viet Nam? Where was the understanding for the lonely life of Frank Blanchette who would never know the touch of a woman unless her lifeless body was lying on a slab in front of him? Why did Kim Jenkins have to suffer so much, both at the hands of George Chamberlain and the man she loved and trusted? And what about Sandra Feeney? She loved her husband and her son unconditionally, only to lose one and be betrayed by the other. And yes, what about me, damn it? Why did I have to give my love to a woman who could never be mine more than that one magical summer? Why was she fated to walk the earth for more than three centuries, unable to find true peace?

Those, and a thousand more like them, were the thoughts that occupied my mind as that big silver bird cut through the darkening skies on the way to California or as my brother Joe liked to call it, the "far left" coast.

As I sat silent with my thoughts, Andrea's enticing voice comforted, encouraged, and laughed with her fellow passengers all the way to L.A. But I didn't fail to notice that one of her hands was always clasped to mine and I was proud. She had finally found me and would never be out of my life again. That was the first happy thought I had on this entire flight, other than that dream about the Cindy with the reds sports car and other *goodies*.

"And you're right, Dad, I'll never be out of your life ever again," she said as she looked into my eyes during the final descent. "And stop asking yourself why bad things happen to good people. You'll have all the answers in time...ye of little faith."

"All right, Young Lady, once and for all, how long have you had that mind-reading ability and don't give me any smart-ass answer."

"Long enough to know that you really love Mother. Long enough to know how much you care about your friend, Jimmy. Long enough to know how much Mr. and Mrs. Allen mean to you. Long enough to know how much you think of Maria and her son. And long enough to know how much you love your daughter." Her smiled broadened. "Just the really important things." She gave me one of her gentle hugs. "I can see other things in that thick noggin (she tapped on my head) but I don't like to invade anyone's privacy."

"Good try, but you could have guessed all that by my actions, not by my thoughts or my daydreams.

"You're right again, Dad, "she confessed as we shuffled down the aisle.

STUNG

I was feeling pretty good about being right for a change until she stopped me in my tracks with a little side comment as we departed the plane. "If her grandfather has free tickets to the Red Sox, why don't you drive down in that little red sports car?"

28

I hadn't been in a hospital for over twenty years, and this was my third one in less than two weeks. First, there was the young Kostenello girl at Maine Medical Center, the only survivor so far in the GREAT CEMETERY SLAUGHTER. Second, there was the unfortunate Kim Jenkins whose life was snuffed out at Portland's Mercy Hospital at the hands of her boss and her lover. Now my old friend and Principal, Barnard Allen, was lying in a hospital bed at Los Angeles County General...his life hanging in the balance.

Andrea and I arrived at Barn's room to find his wife by his side. Two doctors and a nurse were talking with each other about a possible cause that could have brought down this rugged and, otherwise, healthy man. All their medical training up to this point gave them no clue.

"We'll have to run some more tests." That's the standard phrase the medical profession uses when they have no satisfactory answer for a wife who is panicking at the thought of losing her husband.

"Charlie! Andrea! I'm so glad you're here." Georgia Allen jumped up and embraced us. "Mr. Allen will be so pleased if only he would wake up. The doctors say it's some kind of coma. His heart seems to be fine. X-rays show nothing abnormal and he's breathing on his own." Her fingers were nervously bumping against her chin as she fought back the tears. "Oh, I must look like a foolish old woman. He's going to be fine, isn't he?" She continued before I could answer, "Why Mr. Allen has never been sick a day in his life. He hasn't missed one day of school in twenty years...I just know he's going to be fine, Charlie...Isn't he?"

"He's not going anywhere, not without the fifty bucks I owe him," I said as I tried to comfort her with humor and move closer to her husband's bedside. The doctors soon left and ordered up more blood tests.

The old man's eyes were closed and his sunburned face was ashen. His snow-white hair had formed a permanent cow lick, having been shoved up by his pillow for quite some time. I noticed that his fingers were slightly discolored, not a good sign from what I've heard. If I hadn't seen the slight rise and fall of his chest, I might have thought he was just waiting to be placed in his coffin. Would it soon be time for Georgia to pick out a suit for him to wear on that long last journey?

His wife's status didn't seem much better. This tall and thin woman had always prided herself on her appearance. There was never a hair out of place. The gleam in her eyes that seemed to be permanent all the years I had known her was now dim and dull. I had been gone about ten days. She had aged about ten years. Her clothes looked slept in. Whatever she wore was always clean and pressed, to the point where it looked like it had just been purchased. She always wore an apron in the house, but she would have considered it a crime to have been seen in one in public. She was wearing it now, no need to make the ambulance wait while she freshened up. Nothing mattered now, except the husband who had dedicated his life to her...the young Marine she had fallen in love with at a dance when she was just eighteen.

Andrea took a seat on the other side of the bed. She had her rosary beads working. Barn and Georgia weren't Catholics, not even that religious. But the old woman seemed to perk up a bit at the sight of Andrea lost in prayer. I thought of Sarah Peters and her picture of Jesus standing at the foot of a hospital bed and what comfort that had given her. Comfort and that chance to hope was what Georgia needed now.

"Georgia, you've told me before of how you met Barn. Would you tell me again?"

"Oh, Charlie, do you really want to hear that old story again?"

"Well, maybe Barn can't speak, but who knows, he might hear you. If you get it wrong he just might wake up and correct you." I put my arm around her to encourage her. I thought if she talked of happier times it might make the waiting easier...for both of us.

"Yes, that would be just like him." Georgia began her story, her eyes constantly fixed on her husband. "I was fresh out of high school and my best friend Vickie and I were going to a dance that wasn't just with high school boys anymore. We were so excited. We spent the whole day shopping for the perfect dresses in hopes of winning a Prince Charming. You remember how those two girls in that Richard Gere movie were always trying to win the heart of one of those Navy pilots? Well, that was Vickie and me all right, only we were after Marines."

A nurse had come in to take Barn's temperature and got caught up in Georgia's story of young love...first love...lasting love.

The gleam was slipping back into Georgia's eyes as she continued, "The dance was off the base at a Howard Johnson's Hotel. As I later learned, Mr. Allen's friends had told him it was to be a formal dance that would begin at nine on Saturday night. They also said that none of the men would be wearing their uniforms, but rather jacket and ties by order of my father...who was the new Company Commander. Well, the dance actually started at eight and *all* the young Marines were in their dress uniforms. When Mr. Allen walked in wearing a white sport coat with a pink carnation...just like in the song...the whole place erupted in laughter. His black hair was all slicked back and he smiled nervously, like that was his first time out by himself. I felt so sorry for him standing there, frozen like a deer in headlights, wearing a jacket and pants that were way too big for him and shoes...Oh, Lord, those shoes...They had soles that were about two inches high." Georgia paused to hold in a laugh, as if it might appear inappropriate with her husband laying at death's door.

The nurse reinserted the thermometer between Barn's lips. Listening in on this real-life love story had taken her mind off the task at hand and she had to get a new reading. Georgia smiled in understanding and received one in return.

"After everyone had their fun, he sat in a chair in the corner all by himself waiting for the next bus to take him back to the Base. I thought he looked so handsome, even though his clothes were way too big for him. Later on that night, an obnoxious drunk, starting asking me to dance; but I refused each time. After a while he got really loud and started cursing at me. Well, here comes Mr. Allen to rescue me not knowing I was the Commandant's daughter. 'Sir, the lady doesn't care to dance with you, so won't you please leave her alone.' My father and mother were having dinner next door when they heard the commotion. 'Listen, Shorty, I'm gonna dance with this broad, so bug off!!!' Mr. Allen stood in front of me, telling the drunk that he didn't want to have to hurt him so he'd better go. The guy had to be at least six-feet-four and there stood Mr. Allen, all five-feet-six of him willing to be my protector. Well, the big doofus took a swing and knocked Mr. Allen right on his fanny. By then my father had arrived and all the men came to attention except for Mr. Allen. He was having a hard time getting back up on those shoes." She stifled another bout of laughter. "My father helped him up and introduced himself, and then told Mr. Allen that he was out of uniform. Poor Mr. Allen just threw his hands up in the air as if to say, *well throw me in the brig. It would be a perfect end to a perfect evening.* Instead, my father chided the other Marines, who were bigger, for not having the courage that Mr. Allen had. Dad told him the next time he was *in* uniform; he'd have an extra stripe on it. Mr. Allen and I danced the rest of the night. He escorted Vickie and me home afterwards. Mr. Allen and I went out for ice cream sodas that Sunday. Then we took a walk through the park and fed the ducks. When we got to my house, he stood up on the front step and kissed me goodnight. That's how I met Mr. Allen. I fell in love with him that weekend. We were married the following spring. He's been my protector and dance partner ever since. On our anniversary we always go out for an ice-cream soda. Then we walk through the park and feed the ducks. When we come home he stands up on the first step and kisses me, just the way he did back then...Pretty dull, huh?"

The old lady wiped her eyes with a hanky that was already damp and in need of replacement.

The young nurse tried to read the mercury through blurry eyes, sniffling and saying she was going home and dump her self-centered boyfriend, then go out and find a man like Bernard Allen.

"Next May we will have been married forty-five years, forty-five wonderful years." She leaned over the side of the bed and kissed her hero, and tried to smooth out his matted hair. Into his ear she whispered, "I love you, Mr. Allen."

Georgia sat on one side of Barn's bed with her memories while Andrea sat on the other side with her prayers. We all waited for Mr. Allen to find the strength to get back up on his shoes one more time.

Soon one of the doctors returned. He had company. It was the ever-smartly dressed Detective Robert Russell with a donut in one hand and a cup of coffee in the other.

"Yo, Charlie, I didn't know you were back," he said as he stuck the donut between his teeth and shook my hand.

"Hello, Detective, I'm surprised to see you here. Don't they have any other cops in this town?"

"What can I say, Charlie? I'm very popular and it ain't just my good looks." He chuckled to himself and splattered powdered sugar into the air and all over his jacket.

"Mrs. Allen, I'd like to ask you a question," the doctor said as the nurse prepared a syringe and Russell adopted a more professional demeanor.

"What is it, Doctor?" the frightened woman asked as she let go of Barn's hand and grabbed mine...the one not sticky with sugar from Russell's hand shake...She stood up in anticipation of bad news.

"I don't mean to alarm you unnecessarily, but we think you're husband was poisoned. The blood work we did showed a slight amount. We can't pinpoint the exact type of poison, but when he was brought into the emergency room we did find a small needle-type hole in his ear and a small drop of fresh blood that had recently clotted."

The doctor gave the nod and the freshly prepared syringe was gently inserted into a big vein on Barn's left arm.

"Is he going to be all right?" Georgia pleaded to know with fresh hope in her eyes.

We should know in about a half-hour," the attending nurse replied.

"In cases like this, Mrs. Allen, we have to alert the authorities when there might be foul play. That's why Detective Russell is here," the doctor explained.

Russell looked at the perplexed woman as if sizing up a suspect. I sensed his years of repeated assessment told him he did not have his culprit.

"I'll be back to check on your husband in about thirty minutes." The doctor and nurse departed.

Georgia sat slowly back down in her chair and said, "Poison?"

Russell then took charge. I must say he was more gracious with

Georgia than he had been with me that night he pounded on my door, and asked if I had any weapons in the house.

Andrea had finished her prayers and was now standing by my side, listening with true concern.

"Mrs. Allen, can you tell me if your husband has any poisons or pesticides that he might have used around the house?" Russell was prepared to write her answers down on a small note pad that looked like it had been sat on for quite some time.

"Well, we do have some that you can buy at the store to kill weeds and bugs. You know, like Raid and things like that." Her emotions were wrestling with each other. The hope that her husband and protector would be okay was winning out over any fear that she may be a suspect in a poisoning.

"C'mon, Russell, you can't believe that Georgia tried to kill her husband," I snapped.

"Surely not," Andrea said.

"Charlie, please, you and the little cutie pie here, be quiet while I do my job." He wiped his powder-sugared hand on his trench coat.

I felt like saying, "That's Sister Cutie Pie to you, but I held my tongue for the time being and let Russell continue doing his job.

Watching this veteran detective work was a lesson in bad manners in step-by-step interrogation. As he used his car keys to dig out the wax in his ears, he asked, "Mrs. Allen can you tell me what you're husband was doing when he had his attack? Was he doing anything out of the ordinary?...Anything that wasn't part of his normal routine?"

Georgia looked up at me to give her answer. "Charlie, he was getting the mail and had just opened a letter from you. I remember him saying in that gruff voice, 'That Charles will be the death of me yet. He sent me an empty envelope. He forgot to put in the letter!' He was shaking his head and chuckling when all at once he slapped at his ear and fell to the porch floor."

"Letter? But, Georgia...I didn't send any letter."

It was then a voice, I was afraid I would never hear again, spoke softly but clearly, "Yes you did, Charles. Mrs. Allen's right. She's always right!"

"MR. ALLEN, YOU'RE OKAY!!!" Georgia shouted as she turned and hugged him.

Andrea went for the doctor as I looked on in amazement. The color was back in Barn's face and the fight was back in his spirit.

"Barn, I knew you wouldn't leave without the money I owe you," I smiled and teased.

"Damn straight!" he replied more loudly.

The doctor returned and examined his newly-revived patient. "Well, looks like you're out of the woods," he pronounced. As we all thanked him he added, "But, we will keep you overnight just to make sure."

The old Principal objected until his wife assured the doctor he would do as he was told. He might argue with the medical world, but he took his orders from his number one caregiver and his only dance partner. I thought of Maria and the way she laid down the law to Tony, and I smiled.

Even Detective Russell was caught up in the mood. "Glad to see you're doing all right, Mr. Allen. Say, I recognize you. You were the Principal at my kid's school."

"I don't understand about the letter," I went on. Why did you think it was from me?"

"Well, it said Charles Sullivan on the envelope and had a Portland, Maine postmark."

"Do you have the envelope now, Mr. Allen?" Russell asked.

"It's probably on the porch where I dropped it. I remember letting it go when I when to swat whatever it was that bit me, no I should say...stung me."

My face must have given away my feelings as Russell said, "Hey, Charlie, you got that same expression you had when I asked you about that Kostenello girl up in Maine."

Andrea took my hand, conveying the same feeling. I sat down on the side of Barn's bed. "Somehow one of those bees must have been sent to your address."

"You mean one of those killer bees I been seein' on the news?" the Detective asked.

Andrea said, "That Lubuka person must have read Mother's mind and found out who all your love-ones were."

"What's a Lubuka, Cutie Pie?"

"It's a long story, Detective, but someone who's involved in the killings back there has great power and can command the bees to kill," I explained.

"Great!..He must be the life of the freakin' party," Russell commented.

"Yes, he's a real charmer, Detective." Then I reminded Andrea that Lubuka couldn't get to a mailbox or a Post Office, but he could send Mr.Holt or Mr.Nelson to do his bidding. "He must have put one of those bees in that envelope."

My heart was racing as I excused myself while I went to call Joe and everyone else I could think of who might be in danger. I must have spent an hour on the phone, but everyone was warned. As of yet, no other letters had been found, and, pray Dear God, none had been opened.

When I got back to Barn's room he was up, sitting in a chair and eating a steak. His amazing quick recovery was almost unbelievable. Georgia and Andrea were still talking with Russell, who was asking, "Now, who's Holt and Nelson and what the hell is a Lubuka?"

"Tell you what, Detective, let me take you to Hooters when I get back and I'll tell you all about it." He seemed quite pleased with the offer.

"Now you're talkin', Charlie! While you were gone, the doc came back and did confirm it was some kind of venom that might have come from a bee. So Mrs. Allen is off the hook so to speak." He then nodded toward Andrea and said, "You sure your little girlfriend here wouldn't be upset with you if we took in a couple of burgers at that restaurant...What did you say it was called? Hooters? I don't think I've heard of that particular establishment." He feigned an oh-so-innocent look.

Andrea smiled as I turned to Barn and said, "I just don't understand why you're still alive. As far as I know no one has survived the sting of those little killers."

"Well, don't look so disappointed, Charles!" My friend smiled as he took another bite of steak."

"It may have lost some of its potency in the stress of travel, or it may just have been a young bee whose venom didn't pack the full wallop of a full-grown one," Andrea suggested. "Or just maybe it was the power of prayer...hmmmm, Dad? Could that possibly be the answer?" she asked like she was lecturing me for not considering the possibility.

"Well, whatever the reason, I'm just so happy to have Mr. Allen back...my protector!" exclaimed Georgia as she gave Barn a great big kiss.

"Protector! Good grief, has she been telling that story of how we met. I bet she said I was knocked down, but I tripped over my shoes. I slipped and fell down. It was as simple as that, or I would have clocked that guy!"

"Yes, Dear, you were so brave." She kissed him again.

"Well, guess my work is done here," Russell said as he turned to go. "I'll call that Chief back in Portland just to confirm...By the way, Charlie, is this the Rios woman you were talking about? You're right. She is a looker!" He gave me a thumbs-up and left without ever realizing Andrea's profession.

"Say, that reminds me, Charles, have you and Andrea had your little talk? Can I finally put that secret to bed?" Barn continued making up for all the meals he had missed, as he went on feeding his face...never suspecting what he was about to hear next.

"Yes, Barn, I know...But when you feel up to it, I've got a BIG-GER secret! I better hold off telling you that one till you finish eating. I don't want you to choke and turn blue. I might have to give you mouth to mouth resuscitation...UGHHHHH!!!"

"Very funny, Charles! Just let me choke if that happens." The old man suggested with a small laugh. "You mean there's a bigger secret than being in love with a nun! Ha!" He was talking and eating at the same time. Usually that would bring a reprimand from Georgia, but not today.

"Charlie, go ahead if you've got something to say. Don't hold him in suspense or I'll never get him to go to sleep," Georgia lovingly teased.

I couldn't resist doing the similar joke I had played on Maria. "Well, for starters, I love this *nun* more today than I ever thought possible."

"Good God, Charles! Have you completely lost your mind?" Barn asked in surprise, slamming his fork down

"And I love him more than ever too," Andrea said, unable to resist the temptation this time.

"WHAT!!! Andrea, you can't be serious!?! I know Charles has a warped sense of humor, but I must say I never expected such foolishness from you. Where's that nurse? I think my blood pressure is going to explode off the charts!"

Husband and wife now looked at each other like they were watching something wilder than anyone would ever see on Jerry Springer. It was time to spill the beans and put them at ease, before they both went into cardiac arrest.

I stood up straight with Andrea next to me and said, "Mr. and Mrs. Allen, I would like you to meet Sister Andrea, *my*...daughter!!!"

Barn dropped what was left of his dinner. His look of surprise was now that of a state lottery winner. I realized that was exactly how I felt. Having found Andrea, I had won the lottery.

As I explained the secret, Georgia's look of surprise turned to joy as the tears came back. "Oh my God, Mr. Allen, this is like having a son and a grand daughter!" She hugged Andrea. "I thought this day might be the worse day of my life but it's the best!!!" The ten years she had aged disappeared as her world did a 360 degree turn.

The moment was wonderful and we all took the time to enjoy it, but it was just an oasis in the troubled times that surrounded it. The next day Andrea and I would return to what was waiting in Portland. Maybe more envelopes with deadly contents. Maybe more *undead*. Maybe a best friend who had fallen back into his temptations. Maybe the last time I would ever see Cindy again, if I could find the strength to complete her wishes. Maybe is a real big word.

29

My frequent-flyer miles were piling up fast as Andrea and I made our way across country again, back to Portland and the unknown fates that waited for us there. She had received permission from her superiors to extend her vacation. Some vacation! We'll both need a vacation from *this* vacation.

I was doing my best to keep my eyes open, but a six-hour flight was battling against my will. I was exhausted and couldn't put up much of a fight. Andrea was doing her social duties, chatting and laughing with anyone who wanted a kind word and a friendly smile.

It's amazing, but when I get tired, I can sleep through a fireworks display and the blaring brass sounds of a marching band. As I heard the voices of the passengers getting lower and lower, my sleep was getting deeper and deeper.

Soon I was playing ball with Jimmy Peters again. But this time there was no long-legged girl with a red sports car. There was no private plane ready to whisk me and that sexy blonde to Boston and free box-seats at Fenway Park. There wasn't even any junk food. This time there was a new cast of characters, plus some very *old* acquaintances.

"All right, Peters, I'm going to hit this one so far you'll never find it. You'll have to ride your bike to get it. In fact, pack a lunch 'cause you won't be back for a while," I bragged as I stepped up to home plate.

"In your wildest dreams, my friend. Just quit your yappin' and hit the damn thing!" Jimmy said as he spit into his glove and punched it. He was standing at the perimeter of the ball field just in front of some of Maine's Civil War dead.

I tossed the ball up into the air, and as it came back down to waist level I swung my Louisville Slugger. CRACK!!! The bat made the perfect wood-to-ball sound that signaled perfect contact. I swear I could hear that baseball scream as the seams split and the cowhide covering fell to the ground. It climbed into the cloudless summer sky.

Up and up it went passing by bugs and birds, over trees and telephone poles, and...SMASH!!!...through the window of the house directly across the street from the front cemetery gates.

"Eh, what did you hit that one with, Doc, a stick of dynamite?" asked Jimmy "Bugs Bunny" Peters as he scratched his head under his Red Sox cap.

"HA! All us supermen from Krypton can hit a ball like that," I boasted. "Haven't you ever seen that big "S"on my chest?"

"Ya, but I thought that stood for shithead! And, Clark, I hope you got a SUPER wad of cash stashed back at your old fortress of solitude, or you're on real good terms with Lois...Cause that's gonna cost ya some major wampum."

"Oh yeah, well you gotta pay half...cause you couldn't catch it."

"I couldn't catch it? The freakin' Jolly Green Giant couldn't have caught that one. HO HO HO!" Jimmy shouted as he placed his hands on his sides, looking just like that big green logo on the cans of green beans, peas, and corn on the supermarket shelf at the Red & White down on Pine Street

"Well, do you know who lives there? Maybe, it's a nice old lady with a kind heart who won't make us pay," I suggested. "Hey, maybe she's a huge Ted Williams fan. All those old ladies love Ted.

"Keep dreamin', Charlie Boy. I seen a young kid waving in the window a few times. I've never seen his parents, but I bet they ain't going to be too happy with you," Jimmy said as he came back to join me.

"I guess there's only one way to find out. You better go ring the bell and fess up," I recommended. "I'll wait here for you."

"Ya, fat chance I'm gonna' take the fall for you this time, my friend. I got a better idea! Let's go get my sister Polly to go with us. People who get their windows busted go easier on kids if there's a girl involved."

"Geez, I dunno...I already owe her fifty cents. and now she charges a quarter a boob, and that's down right dith-picable"

"Very funny, Daffy, but it will probably cost us more than fifty cents to pay for that window."

Polly Peters hated her name, especially her middle name, Patience.

Polly Patience Peters sounded like a tongue-twister and so she insisted everyone call her Nancy, like her hero Nancy Drew. Of course, knowing her distaste for her full name, Jimmy and I never called her Nancy. Instead we added more "P" words to put in front of her name just to piss her off...as in Pissed-off Polly Patience Peters.

It was getting near dark when we finally found *Nancy* over at a friends house watching TV. On the screen Thalia Menninger was putting one over on poor ol' Dobie Gillis for the umteenth time as his stressed out dad said, "I just gotta kill that boy."

"Speaking of Dobie and Maynard Krebs, this is my goofy brother Jimmy, and his friend Charlie," Polly said, introducing us to her friend Jolene. "What do you two creeps want?"

Jimmy explained our predicament and how we thought the homeowners would go easier on us if we had a girl with us. We even called her Nancy just to make the request more acceptable.

The two girls talked in over in secret, with occasional giggles interrupting their plans. Then they approached us. "Here's the deal. We will both go with you if Charlie takes me to the eighth grade Sadie Hawkins dance this coming fall...and Jimmy you have to take Jolene."

"Sadie Hawkins, no freakin' way. We'll have to wear jackets and ties...and buy you flowers," I said in protest.

"And take a bath!" Jimmy added.

"Ya, and take a bath!"

"Ha Ha! Very funny, but that's the deal. Lump it or leave it!"

It was now our turn to talk it over in secret. Jimmy and I said okay for now. We would find a way to worm our way out of the dance part.

It was a warm late May evening when we approached the house with the broken window. From the outside it looked like there was nobody home, but inside somebody was playing organ music like you hear in church at a funeral. There were no lights on except for two flickering candles burning in the upstairs window.

We stepped onto the front porch and all of a sudden the temperature took a dive. It was noticeably chillier...to the point where you could almost see your breath. Jimmy and I kept blowing into the wind, trying to make it frostier.

"Will you two morons grow up? Get on with it. Ring the damn bell!" prodded Jimmy's sister.

I answered back in an English accent that just seemed to come out of nowhere. "Why, James, the pushy-pissed-off Polly Patience Peters certainly doesn't live up to her middle name now, does she? And would Nancy Drew sound as pernicious as paunchy Polly?"

"Why no, Charles. She's always been pouty, perturbed, particular, and partial to flatulence." Then Jimmy ripped one off. We were overcome with a big case of giggles as the two girls pinched their noses, held their breaths, and threatened to leave us there.

"Jimmy, I'm not sure this is such a good idea. Let's just leave a note with Charlie's phone number on it and an explanation of what happened," a sensible Jolene Beaulieu suggested.

"All right, but no Sadie Hawkins dance," I counter demanded.

"Not fair!" said Jimmy's sister. We came here with you. That's all we promised, so you have to take us." She pouted like a spoiled little rich kid and that made me think of another chain of "P" words but I thought better of it. I was getting too scared.

Buzzzzz. Jimmy rang the bell.

"Screw it! If we still have to go to that stupid dance, then we are going to finish this tonight," Jimmy insisted along with my less-than-supportive backing.

The organ music stopped. The door slowly creaked open to a dark and barren front room. Cobwebs, the size of curtains, hung everywhere. Jimmy said it must have been one huge mother of a spider that spun those suckers.

"Charlie, does this place remind you of another place over on Pine and Carlton that fell down last winter?" Jimmy asked nervously.

"Remind me of it? It looks and smells the same, but it just *can't* be the same.

The big door slammed behind us as we made our way inside, all the while holding on to the girls like they were our security-blankets.

"Hello." I managed to eke out to what look like an empty house.

"Hello down there!" came the reply from the top of the stairs.

It was the little kid that Jimmy had seen waving in the window. "Are you here to see my father?" he asked with innocent eyes.

"That's right, "I said. "Is he mad?""

"Oh...quite mad," said the small boy, and then he laughed an eerie laugh. He beckoned with his long thin index finger for us to ascend the stairs, and we complied as if a strange force was making us do so...pushing us forward with invisible hands.

"Is your mother home?" Jimmy's sister asked, in hopes a woman in that place would make it less terrifying.

"Mother is sleeping, but she should be getting up real soon. After all it's time to feed, or should I say, dine?" Again the little boy laughed in an evil way, like someone might do if he were torturing or killing a cat.

We were now at the top of the stairs as the little kid slid down the banister, "I'll tell Mommy that you're here. I'm sure she's *dying* to meet you." There was that curdling laugh again.

"All right you guys, fuck the dance! Let's get out of here!!!" Nancy screamed.

"WOW! I'm telling Mom what you said," threatened Jimmy.

"Well, if you don't get your ass out of her now you won't be telling no one nothing," proclaimed petrified and heart-pulsating Polly Patience Peters.

As we turned to descend the same stairs we had just climbed, they disappeared in front of our eyes. Behind us we heard a low voice. "Tisk tisk tisk. You'll have to be punished for that kind of talk, young lady. Not very polite for mixed company," he snickered. "You're alive and we're *dead*. Now that's what I really call mixed company." His voice was smooth and baritone.

We slowly turned and there, silhouetted against the broken window, was the figure of a man in a cape wearing an Abe Lincoln stovepipe hat. His face was no more than that of a skeleton and his eyes burned fire-red.

"So, boys, we meet once more. Bet you thought you'd never see me again after my old house was destroyed." He extended his cape, blocking out the light from behind.

I couldn't speak. Neither could Jimmy. Suddenly I could hear pissfizz tinkling down the leg of one of us. There was a lot of crying going on, except from the girls.

"C'mon you two losers, let's go back down before that bony bastard gets us," Nancy Drew commanded.

The girls were in charge. That was fine with Jimmy and me. Anything to get us out of the house. As we turned, the stairs appeared again as if out of nowhere. The little boy was back, along with about a dozen more like him. Joined by what I guess was their mother; they started slowly up the stairs, crawling and clawing at us. The whites of their fangs were dripping blood and they looked hungry for more.

"Come feed, my children," said the beast in the cape behind us. "There's plenty for all, so don't be little piggies." He laughed fiendishly as he closed the gap between us and the vampires ascending the stairs.

Jolene was the first to be grabbed as she screamed in horror. The group of ghouls attacked her like she was a cow that had fallen into a river of barracuda. They tore her limb from limb, their sharp teeth sinking into her tender young flesh. One had her left arm while another had her right. The littlest vampire, the window waver, was sucking all the blood out of one leg while his mother was feasting on the other. A gravy of blood covered the fresh flesh. The rest of the band-of-the-damned tossed Joline's head around like a frisbee. Her eyes were still moving when they threw it up to the bony fiend wearing the Abe Lincoln hat.

With the finesse of Yankee ace, Whitey Ford, he pitched it through the broken window and said, "Here, kiddies, here's your ball back. Now play nice." His fiendish laugh bounced against the walls as Jimmy's sister fell into the teeth and cold dead hands of the vampire band.

Polly Patience Peters punched and poked her attackers like Davy Crockett fighting to the last drop of blood at the Alamo. "Take that you ugly bitch!" she said as she kicked a couple of the tiny vampires, while sticking a bobby pin into the eye of the mother of them all.

The mother screamed in pain and fell all the way back down the stairs. She plucked out her eyeball with the bobby pin still stuck in it, and then ate it like an olive on a toothpick from a martini glass.

"Well, boys," the female fiend yelled up the stairs while licking her lips, "you don't have to worry about going to that sucky dance now."

The vampires descended onto Jimmy's sister until there was nothing left except the ribbons that had been in her hair. The Alamo had fallen. Santa Anna and his army showed no mercy. There were to be no prisoners. "Kill them all and kill them now!"

Jimmy and I were next. We vowed to go out together. We turned toward the monster behind us and rushed him, knocking him to the ground. We were about a foot from the broken window and decided to jump. We leaped and I was free, but the bony fingers of the dead man in the Abe Lincoln hat grabbed Jimmy by the ankles and pulled him, kicking and screaming, back into that house of horrors.

Within seconds there was silence and I kept screaming, "I made it. I'm on the ground! I'm on the ground!!!"

"Wake up, Dad! We're in Chicago. Dad! Dad! We've landed."

I felt my shoulders being shaken, and the pleasant smell of strawberries replaced the musty and decaying smell of the house across the street from the old cemetery.

"Holy moly that was a doozy!!! Andrea, could you tell what I was dreaming?"

"Oh, something about vampires playing baseball...with a couple of girls thrown in. You couldn't have a dream without girls! I was busy talking with another teacher about the upcoming school year and didn't pay much attention to your silly dreams. I don't like to look at your sleeping thoughts. I keep hoping you'll mature and maybe dream about things you can do to make it a better world."

"Why didn't you wake me? That would have made it a *better* world, at least for me," I insisted as I continued rubbing my tired eyes.

"Well, you needed your sleep. Besides, I've heard you weren't supposed to wake anyone during a bad dream. Too much of a shock to the system."

"Whoever told you that never has dreams like I do when I'm on a plane. Next time, wake me. I'll take my chances."

The rest of the trip was routine until we got into Boston where I picked up a copy of THE GLOBE. I had been out of touch with the news for the last twelve hours. I was busy with other things, but the bold black headlines shocked me back to the reality of the day: **PROMINENT PORTLAND LAWYER FOUND DEAD. PO-**

LICE EXPECT FOUL PLAY.

(Portland, Maine) Portland Attorney Sandra Feeney's nude and battered body was found yesterday at the fashionable home she shared with her husband, John, in the upper-class west end part of town. Mrs. Feeney had been under a doctor's care since the recent death of her twelve-year-old son Paul, who was one of the victims in what has come to be known as THE GREAT CEMETERY SLAUGHTER.

John Feeney, who's been rumored to be among the front-contenders for the Democratic Gubernatorial nomination, was said to be in seclusion and grieving his wife of thirty years.

A spokesman for the Portland lawyer said Mr. Feeney had been devoted to his high school sweetheart who was also his law-firm partner. The spokesman said Mr. Feeney had found the body and phoned police. It's reported that the attorney was overwhelmed with grief. "She was my life, my reason for getting up in the morning. All day, whether at the office or in court, I was thinking of Sandra and cherished every moment we spent together," cried Mr. Feeney, according to the officers first on the scene. The police also said the attorney was playing *their song*, <u>I Only Have Eyes For You</u>, as they arrived at the home on the Western Promenade.

Portland Police believe an intruder broke into the home thinking it was empty and came upon Sandra Feeney by surprise. According to the Feeney spokesman, Mrs. Feeney often left the lights off and the home dark while she was in seclusion. Police hope to question Mr. Feeney further when the attorney is up to it. He did say some of his wife's expensive jewelry was missing and would cooperate more fully with Police in the next few days.

The only possible clue was a little gold chain and locket that was found in the hands of the dead woman. There was a sentiment printed on the cheap jewelry making police think it wasn't something that Sandra Feeney would own. The inscription on it is not being revealed to the public at this time. It may belong to her killer.

"SON OF A BITCH!!!" I yelled loud enough to be heard throughout the Delta Concourse.

"Dad, take it easy!" Andrea urged as we handed our tickets to the attendant.

"Feeney is going to try and blame the death of his wife on me! I just know he placed your mother's locket in his dead wife's hand."

"Chief Richardson and a lot of people know you have been out of town and couldn't do that. He also suspects Mr. Feeney in the death of Miss Jenkins. You have nothing to worry about."

"Nothing to worry about?!?" The last time I had nothing to worry about Chubby Checker was twistin' on <u>American Bandstand</u>.

30

There would no more meetings in John Feeney's plush downtown offices. His law practice was over. His clients would have to find new representation. New trial dates would have to be scheduled. He was in seclusion, more likely in hiding, ready to make a break for some far off destination like the South of France where he could con the rich and famous into thinking he was something more than he really was, a cold-blooded killer.

Maria Reza's house was where we gathered now to compare notes and give updates. The house on Melboune Street was in the Munjoy Hill section of town. It was where District Attorney, Brain DeWolfe, and Portland Police Chief, Ray Richardson, also lived. It was where Mr. Holt and Mr. Nelson died...the second time around. Police headquarters was just down the hill.

It was Richardson who spoke first as we settled into our places. "First of all let me tell you that we do have Feeney's house under constant surveillance. Charlie, he had no idea you were out of town and we're gonna let him think that way for now, in hopes that he'll trip himself up. Even a smart lawyer makes mistakes."

"But why would he kill Sandra? She knew about Kim and all the others, and didn't make any noise about it," asked the District Attorney, almost in tears. He had known Sandra for a long time and had quietly been in love with her for years.

"That's just it, Brian. She knew! That maniacal bastard...Ah... excuse me, Sister...He wants to be the next Governor so badly he'll do anything to keep that goal clear of any obstacles."

"But, Chief, a lot of people knew," Detective Reza pointed out.

"That's right, Tony, but the accusations coming from her would be the most damming of all. It would cost him the Governor's job for sure." The Chief speculated. "Remember, lots of people knew about Clinton and the intern and the lies he told, but he kept his job because Hillary 'stood by her man'. Sandra Feeney might not stand by hers forever, at least John wasn't willing to take that chance...not after all that has happened."

"Well, I've called for a grand jury to consider indictments against him in the Jenkins case. He'll never see the inside of the Governor's Mansion as long as I can help it," a defiant District Attorney vowed.

"Just remember, Brian, he's go a lot of influential friends, here and up in the State Capitol...and in Washington, D.C. They all hate him, but they need him. Politics makes strange bedfellows and all that happy horse sh...ah...stuff."

"Chief Richardson, please don't think of me so much as a nun right now, but as my father's daughter. I want to see everyone brought to justice," Andrea said. She took my hand and looked me in the eye and continued, "I also want to bury my mother so that she can finally rest in peace, and my father and I can get back to our normal lives; so that we all can get back to our normal lives."

I knew she was right, but the thought of destroying Cindy was the one thought I fought most to keep out of my mind. The Chief nodded to Andrea in understanding. "One other little tidbit I've learned," Richardson put forth, "Feeney has requested that Sandra's body be cremated and buried nowhere near their son."

It was then the doorbell rang. As Maria answered, Frank Blanchette stepped in. In his hands were two official-looking folders, the autopsy reports on Kim Jenkins and Sandra Feeney.

When I introduced him to Maria and Andrea, two new faces to him, the Coroner acknowledged shyly, as was his nature around attractive women. Frank seemed particularly shy, as if to be extra polite, when I told him Andrea was a nun. He then sought permission from Richardson and Dewolfe to reveal his findings."

"Please sit down, Doctor Blachette, and make yourself comfortable," Maria Reza offered. "Let me get you some coffee."

"Oh, why, thank you. I would like that."

The smell of tobacco followed him though the door and stayed on his breath. His face was gaunt and his eyes had noticeably aged since just a few days ago. I thought to myself that he looked so much older than everyone else who had been in our junior high biology class. They would probably think the same about me, but I don't like that thought. So I don't entertain it too long.

Frank didn't seem to like fresh air or being outside, other than to grab a smoke. He just seemed like he would be more comfortable around a computer screen in the darkness of his room where he could be Tom Cruise to the unknown ladies he chatted with. Even more comfortable surrounded by the dead in the refrigerators of his office. They were his friends, the quiet neighbors who never talked behind his back. He rarely was the center of attention and he relished the moments like the one he had now. We listened carefully as the Coroner made his report.

"First, I would categorically state in any court that Miss Jenkins did not die from the deep bite marks on her chest." He accepted the fresh cup of coffee. "Thank you so much." He sipped it slowly and then continued, "Miss Jenkins had very large breasts." The timid doctor blushed in embarrassment and looked down at the floor.

"Just what was the cause, Frank?" the Chief questioned, losing the patience a good interrogator rarely has...like Joe Friday on <u>Dragnet</u> saying, *Just the facts*.

"I would say she was suffocated, smothered to death by the pillows on her bed. I found tiny fibers from the slip cases in her lungs." Frank's dead eyes began to come alive as he got to the meat of his findings.

"We got the bastard!" exclaimed the Chief. "I can't wait to see him wearing that bright orange and marching into court with cameras capturing every embarrassing moment. I bet I could sell tickets. There's probably a thousand people in this town alone who would pay top dollar."

Dewolfe deflated the Chief's balloon by saying, "No so fast, Ray. The defense will call a coroner who will say that normal inhaling from anyone, lying on or near pillows, could cause the same effect. Plus, there were no witnesses."

"Oh, I beg to differ," Frank said. "There was one witness...Miss Jenkins."

The Coroner seemed to grow in confidence and lose his initial shyness as he saw he had a captive audience who couldn't go further in the case without him. *Anybody need help cutting open their frogs? We do, Frank, we do.*

"Miss Jenkins?" Tony was puzzled.

"Yes, Detective, Miss Jenkins. The dead do talk you know...at least to me." He smiled in anticipation of what he would say next. "There were also traces of an expensive silk, certainly not the kind used in ordinary pillow cases. It was more like the kind found in an expensive tie. The threads were found in her stomach."

"The kind a powerful, rich lawyer would have?" I asked.

"The kind John Feeney *does* have," insisted the excited pathologist.

"For crying out loud!" DeWolfe interrupted. "There are a lot or rich men with expensive silk ties in this town. Even I have a couple. How are you going to prove it was Feeney's?"

Frank, now relishing his role as headliner, grew bolder. He turned to Andrea and said, "They have ears, but they do not hear; eyes, but they do not see. Isn't that something someone in your business was fond of saying?" His voice was now a low smooth baritone, just like the creep in my dreams with the stovepipe hat

Jimmy whispered in my ear, "You think I've been cooped up a long time? This guy has really got to get out more." I think Jimmy could have shouted those words and Frank wouldn't have noticed. The lonely Coroner was in his own zone and he knew where he was going.

"Frank, cut the shit!...show us the proof that Feeney killed Kim Jenkins," a frustrated Chief Richardson demanded, nun in the room or no nun in the room.

Blanchette bathed in his spotlight again and went on, "Like I was saying, the Jenkins woman had the proof you needed. She put up a struggle. As Feeney tried to smother her, his tie must have been dangling near her mouth because I found *this* in her stomach. She must have bitten it off with what little strength she had left." The Coroner literally laid out his proof on Maria Reza's coffee table. Then he sat back down as if waiting for applause.

The D.A. picked up the small piece of cloth that read: Custom made for J. Feeney by Thompson Bros.

Silence greeted the moment and then disappeared. "Justice, sweet justice!" the D.A proclaimed. "Not only will he not be in the Governor's Mansion, he'll be in the jail run by his biggest enemy and opponent, Warden William Dudman. Thank you, Kim!"

STUNG

It was the Perry Mason moment we had been waiting for.

"Good work, Doctor, good work." The Chief congratulated Frank as we all concurred. "I'll have him picked up immediately. No, by God, I'll do it myself. I personally want to slap the cuffs on him and read him his rights. Charlie… You, Tony, and Brian can come along if you want…and you too, Peters. He's caused you a lot of grief as well."

Jimmy smiled in appreciation as I said, "What about the report on Sandra? Frank hasn't filled us in on that yet."

"You're right, Charlie. In all this excitement I almost forgot. Please, Frank, continue with your reports. What about Sandra?" the Chief inquired.

"This is going to be a bit of a bigger surprise. Her body was bloodied and beaten all right, but it was done *after* she had died as if to conceal the real cause."

The room grew silent again as we all sat down in disbelief of what was to follow. The Coroner took a deep breath to get out the words he didn't want to say. "Sandra Feeney is the latest victim in the rash of slayings that started with her son. She was *stung* to death!"

It was then I stood up, "Oh my God! She must have received one of those letters with the bees inside."

Tony then stood and asked, "But why would anyone beat her like that? What did Feeney have to gain by making it look like she died another way? And why would he want to pin this on you, Charlie?"

No one had an answer. As everyone pondered the young detective's questions, Andrea inquired if she might suggest a theory.

"Of course Sister, please. We're at a lost. Any help would be appreciated," the Chief said.

Andrea stood and with a solemn stare said, "Evil seeks out evil for its own sake. Lubuka is confined within the same territorial boundaries just like the bees and cannot do all the evil by himself without the help of willing accomplices. He knows he can hurt my mother by hurting those she cares about the most. That would especially be my father and me."

"Sister, just what is it you're suggesting?" Dewolfe asked.

"From what I've heard and understand, Mr. Feeney would be a

great ally. In return for his assistance, Lubuka could be promising him more power than Mr. Feeney ever imagined."

"But how would he contact Feeney to make such a pact?" I asked, and before the question could complete its thought I said it in unison with the D.A. and the Chief, "Paul!!!"

The front room of the Reza residence grew quiet again. Even Riley and Little Brutus stopped running up and down the stairs as if they sensed the real horror of it all. Could it be that the young son of John and Sandra Feeney was *undead*? Was there some sort of mind control going on where a fiend, confined to a crypt in the old Western Cemetery, was sending messages through one of his previously buried victims? Did the secluded attorney want his wife's body cremated to extinguish all signs of tiny little bee stings? Did he beat her so badly after she was already dead that Frank Blanchette would just assume the cause of death? Did he still really hate Cindy for not being able to prevent Paul's death in the first place? Did Lubuka know all along, that if he spared the life of the Kostenello girl, Cindy would place the locket in her hand and that would result in my return and the return of Cindy's daughter?...That by killing what meant most to her, Cindy would be in such grief that he could overcome all her powers, once and for all?

Yes, I answered to myself. Evil does seek out evil. There is strength in numbers. Birds of a feather do flock together. Misery does love company. And Lubuka and John Feeney would make the perfect partners.

Andrea continued staring into space as she said, "It's like our faith teaches us. The devil is like a chained dog. God has him on a leash and he can only complete his evil desires if we are willing to help. If we would just refuse to go along with him, he would be as helpless as a toothless puppy."

I put my arms around her and kissed her as Brian DeWolfe asked the Chief, "Did you ever interview those boys in the black and white over where Paul was buried?"

"I was on my way to do just that when I got the call that Sandra had been murdered. Maybe we should go over their now, just to make sure Paul is in his grave."

"Or not," Tony added.

It was agreed. Andrea would stay with Maria. The Chief, the D.A, Tony, Jimmy, and I piled into Richardson's squad car while Blanchette followed in his car. We headed for Calvary Cemetery to get the answer about Paul. Then we would get his father. First things first.

The shift change was in progress when we arrived at the front gates. The same two officers who had been on duty the night Richardson called, after he had heard John Feeney talking to his dead son on the phone, were on duty again.

They appeared surprised and nervous at the sight of the Chief's car. They looked at each other as if to say, *we better get out story straight.*

"You two. Over here, now!" the Chief snapped.

"Yes sir. Is everything okay?" one of them inquired while the other looked on, uneasy.

"You tell me," Richarson instructed.

"Well, like we said the other night, everything seems fine, doesn't it?" The one said to the other.

"Yeah, that's right, everything's fine," his partner agreed. "Just normal activity...people stopping by to pay respects to their loved ones."

"Good. Good," The Chief said, "cause you know that John Feeney is about to be arrested for first-degree murder, and if you guys are withholding any information about his comings-and-goings, well let's just say, "YOU'LL BE IN SHIT UP TO YOUR EYEBALLS!!! DO I MAKE MYSELF CLEAR?!?"

I had never seen Richardson in action, except for those press conferences, and I was impressed. Hell, I would have talked if I were holding back, and so did they.

One looked at the other and said, "Well, we really didn't *see* anything."

"That's right," said the other. "He told us that he would be here visiting his son for about an hour and that we should go get a bite to eat."

"Yup, that's what he said all right, and he even said he had squared it with you." The young cop took off his cap and wiped the sweat from the liner, as he had seen his Chief do numerous times. He wasn't mocking his boss. It appeared to be done as a sign of respect, like a young wolf submitting to the leader of the pack

"Mr. Feeney said that new cops who don't cooperate with him never get promoted. We heard that from some of the other guys too. They say he's one powerful man, and you would be better off to cross the devil himself than to tangle with Attorney John Feeney."

"I don't know how you could tell the two apart, except for the horns and the tail, "Brian DeWolfe added sarcastically.

The two rookies were noticeably troubled, hoping they wouldn't soon find themselves in one of the cells at the Cumberland County Hotel with One Eye Wheeler and some of the others they had recently arrested.

"Chief, when we got back, he was gone and there were some new flowers near the kid's grave."

"Honest, Chief. That's all there was, some new flowers."

Richardson then instructed the two young cops to find the Calvary Cemetery caretaker. "Tell him to bring a backhoe and meet us over at Paul Feeney's grave. You two grab some shovels too!"

"Ray, we are going to need some sort of authorization before we can exhume a body," warned the District Attorney.

"Not in an emergency, Brian! Besides, we have the Coroner with us. We can make this look very official."

"Chief, may I suggest we call for a priest. This is a Catholic cemetery. You don't want the church causing us any unnecessary grief."

"Charlie's right about that," the D.A. agreed.

Father Mike Murphy was called and arrived at the same time as the backhoe. We filled him in on the task at hand and the reasons for it. He made a cell phone call, hung up, and nodded his head in approval.

Caretaker Tom Curran sat nervously atop the huge yellow tractor that came crawling down the dirt road next to Paul Feeney's grave. The two rookies had their shovels, and just as Richardson gave the go ahead to start digging, Curran called out, "Wait! That won't be necessary." He climbed slowly down from the big rig. He was noticeably shaken as he twirled his old blue and white striped railroad cap in his hands.

"This has got to stop now. I'll never be able to sleep again if I dig up another grave like that." He started blubbering like a two year old caught with his hand in the cookie jar. "It's that lawyer's fault. He made me and my two sons meet him here the other night. He made us do it"

"You mean, John Feeney?" the Chief asked.

"Ya, Feeney, a real big shot!" Curran blew his nose into a dirty rag as he tried to regain his composure. We all stood there spellbound as he went on. "He said if I didn't help him, he'd have my sons brought up on drug charges. I told him that my boys don't have nothin' to do with that stuff; but he said by the time he got through, he would make them look like they were part of some South American cartel. Now I ain't exactly sure what a cartel is mind ya, but I know it can't be good. So I agreed to do what he asked...But never again! No sir, not for all the gold in Fort Knox. When I told my wife she said I was going straight to hell for sure. She said my boys would be joining me there." The caretaker broke down into tears again.

"Mr. Curran, let me assure you that nothing's going to happen to you or your boys as long as you tell us the truth. I'm the District Attorney and I can guarantee it."

Curran sat down in front of his tractor, still twirling his hat in his hands, and began. "This ain't gonna be pretty and you might not even believe it, but it's the God's-honest truth. It was really dark, round midnight. He said he just wanted to move the casket to another site 'cause he had been threatened by grave robbers or somethin'." The caretaker then threw his hat as far as it would go and jumped up. "You gotta promise me you ain't gonna lock me or my boys up in the looney bin, or I ain't gonna talk no more!"

"Mr. Curran, these men have a very important job to do and nothing is going to happen to you or your sons," assured Father Mike.

"Ya, well, okay, I guess if you say so, Father."

Curran then walked back and forth in front of Paul's stone. He looked at it and was repelled by what he had to say. He turned away and threw up into his dirty rag. We waited. Then the tortured man continued.

"The boys were doing just fine, but when we came to the casket itself, Feeney told us to open it up. We thought he just wanted to move the whole thing to another plot. When he said to open it, we thought he was misspeakin'. My boys looked at me and said we shouldn't oughta disturb the dead like that." Curran started losing control again and Father Mike put his arm around the caretaker's shoulder. "Then the bastard pulled out a big honkin' gun. He pointed it right at me and told my boys if they didn't open it up he would blow my head clean off! And he would have done it too! You should have seen the look in his eyes. He looked like he was crazy...a real sick psycho!"

"Mr. Curran, what happened next? Be sure to tell it exactly as it happened, "the Chief instructed. "We know it wasn't your fault."

"Jesus, Mary and Joseph, Father...is God still in his Heaven? Cause, as sure as I'm standing here, that Feeney kid ain't in his grave."

"Go on, Tom," Father Mike said in a tone that comforted the frightened man. "Yes, God is still in His heaven."

Curran gave himself time to say his words just right. "Eddie, my oldest, he pulled back the lid and my youngest, Willie, shone in a light; and there was the boy laying so peaceful in his suit, a little teddy bear in one hand and his beads in the other. Mr. Feeney then called his boy's name ever so gently, 'Paul, Paul'...and...ah...ah...oh, God...ah... the boy...he...he opened his eyes!!!...Eddie ran into the night and just come home this mornin'. He's only nineteen, but his black hair turned white in that moment of horror. He said he'll never go into another cemetery ever again, said when his time comes just to sprinkle his ashes up there on Mt. Katahdin. Willie, why he pissed himself, and who can blame him? I just leaned over and threw up the Hungry Man I had just eaten...The boy was ALIVE I tell ya. He was ALIVE!!!"

"We believe you, Tom. Please, take it easy. Why don't you sit down for a minute?" Father Mike suggested. "I know this is very difficult, but what happened next?"

Tony was writing everything down in a little note book. I thought of Cindy's journal and her words, *I'm writing this down in hopes that someone will find it someday and know the truth.*

The caretaker continued without ever looking up. "Feeney, he reached down and pulled the kid out...I mean right the frig out! He got him standin' on the ground and he hugged him. The kid just stood there not really huggin' back and then Feeney, he started to cry. When the tears fell on the kid he let out an awful howl and whacked Feeney so hard he almost fell back into the open hole. Feeney got up and took the kid's hand and the two started walkin' out of here. Then me and Willie, we filled the grave back in and made it looked like it had never been touched. I even took some fresh flowers from another grave and put them here on this one."

Curran was at the point of collapse when the Chief thanked him and told him he could go home. "And, Mr. Curran, please don't tell anyone else what happened here."

"I won't," said the caretaker as he fell to his knees in front of Father Mike and asked for his blessing for him and his boys. Mike gladly gave it. "Is this the end of the world, Father? Are all the dead gonna rise out of their graves? Is it Judgment Day?"

"No, Tom, this is just a mistake, a horrible mistake. Apparently, the boy was buried alive. Things will all be better soon. Try and put it out of your mind. I'll keep you and your fine sons in my prayers."

Trembling, the caretaker continued, "Ah, Father, there's something else I should mention." It was like Curran was making a confession and when asked if there was anything else before receiving absolution, he fessed up to one more embarrassing sin. "If that kid was buried alive, shouldn't he pretty much have looked the same if he wasn't really dead?"

"What are you getting at, Tom?" asked the puzzled priest.

The frazzled man looked at Father Mike and the rest of us before he said, "Well that kid...he...he had fangs...you know, the kind you see in those Dracula movies. And one other thing, they was drippin' some sort of goo. I ain't never seen old Bela Lagosi do that. I wasn't gonna mention it cause I thought you'd think I'd really gone off my rocker. But I know what I seen...And they were fangs all right! And there was something drippin' out of them."

"Paul was a sick boy, Tom. It probably had something to do with his condition. Go home. You'll feel better in a few days," the priest assured him. And I thought my old friend Mike might himself be having one of those moments of doubt that are common to all believers.

Curran left his big tractor on the dirt road and his crumpled hat on the ground, but we all knew he couldn't leave behind the memories of what happened there. Who could? Things wouldn't be better in a few days. For Tom Curran and his boys, and for all of us, things may never be better again.

31

The big red brick mansion on Bowdoin Street had been the center of many parties and social gatherings. Anyone who was anyone, in the know and on the go in Southern Maine, would go nowhere with their constituents or clients without the imprimatur of Portland's most powerful family headed by John Feeney. Every winning Democratic candidate, local and national, was expected to make a call to the Feeney residence on election night and express gratitude for the lawyer's help. Brian DeWolfe spoke of one evening when he was there and an obligatory call came in. Feeney, showing his arrogance, shouted to Sandra in front of the crowd, "Tell Bill I can't talk to him now. Tell him to call me tomorrow, and tell him and Al I said congratulations."

If Portland had a Don Corleone, it was John Feeney. The compound's lush lawns and landscape were manicured to perfection. The home itself was bathed in soft lights and Ivy League vines. Ever mindful of first impressions, John Feeney spared no expense to entice and intimidate.

That was then, but this is now. The big house was dark. The vines on this night were more a covering than a decoration. The expensive matching Mercedes sports cars were tucked away inside the garage, not in the driveway where they were usually parked in a bragging display. The whole place was void of any signs of life. As we approached in the Chief's squad car, with black and white backups following close behind, I could here Willie Nelson singing on the radio in my mind, (Turn Out The Lights), <u>The Party's Over</u>. But was the party over for Feeney or for us?

Who or what was waiting inside, we weren't quite sure. But Richardson was now carrying a small squirt gun, tucked in his belt along side his service revolver. The backup boys looked puzzled as the Chief asked, "Charlie, you and Peters got your G. I. Joe's?"

"Ever since that meeting with those two creeps, Holt and Nelson, I sleep with mine and take it everywhere," Jimmy replied as I held mine up.

"Ray, we should still get a search warrant," the D.A. reminded the Chief.

"Brian, do you know a judge in this town who will sign it? This is the almighty John Feeney we're talking about, not some two-bit drug dealer."

"All right, but you could lose your job."

"Damn it, Dewolfe!!! Get your head out of your ass! My badge is the last thing I have on my mind. We have dead people walking around town and some 300 year-old asshole trying to assemble a whole army of those goddamn ghouls. There are little bees down the street that could descend on us at any moment and sting us to death!" Ray ripped the silver badge from his chest and threw it into the night air. "There, now I don't have to worry about losing it. With a save-the-world look on his face, the Chief shipped a shell into the chamber of his pistol. "Throw away your law books, Brian. This is a brand new day."

"Sorry, Ray, you're right. These are very unusual circumstances."

"Charlie, you, your friend, and Dewolfe are still civilians and I just have to remind you I can't be responsible for you. You are under no obligation to go in there with us," the Chief said as he nodded toward the mansion.

"Thanks, but we are more a part of this than most. Besides, you can't keep us out. You no longer have a *badge*."

Richardson smiled. "Charlie, anyone ever tell you you're a wise-ass?"

I thought of how much the Chief reminded me of Bernard Allen. They were both good honest men who did their jobs well, the kind of men you would want in a foxhole with you when the enemy came over the hill and made their charge. They even had the same white hair and moody dispositions.

"Be easier to find someone who hasn't called him a wise-ass," Jimmy quipped.

The Chief then gave the orders, "Detective Reza, take two men and go around back." He pulled the small squirter out of his belt. "Here, take this water gun. The rest of us will go in the front. Now, it's dark in there so make sure you know what you are shooting at before you fire your weapons. Any questions?"

No one replied. Our expressions said it all, "Let's go."

We gave Tony and his men ten minutes to get in position. The Chief took the bullhorn from one of the uniform boys and stood in the lawyer's driveway.

"John Feeney, this is Ray Richardson. You are under arrest for the murder of Kim Jenkins. You have five minutes to come out peacefully...If not, we are coming in. You should know that the whole place is surrounded. We know you have Paul with you. We will do everything we can to see that he is safe."

There was no reply. None was expected. The time passed and the Chief pulled out his revolver as did the others. He rang the bell and knocked on the big front door with his night stick. He let thirty seconds pass and then shot the lock off. He emptied his gun into it before it finally gave up and clicked open.

Reloaded and ready, he kicked in the door the rest of the way until it revealed the dark hallway. The lights failed to come on as the main switch just inside the door was tried. The sophisticated alarm system had been dismantled. It was as if Feeney wanted no attention brought to the house, not even if burglars were about. He had something to hide, something he was willing to sacrifice everything for...Paul... young, dead, alive, Paul.

"Easy men, remember Feeney's no fool and he won't go without a fight...and not without his son. There's no way to figure what a mad dog or a madman will do when he's cornered."

The two cops with us turned on their flashlights, revealing the opulence of the home...crystal chandeliers, a grand piano that would have made Liberace jealous, Persian rugs and rare paintings including Renoirs and Van Gogh's. Above the huge marble mantle with pure gold candle holders was a portrait of Feeney and his son...no Sandra included. And I thought, only if Feeney had gone over the edge of madness, would he leave all this for any looter who happened by.

The Chief and his men took the lead, doing the job they were trained for. They checked and searched each room while the rest of us civilians waited to help in anyway we could. The eerie silence of the big house made each step thunder in comparison. Every door and closet opened revealed nothing out of the ordinary. Everything was in order and in its place, except for the lawyer and his only child. The child was definitely out of *his* place.

Richardson and his men returned and joined us at the front of the house. We then made our way to the back door where the Chief shouted for Tony and his men. They approached with the news that no one had come out on their side.

The Chief holstered his revolver. "If he's in there, he's well hidden."

"He's gotta be in there, where else could he be?" asked one of the cops assigned to keep surveillance on the place. The young officer had Durloo printed on his name plate.

"Tell me, Melvin, are you sure nobody's come out of there since I put you guys here?" The Chief had faith in his men, but they were rookies and rookies make mistakes. Feeney knew that better than anybody. He was prepared for it.

Durloo looked at his partner, "Nobody, Chief...well, except for a gardener and his kid."

Richardson put his face an inch away from the cop. "Melvin, do you ever expect to get a pay raise in this business? 'Cause more than likely you'll be waitin' a long freakin' time!"

"But, Chief, it couldn't have been Mr. Feeney. This guy had long blond hair...and he had a kid with him...And Mr. Feeney's kid was buried a couple of weeks ago."

"Ray, go easy on them. They didn't know about Paul...You know, being whatever he is," reasoned the District Attorney.

"That must have been Feeney in one of Sandra's wigs," mumbled the Chief.

"Oh my God!!!" The words jumped out of my mouth before the thought was finished.

"What is it, Charlie?" the D.A. asked?

"What would be the *one* thing someone like Feeney would want more than power? The one thing that would make him leave all his treasures unguarded? The one thing that he couldn't buy with all his money?"

Everyone looked puzzled, as if I were asking some kind of a kid's riddle. I couldn't wait for an answer. "Immortality!!! What can be more powerful than that?"

"I don't understand," said the Chief.

I continued. "Where could Feeney hide with his son without worrying about anyone looking for them? Where would he find sanctuary for himself *and* his son?"

"Shit! Charlie, you don't mean he's up at that cemetery, in that crypt having freakin' tea and crackers with that Lubuka bastard?"

"JA-EE-SUS!" exclaimed Brian DeWolfe.

"I'll be jiggered!" Jimmy added.

"Chief, who's Lubuka? What are you talking about?" asked Officer Melvin Durloo.

Richardson turned to his surveillance team and the other uniformed cops who had question marks on their faces. "You guys go home. You've done a good job. We'll be holding a press conference in the morning. You'll understand everything then. Go home, hug your families and tell them you love them."

The look now on the Chief's face reminded me of a preacher I had seen on a Sunday morning TV show. "Repent! Get ready to meet your Maker." Only the TV preacher took time to sell his latest tapes. The world may end tomorrow, but he was giving the viewers ninety days to make their payments of $19.95 in three easy installments.

The black and whites sped away and left us standing at Feeney's mansion.

"They may know everything after your press conference, Chief, but you can't blame them if they still don't understand," Tony pointed out. "Hell, I know and I still don't understand how this could happen, especially in a sleepy little town like Portland, Maine."

"Just what are you going to say at the press conference, Ray?" Dewolfe wanted to know.

Richardson walked in front of us, toward his car. He looked like he was already preparing his statement. "The truth, Brian. It's time to tell the truth. Who knows? Maybe it will set us free."

Maria and Andrea prepared a chicken dinner with all the fixins' when we arrived back at the comfortable house on Melboune. We sat around the table, talking about the day and feasting like it may be our last meal. With all we had been through together, I thought maybe we *were* family; and that song by Sister Sledge played on the radio in the back of my mind.

The TV in the living room had been left on almost continuously for any late updates. I mostly ignored the chatter and the repeated reports about the strange and unsolved deaths in Maine. I tried to run away from it, if just for a little while. But there is no escape when you hear, "Breaking news and exclusive footage of what has become known as the Great Cemetery Slaughter...That, and Andy Rooney, tonight on 60 Minutes"...tick tick tick tick tick tick.

I sat there paralyzed by the words. What did Leslie Stahl know that we and the rest of the country didn't?

And there they were, Monroe and his friend, Jeff. The former bellboy and his pal had done it. They had made the big time. They sat there with broad cat smiles, ready for the world to sing their praises. They didn't have film of Big Foot lugging it through the Northwest woods or Nessie from Lochness. They didn't have one of those alien bodies from Area 51 or Shirley McLaine with Elvis on the line. They did have something more unbelievable. They had the *undead*, captured and preserved on film.

Monroe explained as the footage was shown. "Me and Jeff here, we're investigative reporters. We're from Portland, Maine and we was following this government secret agent. He calls himself Charlie Sullivan. At least that what he told me. That's how he signed the register at the hotel where I used to work, but we know that's not his real name."

Jeff interrupts, "Yeah, he's top secret, Man. Probably got a double O in his code name. You know...licensed to kill!"

"You're such an idiot!" I shouted as if he could hear me.

Monroe went on. "What you see here on your TV screen is Sullivan, or whatever his name is, and some other secret dudes pulverizing two guys."

There was the film of Holt and Nelson going up in smoke as their rotted flesh fell away. There was Little Brutus biting off a hand that would never feed him. There was Tony being lifted up into the air.

There was me squirting away at close range and then pouring water over the *undead* as they crumbled to the ground.

Maria Reza was now holding her hands to her heart as she was just learning what her baby had been through during that "fender bender".

"These two guys were the first to get killed by those deadly bees that live in that old cemetery on the Western Prom...and hold on to your wig, Lady, but this video was shot two weeks *after* they were buried." Monroe reported.

"That's some kind of secret weapon they are using," Jeff pointed out as the pictures continued. "The government spent billions developing those powerful weapons, man. Those are probably the only two like it in this world."

"I paid $2.98 for each of them at Ames, you goof-balls!" That was Maria Reza's reaction to their secret weapon theory.

"Who's gonna believe those idiots?" Brian DeWolfe chimed in. "It looks like something from a horror movie."

The District Attorney might have had a point, but the next footage would put the world on notice. Something or someone unnatural had come to live in Portland. Monroe and Jeff will probably get their own show after this.

John Feeney's face was familiar to the major news outlets like CBS. After all, he was rumored to be a shoe-in for the Democratic nomination for Governor of Maine. But he might lose some votes now. The next video showed the powerful attorney helping his dead son out of his grave. CBS did make a disclaimer that they could not yet confirm the story, but a picture is worth a thousand words. They and the rest of the country may still have their doubts, but the local population would have none. They would know the lawyer's face and many knew that the walking corpse was his son, Paul.

After the video ended Monroe and Jeff sat there with smirks on their faces like they were going to be the latest superstars and newsmakers. Goodbye Ben and J-Lo. So long Michael and Koby. See ya later Martha. Hello Monroe and Jeff.

"So, how much are we going to get for the story, Lady...and the video?" the new superstars were asking. "It must be at least a million?"

MIGHTY JOHN MARSHALL

They were told that CBS didn't pay for stories and could be heard yelling, "That's bogus, man. That sucks! We're going to CNN."

The screen faded to black and then McDonald's was touting its latest addition to their menu. Anybody hungry for a Big Mac after seeing rotting flesh and dead corpses walking around? Hold the ketchup! When the commercials ended, CBS was showing a rerun of an old show.

The competition must have been watching because all the news outlets were now back up and running full tilt on the strange happenings in Portland, Maine. THE GREAT CEMETERY SLAUGHTER was back on top as the number one story in the country. Within hours, thousands of local residents would be driving down I-95, away from the condemned city. At the same time, damn near as many reporters would be coming back in.

"Excuse me, everyone," said the Chief. "Time to call the Governor. We are going to need the National Guard and any other help he can muster up. My next press conference will probably get me fired for withholding information or get me an appearance on Larry King. Either way, it's gonna be a pain in the ass."

We had become a family, but now it was time for blood relatives to be together. Brian DeWolfe went home to be with his sister and her two children. Ray Richardson made his phone calls and would spend the night at Headquarters. But first he would make a trip home to check on his wife and grandkids. The young children were spending the summer in Portland while their parents were in Egypt on an expedition to find some long-dead mummies. The irony was not lost on the Chief.

I took Andrea over to spend the night in the apartment where I grew up with brother Joe. It meant a lot to me to have her experience the familiar surroundings of the world I knew when I was young. Joe would drive her crazy with his genealogy findings and his stories of what a great sports star he was in high school. She didn't seem to mind as I explained what he would put her through. She said she looked forward to spending time at the home of her grandparents. I knew that her mother was on her mind as well. Cindy was the only one who couldn't be harmed by Feeney or Lubuka, not yet. And for that Andrea and I were grateful.

However there was one more thing that had to be done that night. It was time for another child to be reunited with his mother. It was time for Jimmy to go home, back to his childhood memories on Danforth Street. I dropped off Andrea with a promise that I would return shortly.

Jimmy had done well avoiding his demons. The helter-skelter events of the last two weeks, along with old and new friends, helped him keep his mind on other things. He started to cry as we drove by the familiar side streets of his youth, Pine, Spring, Brackett, Emery, and Danforth. I could only imagine what he was thinking as he was going back in time, back to when his dad was working at the store, a big man...happy and healthy...who didn't realize disease had taken up residence in his body. Sometimes the monsters aren't in the closet or under our bed...or in a cemetery. Sometimes they are inside of us. And there is nowhere to run. His mother was singing at home while doing the routine things of her day. His sisters were driving him crazy and he realized how much he enjoyed it. After supper he and his dad would watch the ball game on TV. Jerry would have one arm around his son while holding hands with Sarah. She would soon get up to put some Jiffy Pop on the stove. After the game Jimmy would lie in bed and listen to the New York and Boston radio stations that would only come in at night. He would go to sleep and dream of pitching for the Red Sox and winning the big game. The crowd would go wild and call his name. Ned Martin would say that Jimmy Peters was the MVP.

I guess the reason a lot of us never grow up is because it never gets any better than the simple pleasures we had when our world was young and new, and all the people we loved were coming home at the end of the day.

But now, as we approached the house, Jimmy was back in the present.

"Charlie, you have to go in with me, please."

"I will. I called ahead and told your mom I would be stopping by."

"You didn't tell her I was with you, did you?" my friend asked nervously.

"No way, that's your job."

I parked in the same driveway where I had once showed Jimmy

my brand new bike all those years ago. The porch lights were on. We knocked on the door. I don't know which one of us was more nervous or excited.

The door opened and one of life's magic moments unfolded. Mother hugged and kissed her son. Jimmy kissed and hugged his mother. For the first night in a lot of nights there was true peace for both of them. Twice in seven days I had witnessed joyous reunions between mother and child. We had one big group hug and then I left them alone with their joy, their tears, and their memories.

As I drove back to my childhood home, the joy in my heart turned to sadness and fear as I thought of the mother and child reunion of Sandra Feeney and her young *dead* son. Was there the same joy in her heart and eyes as I had just seen in Sarah Peters'? Did they hug and kiss? Did they laugh and share stories as Cindy and Andrea had? Or had Sandra Feeney screamed in horror at the sight of her son's rotting flesh? Did she gag at the smell of death? Did he try to kiss her? Or did dead Paul try to bite her in the same manner as Holt and Nelson when they came at Jimmy and me with drooling teeth that had grown long and sharp as the metamorphous in the grave from dead to *undead* was taking place? Did his eyes burn red as his cold clammy fingers reached for her?...Maybe the bees got to her first with their sweeter kiss of death. I could only hope so.

32

Fear and intimidating monsters didn't stop the presses, and the morning newspaper at the foot of the stairs shouted: **PORTLAND PANICS**. The big headlines needed no more, but, of course, there was more. Pictures of Mr. Holt and Mr. Nelson were on the left side, properly identified as the first of the *undead*; while a smarmy Monroe and Jeff were on the right, along with frame footage of Feeney and his *undead* son walking away from the grave site. You could even see John Curran and one of his boys in the background with frozen looks of fear pasted on their faces.

Staff writer, Lisa Ibrahim, had most of the facts, but not all. There was no mention of Cindy or Lubuka, the witch and the wizard of the Western Cemetery. The city was not yet aware that there were two residents of the West End that had been *living* there since before any of the world wars. Before Teddy Roosevelt went up San Juan Hill. Before Custer's last stand. Before the North and South were ever pissed off at each other. Before Abe Lincoln ever put on his first stovepipe hat. The citizens of Portland had no idea that two of their current neighbors had been born before their most famous citizen had ever told the story of <u>Hiawatha</u> by the Lake of Gitche Gumee or had regaled his readers with <u>The Midnight Ride of Paul Revere</u>. The two neighbors were even alive before Paul Revere himself.

But, there were enough facts to make the headlines ring true. The first two deceased victims had climbed out of their graves, had walked the streets of town, and had died again in a puff of smoke. Just how that happened; the paper could not say, other than to repeat the words of the two new media stars who said it was some secret government weapon that destroyed the zombies. That's what the Paper decided to call the undead, *zombies*. It made the story seem even more sensational. The fact that Portland's most prominent family was involved made the whole thing even more believable. Everyone knew the Feeney's and now they knew the youngest Feeney was a zombie too, out of his fresh grave and out *there*, somewhere, waiting to bite the flesh off anyone who crossed his path.

Below the fold were pictures of the National Guard loading their trucks and arming their tanks. General William Roderick was shown next to Republican Senator Barry Darling. The General guaranteed that his troops would have the situation well in hand by the end of the day.

"Those bastards may have the cops in trouble, but now they'll face the U.S. Army, and by God they'll run back to their holes when Uncle Sam comes a-callin'" was the quote from the story below the photo.

I couldn't see if Roderick had any pearl-handle pistols like General Patton. If he did, they were hidden by his bloated beer gut.

There were also pictures of the traffic jam heading out of town. Other photos showed the looting that had already taken place as opportunists broke into closed businesses and recently vacated private homes. Two photos showed broken storefront windows, one from the Army Surplus Store downtown and the other from Young's Furniture in South Portland.

On the inside of the front page much of the little-known history of the cemetery was revealed. The paper was now sharing the facts that Tony Reza had discovered when he went checking through the archives of the Maine Historical Society and the police and cemetery records. They were all there, all the mysterious killings going back over one hundred and fifty years.

But there was news that I didn't know. Neither did Brother Joe with all his connections. A story that Detective Tony Reza had apparently missed as well, the story of two young boys lost and gone forever. They were the subject of a newspaper article from 1945. They too had played baseball in that old cemetery. Patrick and James Houlihan lived up on Carroll Street near the Western Promenade and often went to practice their hitting and fielding on that same open field that Jimmy and I knew so well.

According to the article in the paper, it was a Friday evening in early July of 1945 when the Houlihan brothers were last seen alive. Witnesses reported seeing two boys, wearing their little league uniforms and carrying bats and gloves, walking through the back gates on Cassidy Hill. When they failed to return at sunset, as they always had, the search was on. Family, friends, teammates, coaches, the police...all walked every inch and by every grave but found nothing, not even a hint that the two boys had been anywhere near there. The search was called off after three days and the Houlihan brothers were listed as "missing persons" with an asterisk. The asterisk indicated foul play was expected. Unlike Paul Feeney, Steve Winchell and all of the other victims, Patrick and James Houlihan were never seen again, dead or alive.

The paper went on to say that the boys had been "detected" and even photographed. The article contained an interview with local paranormal guru, Ken Gilman, who stated the cemetery in the West End has been haunted for years. Gilman went on to say that the Houlihan brothers were very familiar to ghost-hunters across the country.

A hazy photograph, presumably taken on a cold October day in 1956, purportedly shows Patrick and James Houlihan wearing their little league uniforms. The boys had disappeared ten years earlier.

Using electromagnetic field meters and digital thermal scanners, a new expedition to verify the existence of the boys' spirits was to have taken place this summer, but it was canceled due to the recent tragedies and danger.

The bodies of the Houlihan brothers were never found, and the paper said that after a few weeks most folks in town assumed they had just run away. A lot of young people did back then, sometimes on a dare from other kids. *"C'mon let's jump the train and go join the circus."*

However, Ghost-buster Gilman believed otherwise. He said their presence was still in there today. Most noticeably in early July, the time of year they disappeared and in October on their birthdays. The best guess Gilman and his paranormal brethren had was that the Houlihan brothers had stepped through some kind of time-warp and weren't able to cross back over. They were trapped and doomed to wander the cemetery grounds until they found their way out.

I read the story with great interest as I'm sure everyone else did, not only because of its fascination, but it just added to the terror of the current story at hand. Like we all had to have the bejeesus scared out of us just a little bit more.

I showed the article to Andrea who shivered at the thought of how close Jimmy and I might have come to falling through the same black hole as Patrick and James Houlihan.

The TV images reflected the story in the local paper and updated the horror that had come to Maine's largest city. The scroll at the bottom of the screen was now running a total on the number of victims associated with the GREAT CEMETERY SLAUGHTER. My count was nine, including Sandra Feeney, but the number on the screen was twelve. Even if they were still counting the Kostenello girl, that left a discrepancy of two. The difference was closed as the FOX News Babe revealed the names of the two latest victims, Thomas Ryan and David Mason.

She continued, "The two young officers of the Portland Police Department were found dead last night when their shift replacements discovered the bodies outside their patrol car. The following video and details are graphic and some may find them objectionable. We will wait ten seconds for any young viewers to leave the room."

The time passed and the video came up. The bloodied bodies were lying on the grass near the eastern perimeter that had been set up around the cemetery. The white sheet coverings were red with blood. Standing next to the dead was Frank Blanchette, giving the details.

"A preliminary examination reveals that Officers Ryan and Mason died of severe hemorrhaging." Frank looked down as if even he was sickened by what he would say next. "Officer Ryan had his throat slit clean through." Frank put his hand to his mouth as if to hold back vomit and then continued. "He was decapitated...His head has not been located. I'm guessing that there were at least two killers. Officer Mason had his...heart removed, however not by a knife."

The seasoned Pathologist and my junior high frog-splitting buddy took time to remove and wipe his glasses before he spoke further. "There were several deep teeth bites around the area. On each side of the bites were puncture wounds that went much deeper. They appeared to have been made by what I can only describe as *fangs*. We will be conducting autopsies later today to see if there were any sting marks that might have been made by the bees. There were no personal items taken such as jewelry or wallets. This was not a robbery. Just cold-blooded killings." The coroner turned away from the camera and lit up a cigarette.

333

I said to myself, "Now I know how Feeney and his son got by the security guards and made their way to Lubuka."

Andrea and I picked up Jimmy, leaving Joe bunkered in front of his TV, saying, "No shit" every time he learned something new. He had filled the bathtub with water and was going to jump in it and turn the shower on if any uninvited guests stopped by. Joe always had strategies for any occasion ever since those days of making plans to get the most candy, back when the boogie man was a fun part of Halloween.

We took Jimmy's mom over to stay with his sister, who lived farther away from the old cemetery than the house on Danforth Street. The reunion was a great success for both mother and son. A silver lining in the black cloud that now hung over my home town.

The Reza house was where we gathered with Tony and his mother. We watched the latest press conference. There was Chief Ray Richardson with District Attorney Brian DeWolfe. In the back were military types and Fire Chief, Rick Stacey. The world was literally watching now as Richardson stepped up to the gaggle of microphones. The networks broke away from their discussions about zombies and the possibilities of their existence. They brought in psychiatrists, psychics, and all other types of talking-heads, some of whom made Monroe and Jeff look like Harvard grads. Local, national, and worldwide the spotlight was on Portland, Maine and Chief Ray Richardson.

"Ladies and Gentlemen, I want to make the following announcements. Let me state the facts as we now know them. The current round of slayings began a little over two weeks ago with the deaths of Eric Holt and Ross Nelson. The reports from the local and state coroners confirm they died as a result of some very venomous bees that have their hives in the old Western Cemetery. The deaths of the two young boys and the three sorority girls were the results of the same such stings. The MSNBC newsman covering the story was also stung to death."

"We know all that, Chief. What about these so called zombies?" came a voice out of the excited crowd. His question was echoed by the media mob.

"Please, let me finish. I can answer many of your questions, if you'll just let me continue." Ray looked around, sizing up the crowd, hoping what he would say next wouldn't send them heading for a hole they could jump into. "We don't know how it's possible, but we do know that those stung to death by the bees have the ability to get up out of their graves with more strength than they ever had when they were alive."

The Chief, visibly shaken by his own frightening words, paused for what seemed like an eternity. "I know you are scared. We all are, but I have vowed to tell you *all* I know."

The crowd hushed as if their very lives depended on everything the Chief said, and it probably did.

"I have it on good authority that those buried in that cemetery, going back hundreds of years, may also climb out of their graves and from their tombs. We have no idea exactly how many are buried there, but we estimate...thousands."

Mass hysteria was setting in. People began running in the streets as the Chief took a bullhorn and pleaded with them not to panic. Some stopped to listen. Some didn't.

Nevertheless, he continued as he raised his hands to quiet them once again. "Holt and Nelson have been destroyed by water. Water is the only thing that can destroy these *people* and we believe the bees can be eliminated the same way. We also believe that Attorney John Feeney's son, Paul, is out of his grave. When he is found, he will be doused with water so that he may rest in peace. And we have a murder warrant out for his father who should be considered armed and extremely dangerous."

"Chief! Chief! Chief!" The voices started interrupting again but Richardson ignored them, determined to get out the whole truth as he had promised.

"We have called up the National Guard and all the fire departments within fifty miles. Additional help is on the way from several Federal agencies including a special task force being sent up from Fort Bragg, North Carolina. Meanwhile, we will line up all the fire department apparatus we have around the cemetery. When everything and everyone is in place, we will go in and flood the grounds and the trees. I suggest that everyone within the sound of my voice fill bottles and cans with water. Then lock yourselves in your homes. It's your best protection. Don't let anyone in unless you are absolutely sure who they are. And, for God's sake, stay away from that area!"

The Chief stepped away from the mics, and, despite his pleas, the reporters and their expensive satellite trucks rushed to beat the Fire Department to the Western Promenade. In the skies above numerous blimps hovered, laden down with multiple TV cameras. If these were to be the last days, it would be recorded for what ever type of civilization was to follow. This could be evolution of the worst kind... from monkeys to man to the *walking undead*.

"The Chief did the best he could," I said, trying to bring some small bit of confidence to those gathered at the Reza house. "Go in with massive amounts of water." It seemed simple, but nothing was as it seemed anymore. "That will take care of the *undead*, but it won't destroy Lubuka."

I looked at Andrea. I didn't need to speak. She knew that only we could destroy Cindy, and our only hope of destroying Lubuka was with Cindy's help. The question was which of the two had the greater power. Soon we would find out.

After the Chief spoke, the President addressed the nation and pleaded for calm, and to let the authorities do their job. He then declared a state of emergency. Marshal law was in effect on the entire eastern seaboard and would be extended across the country at a moment's notice if needed. Authorization was given for small portable nuclear arms to be at the ready. The states of Massachusetts and Georgia were instructed to open the tombs of the dead newsman and sorority girls and flood them to the top. The same would be done here to the Winchell boy's grave.

The countdown was on until the final face-off when man and machine, armed with water and tactical nuclear weapons, would go up against the powers of darkness and evil, armed with hate and destruction...and powers never witnessed in our imaginations.

Within an hour news cameras were everywhere getting world reaction. If the dead could climb out of their graves in Portland, Maine; then maybe they could do the same anywhere in the world. At the Vatican, the Pope was urging the world to pray for all souls concerned. Churches from Moscow to Manhattan were flooded with those seeking forgiveness before what could possibly be the *end*. In the Middle East, Jews and Palestinians dropped their guns and rocks and were filling their synagogues and mosques. Across the planet old hatreds were put on hold as the world pulled together as one. Pakistan and India were not concerned for the moment over who controlled Kashmir. Every nation, even France and North Korea were offering genuine help. Billions of eyes were focused on a small old cemetery in *my* home town. The world was waiting, praying, and holding its collective breath.

The TV was on but we sat in silence, only half listening, mostly thinking of the way things were before two winos decided to "tie one on" and "sleep it off" in a quiet cemetery where once lasting friendships were formed, ball games were played, and young love was discovered.

I thought of the Houlihan brothers. Were they really in there? Were they seeing from the "other side" all the evil on this side? Were they thinking maybe they were better off where they were? Or had I, like others reading the account today, been suckered in by ghost-chasers and other followers of freaky things. Maybe the Houlihan brothers did join the circus and today are retired down in Florida wearing white belts and white shoes and waiting for the early-bird special with their blue-hair wives.

The Chief broke my train of thought as he came to the door. The last two weeks had been hard on us all, but now his faced looked like Georgia Allen's had just a few days ago when she thought her husband was at death's door. Ten years worth of aging from the last time we saw him indicated that something else was wrong, terribly wrong.

The once tough cop fell onto the couch, asking Maria for a cup of coffee and, if she had something stronger, "pour it in." He waited for his drink as if it were a transfusion he needed to make it to his next breath. Ray was on the verge of breaking down, but whatever it is down deep in his soul that makes a good cop go on in impossible times, was working overtime in Richardson's

"I couldn't stop her, Charlie...I couldn't stop the others...He's dead!"

"Easy Ray, take your time. You couldn't stop who? Who's dead?"

The Chief grabbed me by the arms and said, "Frank...Frank

Blanchette is dead!"

We all gasped and would have grieved further, but there was no time. There may never be time for grieving or laughing ever again.

"How, Ray? Who?"

He stood up now, if somehow that would give him the strength to explain. "I was standing outside watching through the window in the door. Frank always locks that door when he's doing autopsies." The Chief removed his hat and ran his callused fingers through his thick white hair. "I wanted to check on my two dead officers, ya know, to see if there were some other results that could help their families know that they didn't suffer. Something that would say they died before the pain."

Andrea now approached the Chief and held his hand, offering whatever support she could to get him through this.

He clasped one of his hands over hers and continued, "Frank had just removed Sandra Feeney's corpse to ship it over to the funeral home. The two dead officers, Ryan and Mason, were on tables nearby waiting for Frank to do his job...Oh God, Dear God!...She raised her arm!...I had seen other dead bodies do that before, just part of the natural way a dead body can react...but, Charlie, she reached for Frank's throat and held it tight like she had it in a vice. He was trying to remove her grip with both his hands, but she was too strong for him...I was beating on the door and yelling for help...Frank's eyes were bulging out of his head...Blood was running out of his nose and ears. His face turned blue and he fell to the floor...Sandra jumped off that gurney like it was a hot plate and then..." Richardson was at the point of hysteria. "And then she ripped the Adam's apple right out of his throat...and swallowed it!"

We helped the Chief back down on the couch. He was sobbing like a baby. He had more to say, but this time he asked for a drink of water. His voice had grown raspy. Water was now worth more than gold, but we gave him his fill.

"She saw me in the window and started toward me and as she got closer, Ryan's *headless* body got up from the table and then Mason got up. He had a big gaping hole where his heart had been...OH, GOD!...I could see right through it. Sandra and Mason had their mouths open and their teeth were yellow and leaking puss...and they had fangs, like a wolf. It was worse than any nightmare!"

Maria Reza had reached her threshold of tolerance and ran for the bathroom, her hands over her mouth. The rest of us may not be far behind.

"They pushed down that heavy metal door like it was made out of cardboard and started for me. I ran, Charlie. I ran!" The Chief buried his face in his hands. His muffled voice went on, "I don't know where they are. I yelled for the others nearby to get the hell out of there, but I didn't wait to see if anyone made it."

It was Tony who spoke next giving the Chief time to regain his composure. His words were almost paralyzing. "If Ryan and Mason are up and walking around that means you don't need to be stung by those bees. You can also come back from the dead if you're bitten by one of those zombies."

The young detective then paused with a new thought. "You realize that Dr. Blanchette must be considered a zombie now as well."

"That puss or goo from their fangs must have the same venom as those tiny bees," I conjectured. I wasn't good at math, but I knew that could lead to a geometric progression of the *undead* that would be limitless. Time was running out. E*vil* was getting stronger.

33

The hours past and the tension grew. The town seemed divided into two sets of humans, those running in the streets as if there were no place to hide, and those barricaded in their homes or offices, glued to their radios, computers, and TVs. Those were the only two options until first light in the morning when Fire Chief Rick Stacey would open up the hydrants, fill the hoses and flood my old playground.

The fly boys from the Forest Service with their fixed-wing aircraft would join forces with the helicopters from the Coast Guard and drench the cemetery from above. General Roderick from the Maine National Guard would then go in with his men, along with Special Forces being sent up from Fort Bragg. If all else failed, the President had authorized forced evacuation for five hundred miles and then, as a last resort, very last resort...*the bomb*. That's the plan...but no plan is perfect.

Those of us inside the Reza residence, except for the Chief, agreed to hold up there until the assault was completed. The doors and windows were locked and shut tight. It was hot, but hot was better than being cool and dead.

Those running in the streets couldn't tell friend from foe. Who knows how many have been bitten, died, got up, and starting repeating the cycle with the next unsuspecting victims. The running total at the bottom of the TV screen was now at 200 and those were only the number of confirmed zombies. You could look out the window and see the catastrophe unfolding as people were spraying water on anyone who came near. Once in a while there would be screams of pain and puffs of smoke as a once friendly neighbor disintegrated into a bag of bones.

Richardson wished us well as he went to be with his wife and grandchildren. We prayed he would make it home safely. There wasn't much else he could do or we could do, but wait and watch...and pray.

On the screen the totals were climbing, 276, and the blimps over the city were capturing the destruction of both people and property. Stores, like Toys R Us and Wal-Mart; and supermarkets, like Shaw's and Hanniford Brothers, were being ransacked for their squirt guns and water bottles. Cameras everywhere were relaying the horror right to the viewer...no edited tape. It was raw footage with all the blood and guts included. You could see it all. You just couldn't guarantee that your eyes and your mind could believe it all. We were like those people who slow down to see an accident where the maimed and bloody bodies make us convulse with shock. We just can't pass by and say a silent prayer for the victims. We just have to watch and see for ourselves; as if somehow it makes us feel better, that in the Russian-Roulette-game-of-life, we had dodged another bullet. By seeing others dead, we think our own odds of living are improving. But, if what we were now seeing was *living*, we might want to think again about whom the real victims were.

Father was turning against son and brother against brother. Best friends were becoming worst enemies as the panic proceeded to the next level.

Passengers trying to board planes went through additional security and were now forced to be splashed with water. When one old lady went up in smoke and howls, the entire airport became a scene of final desperation as passengers rushed the security agents and fought for a final seat on *any* plane going *anywhere*. The rich were throwing their money at the pilots, begging for even a small space in the belly of the aircraft.

Down at Vermont Transit and over at Concord Trailways similar scenes of desperation were occurring as passengers struggled to get that last seat on the bus.

There was no exception down at the docks where the terrified citizenry was taking over the Casco Bay Lines. In the bay, The Scotia Prince was listing to one side as the weight of the public, with no regard to the plight of women and small children, pushed it to the brink. Chivalry was dead. Another Titanic was sinking.

We were hypnotically fixed on the television, our minds continually fighting hard to believe our eyes. Then, I could begin to hear it. "Wait!" All eyes turned to me as my ears perked up, like a nervous deer hearing the snap of a twig just before a bullet rips through its underbelly...leaving Bambi alone and trembling.

"What is it, Charlie?" Maria Reza asked, her face searching for good news but expecting bad.

"Turn down the volume, do you hear that? Listen!"

"I hear it, Dad. What's making that sound?" Andrea wondered.

"It seems to be getting louder," Tony said.

"I hear it too," Jimmy added.

The ground was rumbling and the vibrations were getting stronger with each passing moment.

"It's an earthquake!" Maria and Tony exclaimed at the same time.

"No...Not quite an earthquake." I said slowly as I listened harder. "Everyone be quiet!"

We were about five miles away from the old cemetery, but, as I looked back at the TV, I could tell the building crescendo was coming from there. The blimps from above were looking down as the impossible that Cindy had feared was beginning to happen. The centuries old stone and slate tombstones were beginning to falter. They were splitting and crumbling apart. Hundred year old oaks and maples and even my old favorite elm near home plate were tumbling as if they had been hit by a giant bowling ball. The ground was coughing up its dirt, opening itself up, and releasing its prisoners from below. At first there were just a few, but soon hundreds of bony hands were blossoming from the earth like some kind of grotesque flowers from a poisoned garden. As the cameras zoomed closer, the flowers grew bigger; and entire arms, bony and rotted away, were pushing themselves up as their skulls bobbed up and down with their new grown fangs. Their mouths were chattering like toy sets of false teeth. Many were now up on their legs and walking toward the old crypt where the evil wizard had his throne. The TV showed just the pictures. The news anchors were like the rest of us, speechless, as we watched in complete and captivating horror.

Then the rest of the world saw him, Lubuka. Standing at least seven feet tall and dressed all in black, he swaggered back and forth in front of the big crypt as his followers gathered around him. Knowing not only they but his enemies were watching, the centuries-old slave rose into the air, hovering about the ground over the heads of the walking skeletons. He had mastered levitation and used it to intimidate and impress. The steady camera work of the men in the blimps was now out of focus as they reacted as the world did, in total shock. As the great wizard descended slowly back down to the ground, the automation of the TV cameras kicked in and the picture was clear again.

Just when we thought we had seen it all, those of us at Maria's house got a new fright. There, next to his new master, was attorney John Feeney. Defiantly, he stood in arrogance with his arms folded like Mussolini at the height of his madness. With a nod from his master, Feeney ordered the new born skeletons and their zombie brothers to spread out into the city and to kill all the people they found, thus creating even more of the deadly fiends.

The scroll along the bottom of the screen was now reporting the numbers of zombies and walking skeletons in the thousands. At the rate they were progressing, they would rule the world in less time than it took God to create it. Despair was replacing hope as my city was being destroyed.

The skeleton army marched out of the graveyard taking two routes to the heart of the city. One band of the dead walked down Danforth Street and toward the Old Port section while the other headed up the Western Promenade and down Congress Street. Many of their zombie comrades joined with them, reinforcing their seemingly unstoppable strength.

Down Danforth, the reign of terror was animated by the screams of those fleeing from the path of the walking dead.

At Ruski's Restaurant, patrons who had made the decision to hold up there put up a brave fight as the skeletons invaded. Water from the faucets and bottles brought many of the bony creatures to a quick end, but in the end there were just too many as more of the *undead* crawled out of their graves and reinforced the troops in front.

Onward they marched like conquering heroes, this vicious army of monsters. They seemed to sense when fresh blood was near. When they stopped at the Victoria Mansion all their skulls turned left in unison. Inside was a frightened group of the Daughters of the American Revolution. The women decided to hide in the historic building until the troubles were over, but now their troubles were really beginning. The army poured through the windows and bashed down the doors. The Daughters were brought screaming and hollering out into the daylight. It was if these creatures knew or were instructed to do their dirty deeds in front of the cameras. One by one the mighty jaws of death brought silence to the squirming group of refined and dignified ladies. One by one they were transformed into killing machines themselves. The effect of the venom was working more quickly than ever.

At Key Bank, the Daughters took over and created more of their kind as they sunk their new fangs into terrified tellers and mortgage lenders who were hiding there.

Across the street, clerks and customers of the new and beautiful Portland Harbor Hotel fought the fiends as best they could. Some were able to hide, some weren't.

By the time the throng marched by the already abandoned Granny Burrito's and Gritty McDuff's, their numbers had almost doubled with the new recruits they had bitten and brought on board.

Past the Custom House the army of dead turned left, as the stock brokers who had opted to stay at Morgan Stanley forgot their commissions and trades and ran for their lives. They filtered quickly throughout the building. Like the Dow itself, some went up and some went down, but all of them would never hear the closing bell again, not in the same human form anyway.

The other band of skeleton storm troopers was wreaking ruin and death as they continued down Congress Street. The elderly at the Lafayette Hotel had no choice but to stay and hope that the madness would pass them by. And for some reason it did. Maybe the ghouls or the one who controlled them figured that they could always go back later and finish off the slow and the weak.

Those hiding out at the Portland Museum of Art weren't as lucky. The skeletons and their zombie comrades made quick work of them.

The marching and the killing continued with more victims at Norm's Bar and Grill, L. L. Bean, DeAngelo's and Subway. The News Department at Channel 8 was next to be devoured as they stayed their post to cover the story to the end...and they did...their end.

At Post Office Square, the postal workers put up one hell of a fight before their lives were stamped and canceled. It looked like they took out about 20% of the skeleton army before they could fight no more.

The two armies now joined up at City Hall and marched toward Munjoy Hill, making a straight and narrow for Melbourne Street and the Reza residence. They must be stopped. It couldn't end like this. As those thoughts muddled in my mind, the unexpected happened again. The TV shut down. The lights went out. The power was off. With only an hour of daylight left, Portland was in complete chaos.

Maria hurried to gather all the candles she could find in the house. The rest of us pushed furniture up against the front and back doors. With lumber and old firewood from the basement, we boarded up the biggest windows. There was only enough for the first floor. We hoped, if any of the *undead* happened to drop by, they couldn't climb or, God forbid, levitate like their master.

We decided to take a page out of Joe's book of ideas and fill the bathtub and sinks with as much water as they would hold. We opened and emptied all cans of vegetables, beans, fruit, even dog food. Anything that could hold water would be used as a weapon.

"Charlie, you remember that basement in the old Buckley place? Remember how we sank into the mud when we climbed into the window?" Jimmy asked.

"Are you saying we flood Maria's basement? That's not a bad idea," I said.

"Hey, you gonna fill my cellar with water?" Maria asked as if the thought was totally out of the question and she was oblivious to the situation at hand. It didn't take long for her to rethink the quagmire we were in. "Tony, don't just stand there! Go get the garden hose and make us a built-in swimming pool." She now looked delighted with her decision and for the next hour the basement filled as empty cartons and old tires took the first dip. Daylight was all but gone. Then, there was another shock to the system. The water faucets ran dry. We had all the ammo we were going to get.

"They must have gotten to the main valves," Tony shouted.

"Something that only a crafty attorney would think to do," I commented.

"Lubuka needs someone like Feeney to do things those zombies can't do...think!" Jimmy suggested. "Lubuka controls them like robots. Their brains are useless to them."

STUNG

"He is their brains," Andrea pointed out. "Those poor souls have no will of their own."

It was going to be a long night, and the possibility that it could be our last night had not escaped us. The thought that one of us, or all of us, could become part of the zombie army before dawn was more horrible than death itself.

With candlelight flickering across the front room, and with wax melting and dripping down the shrinking sticks; we joined hands like we were sitting around a campfire. We weren't telling ghost stories as we might have done when we were kids. We were praying, not only for ourselves, but for the world and people we never knew and would never meet. But at this moment in time we were all related as human beings with one common enemy, *EVIL*.

The streets had grown quiet as neighbors had either made their way to safer non-invaded territory or had barricaded themselves in their homes. They were probably praying like us that tonight or tomorrow would not bring the end of the world as we have known it.

With the sun surrendering its very last light in the west, a strange marching sound could be heard shuffling up the street.

"They are coming!" Tony shouted as he peaked though a punched out knothole in the wood covering the front window.

"Who's coming, Baby?" his frightened mother asked, as she clung to his shirt tail.

"It's the skeletons from the cemetery. There are hundreds of them!"

"Let me see," I pleaded as Tony moved back.

It was like seeing something out of an old black and white propaganda film that showed Hitler's precision marching armies. The skeletons, their fangs dripping with venom, were goose stepping the same way the Nazis did. They had arrived at their destination after stopping off now and then for a "bite". Along side was their General, the insane attorney, John Feeney. He was marching to power with his own private army of ghouls. He was Field Marshal Herman Goering and Lubuka was the Furer. That was the thought that came to my mind. That horror was all too real, and so was this.

The emerging moonlight shone against their bones. Closer they marched, their mouths snapping, just in case something edible in the form of *real* life came their way. Then the sound of bony feet beating against the tar and brick stopped. There was silence as their general stepped in front of the white clapboard house on Melbourne Street.

"Charlie, I know you and your friends are in there," he shouted with his hands cupped to magnify his voice. "Why don't you come out and join us? There is no use in struggling against us. It's just a matter of time before the world is in complete submission."

Those of us inside were doing a small head count. We figured there were just too many of them, with more now marching to the rear. I just couldn't judge if there was enough water to destroy them all.

"Do you know Paul is going to be my vice president? That's right, Charlie Boy, my inauguration will be in just a few weeks...and you're all invited!" Feeney mocked.

"He's really flipped," Jimmy said.

"I gotta say, Charlie...that old girlfriend of yours is a tough competitor, but it will be just a matter of time before King Lubuka has more power than she ever dreamed of. Soon he will control the bees and soon not even water will destroy them or my armies."

Soon, but not yet, I thought.

The ever cool and collected Andrea broke our silence. "Where is my mother? Is she all right?"

"Oh, I see you are in there, Charlie, and with your daughter." She's a pretty little thing. I just might have to make her my first lady!" The mad, obnoxious, lawyer laughed loudly and then added, "Of course she wouldn't be my *first* lady." He laughed all the louder. He had turned into another George Chamberlain...maybe worse.

There was no use in concealing our presence. "Feeney, haven't you caused enough pain and suffering, first with Kim and then with Sandra?"

"C'mon, Charlie. They were both bitches who just wanted to attach themselves to my rising star. Tell you what, you and *sweet thing* come out of there and I promise you safe passage to see your old girlfriend?"

"And just why would you want to do that?" I hollered back.

"To tell you the truth, I just as soon kill you with the rest and make you part of the zombie army. But, Lubuka, he's got other ideas. Guess he just wants to show you there are no hard feelings."

Feeney's frightening laughter was getting more sinister and the thoughts of the fiend from my dreams came to mind. I could almost picture Feeney in that black cape and that tall stovepipe hat.

"I have to bring you back, dead or alive. With you and your kid in his presence, whether you're breathing or not, that witch will just give up and will no longer present any kind of opposition. The choice is yours."

"What about my friends?" I shouted.

"Screw em, they're no good to me," he answered back and then went on, "Of course I just might poke that Reza bitch a time or two before I let the zombies have her. Now, are you coming out or are my troops coming in?"

The crazed lawyer was losing patience with those of us inside. He would have less tolerance after Maria pulled me away from the window.

"Just try it, Fat Boy, and I'll gouge your eyes out," she shouted back in defiance.

"I like a feisty woman!" Feeney yelled as he put his goons back in motion.

"I think Maria just gave you our answer. You give us all safe passage or come and get us. One way or another, Feeney, your days are numbered," I yelled out of the hole in the boarded up window.

"Oooo I'm shakin!!! What ya gonna do? Squirt *me* with one of your little toy guns?" The crazed leader of the skeleton army laughed.

The bony soldiers turned toward the house and followed his orders. With more strength than when they were human, they pounded and bashed their way though the wooden covered windows and shored up doors.

We began tossing, squirting, and throwing water at them. With great howls of pain those in front crashed upon each other as their comrades climbed over them. In the confusion of the smoke that followed, we held hands and formed a link. We made our way down the cellar stairs and into the basement where now the water was at least a foot deep. It was there we would make our stand.

The eerie sound of skeletal feet coming down the steps was enough to make anyone scream, but we had all seen and heard so much by then that the noise of the walking *undead* had no more effect than warning us that doom was getting closer.

Maria and Andrea stood behind as Tony, Jimmy, and I formed a human barricade in front of them. We estimated that most of the zombie army was still outside, just waiting to reinforce those now inside, coming for us like the mindless robots they were. Hope was fading fast. Final prayers were said.

Then, the most wonderful and unexpected miracle crashed through the air. Thunder clapped and the skies opened up. The rain came pouring down. Those skeleton ghouls and zombies outside crumbled into dust. The same happened to those marching toward us as their feet hit the water in the basement. The lightning flashing through the mounds of smoke looked like a strobe show at a 70's rock concert. We stood there as the mist dissipated and the mangled broken bones of the skeletons piled up in front of us. We thought we were safe for the moment thanks to the blessed rain from above. We climbed over the dust and bones, still smoldering at our feet.

As we reached the foot of the stairs lightning flashed again, and we could see the silhouette of John Feeney with his big gun pointed toward us.

"You fools! The rains may destroy this bunch of dead, but there's an endless supply to be had. Soon, with Lubuka's new formulas, water will have no affect and nothing and no one will be able to stop us."

"John, it's not too late to do the right thing," I pleaded. "Let Paul go back to his grave and rest in peace."

"NO! Paul is safe in the big crypt with Lubuka and once water is rendered useless as a weapon, he will walk again in the sun and rain and take his place beside me."

Feeney raised his pistol. The moonlight, now shining though the parting clouds, exposed the look of determination on the demented lawyer's face. There was no going back, not for him.

"BANG!!!" The sound of the pistol blast echoed and bounced back and forth against the concrete basement walls of our water-filled fortress. The bullet hit its mark. The splash of the fallen body covered us all with water and blood.

Tony lowered his gun. It was the first time in his young career the Detective had fired his weapon in the line of duty. The lawyer lay dead in front of us. The horror of this night was over; but as we silently stood there, tired and troubled, we knew there was more terror waiting in that crypt up at the old cemetery. Water could kill the *undead*. Bullets could kill evil men like John Feeney. Neither could destroy the big black slave from Barbados who first came into Cindy's life in 1699, and who first walked the old cemetery in 1820. Over the centuries his power had grown stronger, and now, in our time, he may be unstoppable. His dream was at hand. Soon, all the people in the world may be *his* slaves.

34

With the sunrise came new hope that the crisis was over, or at least that the "good guys" were winning. The power came back on. The words and images on TV reinforced that hope. The pictures showed the smoldering ruins of the skeleton army and the rotting zombies, left melting from the rain like that cake in <u>MacArthur's Park</u>. A faceless voice behind the pictures spoke slowly in a reassuring way, like a father or mother telling their frightened child in the middle of the night that it was all just a bad dream.

There, there, Charlie, there's nothing under your bed or in your closet. That's just Joe trying to frighten you. Here, have a drink of water and you'll feel better. In the morning I'll make some pancakes with extra syrup, just the way you like them.

"Ladies and gentleman, what we have seen in the last 24 hours is something the world has never experienced before. The pictures you are seeing are of men, women, and children who have died, *twice*. Through some kind of unknown power, many were able to burst through the ground that had covered them for centuries. As the migrating horde of these ghouls plunged through the once peaceful seaport town of Portland, Maine, killing and creating more zombies, the world panicked as the television images showed the creatures spreading out farther and farther. Then, like a miracle, the sky that had been clear all day darkened with storm clouds, and opened up, releasing its saving rain. How something as harmless and life giving as rain could destroy what man with all his weapons could not remains a mystery."

More syrup, Charlie?

The cameras from the blimps above now panned around the city, and, at first, it looked like a ghost town with no signs of life. Slowly as the morning progressed you could see people coming out of their homes hugging and kissing neighbors whom hours before they would have sold out for a bottle of water. Old friends were reunited and new friends were made. Bad blood and bad feelings were put aside and forgotten. You could see groups of others gathered on doorsteps and in driveways offering comfort to those families who had suffered a loss. Impromptu prayer meetings popped up as people gave thanks for all they had, for things and family they had once taken for granted. Everyone was sharing food with the cops and firemen who had fought so bravely to protect them. It was like those old black and white movies that showed the people of Paris being liberated in World War II. You know the ones, with a grateful French populus throwing flowers at American G.I.'s and running to kiss them as they marched through the streets.

Another camera angle showed the National Guard trucks being filled with bones, now bleaching in the morning sun. The soft voice behind the pictures said the plan was to re-inter the dead in the same graves they had crawled out from. There was no chance of being accurate in placing the same bones in the same plots they had once occupied, but all would contain some. At least they would all be back together in the same old cemetery where they had rested for so long.

The scroll across the bottom of the screen was no longer showing the number of confirmed zombies, but instead, the number of confirmed dead, not including the previous dead who had fallen again. The latest total was 862. Phone calls to Jimmy's sister and to Joe assured us we were among the lucky families who were still whole.

The soft-spoken announcer continued. "We want to remind all who are watching that those skeletons and zombies caught out in the rain are dead. We are now going to Police Headquarters where Chief Ray Richardson is about to make a statement."

Standing before an American flag with General Roderick from the Maine Army National Guard, the Chief looked tired but in command. "I want to take this time to update the citizens of Portland and the world on all that has taken place under these unusual circumstances. First, I want to thank God for sending the rain."

"Here, here!" General Roderick interrupted.

The Chief continued, "It's important to remember that the main water pumps are still malfunctioning. The computers that operate them have been tampered with, but we hope to have fresh water up and running before nightfall." Richardson looked down for a moment as if searching for that last ounce of courage to say what he had to say next. "You have a right to know that we are not out of the woods yet. There are a few more that need to be destroyed, but they are confined to the old cemetery. Chief Rick Stacey is once again assembling his men and trucks around the perimeter. When water has been fully restored, a number of us will go in there and hopefully destroy the rest of the *undead*. The best thing you can do now is to stay in or near your homes. Listen to the radio and TV broadcasts for updates."

"Don't worry folks, my men will take care of the rest of those bastards," the General boasted as if bucking for another star.

I could tell that Richardson just wanted him to shut up and go away. Ray wasn't a glory-hound. He was just a man, a good man, who wanted to do his job and then go home and play with his grand kids.

"Lastly, and most importantly, I want to extend my sympathies and those of my Department to the families who have lost loved ones. Some I knew personally, some just by name, others not at all. They will all be missed and honored in a special ceremony to be held when this entire matter is brought to a close. I have prepared a list of those names that we have thus far. The list is currently being handed out to the media. On that list are several members of my Department who courageously gave their lives while trying to bring this menace to an end. I ask that you remember them and the families they left behind in your thoughts and prayers."

As the Chief said his final words, the list of those who died in the zombie and skeleton attacks appeared on TV. One name after another slid slowly down the screen. Maria recognized some of her customers from her hair salon. Tony recognized some of his friends from school and from the force. Jimmy and I saw the names of some we knew, some from the old neighborhood, even some we played with back when our world was young and innocent.

With massive holes in the sides of the house, and crumbling bones piled up in the doorway and the basement, we sat silently letting our wet clothes dry as the names flooded us with memories.

We gave a collective hush of grief as we read the name of Brian DeWolfe. I had not known the District Attorney that well; but, like the others, had come to care a lot about him. I remember Brother Joe talking about him when I first came back to town. He said Brian always had a crush on Sandra Feeney, that is, before she was married. But Brian never had the nerve or found the right words to tell her how he felt. Sandra's cousin, Liz Ward, said Sandra knew and waited for Brian to express his feelings, but he never did. So Sandra remained John's girl and eventually became his wife. Her mother urged Sandra to accept Feeney's proposal. The DeWolfe name didn't hold the kind of prestige and power that the Feeney name did.

It was like those *proverbial ships passing in the night*. Sandra sailed by Brian and wrecked herself as she crashed into the Good Ship Feeney. It was another case of love lost, of what might have been had the stars lined up correctly in the cosmos. Joe said Brian was one of the good guys. Joe was right. I wondered how Brian died. Maybe he was bitten by Sandra herself.

"Maybe they are finally together, innocent again." Andrea offered in comfort as she read my mind.

I put my arm around my daughter. She was my strength through all of this...the strength I would need by my side when it came time to say goodbye again to her mother, the love of my life. Many of us have many loves, but there can only be one greatest love for each of us. For Brian it was Sandra. For Sarah Peters it was Jerry. For Frank Blanchette's dad it was his Anne. For Georgia it was Barn. For my dad it was my mom. For me, it will always be Cindy.

The names of the dead rolled on and there was Frank Blanchette. I wished now I had been a better friend to Frank back when he was a nerd in school. I thought of his father who now must be grieving alone with no one to share the loss of his only son.

I was temporarily lost in my thoughts when suddenly there were noises coming from the basement where John Feeney's body was left floating among the scattered bones of the skeleton army. He had fallen in front of us and never got up. We just assumed he was dead. We heard the shot. We saw him fall. We saw the blood.

"Did anyone check to see if Feeney was dead?" Jimmy asked with that same worried look that was on all our faces.

"I kicked him in the balls when I went past him," Maria said, as if it would be something anyone might have done who grew up in her Brooklyn neighborhood.

"He might have been unconscious," I suggested.

"Or faking," Tony offered.

The sound of something heavy was now making its way up the cellar stairs. The vibrations from each step made the glasses and plates in Maria's cabinets shake and rattle. Some of the broken glass that was hanging on in the front window now let go and fell to the floor.

Tony dropped his gun in the water after he shot Feeney. When he picked it back up it was water logged and useless. He tried firing it now at the ceiling, but it was in vain. The sound on the steps was getting closer. Then we heard the yelping noise.

"It must be Riley!" Maria shouted in joy as she ran to the basement stairs.

In the panic of the previous evening we had lost track of Riley and Little Brutus. The two had followed us down the stairs to the flooded basement and then climbed up onto a table in the corner to get out of the water. It was her dog all right, but he was being held in the tight clutches of the wounded, but very much alive, John Feeney. The evil lawyer had a knife on the golden retriever. His grip around the dog's neck was firm and the knife was next to Riley's throat. Little Brutus was now nipping at Feeney's heels. Jimmy hollered out for his dog. Little Brutus ran and jumped into Jimmy's arms, still snarling at the lawyer.

"Nice shot, Reza; but, like most inexperience detectives, you failed to check your kill closely. You were all too busy getting your asses out of there. You got me in the belly, but the bullet didn't go in deep enough to mess up any of the ol' vital organs. I knew someday that extra blubber I was carrying around would come in handy. I floated and played dead till you were out of sight, and gave myself the night to get some of my strength back."

"You hurt my dog and I'll kill you myself!" Maria threatened.

"You numb bitch! You couldn't kick me in the gonads hard enough to make me flinch. I learned to take a lot of pain during my playing days. There's nothing you can do to hurt me." Feeney laughed in his taunting way. "I was the Captain of the Team and I still am...only thing different is we got a new coach, Coach Lubuka!" Feeney's eyes exposed the madness of his mind.

I held Maria back as she lunged toward the attorney. He pulled back and jammed the knife into Riley's hide, just enough to get a yelp and a whimper.

"One step closer and the dog dies!" shouted Feeney in a voice that sounded like he wasn't suffering much from his wound.

Riley was now hanging limp, like all the fight had been taken out of him. His eyes had a look of desperation with that *mommy-I'm-scared* look you might see on a two-year-old when he's first hoisted into a barber's chair.

"What do want, John? You certainly don't want to kidnap a dog," I said.

"Brilliant deduction, Teacher! You can go to the head of the class." Feeney took a quick look outside to see if everything else was normal, or at least as normal as it could be under the circumstances.

"I want to get back to the crypt in that old cemetery...back to my new friend, Lubuka. You should see that place inside, not bad for a tomb."

He moved closer to the front door, kicking away any old bones that lay in his path. Then, almost as an afterthought, he said, "Your old girlfriend sure is a looker. Too bad she's such a pain in the ass, always trying to thwart our attempts to finish the mission before us, you know...to rule the world." His evil grin widened.

Feeney's eyes reminded me of Dr. Frankenstein's when he proclaimed of the monster, "It's Alive! It's Alive." The lust for power flushed away any attempts to reason with him.

"Let the dog go and I'll drive you up there," I offered. "No tricks, I promise."

"You'll drive me up there all right, but I'm swapping this flea bitten dog for Sweet Thing over there. Either that or I'll slit his throat and probably get hers or the Reza bitch before you can overpower me. Hell, I might get you all. You wanna try me?" He squeezed Riley's throat tighter and jumped at us. "HA! You're all chicken-shits!"

Without hesitation Andrea approached the lawyer and said, "You can let go of the dog now."

"Well, Sweet Thing has more sense than the rest of ya. You drive, Charlie. She'll be in the back seat with me. Try anything funny and I'll slit her pretty little throat from ear to ear." Feeney let the knife slide over the tender skin on Andrea's neck, cutting the thin chain that held her tiny cross. It fell to the floor.

"No, Andrea, he's my dog. I'll go," offered Maria Reza.

"No way! I'm taking Sweet Thing. I know you want me, Bitch. Maybe if I get real horny sometime, and there's no one else available, I'll come knocking on your door." The lawyer smacked his lips like Hannibal Lecter eating his farva beans. Then he dropped the dog, all the while keeping the knife next to Andrea's throat.

"Go get the car, Charlie, and remember, no funny stuff or she's gonna bleed all over this nice secondhand carpet. Bet you had to give a lot of shampoos and permanents to those old ladies to pay for this high-quality rug." Feeney laughed out loud at Maria's expense.

The look in Maria's eyes as Feeney teased her grew almost as insane as his. If she ever did get her hands on him, she would kill him. I had no doubt in my mind. I also had no doubt that Feeney would kill Andrea if I didn't do everything he said. I got the car. Feeney got in back with Andrea. We began our journey.

The cameras in the blimps above didn't capture all the death and destruction. As we drove past the Munjoy Hill area of town, there were broken down and burned out cars. Smoldering carcasses of the zombies sent foul stenches into the air, smells worst than those that could be found in any of Maine's mill-towns.

As we past the piles of debris on Congress Street I asked, "How do you expect to get past the cops surrounding that cemetery?"

"The same way I'm getting you to give me this ride. Sweet Thing here! You think they'll take a chance at shooting me with her so close by?"

Feeney gave Andrea a tight hug and tried to kiss her. I had all I could do to keep myself from going insane.

"Once I'm inside those gates, I'll be safe. Those cops won't go in there. They fear the bees will get them...And they're right!"

"How do you know the bees won't get you, Mr. Feeney?" Andrea asked.

"Mr. Feeney! Aren't you the polite one?"

"You don't want to experience the same fate as your son," Andrea warned.

"That's where you're wrong, Sweet Cheeks. Lubuka will see to it that the bees stay friendly where I'm concerned. That witch's powers are equal to his. They kinda battle it out for control, but soon Lubuka will have the upper hand and that witch will be powerless. I have it all figured out. A good lawyer knows the tactics of his opponents, and I am the best lawyer I know!" He smiled, insanely pleased with himself.

We proceeded past the Maine Medical Center, down the Western Promenade and to the cemetery. Tony had already informed the cops about the situation. We passed without problems.

I stopped the car in front of the back gate. I thought about the Halloween night when Jimmy went running out of that very same gate, screaming to Tommy Caine that there was a zombie chasing after him.

Feeney hollered out to Lubuka and the evil fiend appeared from behind that same big crypt and beckoned him forward.

"Okay, John, let Andrea go," I insisted.

"Sorry, Charlie, but Lubuka wants you both inside."

Before I could say anything, I saw Cindy standing in the distance. She raised her arms and commanded the bees forward. Suddenly, thousands of the tiny killers swarmed towards a now frightened John Feeney. Then, in an instant, the bees landed on a nearby fallen stone. They acted confused as Lubuka counter-commanded Cindy.

"Thank you, Master," Feeney shouted out to Lubuka. "C'mon you two. The Master waits."

Then with strength that surprised Feeney, Lubuka, and me...Andrea broke free of Feeney's grip. She raised her arms in conjunction with her mother. The bees again flew up into the air and descended on Feeney without hesitation. Lubuka tried to divert them, but the combined power of Cindy and Andrea was too much.

The bees covered Feeney and invaded his body. The evil lawyer cried out for mercy and help. There was none. What there was, was justice. He fell dead about a hundred feet from the crypt.

The evil wizard retreated into his lair to fight another day. With another wave of her arm, Andrea sent the bees back to her mother.

I hollered to the nearest security cops to bring some water. I wasn't going to give Feeney a chance to do more damage as a reborn-zombie. It was time to finish him off, once and for all. I poured the water on him till everything was burned. His body smoldered and his dust blew away, taking his soul to who knows where. Andrea said a prayer for him. I could not.

As Cindy moved toward us, the cops retreated. They had seen her powers from the road, and although I assured them she would not harm them, they left us just the same. They would wait for the hydrants to be activated and then they would come in to flood the cemetery.

Within moments Cindy, Andrea and I were alone. It was probably the last time we could talk so freely. We learned there were more of the newly-born zombies, including Paul Feeney, still inside that old mausoleum with Lubuka. We still may be able to destroy them and the bees. Even Cindy wasn't sure how we could finally kill the big slave, but with the bees dead he would not have the means to create more zombies.

It was getting near sundown. Soon, the final invasion to destroy the *undead* would take place. We could only hope that Lubuka had not yet found a way to make the zombies immune from the power of water. Cindy wasn't sure. Mother and daughter embraced. We all hugged. We knew the end was near.

35

The word came down from above. How high up "above" was nobody could say, but it was decided that Chief Richardson would covertly lead a small group into the cemetery to eradicate the rest of the *undead* if that was possible. At least to get an idea of what we were up against before General Roderick went in with his troops. The thinking was...destroy the bees and the *undead* with water and confine the wizard to his territorial limits even if he himself could not be destroyed. The decision was made to try the element of surprise, to catch Lubuka unaware before he could send his zombies and the bees to do their killing.

No one on the Special Forces or the cops, dressed in beekeeper suits and armed with huge water guns, could understand why some civilian and his daughter were going along, especially without the protection of the bulky gear. Richardson knew why and that was enough. The Chief also kept secret the fact that we would take the long way in, through the front gates on Vaughn Street.

As part of the surprise, General Roderick would amass his troops at the back gates on Cassidy Hill along with the bulk of the fire trucks. The big mausoleum was closer to the back of the old cemetery, in range of the fire hoses. It was felt that Lubuka would be distracted by all the action going on there.

We waited for dark. It was a clear warm night with a full moon bathing the entire cemetery in a shimmering silvery light. We would quickly make our way over the old baseball field, trying to avoid the open holes and graves recently abandoned by the long-time residents.

We all dressed in non-reflective black. Even the special beekeeper suits had been sprayed with black paint. Anything that was shiny and could be removed was removed. I was given the walkie-talkie to keep us in communication with Roderick and the Fire Chief, just in case we needed their men to come in a hurry.

Also kept secret, especially from the media, was the word had been given; if we fail and Roderick and his men fail along with the firemen led by Chief Rick Stacey fail, a forced evacuation for five hundred miles would commence followed by a small nuclear blast. If water could now longer destroy them, if radiation was not the final answer, then all bets were off. There was no more Plan B.

At 9 o'clock we started on our mission. Everything went smoothly as we made our way over the old ball field. When we got to home plate, the Chief gave the signal to get down. We would crawl slowly from there to the big crypt. The Chief was in front with the Special Forces and some of his men on each side. Andrea and I were in back.

Everything seemed peaceful and quiet...too quiet.

The odd noise I heard next I had never heard before. It was a like the sound of someone dragging a body slowly over a rug. I looked to the side and there, creeping out of a nearby abandoned grave, was a giant slug. It was the size of a rat. It was the last thing I wanted to see, another horrifying weapon in Lubuka's arsenal of terror. It was slimy with no legs, no eyes, just a big gaping mouth that was constantly sucking. Each time the mouth receded it exposed two rows of razor-sharp teeth and fangs.

The slug was continually searching for anything that came near. It was closest to one of the cops on the left. Before I could warn him, the creeping slug attached himself to the cop's left leg and somehow was able to penetrate the heavy material of the beekeeper suit. The panicking cop cried out in pain, loud enough that even the special helmet he was wearing could not muffle the sounds. Blood gushed out like a geyser and the man's body shriveled up before my eyes, like a vacuum sucking air out of a plastic bag.

By now the Chief and the rest were aware that something was terribly wrong. The slug, full of blood, bloated to at least two times its already huge size. One of the cops took out a big knife and hacked the giant bloodsucker in two. The blood of his fallen comrade exploded all over him. Terrified, he got up and ran toward the back gate. He never made it. The ground began to rumble and he found it difficult to stand. More graves opened up. More bony hands appeared and pulled the fleeing cop under the earth. His screams could be heard all over, only adding to the fear and uncertainty that had gripped us all.

Lubuka had kept some of his skeleton army in reserve and had found ways to make other creepy, crawling, stinging, buzzing, biting, bugs as deadly as the bees. He was evil, but he was smart. He laid a trap and we were falling into it. Our plan was to sneak up and surprise him, but the surprise was on us.

We all got up to retreat to the front gate, but crawling slowly and deliberately over the ball field were hundreds more of the giant slugs. In the air above were all kinds of flying insects, buzzing and hissing. There were mosquitoes the size of small birds, and there were wasps with tiny fangs oozing deadly venom. Their size was birdlike as well. And there were more bees...only this variety was as big as bats. And, yes, there were bats. They were the size of eagles. On the ground, crawling next to the giant slugs, were huge spiders like the African variety that had supposedly been in the Old Buckley House when Jimmy and I went running through it when we were twelve.

We were shocked beyond belief, but I managed to say just one word into the walkie-talkie, "WATER!" I prayed that it would come soon, and I wondered if Cindy could halt back these other deadly creatures as she could the bees. Or was Lubuka in complete control? In the distance, I could see her pointing her hands toward the unnatural hoards assembled against us.

Meanwhile, Andrea added her powers to compliment her mother's, and for the moment we were protected. Formerly invisible rays of light were streaming from their fingers and joining forces to combat the evil wizard and the monsters he had created.

There was no going back, and so, carefully avoiding any other grave sites; we made our way toward the big tomb, the den of Lubuka. The oncoming swell of little deadly creatures seemed to have halted but not stopped completely. Slowly but surely the killers came toward us. I could see the look of anguish on Andrea's face as she tried to hold them back. But the sounds of the buzzing beasts got louder and the giant slugs and spiders crawled nearer. Newly risen skeletons marched on us from the other side. Suddenly, the help I called for was answered as a flood of water dropped from the helicopters above, backed up by the gushing hoses from the fire trucks.

The skeletons retreated and smoldered on their way back to their graves. Likewise, the bloodsucking crawlers were burnt to a crisp, and the giant bugs and bats were dropping from the sky like smoke bombs.

As we stood there letting the saving water drench us, I could hear Cindy crying out in pain. She could have remained safely inside the old crypt; but she stayed, with her arms holding back any deadly creatures, until she was sure Andrea and I were safe.

I called to Fire Chief Rick Stacey to turn off the water. Then I ran to Cindy and carried her, as fast as I could to the doorway of the crypt. Dry under its overhang, we waited for the hoses to be turned off. She had lost a lot of her strength and warned us to leave.

"Charlie, I'm not sure I can fight him off in my weakened state. Please, take Andrea and your friends and leave this place."

Then a creeping scarlet light grew brighter as the door to the big crypt opened. Standing there with numerous zombies behind him, including young Paul Feeney, was the object of our hunt.

Richardson and his men stood there in terror. They might have wanted to run, but they had seen what happened to the others who did. Indecision kept them in place. Knowing Cindy didn't have her full strength, we were at the mercy of time and God.

Lubuka smiled a smile that could only be smiled by someone who believed he was in complete control. The ghoul was more grotesque in appearance as he stood closer to us than ever before. His big white eyes were covered with bloody red veins. The sides of his monstrous nose caved in and our as he breathed, like a tired ox or bull. His teeth were huge and rotted. His breath smelled like decaying fish on a hot summer tide. He pointed toward me and then at Andrea.

"You two I will not kill if you submit to my wishes, but I will kill all of you if you don't do as I say." His voice was low and deep, and phased as he spoke like there were several people speaking the same words at the same time through the same mouth.

I could hear Roderick screaming into my walkie-talkie, "My men are ready!!!"

"Hold on, General Roderick. We are okay for now, but stand by." I looked at the menacing eyes of Lubuka as if to say, *there are a lot of guys out there with a lot of water. You better watch out. I'd give a million bucks for a big snowball right now.*

"Charlie, you better watch out. You haven't changed from those first days when you and your little friends came to play your silly little games. You and your friend, Jimmy, always making stupid jokes. I wanted to kill you then, but (he pointed to Cindy) she held me back."

I forgot he could read my mind and the minds of anyone else nearby.

Lubuka then called for young, dead, Paul Feeney to join him in the doorway of the big crypt. The boy came forward like a robot.

"Take your water guns and shoot him," Lubuka commanded.

Chief Richardson looked at me as if I were in charge and not him. "Charlie, should I do what he asks?" He really didn't wait for me to answer as he fired a burst of water at the dead boy.

Even Cindy had a look of shock in her eyes as the water failed to destroy or even hurt the boy. The Chief fired again and the water splashed helplessly down the front of the boy's chest. Paul smiled, revealing his fangs, and his eyes burned red.

Lubuka laughed an evil laugh. "You can shoot him, burn him, stab him or poison him! But he will still *live*. And now that water is no longer their enemy, you can never destroy my followers. You can never destroy me!" And then he mocked, "Not even if you *love* me."

The Evil One's laughter was as frightening as his appearance. Filled with confidence, he stood there in the doorway of his grave and the tiny bees swarmed to him.

"They too, my little friends, are safe from rain and any water you can hit them with." The little killers settled on his massive chest, waiting to do his bidding. "Soon all the insects that crawl and fly will be immune."

The day had come. It had taken over three hundred years, but it was here. Lubuka was more powerful than Cindy. There was nothing or anyone who could destroy him now. We knew it and he knew it. Then, as if to drive home the point, The Evil One stepped out of the tomb and levitated above us.

"Look into the crypt and see what awaits anyone who does not obey me." The sound of his phasing voice was almost hypnotic.

Inside the lair were men, women, and children. All were zombies under the power of the great wizard. They were huddled together, moving back and forth, just waiting for the order to kill. It looked like they were actually aching for the chance to prove themselves worthy servants.

The highly decorated Special Forces, who had seen action in Bosnia and Iraq, were noticeably trembling in fear as the zombies started slowly walking toward the front of the crypt.

"I can hold them back and spare your lives if you destroy her now!" Lubuka, now filled with more noticeable hate and revenge, pointed at Cindy.

"She no longer has more power than you. Why are you afraid of her?" I asked.

Lubuka moved closer to Cindy and spoke with a touch of respect, "She is a crafty one." Then he turned to us and said in a booming voice. "She has lived long enough. If she lives on, she just might find new powers to combat mine. Her time has come. I'm not taking any chances. Besides, that's what she wants...to die one final time." Lubuka grinned and lowered himself to the ground.

Cindy communicated to Andrea with thoughts and then they embraced.

The fiend shrugged as he listened in to what the rest of us could not hear. "Enough!" He raised his arms and said to me, "Will you or your bastard child destroy her or not?"

Chief Richardson then removed his protective helmet so he could speak more clearly. "Charlie, what's to prevent him from killing the rest of us once the Manchester girl is destroyed?"

"You'll just have to take my word for it. You have no other choice, you fool!" Lubuka said more impatiently as he turned his gaze on the Chief.

"Think, Charlie! We have no power against this creep if she's not around. Better some power than none at all." The Chief had reached the point where fear was fading and anger was increasing.

That was the last straw for Lubuka. He raised his arms to send the bees to kill the Chief. But before he could give the command and before the Chief could get his protective helmet back on, another voice was heard.

How she got up there, I couldn't say. She stood on top of the mausoleum, still wearing that heavy woolen dress that came to her ankles just above her tightly-laced high black shoes. With the full moon against her back she looked like an avenging angel. It was Abigail Kostenello, the scourge of Lynnfield, Massachusetts. She held out the giant crucifix that hung like a weight around her neck.

"I command you; spawn of the underworld, to bow before me. My power is greater than yours. You cannot fight against the force of the crucifix!"

Lubuka was startled by the unexpected and he cursed at his new tormentor. His voice was now growling, like that of a mad dog. He slowly levitated himself up again and Abigail Kostenello took a step back. She had not been ready for such a display of his power.

The big wizard looked directly into her eyes, absorbing her every thought. At first there was a faint smile on his lips, and then it slowly broadened into a wider, evil grin.

"Tell me, Abby, may I call you Abby?" he asked in that low phasing voice, "Didn't you like it when young Richard Kostenello fondled you in the back of your father's old Hudson? No? Come now, Abby, you begged him *not* to stop. In fact, it was YOU that seduced him! He was from an upstanding family in the community, not like the real father of your child, not like Cyrus Perkins. Cyrus' family wasn't wealthy enough for you. He ran with a bad crowd. He smoked and drank and diddled all the little girls in town. It wouldn't do for the prim and proper of Massachusetts to think that sweet little Abigail was such a WHORE!!!" Lubuka laughed as if he and Cyrus Perkins were old friends.

"Shut up, you bastard!" the woman demanded as sweat broke out on her lily-white forehead. She held the crucifix higher and demanded that Lubuka take back all that he had just said or she, Abigail Kostenello, would see to it personally that he was condemned to Hell.

Lubuka, still hovering, moved closer to her. "Abby, I could really like you. You are such a hypocrite! Tell me and the rest, before I kill them, how much you have come to enjoy your afternoon visits with Jane Norman. How after your lunch, you retire to her bedroom and satisfy your...desires. Tell us how you groan with pleasure at her

MIGHTY JOHN MARSHALL

touch the way you did with Richard and Cyrus, not too mention the half-dozen other boys you gave yourself to."

Then, in an instant, his big hand grasped her around the neck and lifter her off the top of the mausoleum. They were suspended in air and God's little helper began to scream obscenities that only a sailor could appreciate. Lubuka smiled as if the cursing and the cussing were music to his ears. He then pulled the startled woman to himself and kissed her deep and hard with that dead-fish breath of his. As he pulled back, his sinister smile broadened. He was about to deliver the words that would sicken her to the point of suicide.

"Let me give you some good news, Abigail. Cyrus wasn't the *real* father either...It was your Uncle Roy!!!"

As the woman gasped in horror we were all spellbound, not only at the powers of the great wizard, but at the reality of Abigail Kostenello. The pious-acting woman threw up all over that woolen suit she wore so righteously. She began to choke on her own vomit and the fiend darted out his tongue, pried open her mouth, and licked it up.

"Hmmm, good...just like mother used to make." Then he spit it back in her face, taking much glee from his dastardly actions.

Abigail's strong voice grew weaker as she pressed the crucifix against his massive black chest, but she got out the words she wanted to say. "I command you, by the power of this crucifix, to burn in Hell for eternity. I damn you to the unquenchable fire that awaits the wicked."

Her strength to fight on was leaving. Revulsion was winning out. But Abigail Kostenello, for all her weaknesses and hypocrisies, was fearless to the end. There was something about her to be admired. And I did.

Lubuka looked up at the moon like a baying wolf, while putting forth the most hideous laugh yet. Then, as if deciding playtime was over, he squeezed her neck so hard that the blood dripped out of her eyes.

"You think you can destroy me with your little statue on a stick?!?" The Evil One grabbed the crucifix from is tormentor and tossed it to the ground. Then, with a powerful display of what we were all up against, he flung her almost lifeless body into the night. It sailed about three hundred feet. Her screams could still be heard as her falling body was impaled on a tall spike that was part of the cemetery's iron gate. Abigail Kostenello had become the latest victim in THE GREAT CEMETERY SLAUGHTER.

The cops and those Special Forces who came in the front gate with us were no longer undecided on whether to stay or run for their lives. Some of them made it to the back gate. Some of them failed to run the gauntlet of new bony hands that reached up out of the ground and pulled them down.

Left at the big crypt and looking up at the hovering monster, was Chief Ray Richardson, Cindy, Andrea, and me.

Lubuka lowered himself down and stood at the entrance of his tomb. Behind him we could see his excited zombie followers, anxious to do his bidding. With water no longer effective against them, they were ready to move out into the city, feeding, biting and creating more of their kind. No one would be safe.

According to my fifth-grade teacher, Sister Mary Margaret, we were supposed to see Jesus coming again in the clouds with a band of angels when the end was near. But it was Hell that had come to town.

The Chief spoke stoically as if he had resigned himself to his fate and had made his peace with God, "Charlie, I guess the one thing we can do before the end is to grant the wish of this big freak. Besides, that's what Miss Manchester wants as well. Do what you have to do to release her soul from this condemned world. There is no hope for the rest of us." Ray had reached the moment of despair. All was lost.

Lubuka grinned as he turned to me and said, "Do it now!"

With help from Andrea, I approached the woman I would always love, perhaps more now than I had ever realized. I carried her over to where the big elm used to stand, where infatuation and friendship blossomed into true love those many years ago. Andrea held her hand all the way. The Chief walked along side. Lubuka marched behind us, like the invincible conqueror he had become.

As I laid Cindy down, the bees gathered nearby as if paying their final respects. Andrea and I kissed her. Andrea had picked up the crucifix that Lubuka threw to the ground. She placed it next to her mother's heart and began to say the Lord's Prayer as I prepared to pour the water.

It was then Cindy's green eyes widened and she quickly sat up. "Andrea, My Precious One!!! *YOU* can destroy him with the crucifix!" Cindy picked it up and held it out to our daughter.

The great wizard cursed and said, "Get on with it! Your God has no power over me. You saw how useless it was."

With his rotting boots, Lubuka kicked the crucifix out of Cindy's hands and then stomped on it till it was buried deep in the ground.

The Chief, forgetting the dangerous and depressing predicament he was in, drew his revolver and pumped six shots into Lubuka's massive frame. "I don't go to church as often as I should, but I would never blaspheme the way you just did."

The bullets didn't make the wizard flinch one bit, but now he turned to crush the life out of the defiant Ray Richardson.

With the strength she obviously inherited from her mother, Andrea pulled the crucifix up out of the ground and held it out. "In the name of God, I command you kneel in reverence to His Holy Name."

Lubuka, with his back to her, quickly cried out in excruciating pain. He dropped to his knees. For over three hundred years only water could hurt him. As he got up and turned around he looked stunned and unsure of himself, like a dazed boxer who had finally met his match. Lubuka had just taken the biggest punch of his life. He stepped back as if there were an invisible corner he could hide in. But the new champ was closing in.

"What's happening?" I asked, stunned myself by this turn of events.

Cindy gently smiled and answered, "Pure evil can only be destroyed by pure goodness. The power is not in the crucifix. It is in those who have pure hearts, those who truly believe in justice and mercy and all the crucifix represents."

"In all that is holy, I command you to leave this world and face His judgment," Andrea said in her soft but forceful voice.

Lubuka screeched again in pain. His black flesh started falling off his huge body. With the strength of a mad man he cried out to his followers waiting in the opening of the crypt. "Avenge me and save me, My Children!"

The *undead* moved toward us. Their mechanical mouths began snapping. Their arms extended out to grasp us. Then the ground

STUNG

began to rumble as the last of the skeleton army climbed out of their graves. The Chief and I fired our water guns in vain as the creatures got closer and closer.

Cindy urged her daughter on and Andrea continued with her task, "In the name of the Savior Of The World, I send you from us, never to return." She held the crucifix to the face of the melting monster.

Lubuka screamed so loud the sound was almost deafening. His flesh burned with real fire. His face was now void of any skin. His big skull bobbled back and forth on his bony neck and then the once-great wizard EXPLODED in front of our eyes.

Within seconds there was nothing left but smoldering ash. The zombies and skeletons, without their all-powerful leader, fell to the ground...never to walk again, not in this world.

The explosion brought the army and firemen scurrying into the cemetery. As they arrived by our sides, the Chief simply said, "Go home, Men. Kiss your wives and hug your children. It's all over." As they looked down at the smoking carcasses of the zombies and the burning bones of the last remnants of the skeleton army, they turned and did as the Chief suggested.

It was then I asked Ray if I could be alone with Andrea and Cindy to say our final goodbyes.

He hugged us all, looked at Cindy and Andrea and quietly said, "Thank you."

We waited for all the trucks and troops to exit the area. We gazed around the entire perimeter from Cassidy Hill to Vaughn Street. The silver moon had us in its spotlight. All was quiet again. All seemed peaceful again.

Cindy smiled. She had arrived at the moment she had waited for. She was going home to be with her mother and her father, and the twin brothers she loved so much.

You may think it strange, but at that moment, I was at peace with what I had to do.

Cindy rested her head in my arms.

Andrea kissed the crucifix and put it back down, next to Cindy's heart. She said the prayer.

I poured the water. "I love you. I always will. Goodbye."

During the next few weeks things started getting back to normal, as normal as was possible after living through a horror such as the world had never seen before and, pray Dear God, will never see again.

The army left. The media left. The commercials returned on the TV.

Monroe and Jeff, failing to find another story, were asking for jobs back at the hotels and restaurants down on the waterfront.

Tony was promoted to Chief of Detectives and started seeing that cute emergency-room nurse, Kelly Beane.

Ray Richardson retired his badge. He has taken his wife and grandchildren to Disney World.

Maria returned to her hair salon. She always takes Riley and Little Brutus along. They play at her feet or sleep in the back room. The dogs have become inseparable. If a customer complains, Maria just says that it's too bad. "Get over it!" They were probably as afraid of her as I was.

Brother Joe went back to his genealogy and his teaching. He's still telling the story to anyone who will listen down at O'Toole's, how his little brother once had a three-hundred-year-old girlfriend. "And get this, my niece is a nun. No shit!"

I know it will please you to learn that the locket was recovered. It was found in the dead hands of Paul Feeney. Paul was reburied as were the others, hopefully for ever more to rest in peace.

I gave the locket to Andrea. It was the first time she had seen it. She kissed the words, LEST WE FORGET, and then she kissed me. She wears it around her neck along with a new tiny cross. This morning I put her on a plane back to Oceanside. She still wants to teach at Marshall High for a year and then take her final vows. Barn and Georgia said they would pick her up at the airport.

Tomorrow the city is going to hold, what I guess you could call, an open house up at the old cemetery. Prayers will be said. Fresh flowers and new markers have been put up. All are encouraged to bring their families and walk through from the front gate to the back gate. The city council suggested it would be a good way to bring closure to the horrors of the passing summer. It's a way to show that there is no longer a reason to be afraid to go to the West End of town.

As for me, I'm on my way to Jimmy Peters' house. He has agreed to enter a rehab facility on Monday and lick his demons, once and for all.

I see him and Sara Peters standing out front.

"Where did you steal the old station-wagon?" Jimmy quizzes as I pull into the driveway.

"I didn't steal it, my mother did!" I laugh. "Actually, it's Joe's. He let me borrow it for this special occasion."

"What special occasion?" Sara Peters wants to know.

"Look in the back," I suggest.

As I get out, Jimmy asks, "Why the bicycles?"

"You and I are going to ride them up to the old ball field and play some *flies and grounders*."

My best friend smiles. "I was hoping we would do that. It's a perfect day for it."

"But first we'll eat. One Italian sandwich from Amato's for you and one from DiPietro's for me" I smile as I hold forth the two bags.

"You got Pepsi, right, my friend?"

"But of course. I even have my old glove, bat and a brand new ball! Try not to lose this one."

I can see by the look in my old friend's eyes that he is pleased. So is his mom. She kisses us both as we leave. "Be home before dark," she says the same way she did when were kids and Jerry was holding her hand.

We struggle to keep our balance as we ride the bikes up Danforth Street to the old cemetery playground. There are aches and pains we don't remember having before. We laugh all the way, just like we had when we thought we would be twelve forever.

We sit near home plate, near a new young elm that has started to grow in its daddy's old spot. Afterwards, we sprinkle the crumbs and leftovers on the newly seeded grass by Wendle Bronson's old grave site.

As Jimmy trots out to take his place in the field, I step up to home plate.

MIGHTY JOHN MARSHALL

The air is warm for late summer, with no breeze. I can hear the crickets rubbing their legs and singing their song. Of course, I am thinking of her. There's not a moment that I don't.

"All right P, P, P, P Porky...Hit that b, b, b, ball," Jimmy yells, reverting back to his Looney Tune style.

I acknowledge him with my bat and toss the ball into the air. As it falls in front of me in the perfect hitting spot, I swing and "Wiff". I miss. Jimmy falls on the ground laughing and insulting me.

It is then I hear a familiar voice coming up behind me.

"You call yourself a baseball player? You swing like a girl!" Maria Reza teases as she approaches with her hands behind her back.

"What are you doing here?" I say as if I weren't really glad to see her.

"What!?! You want this whole place for yourself? I can out hit you and Jimmy with my eyes closed. Back in Brooklyn I broke more windows than anyone else on the block, boy or girl."

I believe her. Why shouldn't I? The truth be told, I have come to really care about her. She's a wise-ass, but so am I...at least that's what I've been told.

"Go ahead, Maria, out on the field. If you catch a fly ball, I'll take you to dinner at The Village."

"Well all right! Now you're talkin'. I might even let you kiss me goodnight!"

"Deal's off!" I joke. "By the way, what are you holding behind your back?"

"Oh, close your eyes," she commands.

"Why?"

"CLOSE THEM!!!"

I am definitely afraid of this woman.

"Okay. You can open them now."

I can't speak. I turn to look at Jimmy. He is just standing there like a statue. He can't believe his eyes either.

"What, don't you like it? I found it over there (she points) on top of your bicycles. I think it looks cute on me. What do you call it, a stovepipe hat? C'mon, Charlie. You know!...like the kind President Abraham Lincoln used to wear."

STUNG